Sacrifices for the Sea God, Burash

The assassin kicked bones aside to expose manacles set into the rock, snapping them about Bracht and Calandryll's ankles before cutting the cords that bound their hands.

Bracht stooped instantly, testing the chains. From above came laughter and the priest's booming voice.

"Too stout to break, those bonds. Save Burash grant you mercy, you pay for your affront."

The water rose, creeping up their legs, overtopping their boots. Lapping ripples touched Calandryll's face and he spat salt water from his mouth, craning his head back, seeking to hold lips and nose clear of the flow. He heard Bracht shout, "Courage!," the cry abruptly cut off by a dreadful choking.

In moments, the level was risen above Calandryll's head, his ragged breath sucking in not air, but water. He floated, turned this way and that as blind panic set him to thrashing, arms flailing wild as he sought hopelessly to thrust his head upwards, into the air.

Calandryll felt death touch him. . . .

DARK MAGIC
by Angus Wells

THE GODWARS
BOOK II

Dark Magic

Angus Wells

BANTAM BOOKS

NEW YORK · TORONTO · LONDON · SYDNEY · AUCKLAND

DARK MAGIC

A Bantam Spectra Book / November 1992

Map by Claudia Carlson

ISBN 0-553-29129-7

Published simultaneously in the United States and Canada

Bantam Books are published by Bantam Books, a division of Bantam
Doubleday Dell Publishing Group, Inc. Its trademark, consisting of the words
"Bantam Books" and the portrayal of a rooster, is Registered in U.S. Patent
and Trademark Office and in other countries. Marca Registrada. Bantam
Books, 1540 Broadway, New York, New York 10036.

PRINTED IN THE UNITED STATES OF AMERICA

OPM   0 9 8 7 6 5 4 3

For Janna Silverstein . . .
. . . "Talent alone cannot make a writer.
There must be a (wo)man behind the book."

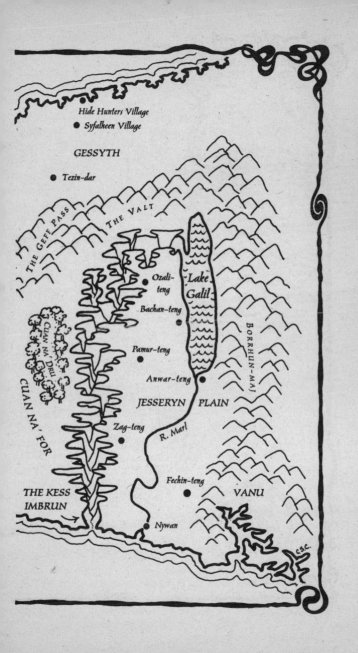

1

NHUR-JABAL meant, in the language of Kandahar, Great Watchtower, and so it seemed the city was. It rose in great terraces of stone against the older rock of the Kharm-rhanna, where the mountains thrust deep into the heart of the land, where the three great rivers—the Shemme, the Tannyth, and the Yst— fell down from the peaks, dividing about the city brooding above like some lithic sentinel, a hypabyssal guardian. Tier upon tier climbed the steep slopes, the buildings like battlements, cut through with roadways and bridges and great sweeps of stairs, all rising toward the single massive edifice that dominated the heights, walled and turreted and towered, the pennants of the Tyrant fluttering purple and gold from the ramparts. It seemed so high that from the topmost towers an observer might stare out across all of the Tyrant's domain. To Kharasul in the west and Vishat'yi in the south, Mherut'yi to the east, on the edge of the Narrow Sea. And it was to that latter direction eyes looked now, troubled. All Nhur-jabal was a defensive wall about the Tyrant's citadel, that great fortress the final bastion of authority in Kandahar, from its founding by Cederus to now, when

Xenomenus ruled. And the rule of Xenomenus was threatened.

To the west the flag of rebellion waved, raised by Sathoman ek'Hennem, Lord of the Fayne, and a wilier enemy than Tyrant or any who advised him had anticipated. Already he controlled the eastern reaches of Kandahar, from Mherut'yi to Mhazomul down the coast, inland to Kesham-vaj and Bhalusteen; already he had defeated an army, proclaimed Xenomenus upstart and usurper; already, in the east, folk hailed him Lord and named him Tyrant. That they would turn as readily against him was small consolation to the hereditary ruler: to achieve that end he must be defeated. Not driven back to his lonely keep, but roundly and soundly—above all, visibly—defeated. Xenomenus wanted the Fayne Lord's head on a pikestaff, to be carried from town to town until all Kandahar knew he was beaten and dead. And yet—the corpses feeding the crows about Kesham-vaj testimony to this—Sathoman ek'Hennem still lived, and triumphed, and threatened to bring down the Tyrant; neither the legions nor the sorcerers at Xenomenus's command able to deliver the rebel to just fate.

It was a dilemma that seemed emphasized by the cold wind that wafted down from the Kharm-rhanna, winter's breath, and Xenomenus shivered as he peered eastward.

Instantly, galvanized by the tremor, a flunky stepped forward, draping a cloak of purple brocade about his master's narrow shoulders. Xenomenus accepted it unaware, feeling no warmer, the cold pervading him less physical than an emanation of doubt, turning from the parapet where he stood to face the throng attending him. Sunlight sparked bright from the rings covering his fingers as he gestured dismissal to the servants and sycophants. He waited until they were gone from earshot into the tower, the doors of glass swung shut, then touched the band of jewel-studded silver encircling his smooth forehead as if to

draw inspiration from that badge of his office and
looked to those who remained.

There were seven, all older than he by several
years, three at least attendant on his father, three who
had known his grandfather. They were of sundry
shape and size: tall and short, most slender, but two
obese, their physiognomy no less varied, their hair
ranging in color from glossy black to age's weary yellow. Some wore a patrician look; others might have
been tradesmen. All wore robes of black, the subfusc
woven with cabbalistic emblems in silver thread.
Xenomenus frowned, not knowing the expression lent
him a petulance that was echoed in his voice.

"Well, gentlemen"—he laid a deliberately scornful
emphasis on the honorific—"it would appear your
colleagues have as yet found this hedge rabble too
much for them."

"My lord, they had not anticipated the gramaryes
left by Anomius." The speaker paused, continuing
when Xenomenus offered no response, "And the Faye
Lord struck with unprecedented swiftness."

"Swift enough he commands the eastern coast."
The Tyrant drew his cloak tighter about him, contesting the nervousness these men, for all they served
him and no other, induced. "Swift enough he holds a
third of my domain. Too swift, it would seem, for
you."

"Our divinations warned of this," said the oldest,
his voice dry as his wrinkled skin, like some wither-
ing tree, "and had . . ."

Xenomenus's hand chopped air, silencing the comment. A younger man glanced warily at the reckless
oldster, clearing his throat to signal caution. "Lord
Xenomenus," he ventured, "what Rassuman says is,
in part at least, true—we divined a stirring in the occult fundus, but vague . . . not of such proportion as
this."

"But you are the Tyrant's sorcerers!" Now
Xenomenus paused and cleared his throat, hearing the
petulance in his voice, carefully deepening his tone.

"If you of all the mages in this world could not discern the pattern, then who might?"

"Indeed," Rassuman murmured, concealing a sour smile.

"The vagueness itself is a portent," the younger wizard said, "a thing we have debated long."

"And do you grace me with your conclusions?" the Tyrant snapped.

The wizard ducked his head, not quite a bow. "In part it was Anomius's doing," he said evenly, fixing Xenomenus with a stare, "but that obfuscation was enabled by some other agency, something within the occult fundus too deep for even our powers to penetrate."

The Tyrant's frown became one of perplexity and he asked, "What do you say?"

"I—we—are not sure, my lord. Such vision was, and is, denied us. It would seem that perhaps the gods themselves cloud the matter."

"Do you say Burash turns against me?" Xenomenus's swarthy features paled, his eyes slitting, a hand rising involuntarily to the coronet. Swiftly the seven sorcerers shook their heads, murmuring reassuring negatives. Xenomenus said, "Then what? Or whom? Do you explain yourself, Cenobar."

The wizard nodded, his face a carefully bland mask. "As best I may, Lord Tyrant, but even we are fallible." He ignored the twisted smile of agreement that met his comment and continued, "Certainly Anomius left behind him such cantrips as gave great aid to Sathoman ek'Hennem, but even so there was a clouding mightier than such as he might produce. It was as if powers greater even than Burash stirred, and in their stirring raised up vapors to blind our occult sight."

"Greater than Burash?" the Tyrant gasped. "What power is greater than our Sea God?"

"There were gods before Burash," said Rassuman.

"The First Gods are gone," said Xenomenus, "gone of their own volition into the Forbidden Lands. And their offspring banished into limbo, bound there by their parents' machinations. Tharn and Balatur play no part in our world."

"Aye, so all know." Cenobar nodded. "But still we could not see, still something clouded these events."

Xenomenus sighed, his shoulders slumping beneath the brocade, and when he spoke again his voice was plaintive.

"And so this hedge lord takes my land? So he flaunts my authority and threatens to bring my realm into civil war?"

"On that we yet have some say, Lord Tyrant."

Xenomenus turned to the new speaker, a grossly fat man, whose beard and robe retained hints of his last meal: "Then say on, Lykander."

"It is our opinion, my lord, that Burash stands with us in this affair, and that while we were not able to prognosticate the uprising we may yet quell it."

Xenomenus cheered at this, his face brightening. "This is such talk as I would hear," he enthused. "How shall it be done?"

"Anomius is the key," said Lykander.

"A dangerous key," said Cenobar, interrupting, falling silent as Xenomenus raised a hand.

"Dangerous, aye," agreed the fat sorcerer, "but not so powerful as to stand against all of us."

"He slew Zytharan," said another, "and left me maimed."

Lykander glanced at the twisted hand offered in evidence and said, "But still you heal apace, Andrycus, and your hand will soon be whole again. I say we must use him."

Xenomenus saw himself usurped, the debate among the wizards, and clapped his hands. "You bear the scars of battle, Andrycus," he said, "and I mourn Zytharan's demise. But still I'd hear how that puking traitor may win us a victory over the rebels he once served."

Lykander smoothed his beard, dislodging crumbs, and said, "There is some dissension among us on this matter, Lord Tyrant. Some adhere to my belief that we must use Anomius to unlock ek'Hennem's hold; others deem him too dangerous."

"Yet all serve me," said Xenomenus softly. "Is that not so?"

"Indubitably," said Lykander.

"Our loyalty is unquestioned," said Cenobar, "but still . . . to free Anomius? Better had we slain him when we took him on the Shemme."

"Then perhaps we should never take Fayne Keep," said Lykander, "for surely Anomius is the only one may open the way to that place."

Xenomenus clapped again. "I would hear this plan," he declared. "The rebels wax stronger by the day, and I'd not waste one listening to your arguments. If Anomius can aid us, then surely you seven can bind him with such spells as must render him harmless. To me—to us!—at least."

"I believe it may be done," said Lykander.

"May I speak, my lord?" asked Cenobar, and when the Tyrant gestured his permission: "I agree that without Anomius the taking of Fayne Keep must be a long and bloody process; even that his aid must surely swiften the downfall of the rebels. But I am uncertain that path is the wiser—I fear that do we free Anomius, we unleash a greater evil."

"Clouded auguries," Lykander grumbled.

"Clouded, aye," said Cenobar, "but ominous for all of that."

"Then enlighten us," said Xenomenus, "as to these auguries."

"I cannot, Lord," Cenobar admitted, scowling as Lykander chuckled behind his hand. "Only say that I fear the freeing of Anomius shall unleash some evil worse even than rebellion."

"What evil is worse than such threat to me?" The Tyrant's eyes flashed affront and Cenobar offered no response, merely ducked his head as Xenomenus motioned for Lykander to continue.

"My lord," the fat man declared, pacing a step forward as though to separate himself from his fellow sorcerers, "we know that Anomius has laid such cantrips about Fayne Keep as to render that hold virtually impregnable; also that it was his skill gave Keshamvaj to the rebels. To take back the one, to breach the other, must cost us dear in time and lives, and for all the time it takes, so Sathoman must wax stronger. Even now hedge wizards flock to his aid . . ."

"Petty charlatans," grunted Cenobar, "weak occultists of no real account."

"Save in numbers," Lykander returned, "and as time passes so their numbers grow."

"Time!" Xenomenus barked. "Always we come back to time! To its lack, to its dwindling—I shall hear out Lykander. Cenobar, you others, be silent."

Lykander smiled through his soiled beard, smoothed his grubby robe over the swell of his belly, and said, "You put it precisely, my lord: time is of the essence. Ere Sathoman can augment his strength we must strike against him—and our keenest weapon is Anomius. He knows Sathoman, knows the rebel's ways, the intricacies of his mind; more, he knows what spells and cantrips remain in force. He set them and therefore can undo them. I say we must use him."

Xenomenus hooked thumbs in silver-chased belt and asked, "Then why have you not? He is our prisoner and you are the Tyrant's sorcerers—why have you not probed his mind for these secrets?"

The smug smile that had decorated Lykander's face dissolved, replaced with a placatory turning of his lips. "He is unusually powerful, my lord. Indeed, against any one of us, singly, he should prove victorious." He paused, preempting the question shaping on the Tyrant's mouth. "Even acting in unison we may not safely extract that information. His skill is such that he has wound defenses about his own mind—do we attempt their destruction we must surely destroy his mind and all it holds. But"—again he stilled Xenomenus's protest—"there is a way. Of that I am convinced. Anomius is mightily ambitious, and already he has turned his coat against Sathoman, fleeing Kesham-vaj even in the hour of victory."

"Aye." Xenomenus interrupted now, furrows vertical between his eyes. "Why did he do that? And were there not two with him then? What became of them?"

"We know not," said Lykander, "only that they were not wizards and seem to have escaped down the Shemme. I deem them of no account, my lord, and Anomius has refused to speak of them."

"So," Xenomenus murmured. "Do you then go on—tell me how Anomius may be safely used."

"His loyalty is to himself," Lykander said, "which is to say, he will serve whoever may promise him the most. At this moment that is you, Lord Tyrant. Offer him freedom and I believe he may be persuaded to our cause. We seven may bind him about with such cantrips as shall consume him should he renege, and thus he shall offer you no harm, but rather serve you in bringing down Sathoman ek'Hennem, the alternative—should he refuse—being execution."

"This can be done?" asked Xenomenus. "You can bind him safely?"

"We seven together," Lykander promised, "aye."

The Tyrant looked to the others and one by one they nodded.

"And what should I promise him? Freedom alone cannot be sufficient, for what freedom I dare offer must be limited."

"That is true," Lykander agreed. "Perhaps a place among us?"

Xenomenus cocked his head, oiled ringlets falling black upon his shoulder, his eyes suspicious. "To become my man? When his bent for treachery is so well established?"

"Bound by our magicks," Lykander reminded, "harmless, therefore. And once Sathoman is defeated and Fayne Keep reduced—well, then his usefulness is done . . ."

Now Xenomenus smiled. "And could you destroy him?"

"Aye, my lord. When he is no longer of use."

Again the Tyrant looked to the rest, his gaze demanding confirmation, and again, one by one, they ducked their heads, murmuring agreement. Xenomenus nodded in turn and spun about, going to the balcony, where he stood staring out across the land, eastward. The sun moved toward its setting and across the broad width of the Yst, fog rose above the water, the walls of the river valley growing misted, the great forest beyond blurring as twilight approached. After a while he faced them again and spoke his decision.

"Offer him freedom. Tell him that his service shall be rewarded. Does he ask for wine—give it. Does he want jewels, or women, or boys—supply them. In return I'll have his allegiance, for what that's worth, and he shall join with you to bring down this Burash-damned rebel. But mark you! Bind him with such magicks as shall ensure my safety and that of all my line: I'd not unleash a viper in my palace! Nor, when his usefulness is spent, nurture it. Once his purpose is served, destroy him."

"My lord is wise," said Lykander, bowing as best his girth allowed. "It shall be done."

"Better destroy him now," muttered Cenobar.

"Better destroy Sathoman ek'Hennem," returned the Tyrant coldly. "Better end this threat to Kandahar."

Cenobar's eyes hooded as Xenomenus nodded confirmation of his own decision, stepping aside as the Tyrant paced across the balcony to the glass doors, pausing the instant it took a servitor to open the portal He disappeared inside, leaving the seven warlocks to mutter among themselves, not hearing Cenobar as he turned to Rassuman and said, "I think we shall unleash a greater threat to Kandahar and all the world than Sathoman ek'Hennem offers."

Lykander heard him and said, "How so? Secured by

our magic Anomius shall be no danger, and do we but
use him to bring down ek'Hennem we are all of us favored in the Tyrant's eyes."

Cenobar offered no reply save a thin and doubting
smile; the fat sorcerer beamed. "The Lord Tyrant has
commanded us, my friends. Do we then prepare our
cantrips and approach our prisoner."

As the Tyrant's citadel surmounted Nhur-jabal with
gold and purple and silver splendor so, nadir to its zenith, the Tyrant's dungeons drove deep beneath, into
the dull and miserable places of the city, catacombs of
suffering. And deepest of all, where weight of rock
dulled sound and spirits, the sheer impenetrability of
the stone leeching hope, stood a door of ancient wood,
set across with rusted metal, bolted and barred, and
inscribed with sigils of dreadful strength. Beyond that
door was a narrow staircase curving down into the utter gloom of a circular chamber, at its center a great
round disc of solid steel, engraved, like the door and
the walls of the place, with the symbols of magic. Beneath that disc was a vertical shaft carved into the
stuff of the mountains, six times the height of a tall
man, its walls sheer and smooth as ice, impossible to
climb, and in that shaft lay Anomius.

The oubliette was lightless save for the brief moment every few days that moldered bread and stale
water were lowered to the prisoner. The stone walls
were damp, trickling puddles over the uneven floor,
and nothing lived there, not spiders or rats or even
those insects that customarily inhabit such dank, forgotten holes. They, at least, would have provided
some diversion from the tedium that, to a sorcerer bereft of his powers, was far worse than mere physical
imprisonment. Anomius had known cantrips were
placed upon the dungeon, but not how strong they
were: mighty enough that he was, in occult terms as
much as physical, blind and deaf. He could work no
magic here, bring no light to brighten the darkness,

nor send out his mind to hear—perhaps sway!—some
nearby mortal; the pouch containing such artifacts as
he used was taken from him, his quyvhal lost with all
his wizardly powers. How long he had lain in the
darkness he was not sure, though it seemed all summer must have passed. That he remained alive was
small consolation, though it occurred to him that
some reason beyond mere vengeance must exist for
that, and he pondered on it when he was not contemplating his own revenge on those he deemed responsi-
ble for this indignity.

It was that cogitation that staved off complete
madness, the wizened mage like some drunken
dancer or acrobat precariously treading a rope
stretched over the pit of insanity.

He thought, as he crouched in his blindness, of
Calandryll and Bracht, his days filled with imagining
of their destruction, cursing them softly, a litany of
raw and pure hatred. He saw now how they had duped
him, tempting him with seditious promises into freeing them and bringing them safe out of Kesham-vaj.
How the Kern had tricked him into using his magic
too close to Nhur-jabal, where the sorcerers loyal to
the Tyrant must sense his powers and set an ambush.
The Kern was more cunning than he had thought; and
the Lyssian youth had been protected by that undefin-
able magic Anomius had sensed in him. The cursed
boy did not even know how powerful he was! Oh, he
wore that stone about his neck and that afforded him
some defense, but not in itself sufficient to withstand
the probing of so great a thaumaturge as Anomius.
No, there was more—some greater power behind it—
and in time Anomius intended to discover what that
power was.

He wondered if they had succeeded in their quest.
Perhaps escaped down the river to Kharasul, from
thence to Gessyth and fabled Tezin-dar. Perhaps they
had secured the grimoire Calandryll had used to bait
his seduction. Anomius did not—could not—believe
the book was a fiction. It must exist: else he was no

more than a dupe, and that was beyond contemplation. He was Anomius! The greatest warlock
Kandahar had known, or ever should know, and he
ground yellowed teeth in frustration as he promised
himself awful revenge, and in the promise found
hope.

He was not slain; he was fed, albeit poorly; therefore he was allowed his life for a reason. What?

He saw it as though bright sunlight pierced the
blankness of the oubliette, and his cursing became
mingled with laughter. Of course: Sathoman pre-
vailed. The ploys and plans and plots he had hatched,
the glamours he had left, the cantrips he had
worked—all were successful. Sathoman held not just
the Fayne, but all Anomius had promised. He was no
longer a mere outlaw lord, but leader of one faction in
true civil war, a valid threat to the Tyrant. And all
Anomius had left behind could be undone only by
him: that guaranteed his life.

Whenever such logic interrupted his vengeful musings his laughter overtook his cursing, rising in shrill
crescendo so that above, where guards and turnkeys
lived in light, men turned to one another, thinking
that at last the prisoner had gone down into utter
madness and sought to shutter their ears, hoping that
soon the Tyrant would order the lunatic's death.

They were, therefore, surprised when the seven sorcerers of the inner cabal came in solemn person to lift
the magicks sealing the outer door and descended
themselves into the gloomy crypt. There, they formed
a circle around the lid of the oubliette and chanted
words of such arcane power that the musty air itself
seemed to hum, filling with the sweet almond scent
of worked magic. A nervous argus was commanded to
draw back the bolts holding the lid and, with two of
his stouter fellows to aid him, to raise the disc. It
came up slowly and thudded noisily over on its
hinges, and as torchlight gleamed about the rim of the
hole there came a single scornful chuckle from out of
the shadows within. For all the stony chill of that

place, the gaolers felt sweat on brows and hands as they were ordered to lower down a rope and bring up the prisoner.

Anomius rose into the light like some pallid grub. Small and sallow when he had been dropped into the shaft, he now seemed shrunk in, his skin pale as uncooked pastry, stretched taut over the bones. His hair had fallen out, his scalp glistening sickly in the radiance of the flambeaux, and his soiled robe was ragged and befouled with the wastes of his near-starved body. Grimed hands hid eyes that seemed huge above his hollowed cheeks, and the watery blue malevolence they held as he squinted at the encircling wizards. He smiled and the turnkeys fell back in alarm behind the protection of the seven warlocks, whose chant grew louder, seven hands pointing in accusation at the crouched figure of the prisoner mage. The scent of almonds grew stronger, and Anomius chuckled and stroked the bulbous protrusion of his nose, and said hoarsely, "So you come at last. I'd have food and wine ere we speak."

Even the sorcerers were startled by this confidence, for though he stood filthy and thin-ribbed before them he radiated a supreme self-assurance that belied his mendicant appearance.

It was Lykander who said, "First we'd ensure safety."

Anomius shrugged, bony shoulders rising beside scrawny neck, but offered no protest or comment beyond another scornful chuckle as the fat mage ushered Cenobar and the one named Andrycus forward to set bracelets of dark metal about his sticklike wrists. They touched the joindures of the circles and white fire flashed briefly, sealing the ensorcelled manacles in place, Anomius wincing as he was burned. Then all seven joined again in the voicing of spells, the almond scent thickening, heady, then dispersing.

"So it is done," Lykander said, "and you are bound to fealty. Raise cantrip or demon against us, or the Tyrant, or any who serve him and you condemn yourself to unpleasant death."

Anomius nodded calmly and asked, "And my powers? When shall you restore them?"

Lykander's round face was bland as he asked, "Think you we shall?"

The question elicited a rattling laugh from the filthy figure. "You bring me up from the darkness," Anomius said, "and for that you must have some reason . . ."

"Perhaps we bring you to the executioner," Cenobar interrupted, then swallowed, taken aback by the look of sheer contempt Anomius flung his way.

"I think not. I think you have at last seen what I saw long ago, and so you must restore me what you took."

"Which is?" Cenobar demanded, seeking to reassert himself.

"That I made Sathoman ek'Hennem," Anomius declared harshly, "and that only I may undo him. That without my aid your Tyrant—and you!—shall likely lose all Kandahar to the Fayne Lord. Ergo, you must restore my power."

Cenobar opened his mouth to speak again, but Lykander forestalled him: "And shall you aid us?"

"Have I a choice?"

Anomius studied the moon-faced mage with lithic calm. Lykander ducked his head and said softly, "Aye—you may refuse and die."

"I am not so great a fool."

The same contempt that had irked Cenobar washed over Lykander. He said, "I have never believed you a fool. A turncoat, yes; a venomous worm inflamed by mad ambition, yes. But not a fool."

"Then you already know my answer." Anomius smiled. "Now bring me out of this foul place and give me wine and food, and after I am satisfied we may speak of civil war and victory."

It seemed almost that he commanded, the Tyrant's sorcerers moving to his bidding, for they parted on his word and motioned him toward the stairs where the gaolers watched in awe, the torches they held trembling as the pale blue eyes swung toward them.

"I am weakened," Anomius murmured, "and I doubt I may climb those steps unaided. Do you give me your arm?"

Swift, his hand clamped upon Cenobar's wrist. The younger mage jerked back as though the hand were a serpent, his fine lips curling in distaste. Anomius smiled satisfaction. Lykander said, "Lend him your strength, Cenobar," and strode ponderously toward the stairs. Cenobar fell into step behind, assuming a blank expression, though fury burned in his dark eyes. Behind them, the rest formed an almost ceremonious procession as they climbed up from the crypt.

THEY brought Anomius to that part of the citadel given over to them, an inner sanctum redolent of their magicks, to a chamber where great panes of leaded glass revealed bright stars, the moon a silver crescent like white fire glimpsed through slit velvet. A generous fire burned in a stone hearth and heavy rugs covered the flagstones. Glass-encased lanterns shed warm yellow light over walls of polished wood and a circular table patterned with cabbalistic signs, large enough to seat three times their number. Cenobar saw Anomius settled in a cushioned chair and ostentatiously brushed at his sleeve. Anomius lounged back, no less ostentatiously waiting. Lykander tapped a bronze gong and while the single note yet hung in the air, a servant appeared.

"Do you have some preference?" the fat wizard asked sarcastically.

Anomius probed a nostril a moment and said, "Good red wine; that quickly. Roasted meat— venison, I think. Or beef. Perhaps a salmagundy; and fresh bread. After, a compote."

Lykander nodded to the servant, gesturing for his fellows to seat themselves. They all took chairs separated by some distance from Anomius, studying him with mixed expression across the great table. He in turn stared back, none of his confidence lost, but rather seeming to wax with each passing moment. After a while Lykander said, "So you foresaw that we should free you? Albeit in limited fashion?"

"I hardly thought you'd set me loose to wander Kandahar." Anomius paused as the servant brought in a decanter of crystal and a single glass. "You do not drink with me?" He filled the glass as Lykander shook his head. "No matter. Aye, I divined that you must eventually come begging my aid."

"Begging?" snapped Cenobar.

"Asking, does it suit your pride better," Anomius returned, and drank deep, smacking his lips. "Aye, that I foresaw. You need me to undo those magicks I laid that have surely brought Sathoman close to victory. To achieve that end you must give me back my power. I suggest you do that now."

"Eat first," Lykander said, "and talk. You must understand our need of caution in this matter."

"Oh, yes," said Anomius, wine-flushed beneath his grime. "But of what shall we talk? The defeating of Sathoman? I'll aid you in that."

"So readily?" asked Lykander.

Anomius raised a hand, turning it so that firelight and starlight alternated on the black metal. "I am bound to serve you," he said. "That, or—as you so delicately pointed out—die. I prefer to live: I have things to do of my own purpose."

For a moment his confident expression shifted, his ugly face contorting, becoming a mask of unsullied rage.

"And what," Lykander said, "might those things be?"

"I was betrayed." As swiftly as it had come, so the rage bled from his face. "And I would have my revenge. You need not concern yourselves—it is not a thing that coincides with the Tyrant's desire to rid himself of Sathoman. In that I shall lend you all my efforts; but in return I'll have your help."

"Unwise," said Cenobar, echoed by Rassuman and Andrycus.

"Refuse and I choose death," Anomius said, extending both wrists to expose the confining bracelets. "Burash! Do you so doubt yourselves that you still fear me while I wear these things?"

"You may not leave this place, save accompanied by two of us," Lykander declared. "You will do our bidding. The consequences of treachery you know—do you accept these strictures?"

"I anticipated no others."

Anomius beamed as servants came in with a platter of roasted venison and the other foods he had requested. He began to eat, grease joining the dirt upon his face and his robe. The sorcerers watched in silence, granting Lykander the role of spokesman.

"Then your powers shall be restored," the fat mage promised. "After you have eaten. Perhaps after you have bathed?"

"The restoration first," Anomius grunted, the words spraying particles over the table. "Then the bath. With perfumed oils and women to tend my needs. A comfortable bed, and robes suitable to my station. After all, do I not become a power in Kandahar? One of you?"

The faces across the marquety displayed offense at this, but none gave argument. Lykander promised, "Those things you may have; now tell me of this other thing, of this revenge you seek."

Anomius broke bread to wipe up gravy, belched loudly and downed more wine.

"I'd seek out two men," he said, his voice grown cold. "A freesword of Cuan na'For who goes by the name of Bracht, and a Lyssian youth named Calandryll den Karynth. They were in my company when you took me, and I suspect they escaped along the Shemme—they sought transport to Gessyth, so Kharasul was their likely destination."

"Were they your acolytes?" Lykander demanded.

"No!" Anomius shook his head. "They were treacherous dogs and I'd see them dead. It was their trickery gave you me."

"Duped by mere mortals?" Cenobar murmured, smiling as Anomius favored him with a poisonous glare.

"Do they threaten our ... alliance ... it may not be," said Lykander.

"They play no part in the affairs of Kandahar," Anomius returned. "This matter is a personal thing— but do you refuse me, then we have no alliance and Sathoman shall run free."

"Assurances must be given," Lykander said.

"Readily," Anomius agreed. "I'll open my mind to you and you shall see this thing poses no threat to your precious Tyrant."

Lykander ducked his head, chins spreading over his chest. "And what help do you need of us?" he wondered.

"A fresh-slain body," Anomius answered, pushing aside the emptied platter of venison and reaching for the salmagundy. "Of preference undamaged, a man or woman in their prime. A strong body to become my hound."

"A revenant?"

Cenobar's dark features paled and beside him Andrycus gasped; Rassuman shaped a gesture of warding. Even Lykander's plump lips pursed in disgust.

"It were best I attend the slaying," Anomius said, undeterred. "Or even perform the act myself, but the corpse must be fresh."

"If these two roam Kandahar they may be found," Cenobar protested. "Their descriptions can be posted among the lictors and the legions. And they may be brought to you."

"And do your lictors consort with Sathoman?" Anomius demanded. "Do your legions have eyes in Mherut'yi and Mhazomul and Kesham-vaj?"

No answer came and he shook his head, turning

from the salmagundy to the compote casually as if they discussed some trivial matter of etiquette. "No. What I need for this is one of my own creation."

"You ask that we aid you in foulest blasphemy," Cenobar cried. "Lykander, this cannot be!"

The plump wizard gave no immediate response but studied Anomius with a mixture of disgust and fascination, as if he looked on something horrifying—that very horribleness rendering it intruging.

"Necromancy is the foulest thaumaturgy," Cenobar insisted. "Shall we stoop to dark magic merely to please this creature?"

"Would you have my aid or no?" Anomius wondered, his eyes on Lykander, unwavering. "Without this you shall have nothing of me."

"Xenomenus bade us give him whatever he might demand," Lykander said slowly, turning from the gaunt figure across the table to study his companions. "And I take him at his word—he'll refuse else."

"Xenomenus spoke of wine and wealth," cried Cenobar. "Women or boys; not this."

"But still Xenomenus would defeat Sathoman," Lykander said. "And without Anomius . . ."

"He'd put all our souls in peril," Cenobar argued.

"Surely mine alone," Anomius murmured, licking the compote's sugar from his lips. "And that I'll chance."

"Let us vote on it," suggested Rassuman.

"Aye," Lykander agreed, "and should the vote be 'nay' and he refuse to aid us, then let those who deny him advise the Tyrant."

Faces paled then and eyes dropped, finding interest in hands and tabletop. Anomius wiped his mouth, smiling, and poured another glass. Lykander drummed fat fingers, summoning attention, and the seven sorcerers raised their heads, the voting silent, the scent of almonds brief on the warm air. In moments it was done and Lykander nodded, turning again to Anomius.

"We'd have your aid, outlaw, so you shall have

your body. But be warned—you shall be held account-
able for its actions! Be they contradictory to our
wishes, it and you shall burn together."

"I ask no more," Anomius declared.

"Then it shall be provided," Lykander said, his
voice somewhat less confident now, "and your magical powers shall be restored."

"Excellent." Anomius sat back, emitting another
belch, his smile satisfied. "You choose well, my
friend."

"I am not your friend," Lykander said softly.

BATHED and perfumed, dressed in a robe of silver-
threaded black, Anomius was a more prepossessing
figure than the sorry creature extracted from the oubliette. He remained ugly and small, but the restoration of his powers invested him with an aura of
strength and a semblance of dignity so that it appeared the ranks of the Tyrant's sorcerers were augmented as the eight similarly dressed men went down
into the dungeons, guided by the chief argus, impressive in his kilt and cuirass of crimson dragon hide.

That official halted, nervous, where a great vaulted
hall was faced with oaken doors, all bolted. At the
center of the hall stood a rack and to the side a wheel,
beyond it the spike-filled bulk of the device called
The Maiden. Braziers filled the place with heat, instruments hung ominous beside them, though it was
the presence of the warlocks that brought sweat to
the forehead of the argus.

"The common criminals lie there, masters."

He indicated a door, hand dropping as Anomius
said, "I want no common criminal. Where do you
keep the worst?"

"There." The argus indicated a second door. "Below this level are the murderers, the child-defilers,
and the enemies of the Tyrant."

"Then lead on."

Such enthusiasm rang in the voice of the little man

that the argus darted a look his way, then averted his eyes from the anticipation he saw. He wondered what transpired: why the other seven were so uneasy; why several wore expressions of such distaste. He did not recognize Anomius, nor venture questions—beneath the Tyrant, these were the land's greatest. He nodded dutifully and drew back the bolt.

Torches shed wan light and oily smoke over the sooted walls of a narrow stairway that descended into the rock. At the foot was a corridor flanked to either side by heavy doors, each inset with a small grille. The stench of unwashed bodies and ordure joined the perfume of the torches as the argus gestured at the first door.

"Within is one Kassium, who slew his father and mother for the pittance they owned. He is scheduled for racking."

"A suitable candidate, I'd think," Lykander suggested, clearly anxious to be gone from this dismal place.

"But perhaps not the most suitable," Anomius returned. "Tell me of the others, gaoler."

The argus shrugged and frowned, confused, and pointed to the other doors, one by one. There lay a cutthroat, next a raper of children, beyond a woman condemned as a poisoner; there a bandit, his neighbor a procurer of unwilling maidens; there one who had preached sedition, a fratricide, a handsome man grown wealthy at the expense of suffocated wives. There were numerous cells and a horrendous catalog of crimes to which Anomius listened attentively, waiting until the argus was done and then saying, "The woman—Cennaire?—tell me of her again."

"A courtesan," the gaoler said. "She stole the purse of an admirer and put a knife in his belly when he threatened to expose her."

"Is she comely?" Pale blue eyes narrowed in interest. "She is not diseased?"

"Aye and nay," the argus said. "She escaped the pox and ere she came here she was lovely. Indeed, she's

sought on more than one occasion to seduce my men,
to offer her body in return for her freedom."

"And was her offer taken?" asked Anomius dryly.

"We adhere to our duty here," the argus promised,
though his furtive eyes denied the implied negative.

"No matter," Anomius said, "so long as she's not
damaged. Bring her out."

The argus glanced at the others and Lykander nodded, the gaoler crossing to the indicated cell and sliding back two heavy bolts. He swung the ponderous
door open and beckoned.

From within a melodious voice said, "So, brave
Gurnal, would you use me again?"

"Silence!" the gaoler blustered, darting a guilty
glance at the watchers. "There are visitors would inspect you. Come out into the light."

"What? No promises to lure me? No blandishments or gifts?"

The argus stepped a long pace forward, raising his
hand. Anomius barked, "Leave her be! Only bring her
out where I may see her."

Gurnal lowered his hand and the woman asked,
"Who are these visitors? Am I now the plaything of
your friends?"

"They are the Tyrant's sorcerers," the argus said,
"and they'd take a look at you. Now do you come out,
or must I drag you?"

"I am, I fear, not at my best," the woman said, "but
if you insist, then so be it."

Gurnal stepped back as she emerged into the torchlight, smoothing tangled hair from the oval frame of
her face, staring boldly at the eight watching men.
Her skin was grimed, but from the dirt huge brown
eyes sparkled defiantly and a wide, luscious-lipped
mouth smiled, exposing white teeth. Her hair was
long and, beneath its coating of filth, a lustrous black,
tumbling about her shoulders, one artfully exposed by
the threadbare gown that also revealed a body slender
save where breasts and hips thrust out the material, a
ragged slit showing a shapely leg.

"Masters, forgive my appearance." She curtsied mockingly. 'But do you only allow me to bathe and I am confident I shall satisfy you all."

"Silence!" Gurnal barked again. "You'll show respect, or suffer punishment for the lack."

The woman favored him with a smile no less mocking than her curtsy and said, "You found softer words before, Gurnal."

"She lies," the argus declared. "She's the tongue of a viper."

Anomius raised a hand, silencing him. "It matters not," he said, staring thoughtfully at the woman; to her: "You are named Cennaire?"

"Aye," she answered, staring back. "And you?"

"Anomius," he said absently. "And for what crimes are you held here, Cennaire?"

Her eyes hooded an instant and then she shrugged. "Doubtless you've an accounting, and were I to tell you I am innocent—the victim of my enemies—you'd name me liar. So: I stand condemned of the slaying of a lover."

Anomius nodded thoughtfully, moving forward to pace around her, as might some farmer examining a heifer offered for purchase, grunting approvingly at what he saw and saying, louder, "She'll do."

"For what?" Cennaire's defiance faltered under his relentless inspection. "Am I to be used by you?"

"Not as you think," Anomius told her, his smile failing to reassure her. "But I offer you freedom from these miserable confines. Shall you accept?"

"What would you have me do?" His scrutiny sent her back a step, closer to Gurnal, as though she sought the comfort of a more familiar oppressor. "What use am I to a sorcerer?"

"Much, I hope," the bald mage answered, "though that I'll explain later. For now—do you come with me? I offer you baths and perfumes; gowns more befitting your beauty; good food, wine. I offer you respite from your cell and the torments of this place. Do you accept?"

Slowly, frowning her curiosity, Cennaire nodded. Anomius offered her his arm, a gnomic courtier, and she took it nervously. Gurnal said, "Masters, how shall I record this?" and Lykander said, "She's given into our charge now, argus. Should anyone come asking, tell them she's taken by the mage Anomius, in service of the Tyrant."

Gurnal mumbled his acceptance and the sorcerers, Anomius and Cennaire in their midst, quit the dungeons.

They went back up from those lower depths of Nhur-jabal to the part of the citadel where the warlocks resided, the black-clad men a living screen about the woman, as if they would hide her presence and the use to which Anomius would put her.

They came to the quarters set aside for Anomius and halted at the door. He said, "Send servants with hot water and such other things as women use. Clothing such as the high-born of Kandahar wear; ornaments. And food."

"No doubt our finest wines, too," Cenobar said, less in mockery than bitterness.

"Aye, that, too," Anomius answered calmly. "And leave us be, for this I'll do alone."

Lykander nodded, his agreement echoed by the rest: none wished for any part of this. Anomius thrust open the door and ushered Cennaire inside with an almost-courtly gesture. She glanced at the seven watching men and licked her lips, hesitating a moment, then stepped into the chamber. Anomius followed her inside and closed the door.

She found some fresh measure of defiance then, a camouflage for her trepidation, and said, "So I'm to be bathed and perfumed and dressed in 'clothing such as the high-born of Kandahar wear'—to what end, if you do not intend to bed me?"

"You recall my precise words." Anomius chuckled approvingly. "You've a good memory, then?"

"I was a courtesan," she said, and a hint of pride entered her voice, "a most successful courtesan. As

such it was important I remember things—to confuse
one lover's name with another was bad for business.
Aye, I've an excellent memory."

"Better and better." Anomius rubbed his hands enthusiastically. "Here in Nhur-jabal?"

"I was born in Kharasul," she said, "and worked
awhile there, but mostly here. I repeat—am I to become your mistress?"

His smile grew sly at that and he gestured at the
chamber. "Is it not enough for now you're free of the
dungeons? Free to enjoy this comfort?"

Cennaire turned slowly round, surveying the room.
Even had she not just come from a stinking cell it
must have appeared luxurious. Panels of pale marble
covered the walls, save where silken curtains were
drawn back from high windows that afforded a view
over the city, and a fire burned in a low-arched
hearth, thickly padded benches set before it. A great
carpet of patterned wool warmed the floor, a table and
two chairs at the center, on that a silver bowl containing sugared fruits. Two doors led to other rooms
and Anomius opened them, revealing a bedchamber
and a bathroom. Cennaire ducked her head.

"I'll agree it is a pleasant alternative. But for how
long? Am I still condemned to death?"

"You've my protection now," Anomius said, pre-
varicating subtly, "and you'll not meet the Tyrant's
executioner if you do my will."

Cennaire fixed speculative eyes upon him, still
wary, but curious now, too. "And yet you say I'm not
here to warm your bed. Then why?"

The tapping of a servant's knuckles on the door
saved him further evasion as he called for the men
and women bearing hot water, soaps and perfumes, a
selection of clothes and jewels, to enter. They came
in, depositing their various loads, and stood awaiting
further instructions. Anomius ordered them gone and
indicated the bathroom.

"Your tub awaits, Lady. Would you not bathe off
that prison grime? After, we may talk of the future."

Cennaire nodded and walked into the steam-filled chamber. Anomius followed her, watching as she carelessly vested herself of the filthy gown, aware that she slid it off with a deliberate languor, seeking, perhaps instinctively, to entice him with her body. That, he was delighted to note, was all he had hoped for: slender and long-limbed, her breasts firm, her hips smooth arcs. No blemishes that he could see marred her form, and had he not another use for her, he would have felt desire stir. *Certainly*, he thought, *she must arouse desire in any other man*. He chortled his approval: all went well. She was beautiful and seemed quick of wit; her memory was good and she met the rigors of her fate with defiance. Aye, he decided, he had chosen well in this one.

He continued to watch as she lowered herself into the water, sighing and stretching out so that her long hair floated about her. She appeared oblivious of his presence, luxuriating in the cleansing warmth, her eyes closed, steam rising in scented clouds. After a while she took up soap and set to scrubbing herself from head to toe, rising up in the tub, still ignoring him as dark, tanned skin shone through the dirt.

Finally she was done, and climbed out to smooth perfumed oil into her flesh, dry her hair with a heavy towel. When she was satisfied, she turned at last to Anomius and asked, "Are there brushes? Combs?"

"In the bedchamber," he replied, and she smiled as if at last he acknowledged his intent.

Naked, she walked slowly past him, hips undulating rhythmically, to find the dressing table where those things were set out in readiness. She seated herself before the mirror, studying his reflection as he halted in the doorway, smiling slightly, and took up a brush, working it with long, slow strokes through her luxuriant hair.

"You are very lovely," he murmured, drawing closer. "A man might lose his heart to you."

"Men have," she said, still smiling. "Shall you?"

"I am a sorcerer," he said, as if that were answer enough.

"Do sorcerers not possess hearts?" she asked. "Are they not men beneath those black robes?"

"Men of higher purpose," he returned.

She pouted then, coquettishly, and thrust back her hair with both hands, the motion emphasizing the jut of her breasts, her eyes still fixed on his reflection. "What higher purpose exists between men and women than the art of love?" she demanded.

Anomius shrugged, not answering directly. Instead he asked, "Would you know power?"

Cennaire's expression shifted at that, becoming for an instant furtive, her long lashes falling over the great brown orbs of her eyes. Then she shook out her hair, the mane cascading about her face and shoulders. "I have known power," she murmured, "over men. It was an enjoyable thing." Defiance set a harsh edge on the melody of her tone.

"A greater power might be yours," Anomius said. "That I can give you."

Interest sparkled then and she turned to face him. "You do not condemn me for that?" she wondered.

Anomius shook his head. "No. It was that—and your beauty—that persuaded me you are the one I need." He touched her cheek, fingers light on the soft skin. "Though there's a price to pay."

"Name it," she demanded, "I'll pay, be it in my ability."

"Oh, it is," he said, moving past her to the bed.

Her eyes followed him and she smiled afresh, starting to rise until he motioned her back.

"No—not that." He poured wine. "Another price, but hard."

"Name it," she said again.

"First prepare yourself," he suggested, indicating the cosmetics left upon the dressing table. "I'd see you in all your glory."

Cennaire ran her hands down over the contours of her body. "Am I not already glorious?" she asked.

"But still, if you desire paint . . ." She swiveled on the seat, facing the mirror again, but with her eyes lowered, hands moving among the pots and brushes.

Anomius watched awhile, waiting until she was done, then smiled his approval and held out a silver goblet, red wine brimming. "A toast," he murmured. "To the power I offer you."

Cennaire took the goblet and sipped daintily, brows arching as she saw he had none.

"You do not drink?"

Anomius shook his head, not speaking, waiting. Cennaire drained the cup and wondered why it felt so heavy in her hand. The figure of the ugly little man swam before her eyes and she smiled languidly, giggling as the cup fell from her grasp to roll across the carpet. Then her eyes closed, and with a careless gurgle of laughter, she toppled from the stool.

With a strength that belied his gnomish stature, Anomius lifted her, carrying her to the bed. Carefully, he settled her on the silken covers, arranging her limbs, then crossing to an armoire from which he fetched two boxes.

One was a pyxis, small and ornately enscribed, that he set aside. The other was larger, and plain. When he opened it, sharp instruments such as chirurgeons use glittered in the light of the lanterns. From that he took knives and scalpels, murmuring the while, his words filling the chamber with the scent of almonds. He set out the tools and touched Cennaire on the lips and eyes, the chest, over the heart, then brought a stick of black wax from beneath his robe and painted on her body a sigil that for an instant glowed with a dark, unholy fire. Then he took the chirurgeon's devices and cut deep into her flesh, down to her heart.

Cennaire cried out once then, but drowsily, bound by his magicks as he excised the living organ and raised it, bloody, in his stained hands. With infinite care, chanting softly all the while, he placed her heart in the pyxis and voiced a spell of containment: within the sigil-scribed box the bloody flesh beat on.

He returned to the woman's body, and from inside his robe brought a lump of clay. He spat on the clay and into the gaping wound, and placed the lump beneath her ribs. Then he touched her, mouthing another cantrip, watching as the clay pulsed and reached out, sending tendrils that connected with the conduits of her body, the wound closing until the flesh was healed and fresh, as though never cut. He knelt over her, breathing into her mouth, and stood back as she shuddered, gasping.

As her eyes fluttered open, filled with panic and the memory of pain, he began to incant a fresh cantrip, staring intently at her supine form.

Cennaire trembled then, racked as if some internal battle were fought between death and life. Anomius's chant died away, the scent of almonds with it, as slowly her chest rose, then fell, the healed ribs expanding as the clay that was now her heart began to beat. Anomius squatted at her side, gently stroking her cheek, smiling triumphantly.

"Now," he said, "you are risen from the dead to do my bidding. Now you are my creature, my revenant. Listen, and I shall tell you what you are to do."

2

LIKE some weary beast the Vanu warboat crept past the cliffs into the mouth of the Yst. Her black sail was lowered and what sound the sweeps made was drowned by the tumult of the river as it fought the sea for mastery of the bay. Salt shone white on the snarling dragonshead of the prow, and on the weather-worn boards of her flanks, the shields hung there; she seemed to limp. Nor were those on board in better shape. The journey south from Gessyth, beating against a contrary wind, the wintry storms, the rounding of the cape, these had taken their toll on a crew depleted by the denizens of the swamplands and the cannibals of Gash. Both Calandryll and Bracht had taken their turns at the oars on that journey, and while that labor had hardened muscle it had also allowed them time to contemplate what lay ahead, to think on the obstacles they must face, the advantage their quarry gained through use of magic while they must transport themselves by physical means. It seemed impossible that they should succeed, but to concede the victory had occurred to none of them. Most likely Rhythamun—or Varent, whatever name he took now—was returned to Aldarin, to gather his resources before commencing his search for the resting place of the Mad God. Therefore they must go back to Lysse, to pick up his trail and follow wherever it should lead. The magical stone Katya wore pointed them in that direction, but before they dared attempt the crossing of the Narrow Sea they needed to haul the boat and take on fresh supplies. On that Tekkan was insistent, and Tekkan was the helmsman—the three questers, Katya, Calandryll, and Bracht, must curb their impatience and hope they were not too late; the quarry not flown.

It was scant solace, Calandryll thought as he scanned the cliffs that fanned to either side of the bay, but the best they had. Varent den Tarl—Rhythamun! he reminded himself bitterly—had thought his seizure of the Arcanum, the demise of its ancient guardians, would close the occult gate, sealing his unwilling dupes forever within the ruins of Tezin-dar. And he might well have been right had Bracht not reacted so swiftly, propelling them back through the portal to re-emerge from the stones close to the Syfalheen village. From there they had returned to the warboat and commenced this journey into new unknowns. He shoved a hand through hair grown long, bleached near pale as Katya's flaxen mane by weeks of sun and sea wind, and wondered what chance they had of victory.

In the body of Varent den Tarl, Rhythamun enjoyed influence and power in Aldarin, and he had told Calandryll that the cantrips of transportation could work only in relation to places already known. Ergo— Calandryll forced himself to think logically, like the scholar he had once hoped to become—Rhythamun must return to his palace in Aldarin. There, perhaps, they would find such clues as might lead them to the sorcerer. That hope was all they had, but between them and its investigation lay obstacles that seemed— at times such as this!—insurmountable.

His eyes narrowed as he saw signal flags along the heights: Sathoman ek'Hennem raised the banners of revolt in Kandahar, and likely the Tyrant's legions would find questions aplenty to put to such wanderers as they, likely find use for the warboat. He raised a hand, tanned and weathered, pointing to the signalers.

"I see them," Bracht confirmed, the black tail of his hair swinging as he raised his head, right hand light on the falchion at his waist. "Likely we'll be met."

"But perhaps not by enemies." The grey of Katya's eyes clouded as she spoke, revealing the doubt behind her optimism.

"I think we've few friends in Kandahar," Bracht returned, teeth gleaming white against the deep tan of his face. "And enemies enough."

"Still, we've a cargo of dragon hides," returned the warrior woman, "and those should win us favor."

Of them all, hers was perhaps the fiercest determination, for the defeat of Rhythamun had been her quest from the beginning. For her there had been no betrayal, no souring of trust as believed-in friendship stood revealed as foulest treachery. From distant Vanu she had come, sent by the northern holy men in quest of the Arcanum that it might be forever destroyed, the resting place of the Mad God lost to those like Rhythamun, who would again bring the world down into the chaos of the godwars. In her that purpose burned with a fierce, bright flame, unsullied.

It burned no less in Calandryll, but in him it was darkened, befouled by treachery, by the knowledge that Rhythamun—in Varent's form and guise of friendship—had tricked him, had played on trust and hope and youthful dreams of glory to make him a dupe. To know that his had been the agency through which the mage had attained the forbidden book was a scouring current of bitterness that stripped away the mantle of innocence he wore when first he fled Secca. His lips stretched in a grim smile as he thought on it: for him this quest meant more than the saving of the world; revenge now played its part.

"What amuses you?" he heard Bracht ask, and answered, "I think on the past; and what I was."

"Best look to the future," advised the freesword, "for it approaches fast."

Calandryll looked to where his comrade pointed and saw two galleys driving toward them, ghostly in the early morning mist. Small arbalests were mounted on the foredecks and bowmen manned the rails. Atop the closer cliff a knot of soldiers gathered. Katya turned, sunlight glinting on her mail shirt, and called in the lilting tongue of Vanu to Tekkan. The helmsman answered with an order that slowed his rowers, the warboat riding the tide as the galleys shifted course to either side.

One hung back, its arbalest menacing as its companion came alongside. Calandryll saw the scarlet puggaree that marked the archers as Tyrant's men wound about the conical helmets of dragon hide. From the foredeck an officer shouted.

"Name yourselves or we sink you."

"I am Tekkan of Vanu," came the answer. "Come with a cargo of hides to serve the Tyrant."

"Vanu?" There was disbelief in the officer's voice. "What do Vanu folk do in Kandahar?"

"Trade, I'd hope," Tekkan returned. "And bring passengers safe home to Lysse."

Across the distance separating the two craft Calandryll saw confusion on the swarthy face and shouted, "I am Calandryll den Karynth, second son to Bylath, Domm of Secca. Do you grant us harborage?"

The Kand's frown deepened beneath the beak of his helm and he stroked his oiled beard. Then he nodded and bellowed, "Move ahead. No tricks, I warn you, lest we send you to Burash."

Tekkan relayed the command to his rowers and the warboat plunged again into motion, flanked by the galleys, the Kand archers staring with unfeigned curiosity at the flaxen-haired Vanu.

"So far," Bracht murmured, "the gods favor us."

"Or toy with us," Calandryll said.

"You become a skeptic." Bracht slapped a hard hand to Calandryll's shoulder. "Ahrd knows, but perhaps I liked the innocent better."

Calandryll grunted and forced a smile: Bracht spoke the truth. "That innocent died," he said. "In Kandahar or Gessyth, I know not—only that he's gone."

"We shall find him." There was no need to name the sorcerer. "In time, we shall find him."

"Shall we?" Calandryll glanced at the Kern and Bracht grinned, nodding.

"Two thousand and five hundred varre, he owes me—aye, we shall find him."

Once Calandryll would have found offense in such pecuniary consideration. Now he grinned back, despite the chafe of impatience, and said, "On my safe return to Aldarin, that was."

"And so it shall be," Bracht promised. "My word on it."

"Does your word hold sway in Kandahar?" A measure of pessimism returned. "Shall the Tyrant's soldiery listen to you?"

Bracht shrugged, leather-clad shoulders rising, and said gently, "We shall see. Ahrd willing, we'll not delay here overlong."

"The Sea God holds sway here," Calandryll retorted. "This is the domain of Burash, not your tree god."

"Even so." Bracht's voice softened, bantering no longer. "I think that Ahrd plays a part in this. Why else send the *byah* to us?"

His intention was to reassure, but mention of the tree spirit that had appeared to warn of treachery served only to remind Calandryll how soundly Rhythamun had deceived him. His mood blackened again and he turned away, studying the escorting galleys.

Bracht looked to Katya and found concern in her eyes. Gently she said, "I think perhaps Tharn stirs, dreaming, and sends doubts to weaken our purpose. We must stand firm."

As with Bracht, Calandryll knew she meant well, but still he could not bring himself to answer or turn to face her. Instead, he grunted a noncommittal sound and fixed his gaze on the city ahead.

They drew close to Vishat'yi now, the cliffs rising steeper, cut through on the west with a great inlet, the settlement spreading upward to either side. A makeshift boom defended the anchorage, heavy chains suspended from moored boats, and where moles thrust out from north and south, huge catapults stood cocked, ready to rain missiles on any approaching vessels. Beyond the moles stood two barbicans, defensive walls spreading back from the harbor to the city proper. That in turn was become a redoubt, streets sealed with barricades and the highlands topped with more catapults. Within the sea walls only a handful of vessels rode the tide, most fishing boats, a few galleys, three wearing the rakish lines of corsair craft. On the moles stood waiting soldiers in dragon-hide armor, their helms and cuirasses marked with the Tyrant's colors.

The boom was drawn back enough the Vanu boat could enter, a galley ahead, the other to her stern, and Tekkan swung her round against a wharf where archers and pikemen thronged, their eyes hard and suspicious.

The commander of the escort—a navarch, Calandryll saw as he sprang ashore—saluted as a tall man whose breastplate and helm were overlaid with golden scales came forward. A scarlet cloak was draped about his shoulders and from his waist hung a sheathed scimitar. He answered the navarch's salute with a peremptory nod, his stern visage turned toward the newcomers. They spoke briefly and the senior officer beckoned the visitors to him. For long moments he studied them, the hook of his nose and his cold green eyes reminiscent of a falcon considering its prey. When he spoke his voice was harsh.

"I am Quindar ek'Nyle, vexillan of this city. You say you are of Vanu? That you come with dragon hides and passengers?"

Tekkan set himself to the front, meeting the cold green stare with no hint of submission as he bowed a formal greeting. "I and my crew are of Vanu," he said calmly. "I am named Tekkan and, yes, I carry a cargo of hides and two passengers."

"Who are?" ek'Nyle demanded.

"Calandryll den Karynth of Secca in Lysse," Tekkan answered. "Son to that city's Domm; and his bodyguard, Bracht ni Errhyn, a freesword of Cuan na'For."

"A curious cargo," ek'Nyle retorted, his voice dubious. "I'd hear of its provenance. Come, you three—you shall explain yourselves."

He spun on polished heels, clearly accustomed to instant obedience, and strode toward the barbican. Katya moved to follow, but Tekkan motioned her back, indicating that only Calandryll and Bracht should accompany him as the soldiery parted, forming an avenue of suspicious faces, pikes held at the ready, as if they anticipated treachery.

The vexillan's stride was long and brisk and he was inside the fortification before they reached the door, seating himself behind a scarred table as they entered. Guards stood outside, and more were stationed along the interior walls, their hide armor dull as old blood in the light that shone down from three high windows. There was an air of palpable tension, increased by the absence of chairs so that the three were forced to stand facing ek'Nyle as he lounged back, studying them, his hands toying with a curved dagger. The place reminded Calandryll of the fortalice in Mherut'yi. He trusted the civil war had prevented any word of his and Bracht's escape reaching this bastion.

"So," ek'Nyle said at last, "explain yourselves."

They had agreed on their story beforehand, and that in such circumstances Tekkan should act as spokesman; he said, "I am a boatmaster, come out of

Vanu to learn what transpires in the world—a voyage of exploration, if you like. Harboring in Secca, I made the acquaintance of Lord Calandryll, who himself was embarked on a scholarly journey and bought passage with us. We cruised your coast and found our way to Gessyth, where we learned no ships had come, thus allowing us to take on a cargo of dragon hides that I'd now trade."

The vexillan's green eyes remained inscrutable as he said, "Trade?"

"Aye," Tekkan answered, "we've need of repairs and supplies, and I understand the Tyrant fights a war—the hides should command a good price."

"You'd profit from our troubles?"

The question was put flatly; beneath its surface lay a threat. Tekkan shook his head, essaying a smile. "I'd aid the Tyrant," he said, "and hope for a reasonable return. No more."

Ek'Nyle grunted, his gaze shifting to Calandryll.

"The son of Secca's Domm, eh?"

"I have that honor," Calandryll returned.

"I think you Lyssians hold scant regard for Kandahar," the vexillan said. "Indeed, I've heard rumors that you build a navy to bring against us."

Calandryll held his face still as presentiment laid cold hands along his spine. "There was talk of building boats ere I left," he agreed calmly, "but only as a measure of protection against those corsairs as harry the trade between our countries."

"There's little enough of that at present," ek'Nyle declared, thin lips curving in a cold smile. "The trading cities of the east coast lay under blockade."

"Indeed?" Calandryll raised eyebrows in what he hoped was a suitably languid expression of aristocratic indifference.

"Indeed." ek'Nyle nodded. Then: "And you lack the appearance of a Domm's son."

Of that there was no denying: the past months had stamped their mark on the youth who had fled Secca. He stood straighter now, his body leaner, hardened, and likely his eyes reflected his impatience and his disillusion. The leathers he wore were beaten by wind and sun, his skin tanned; he was not aware he stood balanced in a fighter's stance, for that was habit now. He smiled and said, "I have traveled far, vexillan, and done my share of boat work. Such things change a man, but you've my word I am Calandryll den Karynth, son to Bylath of Secca."

"You've proof?"

Calandryll's smile faltered. He endeavored to transform the shift into a look of outrage, such as an insulted noble might wear. "I am not accustomed to the questioning of my word," he said coolly.

Ek'Nyle snorted soft laughter. "You've the manner of a Lyssian aristocrat, I'll grant you that. But you've the look of a warrior."

"Is it not your custom, too, that the nobility train for swordplay?" Calandryll demanded, struggling to maintain a disdainful air.

"It is also our custom to walk cautiously about those who may be our enemies," the Kand responded.

"How might you name us that?" Tekkan interrupted. "What quarrel exists betwixt Vanu and Kandahar? Do we not come with hides?"

"As might spies sent by Sathoman ek'Hennem to probe our defenses," ek'Nyle retorted absently; and abruptly turned his questions to Bracht: "You're this one's bodyguard?"

Bracht nodded.

"And you are?"

"Bracht ni Errhyn of the clan Asyth, from Cuan na'For."

"You're a long way from your homeland, Kern."

Bracht shrugged. "I went awandering. I found myself in Lysse. I took employment with Lord Calandryll."

"A horseman at sea?"

Again Bracht shrugged.

"You I'll accept as a freesword," ek'Nyle said, his

voice speculative now. "But a warboat out of Vanu? A roving aristocrat? These things are . . . unusual."

"But nonetheless true," said Tekkan.

"Perhaps," the Kand allowed. "So tell me, boatmaster, where you would go. If I let you."

Calandryll stiffened at the implicit threat of delay. At his side, Tekkan said, "Why, back to Lysse, vexillan. To return Lord Calandryll to his home. Thence to mine."

"The coastal cities are closed," ek'Nyle said.

"Therefore I'd empty my hold of hides and take on such supplies as will see us safe across the Narrow Sea," Tekkan replied, his voice even. "Without touching your coast again."

"Or creep ashore to bring word to the rebels." Ek'Nyle's hands tightened on the dagger, drawing the blade partway from the embossed sheath. Sunlight glittered on the steel. "You present me with a problem, boatmaster. You and your passengers."

Calandryll saw them held here, Rhythamun gaining all the time. He frowned, seeking to emulate his father's manner, to overwhelm objection. "Vexillan," he intoned, making his voice curt, "I repeat that I am Calandryll den Karynth, of Secca, and I'd return home swift as I may. Would you delay me? Such action runs contrary to the accords between our countries and I think your Tyrant must take a dim view."

Ek'Nyle was unimpressed: "The Tyrant sits in Nhur-jabal," he said carelessly. "I command in Vishat'yi and I repeat that you bear scant resemblance to a noble of Secca. Nor do you carry such proof as would confirm your claim. Rather, you've the look of some freesword; perhaps one employed by Sathoman ek'Hennem."

"That I resent!" Calandryll barked, endeavoring still to emulate his father, to summon up that admixture of authority and threat that characterized Bylath.

"Prove me wrong and I'll willingly apologize," the vexillan offered negligently. "But until such proof is forthcoming, you'll remain in Vishat'yi. As my guests, of course."

The dagger thrust hard into the sheath, punctuating the sentence. Calandryll asked, "How shall I prove it?"

"First," ek'Nyle declared, "I shall inspect your cargo. Do you truly carry dragon hides, then, aye, I shall accept you've made the journey from Gessyth. As for the rest"—a hint of malice hid behind his widening smile—"perhaps I must send to Nhur-jabal."

"That would confirm our probity"—Calandryll nodded, steeling himself to patience—"but take far longer than I care to linger here. Surely our cargo will confirm the rest—were we in the rebels' pay, we'd hardly deliver so valuable a cargo to the Tyrant's legions."

Ek'Nyle's smile warmed a fraction, as if he welcomed such debate, or found pleasure in cunctation. He shrugged eloquently and said, "Unless it be subterfuge—a ploy to win my trust. Come south from Gessyth I must ask myself why you failed to offload your cargo in Kharasul."

"We'd word of your war," Tekkan interjected, "and guessed your need would be greater the closer to the fighting."

"This smacks again of profiteering," ek'Nyle responded.

"We ask only that you allow us to haul our vessel and stock our hold with supplies for the crossing of the Narrow Sea," said Tekkan. "Does that sound like profiteering?"

"No," ek'Nyle admitted, smiling, and Calandryll felt hope soar. Then fall as the smile froze and the vexillan added, "Nor like the usual greed of common traders."

"We are not common traders," Tekkan argued, "but explorers. All we seek now is to return home unhindered."

"As shall you," said the Kand, "if I am satisfied."

"Such outcome appears impossible," said Calandryll. "How may we provide the proof you demand?"

"The cargo first." Ek'Nyle's gaze fastened hard with suspicion upon his face. "Then I shall decide."

"And if you cannot?"

"Why, I have two choices." The smile returned, as if the man relished his authority and the power it gave him. "The one is to execute you; the other to send you to Nhur-jabal, that the Tyrant's sorcerers may question you."

Calandryll felt his hands clench involuntarily into fists, aware that ek'Nyle caught the movement, cursing himself for that small betrayal. Then, in the vexillan's words, he saw an opportunity to turn the debate in a more favorable direction; it was a slim chance, and more than a little hazardous, but his patience wore thin and recklessly he asked, "And is there not a sorcerer here in Vishat'yi? If not, a spaewife. Either would surely divine our honesty."

To his right he heard Tckkan's sharp intake of breath; to his left saw Bracht's warning glance. It was a dangerous gambit: sorcerer or spaewife, either might reveal the true purpose of their quest, and in the doing betray them to ambition, perhaps involve them in further delay should the Tyrant's wizards take a hand. Against that danger he balanced the conviction that this officious vexillan would hold them here indefinitely, out of suspicion or spiteful amusement, and each day—each hour!—they lingered weighted the scales heavier in favor of Rhythamun.

"Your suggestion appears to alarm your comrades," ek'Nyle remarked. "Why might that be?"

"I've no liking for magic or its practitioners," Bracht grunted truthfully.

"And you?" the Kand asked Tekkan. "Do you object?"

The Vanu shrugged, shaking his head, his expression bland.

"Then perhaps that is the way," ek'Nyle murmured, studying their faces for sign of further reaction, but finding none for both composed themselves despite their doubts. "Sorcerer and spaewife, we have both. But first, this cargo . . ."

He rose in a swirl of scarlet, snapping orders as he came around the table, a squad of pikemen falling in about the three as he strode from the barbican and back across the cobbles to the wharf where Katya and the other Vanu folk waited, ringed round by watchful soldiers. Calandryll glanced sidelong at his companions as they were herded to the warboat, seeing Bracht's blue eyes clouded with doubt, Tekkan's grey impassive.

Gulls rose raucous as they came near, and over the smooth water of the anchorage the mist faded, a pale sun breaking through the overcast. The air was cold and from the heights above the city a wind skirled, fluttering the banners atop the barbicans and the mastheads of the ships. Tekkan called in his own language and several flaxen-haired Vanus sprang to the warboat's deck, the rest forming a chain as the baled dragon hides were passed onto the quay. Quindar ek'Nyle watched patiently as the hides were stacked, then, nostrils pinching at the pungent odor, inspected the topmost bale.

"In this you have not lied," he allowed when he was satisfied. "And in return you ask for supplies and the use of this anchorage?"

The hides were worth far more. From them armor could be fashioned, tough as any metal out of Eyl, and without the seasonal influx of traders prices must surely rise. Even so, Tekkan nodded and said, "And such materials as we need to make the repairs."

The vexillan smoothed his oiled beard a moment, then shrugged. "You may commence your repairs. After all, are you proven false in the other matter this boat shall become part of the Tyrant's fleet."

"When shall this proving take place?" Calandryll demanded, hard put to conceal his irritation.

Ek'Nyle turned him a speculative glance and answered, "When Menelian is ready. Until then you'll remain here."

His chin jutted in the direction of the barbican and Calandryll saw that they should be held prisoner until the sorcerer came. He sighed in affectation of aristocratic vexation, though frustration gritted his teeth. Across the piled hides he saw Katya watching, unnoticed by ek'Nyle among the other Vanu women. Her grey eyes were troubled but she forced a faint smile of encouragement and he thought that at least she was not held. If worst came to worst, perhaps she might be able to take the warboat out. His gaze traveled past her, across the harbor to the boom, and all his fears returned: while that barrier hung across the exit there could be no flight. He started as a pike tapped his back, urging him away, ek'Nyle already pacing toward the ominous tower.

Reluctantly he fell into step, following the vexillan inside the barbican, where a door of wood and metal was opened, ek'Nyle offering a brief bow devoid of apology as he ushered them into a cold stone chamber.

"I shall ask that Menelian attend you," he declared. "Until then you will remain here."

Before Calandryll had opportunity to protest that such quarters ill befitted the son of Secca's Domm, the door was closed, the sound of oiled bolts sliding into place horribly final. He looked around, seeing a small chamber all of grey blocks, a single window granting sight of a rectangle of brightening sky cut vertically by thick metal bars. Around the lower part of the wall the blocks were extended inward to form a continuous bench and at the center of the floor a hole gaped dark, the acrid stench rising from it attesting to its use. Bracht grunted and availed himself of the facility: a tacit comment on their plight.

Tekkan settled himself on the bench and said softly, "Was it wise to bring a mage into this?"

"Ek'Nyle would surely have thought of it sooner or later," Calandryll retorted, his irritation spilling over so that his response came out harsh. "And if not—would you rather we went in chains to Nhur-jabal?"

Tekkan favored him with an imperturbable look and shook his head, prompting a pang of guilt. "Forgive me," Calandryll asked. "These delays sit ill."

"With us all," Tekkan murmured.

"Your magic would prove useful now," Bracht said, stretching on the stones, head pillowed on his arms.

"My magic?" Calandryll laughed bitterly. "Whatever magic I worked was the gift of Rhythamun, channeled through the stone he gave me and lost with its going. And I thought you had no love of such thaumaturgy."

"I'd sooner put my faith in honest swordwork, true," Bracht answered evenly. "But I come to think that perhaps fire must be fought with fire. Could you wreck that door as you turned those canoes off Gash's coast I'd accept such usage. And in Mherut'yi your magic freed me from a similar prison—I'd not object to another such demonstration."

"I fear I must disappoint you." Frustration set an edge to Calandryll's voice. "I've no magic in me now, nor any answer to this cursed delay save patience."

"Which," Bracht returned, "you lately lack."

Calandryll stared at the freesword with narrowed eyes. That the Kern's comment was true did nothing to assuage the anger he felt rising; rather, it fueled his ire. He clenched his fists and drove them hard against his thighs, fixing Bracht with a stare no less cold than ek'Nyle's.

"I'd halt Rhythamun," he snapped. "I'd hunt him down and slay him before he locates Tharn's tomb and raises the Mad God. I believed you shared that aim."

"Gently, gently," Tekkan said, concern in his voice. "That aim is common to us all. Let us not quarrel over such shared purpose."

Calandryll ignored the boatmaster, his eyes locked with Bracht's. The freesword rose to a sitting position, adjusting his falchion across his knees. "I share that aim," he said carefully, "as you well know."

"I know you'd have the coin promised you!" Inside his head a calmer voice told him he spoke wildly, that these accusations were unjustified, that Bracht was a proven comrade. Even so, he found it impossible to still his tongue; it seemed a madness impelled him to strike out, careless of what he said. "I know you lust after Katya and must pursue this quest until the Arcanum is destroyed and Rhythamun defeated so that you may press your suit. Otherwise . . ."

He shrugged, raising balled fists to slam them, again, hard against his thighs, shaking his head as if in dismissal of the Kern.

Bracht studied him a moment, swarthy face creased by a frown. When he spoke his voice remained soft. "As we entered this harbor Katya suggested that Tharn stirs," he said. "That the god, dreaming, sows the seeds of disruption, of disillusion. I think she was right." His voice hardened then and he added, "Did I not, we'd set blade to blade and I'd slay you."

Calandryll's hand dropped to the hilt of his sword at that, his body shifting unconsciously to a fighting crouch. Then he froze, his mouth falling open so that he gaped at Bracht, amazement in his eyes, and something close to fear. He shuddered, straightening, hand snatching back from the sword's hilt as though from the jaws of a serpent.

"By all the gods!" He heard the words come out hoarse, horrified by his actions. "I think you speak the truth. Forgive me, friend!"

He wiped a hand over his face, sweat beading there despite the chill that pervaded the cell, and folded his arms across his chest, licked at lips gone dry.

"I think Katya was right. Or Rhythamun leaves some foulness in his wake. Or these delays drive me down into madness."

Bracht stood up, crossing the flags to set a hand on Calandryll's shoulder. "You are forgiven," he said lightly, and gestured at their confines. "Imprisonment sits hard with me, too. And I'd no sooner linger here than you; all this serves to shorten tempers."

"Even so." Calandryll shook his head, looking into Bracht's eyes.

"Even so," the freesword said, "we shall not succumb. Does Tharn send magicks out of his dreaming, or Rhythamun lay gramaryes to thwart us, we shall resist them. We must!"

"Aye!" Calandryll nodded enthusiastically, all anger drained away. He felt very weary as he grasped Bracht's hand. "And do I speak such madness again, you'll bring me to my senses, no?"

"Aye, that I'll do," Bracht promised. "And you the same for me."

He led Calandryll to the bench and saw him seated, an arm companionable about his shoulders. Calandryll muttered, "But you take it well. You chafe at imprisonment, I know; yet you hold your temper."

Bracht glanced at the bare walls and grinned tightly. "I like this no better than you," he agreed, "but I've learned the hunter must sometimes be patient. And . . ."

He paused; Calandryll looked at him, seeing doubt in the blue eyes, in the set of the wide mouth. "And?" he prompted.

"Anomius claimed to divine a power in you," Bracht said slowly, choosing his words with obvious care, "the spaewife in Kharasul, too, and you wore Rhythamun's stone for half a year. Mayhap that . . . opens you to occult blandishment."

The words fell like cold water on Calandryll's ears, awakening him to fresh fears. "I've no power," he mumbled helplessly. "Were that so, I'd blast away that door and free us. But I cannot! That power they discerned came from the stone."

"Mayhap," Bracht said, "and mayhap the stone served to render you vulnerable to sendings."

"Then I am a danger to our quest." Calandryll felt moisture on his face, unsure whether it was sweat or tears. "A danger to you all."

"No!" Bracht's voice was earnest; his hand tight on Calandryll's shoulder. "Remember what I've taught you of swordplay—that even the best have some weakness; but aware of it, compensate. This—if it be true!—is no different."

Tekkan moved to his other side, his lilting voice measured: "And if it be true, then likely you still possess the power we've seen you use. Be that so, you've a formidable weapon at your beck."

"Hardly at my beck." Calandryll shook his head. "I say again—that power came from the stone."

"Did you not tell me Rhythamun advised you the art of magic is hard-learned?" Bracht demanded. "Then mayhap you need to learn its usage. Just as you needed to learn swordskill."

"Which benefits us little here," Calandryll returned.

"But later," the freesword said. "Quit of this place do we not go to Aldarin? To that palace Rhythamun used in Varent's form? There was a library there, no? A chamber filled with books, you said. Well, likely we'll find books there that deal with magic, and you may take them and read them and perhaps learn to use the art."

"Think you we'll have time enough, and I the talent?" Calandryll muttered doubtfully, then snorted bitter laughter. "And then I should be a mage, should I not? And you've no love of wizards."

Bracht's answering chuckle was genuine. "For you I'll make an exception," he declared. "Mayhap you'll be the flame to fight Rhythamun's fire. And against that one I'll accept any allies."

"We've yet to escape this impasse." Calandryll was cheered by his comrades' loyalty, but still stone walls stood firm barrier against optimism. "And Quindar ek'Nyle seemed in no hurry to free us."

Bracht shrugged. "I'll not believe our quest ends here," he said stoutly. "We'll be freed ere long."

Tekkan nodded solemn agreement and said, "If Tharn does stir, then surely the Younger Gods must

sense it; if Rhythamun works his magicks to raise the
Mad God, then his successors must sense that, too.
And surely they'll not bow readily to Tharn—mayhap
they'll aid us. Cleave to hope, Calandryll! We live yet,
and living may still hope to succeed."

Calandryll sighed, ducking his head in acceptance
if not agreement. For all their reassurances it seemed
to him hopeless optimism to think they should find
godly aid. Using Varent's body Rhythamun had succeeded in all his aims to date. He had obtained the
chart that showed the way to Tezin-dar; had snatched
the Arcanum; was even now likely on his way to the
resting place that book revealed. And never had the
gods intervened to halt the madman. Not Dera, goddess of his own homeland, or Burash, the god of
Kandahar. Only Ahrd had taken a hand, and that no
more than cryptic warning of deceit. To put their
trust in the Younger Gods seemed vain to him: this
seemed a thing of humankind, of him and Bracht and
Katya, and none others.

Miserably he asked, "What shall Katya do while we
languish here?"

"I told her to see to the warboat's repairing,"
Tekkan advised him. "To haul and caulk as swift she
may. That and lay in those supplies we need to cross
the Narrow Sea. Beyond that . . . well, does this mage
prove us true and we're set free, we sail for Lysse; if
not, she's to take the boat on alone."

"Each augury we've heard has spoken of three,"
Calandryll protested. "In Secca, Reba foretold two
companions; in Kharasul, Ellhyn scried the same. The
guardian in the Syfalheen village awaited three. How
shall Katya succeed alone?"

"She'll not," said Bracht firmly. "I've little enough
liking for magic, but I trust such scryings—three were
prophesied and three there shall be. We shall be quit
of this place ere long."

His tone was positive and Calandryll forced a
smile, even though he could not share the Kern's optimism. A mood of black melancholy gripped him,

heightened by his unusual—and unexpected—display
of temper, and he thought Bracht spoke to reassure,
rather than from any real belief. It seemed to him
their way was fraught with danger, obstacles strewn
in their path to hinder and delay, as if fate itself,
laughing at the gods, contrived to impede their progress. Time was of the essence and yet at every junc-
ture speed was denied them. Perhaps Tharn did stir
and somehow pluck the strings of destiny to hamper
them. If that was so, what chance had they of success? And yet they must succeed, else the Mad God
would rise and all the world come down in ruin. He
shivered at the thought, the specter of despair looming ominous.

Then the clattering of his teeth became a grinding
as anger rose anew, directed now not at his companions, but himself, and Rhythamun; at Tharn, too. If
the god or the wizard worked to set this black mood
on him he would deny them. He would not succumb!
He would not concede them that victory! He
clenched his jaw, his smile grim now, nodding to
Bracht.

"Aye." His voice was hard with anger. "We'll quit
this hole and sail for Aldarin. To the ends of the earth
if need be."

"Aye!" Bracht's hand fastened tight on his shoulder, the pressure comforting. "No pompous Kand
shall halt us. Nor wizards; nor any other thing, be it
of man's making or magicks."

"Amen to that," murmured Tekkan.

THEIR resolution waned somewhat as the day progressed. Outside they heard the city come alive, but
the single window was set too high to afford them
any view save of the sky, wintry and grey, and the
door was not opened until noon, when a single dish of
spicy meat and vegetables was delivered to them. The
soldier who set the bowl down was accompanied by
three others, and beyond them, before the door closed

again, the prisoners saw more standing alert in the chamber outside. They ate and settled back on the bench as noonday passed into afternoon and then twilight dimmed the sky. Neither candles nor flambeaux were brought them and soon the cell was dark, the air grown chill again. They spoke, in increasingly desultory fashion, seeking to maintain their optimism, but for Calandryll each passing hour renewed his melancholy, until it began to seem that they should sit forgotten in Vishat'yi forever. He fought the mood, but it was inexorable as the mounting cold and he felt his spirit numb, hope fading. In time, with little else to do, they stretched out and slept as best they might, the stone hard and cold, inspiring miserable dreams.

Then sound and light intruded and they woke, Bracht and Calandryll reaching instinctively for their swords.

"I'd not advise that."

The voice of Quindar ek'Nyle was aloof, his words emphasized by the pikes angled toward them, torchlight glinting on the blades. The vexillan stood slightly behind five of his men, wrapped in a cloak of fur-lined scarlet now, his expression calm. Straightsword and falchion slid back into the scabbards and he smiled coldly.

"Come—Menelian shall examine you."

Without further ado he turned and quit the cell. The soldiers parted warily, as if they anticipated attack. It felt to Calandryll that they were already tried and found guilty, and he struggled to find some measure of optimism as he rose and stretched, working knots from his stiffened muscles.

"Hurry." The vexillan's command rang impatiently from the outer chamber. "I'd not keep Menelian waiting. Nor, I'd think, would you—save you be afraid of facing him."

"We've nothing to fear," Calandryll declared, hoping that he spoke the truth. "Lead on."

He walked out of the cell, the room beyond warm, braziers set about its perimeters, the scent of wine

mingling with the heady aroma of the narcotic tobacco favored by the Kands to render the air thick.
Ek'Nyle waited by the main door, beckoning them
out, a squad of six armed and armored men forming
around them. A full moon westered toward the
clifftops, setting the hour sometime past midnight,
blanching the city, outlining the catapults along the
heights like gibbets. In the harbor masts swayed
gently and waves lapped softly. Calandryll saw the
single stem of the Vanu warboat, but of its crew or
Katya he saw no sign.

"This way."

Ek'Nyle sounded irritated, irked by the disturbance
of his night, and it occurred to Calandryll that the demands of the sorcerer Menelian must take preference
over those of the vexillan. It was some small measure
of consolation as they were herded away from the barbican into the darkened streets of Vishat'yi.

Soldiers stood alert by the barricade sealing the
street that led inward from the mole, warned of their
coming by the torches of their escort. They saluted as
ek'Nyle approached, a way already cleared, closed behind the nocturnal visitors as they went on into the
city. It was darker there, the buildings close, rising up
the slopes like terraced cliffs, their windows shuttered so that no light shone out; nor were there such
lanterns as brightened the avenues of Lysse's cities,
the brands held aloft by the two leading soldiers and
the glow of the moon the only sources of illumination. They walked through pooling shadows, the
drumming of their boots echoing off the night. It
seemed to Calandryll like a threnody, the darkness
matching his mood, so that he began to ponder the
wisdom of his suggestion.

Pointless, he told himself as they climbed a rising
avenue, it was done and they were committed. As he
had said: sooner or later ek'Nyle would surely have
brought them before the wizard, so sooner was the
preferred option. Whatever the outcome they would,
at very least, know more certainly where they stood,

and that must be better than the limbo of the cell. He
fought his doubts, seeking a tranquillity that eluded
him.

The avenue turned and they ascended a flight of
wide steps, the city falling away below them, the harbor a pool of black and silver, harlequined by the
moon. Then the steps devolved on a small plaza, surrounded by tall, narrow buildings, each walled, and
ek'Nyle halted before a gate. He tugged a cord and an
unseen bell chimed, the sound clean and clear as the
moon's light. The gate opened and the vexillan led his
men through into a paved courtyard, the keeper a
cloaked and hooded shadow that moved on silent feet
across the stones to usher them inside the house.

They entered a vestibule lit by seven lanterns, their
trapped flames giving off a faint resinous perfume.
The floor was tiled in the manner of Kandahar with
colorful mosaics, while the walls were starkly white.
An effigy of Burash stood in a niche. The gatekeeper
disappeared back into the courtyard, the door closing
silently behind him as the inner portal swung open to
reveal a thin-faced man whose robe of silver-decorated
black defined him as the sorcerer. He was, Calandryll
noticed with vague surprise, young, not yet close to
his middle years, his cheeks clean-shaved and his hair
pale for a Kand, more brown than black. His eyes
were dark and confident as they surveyed his visitors,
bright with intelligence and, Calandryll thought,
amusement.

He studied them awhile, that delay visibly increasing ek'Nyle's irritation, then nodded and said, "So
these are the ones."

"Who else?" the vexillan snapped. "Do you work
your art on them and I'll be gone."

"Go now," the mage returned, his voice careless.
"I'd not keep you from your duties . . . Or your bed."

Ek'Nyle frowned, disconcerted, momentarily unsure of himself, his poise threatened.

"And take your men," the wizard added.

"What?" Confusion strangled ek'Nyle's question.

"I am protected well enough." Finely sculptured lips parted in a smile. "Or do you doubt my talents?"

"No, but . . ." The vexillan shook his head, confusion mounting, his discomfort widening the mage's smile. "Is that wise?"

"I deem it so," came the answer. "And doubtless you've tasks aplenty for your men."

Ek'Nyle nodded curtly, attempting to regain his air of authority. "If that be your wish," he muttered.

"It is," the mage declared. "You need not fear for my safety."

"So then." Ek'Nyle cast an angry glance at the prisoners. "As you wish. I leave them in your care."

"And I bid you good night."

The black-robed man watched as the vexillan spun about, barking an order that brought his men trotting hurriedly after him. The door closed on their backs and for a moment the clatter of marching heels drummed in the courtyard. Then there was silence.

"I am named Menelian," the sorcerer announced. "Do you follow me, and we may settle this matter of your probity."

3

POLITE as if he entertained welcome guests,
Menelian ushered them from the vestibule into a
cozy chamber full of warmth and light. Shutters were
closed over windows of colored glass, their panes reflecting the glow of the lanterns ensconced in niches
in the stark white walls, scented like those outside,
and in a hearth a generous fire burned. Two plain
wood settles stood before the hearth, chairs of equally
simple design spread along the walls, which were un-
adorned. At the center of the chamber was a table laid
with cold meats, spiced vegetables, bread and cheese,
a bowl of fruit, four tankards, and a keg. The simplicity of the room surprised Calandryll, his frown registering so that the sorcerer chuckled and asked, "What
had you expected? The paraphernalia of thaumaturgy,
black candles and skulls? Or sybaritic luxury?"

"I was not sure what to expect." Calandryll shook
his head, taken aback by the wizard's casual manner
and unsure how to respond. The sorcerer appeared
friendly, his amusement genuine, but without hint of
mockery, and the gaze he turned upon them seemed
honest. But so had Rhythamun when he posed as a
friend: Calandryll chose to wait judgment. At his side
he saw Bracht staring warily about.

"I cannot blame you for doubting me, knowing Quindar ek'Nyle as I do," Menelian said, his smile hinting at apology. "I assume you were held in that stinking pit he uses for a cell and fed no better than his men. Warm yourselves. Eat, partake of this good ale. Or do you prefer wine?"

His manner remained that of an eager host rather than an inquisitor and Calandryll felt confusion grow. This was a mage sworn to service of the Tyrant—did that loyalty make him friend or foe? "Ale suits well," he murmured. "But . . ."

"Doubtless you anticipated a somewhat different reception." Menelian chuckled, setting a tankard beneath the keg's spigot, filling it and then three more. He passed them round, still smiling as he saw the frank suspicion on Bracht's face, measured doubt on Tekkan's. He raised his own and drank deep, wiping foam from his lips casually as if they conversed in some tavern. "And after Quindar's welcome I hardly blame you."

He drank again, watching them over the rim of the tankard, his eyes bright with intelligence.

"I assure you, gentlemen, that there is no poison in the ale. Nor magicks or potions. Only an honest brew and food I thought you might enjoy."

Calandryll glanced at Bracht and saw disbelief in the Kern's eyes. Neither he nor Tekkan moved to taste their drink. He looked at Menelian and shrugged—the man was a sorcerer: he had no need of potions to work his art—he drank.

The ale was, as the mage had promised, good. It washed away the fur-tongued memory of ek'Nyle's stew and awakened his appetite: he took another draught, deeper this time.

"Your comrades appear less trusting," Menelian said, "so perhaps I'd best lay cards on the table—for I think that trust is important here, and I think we've little time to waste."

He motioned at the settles, and without waiting for them to seat themselves cocked a finger, murmuring softly guttural words. A chair rose from its place against the wall and floated to him as the scent of almonds briefly contested with the lanterns' perfumed vapors. "So," he said as he sat. "Let me be the first to show my hand. Mayhap that will convince you that my intentions are honest, and I am no enemy. Rather, a friend."

Bracht's narrowed eyes argued the suggestion, but still he took a place beside Tekkan. Calandryll lowered himself to the opposite bench, intrigued despite his doubts. From the corner of his eye he saw Bracht take a cautious sip, Tekkan follow suit. His own head felt clear and he thought perhaps Menelian might speak the truth: Rhythamun's duplicity need not mean all sorcerers were hostile.

"I serve the Tyrant," Menelian declared, "let there be no doubt of that. I have pledged loyalty to Xenomenus, but that service does not mean we are enemies—the contrary, I think. Please do not confuse me with such as Quindar ek'Nyle." This directed at Bracht, whose scowling face still registered suspicion. "The vexillan is a soldier, and has the tendency of most soldiers to think in simple terms—black and white, with no shades between. He organizes the defense of a city threatened by civil war: Sathoman ek'Hennem holds most of the eastern coast and is likely to attack Vishat'yi ere long—Quindar perceives a warboat in his harbor and finds no handy place in his thinking to which he might assign it. Ergo, he suspects you of some underhand ploy. Some stratagem of ek'Hennem's he cannot yet discern."

"And you do not?"

Calandryll realized that his tankard was empty. Menelian rose, taking it and refilling it. On impulse Calandryll followed him to the table, helping himself to food as the sorcerer said, "No. I have some idea who you are—or what—and that is why I had you brought here at this ungodly hour."

They returned to their respective seats as Tekkan

climbed to his feet and loaded a platter with meat and bread. After a moment's hesitation Bracht joined him.

"I serve the Tyrant," Menelian repeated. "I am a lesser member of that elect group sworn to prevent the chaos that arose when every petty lordling employed a host of wizards to further his ambitions. You know of the Sorcerers War?"

Calandryll nodded and the mage continued, "And you have already met with Anomius, who served Sathoman."

He raised a hand as Bracht's platter was set aside, the Kern's hand dropping to his swordhilt.

"Put up your blade, Bracht ni Errhyn, for I'm not your foe. More like your friend. Listen to me!"

Bracht frowned doubtfully, but the falchion slid back into the scabbard and he took up his plate again.

"Anomius lives," Menelian said. "He was captured and taken prisoner to Nhur-jabal and cast into a dungeon, bound there by magic. But even so the gramaryes he left behind furthered Sathoman ek'Hennem's cause and the Fayne Lord triumphed in the east. The Tyrant is young, and like most young men takes a short view—in hope of victory over Sathoman he has freed Anomius."

"Who would see us dead, I think," Bracht grunted.

"Indeed he would," Menelian agreed. "And within a few days, Quindar ek'Nyle will receive the Tyrant's orders to apprehend you and deliver you to Nhur-jabal. Anomius launches a plot against you."

He paused dramatically, sipping ale, and Calandryll said, "Why do you tell us this?"

"Because we who name ourselves the Tyrant's sorcerers are pledged to serve all Kandahar," Menelian replied, "and Anomius serves only himself. I received word from certain of my colleagues of his desire to take you; and at the same time, word that those of the inner circle, who are far mightier than I, have seen such stirrings in the occult fundus as must override our immediate loyalties to Xenomenus."

"Sorcerers' riddles," Bracht said dubiously.

"No!" Menelian shook his head. "Warning and aid. The Tyrant sees only the immediate advantage— victory over Sathoman—and to that end will listen to Anomius, who seeks to take you for personal revenge."

"Why?" Calandryll asked, wanting for reasons he could not yet define to trust the sorcerer, but not yet sure he should.

"Because he believes you have obtained some book of gramaryes as can render him supreme," Menelian returned.

"That was a gambit to escape Sathoman ek'Hennem," Calandryll said carefully. "No more."

"Much more, I think," said Menelian. "I think you went to Tezin-dar to find the Arcanum."

Calandryll's platter hit the floor, what little food was left spilling unnoticed over the polished planks. Menelian gestured, so that the spillage was flung into the fire, where woodsmoke became mingled with the perfume of almonds.

"Anomius does not yet know that," he said earnestly. "But whatever tale you spun him, his ambition prompts him to believe you sought a tome that would reveal such ancient spells as must make him master of all Kandahar. He'd have it, and his revenge, too. He's crazed, but like some beast with a taste for human flesh—cunning and dangerous."

"And you know its true meaning?"

Calandryll stared at the sorcerer. Menelian nodded. "The masters of the inner circle discerned the true import of your quest," he said solemnly. "Once they had probed Anomius and thought on what you did." He looked to Tekkan then, his expression curious. "Did the holy men of Vanu not realize that what they divined must likely be known to others?"

Tekkan shrugged. "I am not of that circle. I do only what they said I should."

"Which was to hunt down the seekers of the Arcanum and bring the book to Vanu that it might be destroyed?" asked Menelian.

Tekkan nodded. "How do you know that?" he asked.

Menelian smiled a shade ruefully and answered, "Vanu folk wandering so far south? It needed only an educated guess to reach that conclusion—but heed me, for as I said, we've little time. I'll tell you all I know and you may judge then whether or not you'll trust me."

He looked them each in the eyes, his own no longer amused, but filled with a fervent seriousness that spoke of honesty; and more than a little trepidation.

"The existence of the Arcanum was—indeed, still is—a close-kept secret. Had we Tyrant's sorcerers believed we might find and destroy it, we should have ventured to Gessyth long past; but Tezin-dar was a legend and all the prophecies concerning that fabled city confirmed that only those chosen by the gods might survive the journey. Sometime past those of the inner circle sensed such flux in the occult fundus as suggested some stratagem was afoot concerning the book, but not the where or how of it. With so little knowledge, we could not act, only await events. But then Anomius was taken and the outlines of his ambition and his belief became clear—we learned that he had encountered a young man come out of Lysse and a warrior of Cuan na'For, bound for Gessyth in search of what he believed was a grimoire of supreme power. Though he had not, the masters of the inner circle guessed this must be the Arcanum, but from what Anomius revealed, it seemed neither possessed such knowledge as would make them the designers of such a quest, and so it was felt some other agency lay behind them. Word came of a Vanu warboat traveling from Kharasul to Gessyth, and when Anomius was freed he spoke of Calandryll den Karynth and Bracht ni Errhyn. The rest is simple logic—those two appear in Vishat'yi on board a Vanu boat, but . . ." He paused, studying their faces with dreadful intensity, "You do not have the Arcanum with you."

Calandryll shook his head: "No."

"Then," said Menelian slowly, "either you failed, or the book was wrested from you. Not by Anomius, for he still lusts after it. Then mayhap by the one who sent you?"

Now Calandryll nodded: "Aye. By Rhythamun."

"Rhythamun?" Menelian asked.

Calandryll heard Bracht's sharp intake of breath, ignored it. "He is a mage," he said. "He tricked us. We believed him honest when he told us he sought to destroy the book. We reached Tezin-dar and the Guardians gave it into our keeping, but then Rhythamun appeared and seized it." He paused, grimacing, anger and disgust in his voice as he added, "He gave me a magical stone to wear. To aid me and guide me, he said. The stone brought him there! Now we go after him."

"And he knows what the Arcanum is?" The sorcerer's voice was low, harsh with horror.

Calandryll ducked his head. "Aye. He'd raise the Mad God."

"Insanity!" Menelian's aplomb was vanished; suddenly he looked young and frightened. "Are his wits addled?"

"By lust for a power he believes he can control." Tekkan set down his tankard, his soft voice somber. "The holy men of my land scried this—that Rhythamun sought the book, but could not approach Tezin-dar himself, only through the agency of others. Calandryll was one, Bracht another, my daughter the third."

"Your daughter?" Menelian frowned confusion.

"Katya," Tekkan said, "who waits now in the harbor."

Menelian nodded slowly. "The three," he murmured. Then, louder, "And know you where this Rhythamun has gone?"

"He wore the form of Varent den Tarl of Aldarin," Calandryll said, "and likely returned there. Beyond that ..."

He shrugged helplessly. Tekkan said, "Katya wears a stone given her by the holy men that points us to the one Rhythamun gave Calandryll. The wizard took it when he seized the book and now it points to Aldarin."

"Then you must go there," Menelian said urgently. "With all haste! I'll send word to ek'Nyle that you're to be given all assistance, that no hindrance be set on your departing."

"Why?"

Bracht's question cracked out like a whip. Calandryll and Tekkan swung to face him, seeing a visage set in lines of doubt. Menelian frowned and asked softly, "You ask me why?"

"I've scant love of magic," Bracht returned coldly, "and little enough for its practitioners. You and these other sorcerers—do you not lust for that power the Arcanum can bestow?"

"Burash, no!" Menelian raised hands in rejection. "To raise the Mad God is rank insanity."

"Rhythamun thinks not," Bracht said. "And if Anomius knew that what we sought was no grimoire but the Arcanum, I think he'd harbor the same mad lust."

"I think Rhythamun must be insane," Menelian retorted, "and Anomius . . . Anomius is a miserable worm."

"A worm your Tyrant has freed," Bracht pressed.

"Because he holds the key to Sathoman ek'Hennem's defeat," Menelian sighed. "Without his aid Kandahar must suffer the ravages of civil war. Only he can unlock the gramaryes he left to defend the Fayne Lord; without him the Tyrant must fight a long campaign . . . a bloody campaign that must surely cost Kandahar dear. Listen, warrior! If I were your enemy—if I sought the Arcanum—do you think I'd free you? No! I'd use my power to bend you to my will, not aid you. Not warn you."

"I've heard no warnings yet," Bracht said.

The sorcerer smiled grimly. "No, so hear me now—

Anomius set conditions on his aid, and against the better judgment of wiser men there were those who agreed to them. My masters are divided on this and did those who spoke for Anomius's release know what I tell you, or what I do here, my life should be forfeit. More than my life! So hear me and trust me, for the sake of all the world."

His eyes locked with Bracht's and after a while the freesword nodded.

"One of Anomius's conditions was that word be sent to all the vexillans and lictors of Kandahar—to watch for a black-sailed Vanu warboat carrying you two. That you be apprehended and sent under guard to Nhur-jabal. The other, that he should have a criminal condemned to death."

His gaze shifted from Bracht's stern face to Calandryll, to Tekkan, and the look chilled Calandryll.

"That demand was met and he took a woman to make his creature. He made of her a revenant. Do you understand what that means?"

Tekkan frowned, shaking his head; Bracht shrugged and murmured softly, "A creature undead, no? Slain and resurrected to serve its master."

Calandryll felt the ale he had drunk curdle in his belly. In Secca he had read something of revenants, in the ancient tomes and erudite manuscripts that had occupied so much of his time before fate cast him as a hunter, and the memory filled him with dread. More modern scholars denied the existence of such creatures, and even in the old texts they were infrequently mentioned, always with loathing. Their creation was deemed a guarantee of hellish suffering for the maker, the act considered an abomination that must ensure eternal damnation, while the creatures thus made were possessed of superhuman powers. He felt chill fingers trace his spine: to fear the Chaipaku was dread enough; to find himself the object of a revenant's quest was raw terror.

"You know," he heard Menelian say, and nodded, his mouth suddenly too dry that words might form.

"And shall you trust to blades to protect you?"

The sorcerer looked to Bracht, his voice hollow, not waiting for an answer before he explained: "I know not how the mages of your land do it, or even if they stoop so low, but a revenant is a creation of foulest necromancy, and that an art spurned by all civilized sorcerers. The creature's heart is cut from the living body, ensorcelled, and held hostage by its creator. It answers only to its creator and must do his will. It knows not human hunger nor thirst—only the fulfillment of its purpose, which is the satisfaction of its creator's wishes. A blade offers it no harm—it is dead! That falchion you wear, Bracht, you might carve its head from its body and still its arms would seek you, the teeth look to bite you. Bind it and it will snap the ropes like thread, chains as easily. It has no life you can take from it! Only by finding its heart and destroying that can it be slain. And that heart will be well hid by the revenant's maker. It is an obscenity!"

He paused, seemingly stilled by the enormity of what he described. Bracht stared at him, his own face grim now. Then he smiled thinly and said, "I have never met anything that cannot be killed. You speak of warnings and tell us that we are hunted by some undead creature Anomius made. You say it cannot be slain—this is no warning: it is a threat."

"A dreadful threat," Menelian agreed, "but not of my making. And still I say it is a warning."

The Kern's tanned face creased in disbelief. The chill fingers that had tracked Calandryll's spine encompassed his body, tapping against ribs and chest, clutching hard about his throat as he gasped, "How so?"

"Aye," Bracht echoed. "How so?"

"Because it must yet find you!" said Menelian. "Anomius raised her—raised it!—in Nhur-jabal. He knew only that you had sailed for Gessyth. Not where you might reappear, nor, I pray, where you go. Until he knows that, he cannot set his creature loose, for it must have some scent to follow, some clue to your whereabouts."

"Then prove your honesty and leave him wondering," said Bracht bluntly. "Let this undead thing seek us. Set us free and we'll sail for Lysse and leave it behind."

"We must repair the warboat," Tekkan reminded, "and that will take some while."

"And ere long messengers will bring word from Nhur-jabal," Menelian said. "And my authority is not so great as to override the orders Quindar ek'Nyle will receive."

"So you say we are doomed," Bracht returned. "Is this a warning that proves your friendship?"

"If you cannot sail before word comes, mayhap I can delay Quindar's response." The sorcerer nodded. "Perhaps long enough you might sail free."

"And if not?"

Bracht's right hand touched the hilt of his dagger, eliciting a wan smile from Menelian. "You say I threaten you?" he asked.

The Kern smiled back, coldly, and said, "In this matter I think any man who fails to aid me must be my enemy."

"Burash, but I'd heard the folk of Cuan na'For think in straight lines!" Menelian snorted. "But not so blindly. Listen—the season hinders travel in Kandahar and word will be slow in coming. I'll buy you what time I can, but once the Tyrant's proclamation reaches Vishat'yi, the vexillan will hold you and send word back. When that word reaches Nhur-jabal, Anomius will unleash his creature and she'll come for you."

"Use your magic to destroy her," Bracht said. "That will prove you friend."

"If that were possible I would," returned Menelian, "but I am uncertain I possess such power. A revenant is a hard enemy, my friend, and this thing is created by a talent greater than mine. Magic works better against the living than the dead and I do not know if I should succeed."

"Surely there is some defense." Calandryll shook off the cold dread that held him, gesturing Bracht to silence. "I have read something of such creatures, and it is not impossible. Is it?"

The question hung plaintive on the warm air and as he voiced it he realized he trusted the sorcerer.

"Could the heart be found," Menelian agreed, "then it might be controlled. But Anomius holds its heart, and while he enjoys the Tyrant's favor none may move against him. Until Sathoman ek'Hennem is defeated, and Anomius no longer of use, I think he's the better hand in this. While he has that organ, the revenant will do his bidding—it has little other choice, save to have him end its existence. Likely, it will have no love for him, but still it must obey."

"But it has no sorcerous power, if I remember aright," Calandryll said. "It need not eat or drink or sleep, save that it chooses, and it's possessed of great strength, but otherwise it commands no magic."

Menelian nodded confirmation as Bracht barked cynical laughter and muttered, "How much more should it need?"

"You say it's a woman?" Calandryll asked. "Know you how she looks?"

"No." Menelian shook his head. "Only that Anomius has created her."

"But knows not where we are." Calandryll forced himself to ignore the naked dread the thought of the revenant induced, forced himself to think calmly. "And if we depart Vishat'yi before she comes, then we've the Narrow Sea between us and her."

"There's that," the mage allowed.

Bracht grinned then and said, "Then delay word as long as you can. Let us sail free to Lysse's coast and we'll look to stay ahead of this monster."

"You choose to trust me then?" Menelian asked.

Bracht shrugged. "What other choice have I?" he asked.

"None, I think," the sorcerer replied, "but to convince you further . . ."

He rose, going to the door, through which he called, bringing a servant to whom he spoke briefly. The man saluted and Menelian returned to the fireside. "I've sent my man to the harbor," he explained, "with word that you are proven friendly in my eyes and Quindar ek'Nyle is to offer every assistance in readying your warboat. I suggest you remain here tonight, and in the morning I'll bring you to the waterfront."

"Katya remains with the boat," Bracht murmured, his blue eyes troubled. "Shall she be safe there?"

"I believe so," Menelian said. "As best I know Anomius seeks only you and Calandryll—and as I said, it will take a while before word comes, longer to return it to Nhur-jabal."

"Do we work the clock round we can sail in two days," Tekkan said. "Shall that be sufficient?"

"I believe so." The sorcerer nodded. "In Nhur-jabal there are those who will delay Anomius as long as possible, though even so he'll set his hound on your trail eventually. All being well, she'll come here, seeking to sniff you out."

"And when she finds us gone?" asked Bracht.

"She'll likely learn enough to follow," Menelian told him. "But even then she must still cross the Narrow Sea. Your best hope is to stay ahead of her. Does opportunity arise, there are those within the inner circle will destroy her heart if they can."

The Kern ducked his head, grinning sourly. Calandryll asked, "What of you? Shall you not find yourself in danger?"

"Perhaps." Menelian shrugged. "But leave me that worry—that you go free to hunt down Rhythamun is of greater import."

Calandryll studied the mage, still more than a little surprised to find aid from such a quarter, but now more ready to accept his sincerity. "There's another thing," he said. "The revenant is not the only hunter on our trail—the Chaipaku seek us, too."

"Burash!" Menelian shook his head, brows arching. "You collect enemies apace. What part does the Brotherhood play?"

Succinctly Calandryll explained the attack in Mherut'yi and the ambush in Kharasul. When he was done, Menelian sighed and said, "So your brother would see you slain, eh? And with so many Chaipaku killed, they'll claim blood debt now. Still, so long as you remain with me you're safe."

"But Katya is not," said Bracht. "Can we bring her here? Or do you let me go to her?"

"Best she come here," Menelian returned. "A moment, if you will."

Again he rose and summoned a servant, giving instructions that Katya be fetched. His face no longer wore its cheerful expression, but was etched with concern, his mouth downturned as he resumed his seat.

"I think," he murmured glumly, "that Rhythamun's desire to awaken Tharn communicates, and even from limbo the Mad God influences our world."

"Be that so," asked Calandryll, "does Balatur not feel it, too? Or Yl and Kyta? Surely if Tharn can affect the world even as he dreams, then so must his brother god; the more their parents?"

"I think that Yl and Kyta are passed beyond caring of this world," Menelian answered sadly. "I suspect that gone into the Forbidden Lands they think no more of what men do. And Balatur? Mayhap your very quest reveals his influence."

"Which seems little enough," Bracht grunted.

Menelian smiled wanly and shrugged. "Do you evince the same mistrust of the gods as you apply to sorcerers?" he wondered.

"I trust in Ahrd, not your southern gods," the Kern

returned, "and in all our wanderings only he has sent us aid."

Menelian's eyes narrowed, framing a question. Calandryll told him of how the *byah* had appeared to warn of Varent's treachery and the sorcerer nodded. "I suspect the Younger Gods are weakened by man's indifference," he said. "They were ever less powerful than those who preceded them, and since their genesis we have turned more and more to our own resources, paying only lip service to the effigies of the gods. But still ... if Ahrd sent a *byah* to warn you, then mayhap Burash will aid you now; and Dera when you reach Lysse."

"If we reach Lysse," Bracht muttered.

Menelian turned toward the Kern at that, his face grave. "You must!" he said. "And with all my power I shall seek to aid you—Rhythamun cannot be allowed to raise the Mad God."

"We're pledged to halt him," Bracht said dourly, "and if that be possible, we shall. But it seems we receive little enough help from those gods Tharn would destroy."

"Or help so subtle you cannot see it," said Menelian, that response eliciting a shrug from the freesword.

"We do what we must," Tekkan offered. "What we can."

Calandryll nodded and stood up, taking Bracht's tankard to the keg and refilling it with his own. "What else is there?" he asked.

"Aye." Bracht took the pewter mug and drank deep. "What else?"

"Only hope," Calandryll said, realizing that the dark melancholy had left him, replaced by resolution, albeit grim. He wondered if that were some spell of Menelian's, but decided not: no magic scented the air and the sorcerer appeared as rueful—as wary!—as any there. Perhaps it was the knowledge that men who had previously seemed hostile now came to his aid, that even among the Tyrant's sorcerers, allies were to be found. He was not sure, only of the fact that he felt more optimistic, despite all the weighting of the odds against them.

"I drink to hope," he said, raising the tankard to his lips.

"To hope," Tekkan echoed.

"Aye," said Menelian. "To hope and victory."

Slower, Bracht followed suit, lifting his tankard and muttering, "To hope and victory."

Then the door opened and Calandryll recognized the source of the freesword's hesitancy: Katya entered, a dampened cloak about her shoulders, the hood thrown back to reveal the flaxen splendor of her hair. She looked at them, her grey eyes solemn, then lighting with laughter as she smiled and said, "So. While I attend needful duties you three sit drinking ale."

Menelian rose, bowing graciously. Bracht was already on his feet, his dour expression gone, burned off by her smile.

"We spoke of the Chaipaku," he said, "and I got to fearing that . . ."

"They might come for me?" The warrior woman shook her head. "No, not yet. And with all my folk about me? And that pompous vexillan's soldiers, too? Sit down, Bracht. No! While you're on your feet, fill me a mug and bring me a platter of that meat."

"My daughter, Katya," Tekkan said. "Katya, this is Menelian, a sorcerer in the Tyrant's employ."

She smiled at the mage, murmuring a greeting. It occurred to Calandryll, as she draped her cloak carelessly over a chair and took a place beside her father, that she enjoyed the subservience of the Kern as he dutifully forked food onto a plate and filled a tankard with ale, bringing both to her like some serving man, or love-struck swain. The sorcerer, too, he saw, studied her with open admiration.

"My thanks," she said as Bracht delivered her a platter and a mug, stretching leather-clad legs toward the fire, light glinting bright off the fine mail of her hauberk, "this is better fare than Quindar offers."

Bracht said, "Quindar?" in a tone that announced suspicion of so casual a use of the vexillan's first name.

"Aye, Quindar ek'Nyle." Katya smiled. "And most helpful since word came from Menelian."

The wizard succeeded in bowing from a sitting position and said, "I offer what aid I can, Lady."

"Which is much, I think." Katya's smile was radiant and Calandryll saw Bracht's face flush with jealous anger as Menelian beamed a reply. Dimly, as if dredged from some deep and almost forgotten receptacle in his mind, he remembered that once he had experienced that same jealousy when Nadama den Ecvin had favored Tobias with such smiles. Now Nadama's face was blurred in his memory and he felt only a vague alarm that the Kern's love of Katya might jeopardize their quest as she said, "Since your man brought word, Quindar has granted us freedom of the harbor. Even set his men to helping us, so that lanterns are strung and repairs already started."

"That's good news," said Tekkan.

"Aye." Katya nodded, glancing at Bracht as she added, "Though I'd sooner have stayed with the warboat than taken dinner with Quindar."

Calandryll saw the Kern's flush darken, the muscles lining his jaw bunch tight as he ground his teeth. In other circumstances so dramatic a reaction from a man more usually taciturn might have amused him; now he felt only frustration with the freesword, and with Katya for the game she seemed to play. "We've news," he said, his tone ominous enough that Katya's face grew solemn.

Succinctly, Menelian outlined their conversation, his words freezing the smile on Katya's lips, her eyes growing stormy grey as she heard him out. When he was finished, she nodded and said solemnly, "If all goes well, we can be ready to sail before two days are passed."

"It should be enough." The sorcerer nodded. "Do the gods favor us, you'll be gone before Quindar receives orders to apprehend you. And in the other matter"—his lips stretched in a thin smile—"I'll do what I can to delay the hunt."

The flirtatious gaiety that had possessed Katya was dissolved by the ghoulish threat of the revenant. Her own smile was no longer bright, but become grim, and Calandryll saw her suppress a shudder. Still, he was surprised to see her look to Bracht, not Menelian, as she murmured, "I'd not thought such creatures existed. In Vanu they are tales to frighten children."

Kern and Kand spoke together. Bracht said, "Ahrd willing, we'll leave her behind," while Menelian said, "They seldom do. Only the foulest madmen raise them."

"And likely stay ahead of her," Bracht said.

"And I'll use my magic to confuse her," said Menelian.

"And if she finds us I'll slay her. Somehow."

"Though I'll likely keep her off your path. Would that I might accompany you, to ward you."

Calandryll looked from freesword to sorcerer, torn between amusement and a feeling of disgust. Had he once vied so with his brother over a woman? Did neither realize that the import of their quest outweighed Katya's smile? Or would they each boast away the hours until the revenant came, or Xenomenus sent word to bring them prisoner to Nhur-jabal? Would Katya allow that?

His answer came on her widespread yawn. "Forgive me," she said, "but while you talked here, I worked; and now I'm mightily tired."

Instantly, Menelian was on his feet. "I've rooms at your disposal, though I'd ask you to linger a moment. Your father spoke of a magical stone . . ."

Katya glanced at Tekkan, and when he nodded, she drew the dull red fragment from beneath her shirt. "This?"

The sorcerer stepped closer, his eyes moving from the stone to the collar of her hauberk, where tanned flesh was exposed. Bracht frowned as he asked, "May I?" extending a tentative hand.

Katya ducked her head and Menelian touched the stone, eyes closing a moment. From between his fingers, Calandryll saw a faint red light glow, then fade as the wizard released his grip.

"Rare, indeed," Menelian said softly, "and imbued with a singular purpose. The holy men of Vanu must possess much power—this is, as you say, a lodestone of the occult. None in Kandahar could create such a thing."

"It guides us true?" Bracht's voice was harsh, his eyes angry as they fixed on the mage.

"It is locked with another," Menelian said, addressing the Kern, but his gaze on Katya as she slid the gem back beneath her shirt, "and in such a way as must surely hold you on course."

"To Lysse, then," Bracht said. "Away from here."

"So it would seem," agreed Menelian, a measure of regret in his voice as he studied the woman. Then he smiled, shifting his gaze to enfold the others. "Allow me to show you to your chambers. The hour is, indeed, late."

"Aye." Tekkan rose, his weathered features grave. "And we'd best make an early start."

"Come then." Menelian offered Katya his arm. "I've chambers enough for all. Four?"

The warrior woman glanced at Bracht and said lightly: "Aye, four."

Bracht's face was sullen as he watched her take the sorcerer's proffered arm.

Menelian escorted them to rooms on the upper level of the house, set side by side along the inner wall, with tall windows opening onto balconies that overlooked a garden where fading moonlight shone on the fog that coiled dense grey tendrils about luxuriant shrubbery and tiled walks. Calandryll found himself mightily tired, wanting only to fall into the wide bed and sleep, confident now of Menelian's honesty. Dawn was not far off, the sky already paling, and he knew that the rising of the sun must see him on his feet: the repairing of the warboat would need every willing hand, and the sooner that was done, the sooner they might quit Vishat'yi; leave Kandahar behind and go on after Rhythamun. He unbuckled his swordbelt and tossed the sheathed blade onto the bed. Beside it stood a table with an ewer: he splashed water on his face and sighed. His eyes were heavy, his limbs leaden; he wanted only to sleep, thinking that for at least a day or two he might enjoy such luxury unhindered by dread—after that he must think of Anomius's creation and wonder how far behind she was, what form she might take. He dried his face, staring blankly into the past as he struggled to recall what he knew of revenants, of their strengths and the weaknesses through which they might be undone. The texts, once so important to him, seemed vague now, misted over like the garden below by all that had transpired since his departure from Secca. He yawned again, hugely, deciding to set concern aside awhile and find refuge in sleep.

He started as the door opened, surprised to find the straightsword in his hand, the point directed at Bracht's belly as the Kern entered.

"Dera!" he grunted, little pleased with the intrusion, "but I might have stuck you."

Bracht shrugged. "Perhaps—I've taught you well."

He brushed the angled blade aside and walked to the window, bracing his hands against the frame as he stared moodily out. His stance was unusually slumped, as if a weight rested upon his shoulders. Calandryll sighed and sheathed the sword. "Are you not tired?" he asked.

"Aye." The Kern turned from his inspection of the garden to seat himself upon the bed. "But I'd speak awhile before I retire."

Calandryll saw that he was intent on talking and resigned himself to a night with little, or no, sleep.

"About what?"

"Our quest," the Kern answered, "and Menelian."

Calandryll stifled a burgeoning yawn, gesturing for Bracht to explain.

The freesword leaned back, one heel hooked against the bed's edge, his sinewy hands cupped about his knee. "Do you trust him?" he demanded.

Calandryll nodded. "Aye. I see no reason we should not; I thought you shared that."

"He's a mage," Bracht murmured, as if that were response enough.

"But one who brings us warning of danger. One who aids us in readying the warboat. One prepared, it seems, to risk his own life to further our purpose."

Bracht nodded reluctantly, his swarthy face etched with lines of doubt. "Why?" he demanded. "What wizards we've yet met have sought to bend us to their own purpose—first Rhythamun, then Anomius. Why should this one be different?"

"Mayhap for the very reasons he stated," Calandryll returned. "Because he'd no more see the Mad God returned than you or I. Because he serves the Tyrant, and if Rhythamun succeeds, then likely all the Tyrants and Domms, the Khans and the Kings, will be thrown down. It's in his own interest to prevent that."

"Mayhap," Bracht allowed, "but still . . ."

"Dera!" Calandryll shook his head, bemused by the freesword's obstinacy. "Did he seek to obtain the Arcanum for himself, then why send word to ek'Nyle to aid us in repairing the boat? Why not use his magic to bind us here and leech our minds of all we know? He could do that easily, I think; but he has not. Rather, he seeks to speed us on our way."

Bracht grunted. "Time shall prove that," he muttered.

Calandryll studied his comrade's glum face, sensing some other reason behind the Kern's doubt. "It shall," he agreed. "If Menelian aids the repairing, then we'll be gone from Vishat'yi ere long—come dawn we'll go to the harbor and see for ourselves."

"And meanwhile?" Bracht muttered. "Do we remain here as his guests?"

Realization came gradually, drawn slowly from Calandryll's memories of his own feelings as he had watched Nadama and Tobias. He felt a flush of irritation, followed swiftly by amusement—Bracht was disconcerted by the attentions Menelian had paid Katya, and by the woman's response. He felt strangely aged as he set a hand to the Kern's shoulder, their positions curiously reversed.

"You do not believe Menelian will betray us," he said gently.

"No," Bracht allowed, "not really. But . . ."

"And can you believe Katya would betray our quest?"

The Kern shook his head, staring resolutely at the far wall.

"She's pledged to bring the Arcanum to Vanu," Calandryll said, "to the holy men, that they may destroy it."

"Aye." Bracht nodded. "But . . ."

"But what?" Calandryll demanded. "Your feelings are known to her and she has not rejected them—only asked that you do not press her on that matter until our quest is done."

Again, Bracht ducked his head in acceptance, but now he turned his face to Calandryll and in his eyes the younger man saw genuine concern.

"He's a handsome man, Menelian," the Kern said morosely.

"Aye." Calandryll suppressed laughter, making his voice solemn. "And wealthy, I'd wager. Cultured, too."

"He admires her," Bracht said. "You saw the way he looked at her."

"I did," Calandryll agreed, "and I believe she enjoyed that attention. Quindar ek'Nyle, too, would seem impressed by her."

"She's beautiful," Bracht said glumly. "Who'd not be?"

"Indeed," said Calandryll, still solemn. "Just as you are."

"I love her," Bracht said.

"She knows that," Calandryll replied.

"Then why . . . ?" the Kern demanded, cut short by Calandryll's raised hand.

"Why does she not spurn such small attentions? Arouse ek'Nyle's anger by refusing to eat with him? Glower at Menelian's smile? Reject the arm he offers her?"

"Aye," Bracht declared fervently.

"Because she enjoys them," Calandryll said, no longer able to hide his laughter. "Dera, man! She's spent more than a year on board that warboat—do you not think she could have found herself a lover among the crew had she wished?"

Bracht frowned, then shrugged his agreement.

"But she did not," Calandryll said. "And even though it's plain to any with eyes in their head that she'd accept your suit, she sought your vow to hold off until our quest is done. Do you truly believe she'll now renege because Menelian pays her a compliment or two?"

"I . . ." Bracht grunted, then shrugged again.

"Am sometimes a fool," Calandryll finished for him. "I do not think that wealth or power sway Katya. I think she's a woman with a mind of her own, and that's made up on such matters."

"Truly?" Bracht asked.

"Truly," answered Calandryll. "And in your favor."

The Kern's mouth hinted a reluctant smile. "I'm more at home on the grass of Cuan na'For," he said slowly, gesturing to encompass the room and the building beyond, "than among such surroundings."

"As, I suspect, Katya would be," said Calandryll.

"Then you think I've nothing to fear?"

Calandryll stared at the freesword, shaking now with laughter. "Save the Tyrant's soldiery, the Chaipaku, Rhythamun, Anomius and his revenant" —he chuckled—"no. Nothing at all."

Bracht's face was solemn as he stared back, then he, too, began to laugh. "Then all is well," he said.

"Good." Calandryll shook his head, both amazed and amused that in the midst of their perils Bracht should find that one thing so troubling. Had he once thought a woman's regard so important? "Now, shall we sleep?"

The freesword nodded cheerfully, rising to glance at the window, where tendrils of mist curled, the sky a pearly grey. "There's little point," he said, "the sun will be up ere long."

Calandryll groaned and stretched full-clothed on the bed, determined to snatch what sleep he could.

4

THE fog that had risen in the early hours was drifted thick throughout Vishat'yi by sunrise, layered across the cleft holding the city in a moist, grey-white blanket that hid the heights with their catapults and the harbor at the mouth of the Yst alike. The streets were ill-lit ravines of shade and shadow, ghostly as Calandryll and his comrades left Menelian's home, silent at this hour, and tinged red by the dull glow of the hearth fires and lamps that showed around the edges of shuttered windows and blank-faced doorways. Lanterns made scant inroads on the brume, and footfalls were muffled as they made their way to the waterfront, Calandryll red-eyed from lack of sleep, clutching the cloak Menelian had provided tight about him, grateful to the sorcerer for the ample breakfast that had awaited his rising. Warm food and the bitter herbal infusion the Kands favored at that hour had done enough to dispel his weariness that he was at least able to attempt civilized conversation, though he could not match his companions' cheerfulness. Bracht, seemingly invigorated by their discussion, was once more his dourly confident self, while both Tekkan and Katya had enjoyed several hours of slumber, and Menelian evinced an energy

Calandryll suspected must derive from magical sources. Forgoing any escort, he bade them wait a moment at his gate, murmuring softly as his hands wove shapes in the air, producing a corona of bright yellow-silver light that pierced the gloom surer than any lantern. With that radiance probing ahead, he brought them unhesitatingly through the fog, down flights of narrow stairs and along winding, grey-shrouded alleys, to the sea, where dim torches glowed and sounds came faint from the wharves. He led the way, Katya to one side, Tekkan to the other, Calandryll and Bracht bringing up the rear with hands on swordhilts and heads swinging constantly from side to side: even under the protection of a sorcerer, it seemed that in such obfuscation the threat of attack was dangerously present.

Indeed, the sight of Quindar ek'Nyle was welcome reassurance, waiting as he did at the head of a troop of armored soldiers, affecting a deep bow as he greeted Katya, a more cursory salute to the others.

"Your Vanu folk work hard," he said, addressing the woman but glancing sidelong at Menelian. "Since word came down they've not halted."

Katya smiled graciously. Menelian said, "I'd not see potential allies delayed longer than need be, vexillan."

"Allies?" Ek'Nyle's saturnine features framed a question and the sorcerer answered, "Indeed. As I advised you, Lord Calandryll is a prince of Lysse and might well persuade his father—the Domm of Secca!—to lend us ships to use against the rebels."

The vexillan's eyes swung to Calandryll, who nodded, thinking that this explanation they had devised over breakfast was as good as any to justify such haste to work.

"Indeed. As you know . . . Quindar . . . Secca and Aldarin raise a navy to defend our sea lanes. Those ships might well be put to your aid against this tiresome rebel lord."

It was easy to affect the somewhat bored drawl of a princeling with his head still fogged as the air

around him, the vacant smile he assumed not entirely
unfeigned.

"Aye." Ek'Nyle ducked his head, the plume surrounding his helmet shedding droplets of moisture. "I
trust you'll forgive my earlier suspicion, Lord
Calandryll. I had no way of knowing . . ."

Calandryll raised a negligent hand. "No matter,
vexillan. Not now that we understand one another."

Ek'Nyle forced a smile. "May I offer you warmer
quarters?"

"I'll stay with my vessel," Tekkan said.

"And I," Katya added.

"I think perhaps I shall remain, too," said
Calandryll. Then thought to maintain his part:
"Awhile, at least. Such ship work might prove inter-
esting."

"As you wish." The vexillan bowed, though his expression was curious. "I'll leave you to it—I've duties
to attend."

Menelian said, "Go to them, Quindar. I'll see our
guests have all they need," and after a moment's hesitation, as if he debated with himself, the soldier nodded, beckoning his men away.

In moments they were hidden in the fog, the clatter
of their boots dulling rapidly, like faint footsteps receding down a tunnel. Menelian smiled, gesturing at
the lanterns.

"So you've the freedom of the harbor—shall we see
how work progresses?"

Once more he offered Katya his arm, and Calandryll was dully thankful to see Bracht accept the
gesture without argument. He followed the sorcerer
along the wharf, braziers marking its edge with sullen light, the slow slap of waves its foot, to where
brighter radiance glowed out of the pervading fog.
This light came from far larger fire buckets, set along
three sides of a stone-walled anchorage, and from
glassed lanterns strung on lines across the depths between the walls. It was, he saw, a dry dock, cut off
from the tide's aggression by a lock of stout timber,

and in it stood the Vanu warboat, held erect by a framework of solid piles. The crew moved like busy ants about the clinkered flanks, their industry arousing feelings of guilt for even what little sleep he had enjoyed. The odor of heated tar mingled with the scorched smell of the braziers' coals and the salty thickness of the harbor fog, and to that was added the cleaner scent of fresh-cut wood, rising from the saws of carpenters, their buzz joining the dull echo of hammers and the lilting voices of the Vanu folk.

"It would appear that all goes well," Menelian said.

Tekkan grunted, more intent on his vessel than the mage's comment, and went down the steps that descended into the dock.

He returned a while later, his weathered features evincing satisfaction at what he had seen.

"You vexillan took you at your word," he said. "Does nothing interrupt, then we can sail with tomorrow's dawn."

"Excellent." Menelian smiled approval, then turned to Katya. "Though I confess myself loath to lose such pleasant company."

"So things go." Katya favored him with a bland smile and wrapped her cloak about her shoulders in such a way as to deny him her arm.

Calandryll saw Bracht grin. "What may we do?" he asked.

"Little, I think," said Tekkan. "Boat work's needed here, and unskilled hands are more hindrance than help."

"Mayhap, then, I may make a suggestion," Menelian offered. "This fog will not lift for a while and my home is more comfortable than this cold harbor, also I've a small library that may provide some clue to the defeating of Anomius's creation. Shall we return there?"

"I'll remain here," Tekkan said.

"Best we three stay together," Bracht suggested, his tone casual, but his eyes seeking Katya.

"Shall it be safe?" wondered Calandryll. "Should we not all stay close by the harbor?"

Menelian shrugged. "I believe you're safe enough under my protection, and I can ward you better within my own precincts."

"We've our archers here." Tekkan nodded. "Surely enough to defend the warboat. I think our friend is right, and I've sufficient hands at my disposal that yours will make no difference."

"Then it would appear you are superfluous to this task." Menelian smiled, his gaze encompassing all three but the comment clearly directed at Katya. "I repeat my offer."

The woman looked to her father and they spoke briefly in their own tongue, then she turned to the sorcerer and said, "Very well. Let us return and study this library of yours."

Menelian bowed and turned again to Tekkan. "Quindar ek'Nyle will provide anything you require," he said, "and should you need to send word, you've only to ask him."

"I think we've all we need."

The boatmaster gestured at the equipment set out around the dock and the sorcerer ducked his head, his cloak swirling as he swung about.

"Then let us return," he declared.

THE shrouding blanket of fog held sway over the city until midmorning, and by then Calandryll had decided that Menelian's library was poorly served with any tracts on necromancy and its creations. He and the sorcerer had spent the hours ransacking the shelves for such works as might prove useful, but found so far only the vaguest references, more forklore and legend than reliable facts. Bracht and Katya, the one cheerfully unlettered and the other unfamiliar with the written language of Kandahar, engaged in sword practice in the garden, the sounds of their combat dulled until at last the winter-hard sun force a way through the mist and servants threw back the shutters.

Menelian rolled the parchment he studied and pushed it away, looking to the window, its thick glass distorting the figures beyond to render hem fantastical, like images from a dream. The brightening sun struck sparks off Katya's mail, the dancing column of her blade. Facing the black-clad Kern she was all gold and silver, her laughter bright as she parried an attack.

"A man might die for such a woman," the sorcerer murmured. "I've not met her like."

"Nor Bracht." Calandryll set the intricacy of a dried leaf between the ivory-tinted pages of a tome bound in cracked leather as he followed the sorcerer's gaze.

"She's promised?"

Menelian's voice was wistful: Calandryll nodded. "In a way. Bracht lays claim to her, but until this quest of ours is done, Katya will accept no man's suit. Not until the Arcanum is destroyed and Rhythamun's threat ended."

The sorcerer smiled. "Then hope exists."

"You'd face Bracht's blade," Calandryll warned, "and I believe Katya's mind made up."

"Blades are of little consequence to me," Menelian returned absentmindedly, though his smile lost a measure of its optimism. "But if she's already chosen . . ."

Calandryll shrugged. It had barely occurred to him that wizards experienced the common emotions of mortal men, but this sorcerer, gazing wistfully at the warrior woman, showed all the signs he had seen in Bracht; all those, he supposed, that he had shown to Nadama.

Menelian's voice was thoughtful as he studied the pair. "Folk think us above such matters. They think because we practice the occult arts we lose ordinary feelings. But we do not! Sometimes, my friend, it is very lonely. The common folk fear us; others regard us with suspicion. To encounter a woman such as Katya is rare." The smile he still showed was rueful and it seemed almost that he read Calandryll's mind. Then he snorted laughter, his good humor returning. "No matter, we must each accept our destiny, and though I'd see her stay, I shall do as I promised—all aid to your quest."

"And my thanks for that," Calandryll said. "I'd not anticipated such help from a mage."

"Why not?" Menelian shifted his eyes reluctantly from the window to Calandryll's face. "Because of past betrayals?"

"Those sorcerers I've so far met have proven"—Calandryll paused, not wishing to offend—"unfriendly."

Now Menelian's laughter was genuine. "Unfriendly?" He shook his head, amused. "You've a talent for understatement, Calandryll. But you trust me, do you not?"

He grew serious again, and it seemed, from the expression on his face and the earnest tone he employed, that he needed reassurance. Calandryll nodded and said, "Aye."

"I discern a limitation." Menelian rested his elbows on the table, hands cupped beneath his chin, his eyes firm on Calandryll's. "Do you explain it?"

Calandryll thought for a moment, then said, "I trust you. But you have spoken of factions among your fellow sorcerers, and those two with whom I've had the closest acquaintance have proven far less than friendly."

"Of Anomius and Rhythamun we've already spoken," said Menelian, "Of the Tyrant's sorcerers ... aye, there are factions, differences of opinion. Were that not so, you'd not receive my help now. But is that not the way of the world? Did men not disagree, we'd all follow like sheep after whoever speaks the loudest; did we not accept the dictates of our conscience, then surely the strong should always force their will on the weak. Those of the inner circle who'd pander unreservedly to Anomius's demands would ignore the greater imperative—to prevent Tharn's raising."

"How can they?" asked Calandryll, and Menelian sighed and shrugged, his eyes clouding.

"They see only the immediate future," he answered slowly, "not the greater picture. They are not evil men; only given to swift answers—Sathoman ek'Hennem threatens the stability of Kandahar and must be halted. Anomius offers a speedy answer to that threat—therefore they accede to his terms."

"And would sacrifice us to his ambition." Calandryll's gesture encompassed himself and the two duelists in the garden. "Is that not evil?"

"They think not," Menelian returned sadly. "To them, the end justifies the means. And if they may end this civil war, what are the lives of a Lyssian and a Kern?"

"Important enough to us," Calandryll declared.

"But would you not give them up to halt Rhythamun?"

All vestiges of mist were gone now, the sky grown an icy blue from which the sun shone with cold brilliance, refulgent against the windowpanes. Through the thick glass it sent lambent rays over the sorcerer's face, lighting bright points in his keen eyes. Calandryll ducked his head. "For that, aye," he allowed. "Not for Anomius's ambition."

"You perceive the larger picture." Menelian's eyes narrowed against the glare. "As do I and those whose orders I follow; the others do not, and we must defeat them."

"Even though, by aiding us, you perhaps fail Kandahar?"

The sorcerer chuckled, shaking his head. "I believe that by aiding you I aid Kandahar and all the world," he said.

"And if your aid is discovered?" Calandryll stared at him, curious. "You spoke of retribution."

Now Menelian's expression grew solemn. He said: "Aye. Save that you sail free ere word comes down to hold you, my life is forfeit. Does Xenomenus send word to take you, then I am exposed—a traitor to the Tyrant. And that has but one outcome."

"Your Tyrant would seem a hard master," Calandryll suggested.

Menelian smiled thinly and said, "He is—but he is the only master Kandahar knows. Without him there is only anarchy; without the rule of the Tyrants this land would surely be plunged into chaos. Burash! Did the sorcerers not work in semblance of union under the Tyrant's aegis, Sathoman ek'Hennem would likely take Nhur-jabal. And after that? Why, there'd be some new Sathoman to contest his rule, and then another and another until all Kandahar be torn apart."

"It seems a poor choice, still," Calandryll murmured. "One made of expediency."

"Save the gods step in to govern our affairs it is the best we have," Menelian replied. "We are but men—even we who possess the occult talent—and men are fallible."

Calandryll could find no answer against that, and the mage's comment ignited a new thought, one not entirely welcome. He frowned as it took hold, a hand rising in doubt to his mouth, his teeth worrying at the joint. Menelian, too, frowned, seeing his expression. "What troubles you?" he wondered.

Calandryll paused, thoughts of what Bracht and Katya had said as they entered Vishat'yi flashing fast through his mind. Menelian waited patiently until at last he said slowly, "You speak of occult talent, and I've told you of the stone Rhythamun gave me . . . He told me then that he saw that talent in me. And in Kharasul a spaewife claimed to discern the same."

His voice trailed off as interest flashed in the sorcerer's eyes, not sure he wanted confirmation or denial: not sure what he wanted.

"And have you?" asked Menelian.

Calandryll grinned humorlessly, his gaze distant as he reviewed the past. "When the Vanu warboat first came close, a storm rose," he said, his voice almost a whisper, "and when the savages of Gash attacked us, their canoes were driven back by a great wind. In Mherut'yi I made myself invisible; and when the Chaipaku attacked us, those who came against me were thrown back. I believed it was the stone that made all that possible."

"Such stones may channel talent," Menelian said, "but only that. Save the wearer be imbued with the gift, they are no more than ornaments."

"Then you say I am a sorcerer?" asked Calandryll. The Kand's lips pursed as he contemplated the question. Then he said carefully, "There are some who have the gift and never know it; more who realize it only at the lowest levels. Spaewives, seers, hedge-wizards ... all possess the talent to greater or lesser extent. But a sorcerer—a sorcerer is one who has studied the occult and learned the full extent of his, or her, talent and the sundry ways in which it may be invoked, employed. That is a long road, of years spent in study, learning the correct usage of the cantrips and the glamours."

"I have learned none," Calandryll said. "Save that one taught me by Rhythamun that I might become invisible."

Menelian's eyes asked a question and Calandryll shook his head, saying, "Since he took the stone I have not used it."

"Attempt it now," the mage suggested.

Calandryll began to shake his head. What had transpired with Rhythamun—that soul-sickening betrayal—and what he had learned since of Anomius persuaded him against such experimentation. For all that he accepted Menelian as a friend, he found himself swung more to Bracht's way of thinking: that his faith was sounder based in blade and cunning than thaumaturgy; that magic was not to be trusted. Though he could not exactly define it, he recognized in some inarticulate manner that his distaste stemmed from disillusion, from the knowledge that so far magic had been used to trick and dupe him, and that persuaded him against accepting the talent in himself. It felt as if such admission must rank him with the likes of those he abhorred. Yet here he sat, engaged in debate with such an occultist who proved himself by word and deed an ally, and if he possessed the power, surely it must prove an advantage in the quest: he forced aversion back, imposing a more scholarly discipline on his rebellious mind.

Again it seemed that Menelian read his thoughts. Or perhaps merely interpreted the expression on his face.

"The talent in itself is neither good nor evil," the wizard said gently, "it only is. The manner of its employment determines whether it be beneficent or baleful."

Calandryll nodded and slowly voiced the cantrip.

No scent of almonds wafted, nor shimmering of the light. From Menelian's face he saw the glamour was not effective: he felt relief. It seemed, in that instant, that had the spell worked, he should have been proven something other than he believed himself to be.

"I think," he heard Menelian say, "that Rhythamun laid such glamours on the stone as would aid you on the way to the Arcanum and no more than that."

"Thus aiding himself," Calandryll grunted bitterly.

"That, certainly," the wizard agreed, "but even so . . ."

"What?"

Calandryll felt emotions rise, unsure whether they were optimistic or fearful, staring hard at Menelian as the Kand said carefully, "But without some power that you possess the glamour could not have worked at all, the stone been no more than that—a stone."

"I know the words," he retorted, hearing anger—or fear?—in his voice, "I learned them well enough, but now they have no effect. What mean you?"

"That some kind of power rests in you," said

Menelian. "Latent, save when directed through a magical object."

Calandryll exhaled sharply, the breath whistling through his clenched teeth like a cry of denial. "As Bracht remarked," he said, "these are sorcerer's riddles."

"No," Menelian demurred, "only supposition based on what you've said. Do you allow me, there is, perhaps, a way I might arrive at some clearer understanding."

"How so?" demanded Calandryll.

"I must use my own talent," came the answer. "Do you allow that—do you open yourself to me—then I may be able to define yours."

He closed his mouth on the instinctive rejection that arose. For all the antipathy he felt, he recognized that he faced a near-impossible quest. He was sworn to hunt down Rhythamun—a thaumaturge ages old and steeped in power, whose own occult strength was indisputable—with only Katya's stone to guide him, and that for now pointing only to Aldarin. Would it lead them on from there? To where? And should they succeed in forcing a confrontation—what then? Their blades were already proven useless against the warlock: no matter what he felt, had he the right to ignore any means by which he might gain advantage?

He sighed and said, "So be it, then."

Menelian's smile was reassuring as he rose to his feet. Sunlight lost itself in the subfusc of his robe, but where the symbols of his status were embroidered the cabbalistic emblems glittered brighter and Calandryll stared at them, not sure that he truly wanted this. He steeled himself as the mage beckoned him closer, moving to meet him so that they stood facing each other before the hearth, the crackling of logs unheard as Menelian said, "Give me your hands."

Silently, Calandryll obeyed. The sorcerer's grip was firm, his skin cool and smooth. Calandryll asked, "What must I do?" and Menelian answered, "Nothing. Only look into my eyes."

Again Calandryll did as he was bade, staring into orbs that he saw were dark violet, lightened by the sun. They seemed to grow as he watched them, expanding and merging until the handsome face that owned them was lost and he felt that he looked down into a well of of deep water. He felt himself drawn in, resisting an instant, then, remembering the sorcerer's words, giving himself over to that weird suction, plunging into the unknown. He was reminded of the utter darkness through which the gates in Gessyth had transported him, his senses reeling, the sensation of falling mounting. Faintly he caught the scent of almonds, but that seemed distant, a mere trace, swiftly fading, as if only the tunnel of the sorcerer's eyes existed, eliminating all else, and he fell or rose—he was no longer sure, direction became meaningless as his physical surroundings—into that dark gaze. His mind swam, floating somewhere beyond himself, a thing detached from his corporeal being, drifting on a dark current that turned him helplessly this way and that. If Menelian intoned some cantrip, he did not hear it, no more than he any longer felt the touch of the mage's hands, or the heat of the fire. His own body was a thing forgotten: nothing existed, save the insubstantial essence of his being and the strange tide it rode. He was a mote blown on the wind; a fetus wrapped in uterine peace. Time was meaningless. He felt afraid, and then calm, and then felt nothing.

Then, abruptly, reality impinged and he staggered, his knees weak, his head reeling as he fell against the sorcerer and Menelian let go his hands to take him securely by the shoulders and turn him slowly round until he was lowered into a chair. The image of a babe, newborn and protesting its descent from the security of the womb, imposed itself on his mind and he thought perhaps he wailed the same blind protest. For long moments his vision was blurred, the almond scent strong in his nostrils as he shuddered uncontrollably, experiencing an indefinable sense of loss. He fought the tremors, drawing shaking hands across his eyes, feeling the dampness of shed tears, and gradually his sight returned to normal.

The fire still burned cheerfully in the hearth; sunlight still shone radiant on polished wood and scattered scrolls, the ancient leather of books' bindings. Menelian once more sat across the table and through the window he heard the clamor of steel on steel. Within himself he felt no difference, no sense of power, only that strange sensation of loss. He shivered and faced the mage, seeing the violet eyes observing him gravely.

"Well?"

The single word sounded harsh and nervous. Menelian studied him a moment longer, then frowned, doubt showing in his eyes.

"There is power in you, of that there can be no doubt." The sorcerer's voice was soft with a kind of wonder, trailing off as though he felt unsure of himself, uncertain of the ground he trod, or that he had explored. "Not such as I possess, or any other mage I know."

"Then I am not a sorcerer, nor can be?"

It seemed to him he said it with relief—better, somehow, to be an ordinary man, no matter the odds weighted against such mere mortality.

Relief dissipated as Menelian shook his head, less in negation than doubt, or wonder.

"Did you apply yourself, perhaps."

There was trepidation now: it appeared the mage had observed something that ... Calandryll was not sure ... frightened him, perhaps, from the uneasy set of his features, the hesitation in his voice.

"What? What have you seen in me?"

Menelian's frown deepened, twinned creases rising vertical on his smooth forehead. He licked his lips, pausing as though he selected his words. Then: "I saw in you a power I cannot define. It seemed as if I looked into the core of the world—or the stuff from which the First Gods fashioned worlds. It is not such power as we sorcerers possess, but something stronger, something . . . primal; raw . . . an energy beyond naming."

He halted again. Calandryll felt a dryness in his mouth, a great desire for wine. The sense of loss defined itself: he was, in a manner he could not understand or articulate, no longer himself. No longer simply Calandryll den Karynth. A ragged breath burst from between his compressed lips, almost a cry of mourning. He forced himself to speak again.

"You can define it no better?"

Menelian shook his head.

"Nor tell me how I may use it?"

Another negative: Calandryll felt his hands clench unbidden in angry fists. Bracht was right—to deal with sorcery was to wander into a maze of unknown proportions, of tortuous circumventions designed solely to deceive and confuse.

"Only that it is there," he heard Menelian say, "a power beyond my comprehension, larger than my understanding. Whether it has always been there, or whether you have been gifted . . ."

"Gifted?" His fists rose briefly, descending hard against the table. Scrolls and parchments jumped on the impact. Menelian started back in his chair, alarmed at the fury in Calandryll's voice. "How gifted? With some power . . . some primal energy . . . beyond your comprehension? Beyond my using? Is that a gift? You tell me I am no longer what I believe myself to be and say that is a gift?"

"You are still yourself," Menelian returned softly. "And I believe it a gift."

"Bracht taught me to use this." Calandryll slapped angrily at the hilt of his sword. "That was a gift. You voice only riddles."

"I tell you only what I perceived, and what I can." The sorcerer's voice was apologetic. "And you are not changed."

"No?" Calandryll shook his head helplessly. "But I am no longer what I was."

"Is any man?" asked Menelian. "Do we not all

change? Do we not all of us become something other than what we were, and yet remain ourselves? Why are you so . . ." he began to say "frightened," but amended it to ". . . angry at this?"

His tone was conciliatory, and on his face was an expression of genuine confusion. Calandryll sighed, not certain himself. His mouth stretched in a sour smile and he shrugged as he answered honestly, "I am not sure. Forgive my ire? I believed myself an ordinary man, but now I hear I possess some power neither you nor I understand. That would seem to . . . set me apart, to make me . . . different."

"You are," said Menelian, slowly and solemnly, "you and Bracht and Katya, Tekkan—all of you are different to the common ruck. Does this quest you undertake not render you different? I think perhaps the gods themselves imbued you with this power."

"And shall they teach me what it is? Shall they show me how to use it?"

"Mayhap they shall." The sorcerer nodded. "I cannot say; only that it seems a power of almost godly proportions."

Calandryll lurched back in his chair, staring at the wizard with rank disbelief in his eyes. Then he laughed; once, and cynically.

"Am I now become a god?"

"Not that, I think," Menelian said, "but perhaps their vessel."

"I'd sooner be a man."

"Most would prefer more."

"Not I." Calandryll shook his head. "I'd be myself and nothing else, nothing more."

Now Menelian shrugged, leaning forward, his dark eyes intent. "I've heard your story," he said gently. "When this quest began you were a prince of Secca, destined to become a priest of Dera. You fled that fate and learned to use a blade along the way—that, you say, was a gift. When you wore Rhythamun's stone you summoned up storms, sent waves against your enemies—you accepted that as a gift. You are no

longer that scholarly youth who rummaged through
your father's library—and yet you are still Calandryll
den Karynth. Perhaps now even more yourself; not
what your father would have you be, but your own
man. I say to you that even though I do not understand what I saw in you, it is a gift!"

Calandryll watched the earnest face with narrowed
eyes, not doubting that the sorcerer spoke candidly;
wanting to believe him, to accept. And yet, lingering
like the fading aftermath of magic, he felt that sense
of loss—as if, with the donation of this knowledge,
something had been taken from him. He could not set
words to it: it was a thing indefinable as love. Perhaps
in time it would fade. Perhaps in time he would accept; perhaps even learn what it was Menelian had
seen within him.

"Mayhap," he allowed reluctantly.

"Listen," Menelian urged, still resting forward
across the table, his elbows crushing an antique
parchment, unnoticed, "I was born to farmers in the
Ryde, folk neither poor nor wealthy. I was their first
son; I had a sister and two brothers, and at the age of
seven years a sorcerer came by our farm and discerned
my talent—I was brought to Nhur-jabal to learn the
art. I was taken from my family and all I knew to a
strange city, where strange men educated me in
things I barely understood. For a year I wept each
night, longing for the life I'd known and cursing those
who'd taken me from it. They explained the need to
me, but I did not—could not, then!—accept what they
said. But that was my destiny—I had the occult talent, and that power decided my future.

"In time, when I had reached a better understanding of my talent, they offered me a choice—they
could remove my power and return me to the life I
had left, or I could join the ranks of the Tyrant's sorcerers. As it is with all adepts, I was allowed a year in
which to decide." He smiled, plucking at his robe. "I
accepted—as will you, in time. Sometimes we have

no choice: the gods decide our fate and it is hard to ignore their wishes."

"And are you happy now?" demanded Calandryll. "Or had you sooner remained a farm boy?"

"I am happy." Menelian nodded. "And my family, too. They are proud to name their son a mage."

"In time, then," Calandryll allowed, "perhaps I, too, shall accept this."

"It is there," Menelian said, "in you. You have no more choice than did I."

"A plaything of the gods?" Calandryll murmured, though less angrily now. "Their—what did you say?—vessel?"

"Mayhap." The sorcerer shrugged. "I saw no evil in you, and so I think you hold a power for great good."

"Mayhap," Calandryll echoed, "do they but reveal its usage to me."

"If the gods gave it, then they will, in their own good time." The Kand smiled, more confidently now. "But still you are a man and I think perhaps you would benefit from such sustenance as men enjoy. Shall I send for wine?"

Calandryll nodded enthusiastically and the sorcerer rose, going to the door, asking that the servant waiting outside bring them a flask. It came in moments, a fine red vintage: Calandryll downed a goblet in two swift gulps. Menelian refilled his cup and looked to the window. Calandryll followed his eyes, seeing Bracht and Katya, framed like figures in a portrait; they were laughing.

"Shall you tell your comrades?" asked the mage.

Calandryll swallowed, following his gaze, and felt a pang of doubt. Would such revelation change his friendship with Bracht? The freesword appeared to have accepted Menelian, but still he held little love, and less trust, for sorcery and its practitioners. His approbation had been hard-enough won and Calandryll found the thought of its loss unbearable. He shook his head slowly, doubtfully.

"Not yet, I think. After all, what is there to tell? That I possess some unknown power?"

Menelian saw the direction of his thinking and ducked his head once in agreement. "Bracht holds sorcery in poor regard," he murmured, "and you value his comradeship. But that's surely won now—would this knowledge change that?"

"It might," Calandryll said, "and I'd not take that chance."

"So be it," said the wizard. "The decision is yours."

Calandryll smiled his thanks and emptied his goblet, gesturing at the cluttered table. "Do we continue, then? Or admit that your library holds scant information on revenants?"

Menelian's face clouded at mention of that hunter and he sighed. "Let us eat," he suggested. "Few enough volumes remain that one of us may peruse them ere twilight."

"Save you object, I'll leave that task to you." Calandryll rose, stretching. "I'd exercise this afternoon on solid ground."

"Willingly." The sorcerer gestured his agreement, pushing back his chair. "So, let us call your comrades in and see what my kitchen can offer us."

IT offered a most excellent luncheon of soup, thick and gamy, then roasted beef with what fresh vegetables the season allowed, followed by several cheeses. Enough wine was drunk that all felt cheered, despite the news that Menelian's library had provided no useful knowledge of Anomius's creation. The sorcerer remained a gracious host, but Calandryll noticed that he was careful to avoid extravagance in the attentions he paid Katya, respecting Bracht's prior claim, though when neither observed him his eyes were drawn admiringly to the warrior woman. It occurred to Calandryll that their quest was likely to bring them into such situations wherever they landed, and that

Bracht's prickly jealousy was likely to flare up on each occasion. He determined to raise the matter with his friend at some suitable time, out of the woman's hearing.

He found the opportunity as they practiced their swordwork.

Katya joined them for a time, engaging him in a bout that Bracht declared drawn, then expressed a wish to refresh herself. Her desire was communicated to Menelian, who immediately sent servants to prepare a bath, and she disappeared into the house, leaving Calandryll alone with the freesword. They fought awhile, carefully without practice armor, the exertion welcome after the long months at sea, with only the limited space of the foredeck on which to engage. Calandryll gave himself over eagerly to the exercise, aware that he was still no match for Bracht, but nonetheless flattered by the Kern's laconic approval as he showed himself adept enough for most swordsmen.

Despite the sun, the afternoon was chill, their breath steaming as they parried and riposted, their blades meeting to fill the garden with ringing sound. Calandryll worked until his muscles were loosened, and then, urged on by the seemingly tireless Kern, until they began to ache. He felt sweat run moist down ribs and chest, beginning to pant as the freesword pressed him, driving him back until bushes brushed his shoulders and Bracht, smiling, gestured a respite.

"You're a trifle rusty," the Kern said, grinning, "but you'll do."

"My thanks." Calandryll lowered his blade and wiped his brow, wondering how to voice his concern. Directly, he decided: "I'd speak with you of Katya."

Bracht stared at him a moment, his gaze suspicious, then grunted his assent. "As we fight," he said curtly, returning to the attack.

"I spoke with Menelian of your interest." Calandryll turned the lunge, finding his riposte countered. "He curbs his own."

"Good." Bracht feinted, the flat of his blade tapping Calandryll's ribs.

"But as I told you—to fault his admiration is hard."

He succeeded in evading a second blow, even scoring a point as he countered.

"Aye. So?"

Steel clashed. They closed, face-to-face: their strength was evenly matched, but Bracht was the more deft, withdrawing suddenly enough that Calandryll stumbled, hard put to repel the fresh assault his friend commenced.

"It will likely happen again."

He danced back, intent on drawing the Kern into a mistake, failing. He wondered if Bracht's blows grew fiercer.

"Mayhap."

"Men will always look at her. Seek to win her."

"She's mine. Or shall be."

"Aye." Sparks flew as their swords met. "None question that."

"Best they do not."

The Kern's tone was threatening. Calandryll sprang aside as he thrust, the flat of his shortsword striking Bracht's ribs.

"And best you curb your temper."

"My temper?" Surprise showed in the dark eyes.

"Aye, your temper. Do you fly into a rage each time a man pays Katya some small attention, we'll earn ourselves more enemies than even your blade may defeat."

He parried a blow and found himself forced down the garden. The freesword's strokes strengthened: he felt a doubt, tempted to call a halt before real injury resulted.

"You think I've a temper?"

Bracht eased away, frowning slightly. Calandryll felt concern begin to fade, replaced with a desire to laugh.

"Dera, man! Where Katya's involved, aye!"

"Mayhap I have," the freesword admitted, and

thrust abruptly forward. "And I'd fight any man for her."

Calandryll was taken by surprise. His blade was flung uselessly out to the side, Bracht's suddenly at his throat. He found himself staring into eyes gone hard and cold. "I've no doubt," he gasped.

The cool press of the steel was gone in the instant it would have taken to sever his windpipe. Bracht stepped back, saluting.

"You speak true, however," he declared, and shrugged. "I find it hard to watch another pay her court."

The moment of outrage was passed; Calandryll sighed and said, "Even though you know she ignores it?"

"Even so," Bracht returned. "In Cuan na'For such a thing is not done. There arc . . . rules, customs."

"We are not in Cuan na'For," Calandryll pointed out, "but Kandahar. And soon—Dera willing!—we shall be on our way to Lysse. There, a woman is free until formally betrothed."

"Like your Nadama?" Bracht asked.

Calandryll was vaguely surprised that he felt no pang of regret at the blunt question. Nadama seemed unimportant now: a memory dredged from his past, dim, his feelings for her, once so passionate, now remote as some near-forgotten impression of childhood. He nodded and said, "Aye. Like Nadama."

"And Katya will not permit such announcement until our quest is done. Until Rhythamun is defeated and we bring the Arcanum to Vanu."

Bracht ducked his head and sighed. Calandryll said, "Such is your agreement," thinking that his comrade's understanding was fashioned by desire, shaped by his own emotions: the precise agreement was that until then Bracht would not formally press his suit. It seemed the wiser course to omit that correction.

"Your southern lands have strange ways," Bracht grunted, then grinned ruefully. "No matter—so be it. I shall endeavor to curb this temper you see in me."

"For the sake of our quest," Calandryll said tentatively.

"Aye," Bracht agreed, "for the quest's sake. But it will not be easy. To watch foppish southerners lusting after her. . .?" He shook his head.

Calandryll, not entirely pleased by his description of southerners, murmured, "Mayhap they'll not. But if they should, best you not make enemies of them."

Bracht chuckled then and flung an arm about his shoulders. "I do not count you foppish, my friend. And you've my word I'll set a tight rein on my irritation."

"Good," Calandryll returned, his spirits lifting. "Now—do we resume our practice?"

"No." Bracht glanced at the sky, darkening now as twilight approached, cloud driven by a wind off the sea building over the city in layers of fuliginous rack. Inside the house, lanterns gleamed. "Evening nears, and Katya would go down to the harbor."

With all that had happened, Calandryll had thought little of the warboat and he assented readily. They went first to the library, where Menelian sat among his books, though still with scant success, he advised them. Katya found them there, trailing perfume from her bath, her fresh-washed hair gleaming like white gold in the lanterns' light. On her arrival, the wizard closed the tome he studied and declared his intention of accompanying them.

"In Vishat'yi I am likely your best protection against the Chaipaku," he explained. "Even the Brotherhood would hesitate to attack one of the Tyrant's sorcerers."

None argued with him at that and they donned cloaks, going out again into the streets of the city. At this latening hour, the sun was fallen beyond the western rim of the cleft, and lamps were lit, but still the sky was light enough they gained a clearer impression of the place. It was far larger than Mherut'yi and more imposing than Kharasul, its terraced streets busy with folk who parted deferentially at sight of

Menelian, whose cloak, like his robe, was sewn with
the symbols of his office. Some called greetings that
he answered courteously, and none appeared much
troubled by the war. Indeed, save for the gaunt outlines of the catapults along the heights, the barricades
about the harbor, and an occasional patrol, there was
no sense of a city facing siege or attack, but rather of
a prosperous settlement going about its usual business.
Merchants extolled the virtues of their wares and tavern doors stood open, revealing a bustling trade; from
eating houses came the smells of cooking food, joining the pungent odor of the narcotic tobacco that
seemed the hallmark of all the Kandaharian towns.

"When first the news came there was a great
to-do," Menelian elaborated when Calandryll questioned the seemingly carefree atmosphere. "Quindar
ek'Nyle was in his element—he had half the popula-
tion building catapults and mangonels, the other er-
ecting barricades. And when that was done, militia
squads were organized, but save for the absence of
trade ships the war has not yet touched us and mayhap it never will. After a week or two of rumors folk
settled back to their normal lives."

Calandryll, who had studied histories of the
Lyssian wars, found this odd at first. In his homeland,
a city apprehensive of attack would show none of the
gaiety he saw around him. But that, he decided, was
because the cities of Lysse were walled, each ruled by
its own Domm, whose fortress, in effect, the city became. In Kandahar, the Tyrant ruled alone, and he
thought that perhaps the folk of Vishat'yi delegated
their concern to that personage; he wondered which
system was the better.

In other circumstances—in his previous life—he
would have found such speculation fascinating and
sought to draw Menelian into debate on the matter,
arguing the pros and cons of monocracy versus repub-
licanism, but now such philosophical considerations
seemed idle. Far greater currents stirred and, more immediately, personal danger was ever-present. Even

under the sorcerer's protection, he was not entirely confident the Chaipaku would hold off—assuming the Brotherhood learned of his and his comrades' presence. He made that assumption: from past experience, it seemed the assassins had ways beyond his comprehension of gaining knowledge, and by now, he thought, they would surely know their prey was in Vishat'yi.

He found himself studying the crowds warily, his gaze moving from face to face, traveling to high windows and rooftops, into the mouths of alleys. In a place like this ambush would be easy—bowmen along that overhanging balcony, or swordsmen there, hidden in that alleyway. Beneath his cloak, he clutched his swordhilt, aware that Bracht and Katya did the same. Only Menelian appeared entirely at ease, and Calandryll assumed he had set some defensive glamour about them.

Whether by that or chance, they came safely to the harbor and passed through the barricades. Quindar ek'Nyle was not about, but along the wall of the dry dock a squad of soldiers under the command of a serask stood watching the Vanu folk at work, their dragon-hide armor as dully red as old blood in the dying light. The serask saluted at sight of Menelian, his men springing to attention with a great clattering of pikes. The Vanu archers standing with them called greetings and Tekkan appeared to investigate the noise.

His canescent hair was sweat-plastered to his head and despite the chill his shirt clung stickily to his broad chest. Sawdust and patches of tar decorated his leathern breeks, but on sight of the visitors his weather-beaten features creased in a wide smile.

"Less work than I'd feared," he said without preamble, "and with ek'Nyle's aid, we've done it faster than I dared hope—we can sail on the dawn tide."

"Not earlier?" Menelian asked.

Tekkan shook his head, the movement dusting his shoulders with wood chips. "The race goes against us now." He gestured at the river's mouth, where waves foamed angrily against the stream of the Yst, ocean and river contesting. "And my folk are weary. I'd give them a night's good rest ere they take up the oars again."

"Wind'll be favorable at dawn, too," the serask offered. "By night it's off the sea; dawn'll bring it round, and once you clear the anchorage you can set your sail."

It was on Calandryll's lips to ask the sorcerer if word might not come down from Nhur-jabal by then, but with soldiery to hear, he thought better of it. Likely not, he decided, not until they were gone. He was reassured by Menelian's smile: it showed no hint of worry.

"How early?" Tekkan asked of the serask, and the man sniffed and said, "Before the sun's above yonder cliff," his chin jutting in the direction of the eastern rim. "Tide shifts around the second hour, but the wind won't get up before the next watch."

"And the boom?" Tekkan eyed the massive chain slung across the harbor mouth apprehensively.

"Instructions are given," Menelian assured him. "The boom will be lowered whatever hour you sail."

"By your leave?" The serasak looked to the sorcerer, who gestured for him to continue. "Fog'll be thick as a dog's fleas at that hour and there're rocks like a dragon's teeth out there. Best you take a pilot to see you clear."

Menelian nodded and asked, "You know of one? A reliable man?"

"Kalim ek-Barre'd be my choice," the serask returned. "If you can persuade him to stir that early."

"Where may I find him?"

The serask pointed toward a row of taverns. "In one o' those. Most likely the Tyrant's Head."

"I'll seek him out," the sorcerer declared, as if the pilot's agreement was not in any doubt. "My thanks for your advice."

The serask shrugged, smiling, and Menelian turned

to Tekkan. "Leave that to me—you'll have your pilot."

"Then we chase the morning," the boatmaster declared firmly and turned his pale eyes to Katya. "I'd ask you be here by the third hour."

His daughter nodded, replying in their own language, and Tekkan chuckled, reverting to the common tongue so that the others might understand. "My thanks, but no—I'll find a place on board. Still wiser, though, that you three remain with our friend Menelian."

The sorcerer murmured agreement and gestured at the warboat. "I'll see them safely delivered at the appointed hour," he promised. "You'll not dine with us?"

Again, Tekkan refused and Menelian bowed compliance. "I'd speak with the vexillan," he said. "Then, if there's no need of us here, I suggest we return."

It was agreed, and after securing directions from the serask as to ek'Nyle's whereabouts, they went to find the officer.

He was inspecting the arbalests on the farther mole, his manner less peremptory but still aloof as he spoke with Menelian, the glance he gave them cursory, save as it lingered on Katya. Calandryll studied Bracht's reaction and was pleased to see the freesword's dark face set immobile, his only reaction a tightening of the lips. Menelian was smiling as he turned away, beckoning them to follow and speaking only when they were out of earshot.

"No word has come from Nhur-jabal yet," he told them, "and therefore won't before you depart. On that score, at least, we may rest easy. So, let us make arrangements with the pilot."

They went to the Tyrant's Head where, as the serask had guessed, Kalim ek'Barre sat drinking. He was a short, thickset man, his eyes small beneath hirsute brows, his voice roughened by the pipe he puffed between swigs of ale. Menelian's presence overcame his reservations and he agreed to meet them at the appointed hour and bring them safe to the egress of Cape Vishat'yi in return for two varre.

"Excellent," Menelian declared as they left. "All goes well and I suggest we repair now to my home, to feast your going and drink a toast to your success."

He almost offered Katya his arm as they quit the harbor, but thought better of it, contenting himself with an elegant bow as he ushered her through the barricade, leading them back through the mazed tiers of the city to his home.

There, he gave instructions that a lavish meal be prepared and breakfast readied early. Calandryll expressed a desire to bathe, and after a moment's hesitation, Bracht did the same, though his ablutions were far swifter and Calandryll emerged to find the Kern seated possessively at Katya's side before the hearth in the central chamber, Menelian facing them. Their conversation was of the Arcanum and Menelian was saying, ". . . no easy journey. If he goes in search of Tharn's tomb he'll likely not find it in any known land." He looked up as Calandryll entered, his expression grave. "You can guess of what we speak—I was agreeing that Rhythamun's palace might yield some clue. If not"—he frowned, his eyes troubled—"then I urge you to seek the help of some other mage."

That eventuality had not occurred to Calandryll. "There are few enough of your talent in Lysse," he said, the excitement that had arisen with impending departure dulling somewhat.

"Then seek help where you may," the wizard replied. "Call on the Younger Gods if men fail you. Ahrd sent a *byah* to you once . . ."

"If we must," allowed Bracht, "but for now we've the stone for our compass, and that points to Aldarin."

"Aye." Menelian smiled. "And you've done well enough so far."

Calandryll felt the chagrin that had dulled his spirit earlier returning. "You say that leading Rhythamun to the Arcanum is well done?" he asked.

"I say you did what no others could," the sorcerer returned stoutly, his violet eyes intent on Calandryll's, in them a reminder of the secret they shared, the words, though addressed to all, intended for him alone. "And more, I say that the gods go with you. That their power stands at your shoulder. That power will not let you down."

Calandryll shrugged. Bracht raised a goblet in toast. "We've come this far," he said firmly, "and I say this is no time to lose spirit. Drink to success! Drink, Calandryll, and put off that grim look."

It was hard to feel disconsolate in the face of the Kern's optimism and Calandryll raised his goblet, drinking deep. He saw Menelian watching him and nodded, trusting the wizard understood.

"Aye," he said, "we'll quest to the ends of the world. And beyond if we must."

5

T HEY came like wraiths to the harbor, wrapped in
cloaks against the damp bite of night and fog,
the subtle nimbus of Menelian's protective glamour
the only light in that stygian gloom until the dull
glow of braziers showed where soldiers stood their
watch, bored and miserable, the arrival of the little
party a welcome interruption of the tedium. Moisture
spat and sizzled on coals as the sorcerer's authority
passed them unquestioned through the barricade, the
cobbles beyond slippery underfoot. Quindar ek'Nyle
emerged from the gloom, muffled in his fur-lined
cape, droplets glinting on his helmet's plume, reflecting the flames of the torches held aloft by his escort
like tiny crimson stars. He greeted them in a voice
thickened by recently quit sleep and without further
ado brought them to the wharf, where Tekkan waited,
conversing with the pilot.

Kalim ek'Barre stood swathed in a sheepskin jerkin, looking, Calandryll thought, like some great ape,
such as were rumored to inhabit the interior of Gash.
His head and arms were bare, the fog's bedewing like
oil on his swollen muscles, dripping from his dense
brows so that he seemed almost to weep. The skiff in
which he would return from his task dipped on the

tide behind the bobbing warboat, tethered on an umbilical rope.

"Soonest gone, soonest I may return," was his only greeting, and with it, he strode the plank to the warboat's stern.

Quindar ek'Nyle's farewell was little warmer, though he lingered as he bowed over Katya's hand, and to Calandryll said, "I trust you'll broach the matter of Lysse's navy on your return."

"Indeed I shall. And my thanks for your assistance."

Calandryll remembered that he played the part of a noble, affecting a languid tone, grateful when the vexillan excused himself, marching off with his men into the brume to order the lowering of the harbor's boom.

"Farewell, then," said Menelian. "Were the affairs of Kandahar in more secure order I'd accompany you. As it is, you go with my prayers—I'll make offering to Burash that he grant you safe passage."

"Our thanks for all you've done," Calandryll replied, taking the sorcerer's hand in a firm grip. "In turn I'll pray no harm comes you for the aid you've given us."

"How should it?" Menelian's gravity disappeared as he smiled. "When word arrives from Nhur-jabal Quindar will fume, but there's nothing he can do to me. After all, have I not dispensed my duty? I was asked to examine you and discern whether or not you threatened Kandahar—that I did, and you do not. Burash knows you do not! May all the gods go with you, my friends."

"And with you," Calandryll said, hearing ek'Barre call grumblingly from the warboat.

"Best we depart," suggested Tekkan, bowing solemnly. "My thanks, mage."

Calandryll moved with him toward the plank. Bracht ducked his head in Menelian's direction, murmuring his good-byes, but not moving until the sorcerer released Katya's hand and the warrior woman came to his side.

Their last sight of Menelian was his shrouded figure, black within the greyness, standing with arm upraised until the fog hid him.

"Man your oars, boatmaster," ek'Barre commanded, "for we'll need the sweeps until we clear this anchorage."

Tekkan relayed the order and the Vanu folk began to sing, their lilting voices setting the stroke as the black ship drifted clear of the wharf and turned the dragonhead of her prow toward the boom. Calandryll, Bracht, and Katya made their way to the foredeck, peering into the gloom, suddenly aware that they were entirely in the pilot's hands. The advent of dawn brought a fractional lightening of the sky, but still the fog hung thick, reducing vision so that save for the sway of the boards beneath their feet and the steady slap of oars in water there was no sense of motion. They might, for all they could tell, be riding stationary, only ek'Barre's knowledge of the harbor and its environs to guide them out.

From ahead came the creaking of winches and the groan of timbers. A shout in the language of Kandahar announced the boom was lowered and ek'Barre swung the tiller over. Dimly, Calandryll saw shapes pass by to either side, the rhythm of the warboat shifting subtly as they left the calm water of the harborage and began the passage out from the protection of the enclosing cliffs. The fog stirred here, roiled by an increasing breeze as they drew nearer the chasm's mouth, but still it was too thick to see even to the stern. The watchfires along the cliffs were invisible and the walls themselves, though he felt their presence as a looming weight just beyond the perimeter of his vision.

"As well we have a pilot," Katya murmured. "Unguided, we might well have foundered."

Her observation was confirmed by an abrupt quickening of the wind. It tattered the obscuring grey curtain, admitting sufficient burgeoning light that momentary glimpses of the headland they navigated were revealed, the level of the turned tide exposing jagged rocks.

"As well you found a remedy for my seasickness," Bracht responded, clutching at a stay as the warboat heeled hard over.

Calandryll in turn found a handhold, seeing in dreamlike snatches that they emerged from the cleft holding Vishat'yi into the main channel of the Yst, tide and wind both strengthening, the oarsmen working harder to hold their course. The fog was banked out here, hanging in great clouds at some points, riven in others by the draft. Rock walls loomed close to starboard, what little sky was visible above them brightening further with the approach of dawn. From ahead he heard the sullen thunder of the open sea, magnified by the channel, as if some great beast lurked there, awaiting their arrival.

Then, ghostly, he thought he saw a shape off the port bow, a second close by. He was uncertain—in such poor light, with the fog still coiling and clouding in smoky billows, it was difficult to be sure. He turned to his companions, gesturing.

"Do my eyes play tricks? Or does something lie ahead?"

Katya and Bracht looked to where he pointed. The Kern, whose sight was perhaps the keenest, shook his head. "I see nothing." Then, as the wind rolled back the curtaining mist a moment: "No—wait! Is that a boat?"

"Best alert the pilot," Katya said, and sprang from the foredeck to the central aisle, striding surefooted to the stern.

"Fishermen?" Calandryll wondered as the brume shifted again, obscuring the shapes. "Or do the rebels come? Does Sathoman attack Vishat'yi?"

"That was no warboat," Bracht grunted.

The wind contrived to skirl then, twisting back on itself so that the fog performed an ethereal dance and

cleared awhile, and with its parting Calandryll saw
more clearly that a pair of lean, low cutters rode the
tide to port.

"There's more," Bracht snapped.

Calandryll followed the freesword's outflung arm,
seeing three similar craft to starboard. "Nor are they
fishing boats," he muttered.

"Does Sathoman mount a raid?" asked Bracht.
"Look to sneak in?"

"With dawn approaching and the tide against
them?" Calandryll shook his head. "It seems, rather,
that they wait."

Bracht braced himself against the warboat's pitching, right hand fastening on the hilt of his falchion.

"Neither corsair vessels. Whose then? And do they
wait for us?"

Calandryll felt apprehension grow as he gauged the
numbers each boat might carry. Their masts were
lowered and they rode close to the waterline, rakish,
the dim light rendering assessment difficult. It
seemed to him that they mounted six, perhaps eight,
oars to a side, with more men clustered between the
thwarts.

"I think there's no other craft abroad."

Bracht's voice was grim; Calandryll loosened his
sword.

"The pilot says likely they're returning fisherfolk."

Both men spun round as Katya rejoined them.
Bracht grunted, "Ahrd knows, I'm no mariner, but I
doubt such craft belong to fish catchers."

From the stern, Tekkan called an order: the
warboat slowed.

"No!" Calandryll shouted, suddenly aware that he
could see the stern. "Faster! Run them down!"

Katya stared at the cutters. Then echoed
Calandryll's warning in her own language. The oarsmen faltered, their stroke confused by the counter-
manding shouts. There was a flurry of desperate
activity as the Vanu archers sought their bows,
wrapped in oilskins against the penetrating damp.

Had they been ready the cutters would have stood little chance: the warboat rode higher, her bulk easily capable of ramming and sinking any one of the smaller vessels, while her archers might have picked off the crews before they drew close.

But fog and time were against them: the cutters were close now and no longer held station but drove forward, converging like a wolf pack as the warboat wallowed, indecisive.

"They attack!" Bracht yelled. "Ahrd curse them!"

Calandryll saw men all wrapped in concealing grey, cloth shrouding their faces so that only the eyes showed, crowding the boats. He risked a glance sternward, in time to see Kalim ek'Barre draw a cudgel from beneath his sheepskin and swing the club at Tekkan's head. The boatmaster staggered, still holding his tiller with one hand, the other raised against the second blow. He fell at that, slumping to the deck, the Vanu boat heeling over as his weight turned the rudder.

Then the cutters were alongside and the grey-clad figures were swarming over the sweeps with simian agility, surprise and weight of numbers in their favor. Calandryll realized the straightsword was in his hand; heard Bracht shout, "Back to back! Hold them off!"

The Kern's falchion flickered like a serpent's tongue toward the hooded head the showed above the forecastle and the attacker gasped, grey painted with red as he fell down between the warboat and a cutter. Calandryll slashed at another, driving him back; saw Katya carve a bloody swath across a chest. He feinted as three masked shapes came close, turning his blade to hack viciously against an arm, and felt the steel meet mail beneath the concealing sleeve. He kicked at the man and swung the straightsword round, over another's belly. This one wore no armor beneath his tunic and Calandryll experienced a savage satisfaction as the man screamed, his cry rising shrill above the clamor.

It seemed the warboat was overrun: the masked

men disgorged from the cutters with such speed that
few among the peaceful Vanu folk had time to reach
their weapons. They fell beneath the onslaught, victims of ek'Barre's betrayal, and Calandryll mouthed a
furious curse, determined that if he was to die now he
would sell himself dear.

He was prepared for that; not for the realization
that none among the raiders carried blades. There
were no swords, nor knives nor cutlasses, in their
hands. Instead, they carried such weapons as might
disable or stun without killing: cudgels and flails,
metal-shod staves, mail gloves. And nets, he saw, in
the instant a fine web rose before his startled eyes and
dropped to entangle him.

There was not enough space to escape it. It fell
upon his head and shoulders, trapping him, dragging
down his sword arm. At his back, he heard Bracht cry
out, the Kern's weight landing against him as the net
drew them together. Katya, too, was caught; all of
them like fish hauled in by a skein. He lost his balance, his comrades falling with him to the deck.

And a flash of pain exploded in his skull, its brilliance like the rising sun, followed on the instant by
overwhelming darkness.

His first instinct was to groan at the throbbing of his
head, his second to vomit. It was irresistible and he
felt bile rise, turning his face to disgorge the contents
of his stomach into a pool of brackish water. His belly
emptied, he sought to wipe his mouth and found he
could not: his hands were lashed securely behind his
back, cords dragging elbows achingly tight, his wrists
held by a loop around his waist. Likewise his legs
were fastened at knees and ankles, bent by the short
cord linked to the engirdling rope: all movement save
that of his head was denied him. He opened his eyes
on darkness and through the stink of his own sickness smelled oily canvas. Panic gripped him and he
struggled to sit up, fresh needles driving through his

skull as it struck wood. He cried out and on his lips
and tongue tasted tar. He forced the panic away, fighting paranoia to tell himself he lived still and therefore
might still hope, ordering his thoughts to a semblance
of calm. It was hard-won and harder held, but through
the involuntary trembling of his pinioned limbs and
the dreadful aching of his head he assessed his situation. He was tied beneath a canvas, supine in a pool
of salty water; wood surrounded him and it rocked
with the undulating rhythm of a moving boat. Concentrating, he heard the steady splash of oars sweeping water, the alternating cadence of waves on prow.
So: the cutters had come out of the fog in marine ambush; Kalim ek'Barre had downed Tekkan; grey-
shrouded figures had attacked; held him now in a
boat.

Hope dissolved like ice tossed in fire as certainty
dawned: they were Chaipaku!

His stomach churned afresh, filled with new and
awful dread: they could be only Chaipaku. Had he not
already voided his belly, he would have spewed again;
as it was, he began to shiver, his teeth rattling like
the tiny finger-cymbals dancing girls employed. He
was taken by the Chaipaku!

Worse, he was taken alive. They had attacked without intent to kill—why? Answer followed question as
lightning links with thunder: because they planned
no swift death at sword's point, but something
slower; something doubtless drawn out, long and agonizing.

He tasted blood as his chattering teeth met about
the tip of his tongue and a numbing bitterness joined
his dread. Where was the power Menelian had
claimed to see in him? Where was that occult talent
that had driven Katya back, turned the canoes of
Gash, aided him before against the Brotherhood? Un-
leashed only by Rhythamun's stone, it seemed, for it
had failed him now—left him helpless. He laughed,
close to hysteria, the sound sour as the taste in his
mouth, the filth in which he lay. Power? There was

no power in him, no talent save that of running blindly into danger. He spat blood and bile, terror and resentment fading as hope leeched out, replaced by numbing enervation. The end was settled now: he would meet whatever hideous fate the assassins had planned for him and Rhythamun would go on to raise the Mad God unhindered. Thanks to his brother's blind ambition Tharn would once more walk the world; thanks to Tobias all that men deemed civilized would be thrown down into chaos, trampled under the heel of an insane god. It was almost—obscenely—amusing that it should end this way, the fate of the world decided by his brother's pointless fear.

His laughter choked off. Had his bonds allowed, he might have curled in a fetal ball; as it was, he closed his eyes, weary now, and gave himself up to despair and a kind of sleep.

How long it lasted he could not tell, for when next he opened his eyes the boat still rocked beneath him, the oars still swept and the waves still splashed, though beneath the edges of the canvas shroud he discerned faint light, and it seemed the tempo of the water had changed. He groaned, for a little while seeking to immerse himself once more in the refuge of oblivion; but that was denied him and for want of occupation other than contemplation of his fate, he sought to define what he could about his immediate circumstances.

He thought then of Bracht and Katya, presumably in similar condition, though whether with him in this cutter, or held in others, he could not know; only that neither had escaped the net. And Tekkan—the Vanu folk on the warboat and the vessel itself—what of them? The traitorous ek'Barre had clubbed the helmsman down, not slain him; at least not as best Calandryll could tell. Nor were the cutters of a size to hold all the crew—so, did they sail free? It seemed likely, for surely the Brotherhood of Assassins had neither commission nor quarrel with them, only with him—on Tobias's contracting—and with his comrades

for the slaying of Mehemmed, Xanthese, and the rest.
He wondered what the Vanu folk would do. Return to
Vishat'yi, perhaps, to seek help of Menelian; or not,
for fear of seizure when word came down from Nhur-
jabal. And did they, could Menelian aid them now? It
seemed unlikely: more probable that Tekkan would
sail on, to Aldarin or back to Vanu. Perhaps the holy
men of that unknown land would send out some
other quester, but in time to deny Rhythamun his
victory? What time was left?

He pushed those thoughts aside, concentrating on
physical matters. The canvas beneath which he rested
was not tied down; by shifting wormlike he was able
to raise an edge enough that sunlight and fresher,
mightily welcome, air intruded. Close to his face he
saw felt boots, presumably those of an oarsman, and
from the different rhythm of the craft on the water he
guessed they traveled upstream, along the flow of the
Yst. Past Vishat'yi, then, to some place farther inland.

The sunlight was strong enough to suggest the day
was well advanced. Likely, therefore, they had slipped
past the city in the concealing fog and now toiled up-
river to . . . With great reluctance he made himself re-
view all he had read of the Chaipaku, that once they
had been dissident worshippers of Burash, a sect de-
plored for their bloody sacrifices, schism isolating
them from the orthodox church. Still they maintained
temples—he remembered mention of that in
Sarnium, or Medith, no longer sure which historian
was the more detailed—and in those temples—this
with horrible certainty—they retained the practice of
human sacrifice. He clenched his teeth as they threatened to clatter anew: death at sword's point he could
face—had faced!—but to think that he should go
bound, helpless, into Dera's arms was another thing
entirely. Nor, it came to him, could he be certain of
finding the goddess. Did the Chaipaku sacrifice him
to Burash, would he be taken by that god? Or wander
for eternity in limbo, claimed by none? He steeled
himself against such theological doubts—of more im-

mediate relevance was his physical fate, and all he could do toward preparation for passage from this world to the next was hope that he should be claimed by his own goddess. He whispered a near-forgotten prayer and sought to nudge the canvas higher.

A curse greeted his effort, and a boot that might have shattered teeth had the user not been more intent on his oarwork. As it was, the boot pressed down on the canvas, sealing him again, locking him back in the reeking darkness. He cursed in turn, but made no further attempt to shift the oily cover.

Slow time passed before he felt the cutter change direction, water slapping louder now against the flanks than the bow. Then the craft juddered and he heard the grating of planks on gravel, shouts, and the splashing of feet in water. He was rocked as the boat was hauled ashore, and then the canvas was thrown back and he was hauled roughly from the bilge, dragged unceremoniously to a narrow strand of dark yellow sand, and let fall. Boots went by his face, sinking in the grit, each footstep filling swiftly with water, the inundation and the shells that littered the place suggestive of a tidal cove. He guessed they were not overly far from the sea and lifted his head, looking around.

Immediately before him was a sheer cliff of dark basalt, pocked in places with the scars of old rockfalls, their detritus strewn about the base. Descending thrusts of stone formed horns that curved protectively about the beach, concealing the bulk of its interior. His captors were hauling the boats up, hiding them from sight. To his right he found Katya, trussed as he was, her flaxen hair plastered about her face in damp tendrils, her swordbelt gone. Her eyes opened as he stared—that confirmation that she lived still a relief—and he saw them flash stormy grey with fury. He essayed a smile that she met with a tentative shifting of her lips, her own head moving as she, in turn, looked to define their whereabouts. Of Bracht he saw no sign until he craned his head round and found the Kern a pace or so behind him on his other side, closer to the river. An ugly bruise purpled the freesword's cheek, swollen so that his left eye seemed to wink, his mouth distorted in an expression both smile and snarl.

More snarl, Calandryll decided as he saw the Kern strain against his bonds, that useless effort noticed by a Chaipaku, who paused in his labors and kicked the struggling warrior in the belly.

Bracht gasped, teeth gritted, and twisted his grimacing face up toward the kicker.

"Put a sword in my hand, fish-lover, and you'll not do that again."

The only response was mocking laughter and a gesture that brought two of the Chaipaku to lift the freesword. They thrust a staff beneath his arms, each taking one end, and dragged him, like a beast to slaughter, toward the cliff. Calandryll saw his comrade's face pale as his shoulders were wrenched upward, but he bit back any cry. Then he and Katya received the same rough treatment, both following Bracht's example, refusing to cry out as the joints of their shoulders took their weight and their bearers trotted swiftly across the strand to a low-arched cave mouth hidden behind the rockfall.

The sun lay just beyond the cliff's rim, the entrance to the cave shadowed. It looked to Calandryll the kind of hollow the sea might scoop out, confirming his impression that they remained within the ocean's sphere of influence, and when torches were lit he saw wrack littering the floor, the air within the confined space tangy with the smells of salt and seaweed. It was more than just a hollow, however, for the grey-clad men went confidently forward, the cave proving far deeper than cursory examination suggested. At its farther end was a hole, waist high from the floor and small enough the Chaipaku must go through singly, on hands and knees. The captives were dragged through and set upright where the tunnel opened into a far larger cave. Here the torches re-

vealed a vaulting roof and a flight of roughly carved
steps that climbed up one side to a ledge beyond
which lay another tunnel mouth. This was wide
enough three men might walk abreast, and several
handspans higher than the tallest present. It turned
sharply leftward, suggesting to Calandryll that it ran
back parallel to the river, and along its length unlit
flambeaux stood in rusted metal fixings, suggestive of
regular use. It ended at a metal door, the leading
Chaipaku producing a key that turned smoothly in
the lock, the door swinging open on oiled hinges. Beyond, flambeaux spread fitful light about a vast cave,
shadow and flame locked in intricate dance, the far
reaches, the roof, all lost in darkness. Below,
Calandryll caught brief sight of a fiercer brilliance,
startling amid the lesser play of the torches. The door
clanged shut with a dreadful finality and the captives
were borne down the length of more steps, to where
the light burned brightest.

They were deposited within a ring of massive slabs,
each one surmounted with a wide silver ashet in
which pungent oil flared, filling the interior of the circle with merciless white light, on stone that seemed
too smooth to be natural. The staffs were removed
and the cords connecting ankles to waists cut, allowing them to stretch out cramped legs, their muscles
protesting. Calandryll saw that Bracht and Katya lay
to his right and that the Chaipaku gathered about
them, studying them as might butchers examine
pieces of meat prior to carving.

They said nothing, and their silence was more
menacing than blows. Bracht cursed them and found
no answer; Katya lay silent, though anger still sparked
in her eyes. Calandryll, cold dread in his belly now,
stared around, aware that he gazed on sights denied
all the learned scholars he had read, such sights as
only the Brotherhood of Assassins had seen. The
stones were carved with images of Burash in all his
manifestations, as man and sea beast, and hybrid min-
glings of both, inscribed in antique language, and he

recalled, briefly and bitterly, Reba's prophecy: You will travel far and see things no southern man has seen. That much, certainly, was true, for this, he realized, was a sanctum of the Chaipaku, one of their secret temples, forbidden all save the initiates of the Brotherhood: none save the Chaipaku might look upon it and live.

The deep-cut images were hypnotic in their implicit threat and he found it hard to tear his gaze away, to look from them to the cold eyes observing him. They held neither compassion nor compunction, only the awful certainty that their owners looked upon victims so close to death as to be already beyond consideration. He felt a great urge to cry out, to protest his fate, to tell these implacable watchers of the quest he essayed, the terrible outcome of the sacrifice they so obviously intended. He stamped his teeth closed on the desire—there was no mercy to be found here; those eyes offered no hope—and instead spoke to his companions.

"What think you they intend?"

He was more than a little surprised that the question elicited no response from the Chaipaku: such indifference was more unnerving than a blow, but none came, nor when Bracht snorted grim laughter and answered bluntly: "To slay us."

"Aye, that I know." His surprise grew as he heard his voice ring firm, tinged with regret, perhaps, but neither shrill nor quaking. "But in what manner?"

"Not as warriors would," returned the Kern, favoring their silent watchers with a contemptuous glare. "Such fish-worshippers fear honest swordwork, I think."

"Did my folk sail free?"

Katya's question was directed as much at the Chaipaku as at her comrades, and met the same stony silence; it was Calandryll who said, "I saw ek'Barre club Tekkan down."

"May all the gods deny him rest," she snarled.

"But I believe their quarrel is with us," he continued. "Not with your folk. Mayhap the boat sails on."

"We've that hope, at least," she muttered.

"And little else," said Bracht. His damaged eye was almost closed now, his mouth curled in a rueful grin as he turned the other toward her. "A pity, that."

"That Rhythamun shall succeed, thanks to this scum?" Katya ducked her head in fervent agreement. "Aye."

"That, too," Bracht murmured, "though I thought on other matters."

Katya frowned. "What mean you?" she demanded.

"That now we shall never reach Vanu," said the Kern. "That now I may never hold you to that promise."

Calandryll stared at the freesword, amazed that even now desire could motivate his words. He saw Bracht's grin widen as Katya's frown became a hesitant smile, a blush suffusing her tanned face.

"No," she said softly.

"Had we," Bracht pressed. "How might you have answered?"

For long moments the warrior woman looked into the Kern's eyes, then her gaze faltered, lowering as she said, almost too softly to be heard, "Aye."

Now Calandryll's mouth gaped open in naked shock as Bracht roared proud laughter. The Chaipaku, too, looked on in wonder. "Then I shall die happy," declared the Kern, and grinned again as he added, "albeit not so happy as I might."

Katya shook her head, but now she, too, was smiling, and Calandryll found his own lips were curved. He drew strength from Bracht's calm acceptance of the inevitable, determined that whatever manner of death awaited them he would meet it with a fortitude to match his comrade's.

That resolution wavered somewhat as his captors stirred, bowing reverentially as they parted to allow a new figure entry into the stone circle. This one was not dressed in concealing grey, but wore a flowing

robe of deep sea-green that rippled like wind-tossed
water as its wearer strode forward, towering above the
three prone captives. The hem and sleeves were embroidered with depictions of predatory fish and a silver rilievo hung upon his chest, suspended from a
golden chain, the face of Burash glowering from the
metal, that image echoed by the mask he wore. Age
had tarnished the gold, lending it a greenish tint that
emphasized its relationship with the seas, and its expression was angry, the lips downturned, the eyeholes
slits. From them glittered orbs of menacing black.

A hand of indeterminate age, black hairs curling
over the back, thrust out, a finger pointed in accusation.

"These are the ones." The voice seemed amplified
by the mask, booming out like waves crashing on
rock. "Those who slew our brethren."

"Who slew brothers," cried the audience. "Who
slew the chosen of Burash."

"Who slew Mehemmed," cried the masked man; a
priest, Calandryll realized, or at least hailed as such
by the Chaipaku.

"And Xanthese," returned the others. One by one,
ritually, they recited the names of the Chaipaku slain
in Kharasul and when they were done the masked
priest cried, "How shall they atone?"

"Let Burash judge them," came the response.

"Aye. They have offended against our god—so let
our god decide their fate." The priest gestured. "Lift
them up."

Roughly, the Chaipaku hauled them to their feet.
The priest touched them each in turn upon the chest.

"Burash shall judge," he said. "For none may harm
his chosen ones, save on pain of his wrath."

"Return me my blade," Bracht rasped, "and I'll
teach your fishy god how a warrior of Cuan na'For
judges him."

The priest ignored the challenge, merely beckoning
as he turned away, his robe rustling as he passed between two stones into the darkness beyond. Hard

hands gripped Calandryll's arms as he was urged to follow, his captors chanting softly now, their voices rising and falling in vocal emulation of the ocean, the words too low that he might understand, but the intonation chilling as the winter sea itself. He was brought after the priest, between the great slabs and along a kind of avenue of lesser stones, unlit save by the receding brightness of the ashets, the way sloping downward so that he thought they must approach the river. Katya and Bracht were at his back, the remaining assassins forming a procession behind. The path steepened, then leveled, running straight and smooth toward a low-arched opening through which pale radiance glowed.

It was not the light of torches or flambeaux but a softer, more regular illumination, as if moonlight played on calm water, green and silver mingled, each color vying briefly for mastery before conceding dominance to its fellow. The pungency of burning oil and the sooty odor of the torches faded, replaced by the sharper perfume of the ocean, such as comes from rock pools, from seaweed and shellfish. Calandryll felt it smart in his nostrils as he was hauled beneath the arch into a cavern vaulted round and smooth as the carapace of an oyster. The priest halted and Calandryll saw clearer where he had been brought; where he was to die. The light came from all around him, some natural phosphorescence, glowing like witchfire from the algae that covered the walls and roof. Immediately beyond the arch a shelf of rock jutted over a deep bowl, wide steps carved in its side, going down to where water puddled, scattered with shells and weed, the ocean smell heady now. Among the smaller items lay larger pieces, bleached white, some straight, others curved, some . . . were skulls, he saw, separated from rib cages, the bones of legs and arms.

He steeled himself against the involuntary shudder of horror that threatened to tremble his as-yet fleshed limbs as he recognized the manner in which he was to be sacrificed: he sensed that the priest anticipated such reaction, and refused to grant that satisfaction.

Across the bowl, lower than the rim of the ledge, the phosphorescence was broken by a single dark eyelet. It seemed to stare at him, or he at it, for he saw its purpose and it drew his gaze with horrid fascination. His surmise that their journey inward from the cove had run parallel to the river was correct. The descending path from the cavern temple had wound counter to that, bringing them close again to the water, but dropping, bringing them to the tidal levels of the Yst, within reach of the sea, into the domain of Burash. The Vanu warboat had quit Vishat'yi on the outgoing tide; by now the race must be turning, incoming. Ere long, it would reach this place, the ocean flow down whatever tunnel ran from shore to cave to flood out through that eyelet. It would be a slow death.

Dimly, an intrusion on his horrid speculation, he heard the priest intone some plea that Burash deliver judgment. He looked about, fighting rank fear, and saw that the shelf bore no sign of flooding, presumably standing above the water's highest level. Victims, then, must be taken down those steps, likely chained there, to await the salty caress of their fate; likely, too, the Chaipaku would wait upon the ledge, gloating. He clenched his teeth, standing straighter, hoping that he could deny them the reward of his terror. He caught Bracht's eye and the Kern grinned. Past him, Katya stood grim-visaged, her grey eyes stormy.

Then the droning of the priest's voice ended and they were bundled down the slick steps. The Chaipaku kicked bones aside to expose manacles set into the bowl's rock, snapping them about ankles before cutting the cords that bound their victims' hands. Katya was fastened between Calandryll and Bracht, he to her left, the Kern to her right. Bracht stooped instantly, testing the chains: finding them solid. From above came laughter and the priest's booming voice.

"Too stout to break, those bonds. Save Burash grant you mercy, you pay for your affront."

The Kern swung round, as much as he might, and said, "Affront to rid the world of such as you? For such duty I think the gods more likely to reward us." Through the mouthpiece of the concealing mask he was answered with laughter. He spat and turned away.

"I think this will be an unpleasant death," Katya murmured, her tone carefully controlled, so that Calandryll was unable to decide whether she felt the same terror and hid it, or was truly unafraid.

"I'd not envisaged so watery an ending," Bracht admitted. "But we all must die, and at the least I face it with true comrades."

Calandryll could think of nothing to say. He stared at the opening, wondering how long before he saw it spout, how long the bowl would take to fill. He felt frustration join fear, that their quest should end thus, pointlessly. That likely his murderers would suffer the weight of Tharn's madness was poor consolation. "Dera be with us all," he muttered.

"I think your goddess has little to do with this place," Bracht said. "Neither she nor Ahrd. I think we rest on Burash's mercy here."

Calandryll snorted. "Burash is not a god known for his mercy," he grunted.

"Would that you yet possessed that power," Katya offered. "Mayhap with that, you might turn back the tide."

"Gone with Rhythamun's stone," he replied, and added, unthinking, "And whatever Menelian saw in me is useless."

"What did he see?" demanded Bracht.

Calandryll experienced a moment of embarrassment, guilty that he had withheld that knowledge from his friends. It had seemed the wiser course then, for fear some mistrust might arise, product of Bracht's instinctive dislike of magic. Now it was pointless to hold back; preferable that he die without secrets, he

told them of the sorcerer's examination and the indefinable power Menelian had claimed to find in him.

"Why did you not tell us?" asked the Kern when he
was done.

"I was afraid," he explained, not sure if resentment
or curiosity sharpened Bracht's tone. "You've little
enough love of magic and I feared such knowledge
might change your opinion of me."

For a while Bracht stared at him, head cocked, his
good eye bright. Then he laughed, shaking his head so
that the long tail of black hair swung wildly from side
to side. "In Ahrd's name, Calandryll!" He chuckled.
"We've come too long a road together that I'll change
my thinking now. Are we not comrades? Should I
think ill of you for some talent you've no knowledge
of? Rather, I begin to change my opinion of wizards."

For the Kern, it was a lengthy speech, and
Calandryll's guilt dissolved, though his embarrassment grew for so misjudging Bracht's loyalty. "Forgive
me," he asked.

"There's no need," said Bracht. "But if you wish
it . . . Aye."

"And you cannot use it?" asked Katya, hope and
resignation vying.

"I do not understand it." Calandryll shook his
head. "I do not feel it. All I know is that Menelian
said it was in me—whatever it is."

"Try it on these chains," Bracht suggested. "And
on the fish-lovers. Reive them all."

He shrugged—why not?—and turned his gaze
downward, focusing his attention on the manacles,
concentrating his will. *Break*, he told the iron, *burn*,
dissolve. Nothing happened: he shrugged again. What
use a useless power? Then he heard Katya's sharp intake of breath; another sound beyond it. He looked
up, and saw the eyelet was no longer entirely dark.
Foam frothed white about its lower rim now as water
entered. Behind, he heard the priest announce,
"Burash comes," and with the uttering of the words
saw the gurgling drip become a jet, lashing fierce from

the hole, spouting furiously across the declivity. Dread gripped him as anticipated fear assumed the dimensions of physical reality. Salt water splashed his boots; he saw the puddles in the bowl enlarged. Some distant, still rational part of his mind told him that the bore of that tunnel was narrow, the rising tide unable to throw its full weight into the hole. Such an onslaught would be preferable, a swifter death: this way, as Bracht had said, would be slow. He stared at the water, wondering how long it would take to reach his mouth, to block his nostrils. Likely he would float awhile—the chains that bound him held sufficient play that the incoming water would lift him up, that a cruel embellishment of the Chaipaku. He saw the base fill, the level rising up his boots now. A skull stirred, rolled by the pressure, the empty sockets where once eyes had been gazing blindly at him. He shivered, wondering if the denizens of the sea, the crabs and small fishes that must surely enter with that spouting, would being to feed before his thrashing ceased, if he would feel their nibbling before his lungs emptied. It was academic: he would be dead soon enough and his bones, in time, join those others.

The water rose, creeping up their legs, overtopping their boots. It was cold with awful promise. It reached their waists, and slowed. Hope flared. Bracht cried, "Does it halt?"

"No." Calandryll looked across the bowl. The level within was above the eyelet now and the tide must fight the pressure of its own deposit: a further sadistic refinement. "It only slows. This place must lie below the upper tide line—the tide is pitted against itself, but it will still come in. Only slower."

Bracht grunted. Katya said, "What manner of man devises such a thing?"

"Chaipaku," answered Calandryll.

"May their own god deny them rest," returned the warrior woman. "May fishes eat their eyes."

It seemed to Calandryll a fate far more likely to apply to them than to the Chaipaku who clustered along the shelf, eagerly watching their victims, silent now as they anticipated the slower, but still steady, rising of the water level. Nonetheless he nodded silent approval of the curse, willing the flow to halt, willing debris to block the tunnel, some freak of nature to turn back the implacable sea.

Uselessly, for where the eyelet lay there was a steady gurgling, the water bubbling and splashing as external pressure proved the greater force, driving ever inward, steadily lifting the interior surface.

It was above his belt now and it seemed time slowed as he watched it rise, climbing upward, chill, to lap against his chest. When the level in the bowl reached that of the tide line outside he knew it would halt, but that level was surely above his head, and by then he would float, an anchored corpse. Anger joined his fear and he mouthed curses of his own as he stumbled to hold balance, shivering in the cold, inexorable embrace.

Lapping ripples touched the skin of his face and he spat salt water from his mouth, craning his head back, seeking to hold lips and nose clear of the flow. Rank fear threatened to void his bowels and he fought the impulse, unwilling to thus express his terror. He heard Bracht shout, "Courage!" the cry abruptly cut off by a dreadful choking. He turned, looking past Katya, to see the freesword spitting, coughing, his dark features furious. The woman met his eyes briefly, smiled thinly, and turned toward the Kern. He heard her say, "Bracht," before she, too, was silenced by the rising tide. Then both were lost behind wavelets of freezing silver that draped a stinging curtain across his vision. He clamped his lips tight closed, instinctively fighting to ride the flow, to tilt his head back so that his nostrils remained as long they might above the water.

That respite was brief. In moments, the level was risen above his head, his ragged breath sucking in not air, but water. It burned his nostrils, seared his throat. He choked on cold fire, his mouth opening involun-

tarily, and pain exploded in his chest. He held what
breath remained, a miser hoarding the very last of his
valuables. His feet no longer touched the bowl's floor;
he floated, turned this way and that as blind panic set
him to thrashing, arms flailing wild as he sought
hopelessly to thrust his head upward, into the air.
The panic grew as his oxygen-starved brain began to
pound, and with it a tremendous rage, a fury at this
injustice, at this pointless ending of the quest. Red
light danced across his eyes, daggers stabbing into the
nerves, driving deep. He felt his mouth open: he could
not prevent it; no more than the inrush of water that
came down his throat in place of air to fill his burst-
ing lungs.

He felt death touch him.

In that moment he lost himself. He was no longer
Calandryll den Karynth, but a single spark of being
that raged against the Chaipaku, against death itself,
that screamed insensate fury, demanding to live.

And hands, cold and immensely strong, lay on him,
lifting him. He felt the manacles snapped, the cold
green submarine light replaced with the glow of phos-
phorescent algae. Water spouted from his mouth and
nose and he drew in great sobbing gasps of air. His
sight cleared and beside him he saw Katya and Bracht
raised up, supported by a massive arm. Muscle rippled
beneath skin akin to fish scales, green and blue, like
deep seawater, and where the arm joined the spectac-
ular shoulder, weed hung, robelike. He blinked stinging salt from his eyes, aware that his comrades stared
in awe at the creature that brought them to salvation,
and his own gaze rose, up a columnar neck to the gills
that fanned where ears should be, seeing that what he
had thought was weed was hair, long and wet and
dark as the fronds that wave in the ocean's depths.
The face turned toward him, human and piscine, together, the eyes round orbs of aquamarine set deep in
their centers with pupils of cold yellow, the nose
broad and flat above a lipless line of mouth. He was
reminded of Yssym and the reptilian Syfalheen of

Gessyth, though he knew, even before the voice spoke inside his head, that this was none other than Burash.

That knowledge sparked amazement, and a fresh bout of coughing that left him weak, hanging like a child in the god's embrace, grateful and afraid, not knowing if this was salvation or merely a continuation of the sacrifice.

You shall have no harm of me. Should I not sooner help those who seek to aid me?

The question was soundless, yet still it rang within his skull, booming like waves breaking on rock, imbued with all the terrible power the Lord of Waters commanded. Helplessly he shook his head, as yet too numbed by death's proximity, too confused by this intervention, to offer any coherent answer.

Do you not quest against Tharn's rising? Do you not think I favor that; would see you victorious? I and all my kindred gods?

Calandryll could only nod and stare.

You called out, man. Did you not know you called me?

Again he shook his head.

No matter. You did: I heard, and came. That suffices. The cold piscatorial gaze altered subtly, the great head turning toward the others, an element of amusement in the silent voice as the god directed a question to Bracht. *And you, warrior of Cuan na'For, would you still pit your blade against me?*

Bracht pushed strands of soaking hair from his face, meeting the god's eyes. "Against a friend? No," he said carefully.

Unheard laughter rang out, approving.

You've courage, warrior! All of you—and that commodity you shall need aplenty where you must go.

Calandryll gathered his reeling senses. His attention was focused entirely on Burash, but from the corner of his eye he saw that the water receded, lapping now, as if in homage, about the god's waist. Below the surface a great tail seemed to stir. On the ledge, the Chaipaku stared in awe, frozen and silent. He asked hoarsely, "You aid us, then?"

Have I not? These fools—a jut of square, flat jaw indicated the assassins—*would wreak their petty vengeance unknowing what they do. That I shall not allow.*

"Lord Burash!" The priest's voice no longer boomed, but emerged frightened; he fell to his knees, arms flung out in supplication. Behind him the rest dropped in obeisance, cowering. "These three slew brothers. Their blades have drunk the blood of your chosen followers—this sacrifice was surely merited."

Burash changed shape. Calandryll was no longer supported on the arm of a merman, but in the embrace of a huge tentacle, the eyes no longer greenish-blue, but unfathomable black, vast discs set above a cruelly hooked beak, the body's bulk hidden beneath what water remained. A tentacle lashed out, snatching the priest from the shelf; another tore the golden mask from his head. Behind it was a face lined by age, the hair on head and chin streaked grey, the eyes widening in horror as they surveyed the god's threatening beak.

You dare to question me?

"No, Lord!" The protest was a whimper. "Never!"

Then speak not of merit when you talk of revenge. Did I ask it? No! These three serve me and all my kin far better than you who name yourselves my chosen. Did I choose you? Rather, you choose yourselves, for petty reasons beneath my consideration. And you—not these three you would slay—have earned my wrath.

The priest's eyes bulged as the tentacle squeezed tighter. His mouth gaped wide, the tongue protruding, and his hands beat uselessly against the rubbery flesh. Calandryll heard the dull sound of breaking bones and saw blood jet from between the parted lips. Then the tentacle hurled the limp body away, tossing it like flotsam to the ledge. The golden mask followed, striking the wall, the image dented by the force, and rattled to the floor among the cowering assassins. A Chaipaku wailed in fear and fled into the cavern.

Let some other wear this bauble. Burash shifted shape again, assuming more human form. Calandryll found himself standing beside a tall figure whose leonine head approached the roof of the chamber, a massive, corded arm protective about his shoulders. *And let wisdom guide your choice. But hear me! These three I name my wards, and all who move against them move against me and shall feel the weight of my anger.*

Those of the Chaipaku capable of voicing a response mumbled nervous agreement. One, braver than the rest, asked, "What shall we do, Lord Burash?"

Call off your hunt, the god commanded. *Raise no hand against these three; neither, be it in your power, let any other harm them.*

"It shall be so, Lord."

Along the shelf the grey-clad assassins groveled, ignoring the body of the priest. The god studied them a moment, then turned, his head ducking toward Katya and Bracht, to Calandryll. His features resembled those of the mask, but smiling.

So, best I reunite you with your vessel. It sails for Lysse, and there you must go if you are to succeed.

His visage was benign, prompting trust, and while Calandryll could not forget the multitentacled image of oceanic wrath, he was no longer afraid. He dared to ask, "Shall we find Rhythamun in Lysse, Lord Burash, or must we go farther?"

Such knowledge is not mine to give, the god replied. *The one you seek has quit my domain and I cannot tell you where he may now be.*

"You know he seeks Tharn's resting place," Calandryll ventured. "Do you tell us where that is, then we may go there; await him there."

Neither is that knowledge vouchsafed me, Burash returned gravely, voice and visage solemn, *for only the First Gods know where their sons lie. Tharn and*

Balatur both were hidden well before I and my fellows were made, and Yl and Kyta alone know where those sepulchres may be.

"The Arcanum holds that knowledge," Calandryll protested, emboldened by the god's obvious goodwill, "and Rhythamun holds the book."

It had been better the Arcanum was never made, the god replied, his tone regretful now, *but Yl and Kyta allowed it, or cared no longer; I know not which, nor is it my place to question what the First Gods do. I cannot tell you where, only grant you what help I may. This much is mine to offer—to bring you safe to your vessel and speed that craft to Lysse. My domain is the sea, and all those places touched by the sea. On land, where salt water holds no sway, I have no power. To Lysse I shall bring you, but there you had best seek help of my sister, Dera, or Ahrd, my brother.*

"How?" Calandryll asked.

Burash laughed afresh, the silent sound like rippling water splashing merrily upon a strand.

As you asked me, man. They shall hear if your voice is loud enough. Now come—time wastes, and god though I be, even I must bow before that passing.

Calandryll would have pressed further, but Burash allowed him no opportunity and he sensed the god deemed enough was said and would reveal no more. He stood silent as the great arms curled about them all, encompassing them in sea scent, and between the closing and opening of a fast-blinked eye they were speeding underwater, fishes darting from their path as the god carried them through the depths of his realm.

Past shoals and shipwrecks they sped, over reefs and wrack, sharks and other great fishes sometimes swimming awhile in escort, but all left behind by the god's tremendous speed. Lost in wonder, aware of little more than that they were saved from certain death, Calandryll stared about, his eyes wide as he observed Burash's oceanic domain. He saw that Katya and Bracht clung together, and that the bruising of the

Kern's face was healed, his expression mute evidence
that he marveled no less than Calandryll. Whether
they breathed air, or were imbued with the god's own
amphibian dexterity, none knew, only that Burash
brought them far swifter than any ship might sail
through the deeps of the Narrow Sea.

How long that wondrous journey lasted they could
not tell, but it seemed little time before they broke
surface and saw the Vanu warboat before them,
Tekkan's face gaping as he watched them raised up
and deposited on the aft deck. Archers held bows
readied for defense and Calandryll shouted for them
to lower their weapons, his cry echoed in the Vanu
tongue by Katya.

"What . . ." Tekkan mumbled, his customarily impassive features twisted in amazement. "Who . . ."

"Lord Burash aids us," Calandryll explained. "The
rest we'll tell you as we travel."

Bring down your sail lest it tatter, the god advised,
and take firm hold—to Lysse I bring you.

Still gaping, Tekkan relayed the command and
Burash sank beneath the waves. Then the warboat
shuddered and, like an eager horse springing into
stride, began to rush across the sea.

6

COLD no longer held any meaning for Cennaire, save as an abstract sensation. No more than hunger or thirst; neither light nor dark, which now were equal in her eyes. Like all the fleshly limitations she had known, they were shucked off in her reincarnation, memories of what she had once been, left behind like a snake's shed skin. Though she still wore the delineaments of mortal flesh, and those seductive as before, she was now more than human and she gloried in her newfound powers. Had Anomius not commanded that she conceal the reality of her being from mortal eyes she would as readily have come naked to Vishat'yi to do her master's bidding as assume the accoutrements of normality that he ordered.

As it was, she wore a tunic and pantaloons of fine green silk such as high-born ladies favored for traveling, and over them a cloak of darker green, lined with silver-tipped black fur, a cap of matching shag upon her head and dark green boots upon her feet. All this she adjusted with feminine care after descending from the winter night into an alley not far from the harbor, composing her pale features in an expression she deemed suitable for the role assigned her. Quindar ek'Nyle was vexillan here, Anomius had told her, and as such would surely know if her quarry had come to Vishat'yi; might even hold them, or know where they went. It was possible she must also seek information of the sorcerer Menelian, though it were better she avoid him, for if he thought to use his talent, he might discern what she truly was and perhaps seek to destroy her. If he could—her master had been confident that it would take considerable magic to thwart her and she herself felt such dread strength within her seemingly frail form that she believed she could likely best even one of the Tyrant's sorcerers. Still, her master had commanded and she was his creature: she would present herself to the vexillan as a lady, an emissary sent down from Nhur-jabal, complete with the letter of marque Anomius had supplied her, and hope to find the three; if not, then learn where they had gone and follow after.

She composed her dress and features and trod delicately through the garbage littering the alley to the plaza beyond. From among the detritus a cat watched her, hissing viciously as if it sensed her wrongness, its fangs exposed and its tail fluffed huge. She glanced toward the sound and returned the sussurant threat: the feline slunk back, seeking the refuge of the shadows. Cennaire smiled and proceeded on her way.

Lanterns blazed around the plaza, defying the dull twilight of a season no longer fully winter, but not yet spring, gleaming from the lintels of tavern doors and the windows of eating houses. Hints of fog wreathed serpentine above while below moisture glistened on cobbles: Cennaire drew her cloak closed across her full bosom, pretending to feel the chill as she negotiated a way through the citizens thronging the square. Most, this close to the waterfront, were sailors or longshoremen, a few soldiers, as many doxies; all glanced at her as if surprised one clad so well should venture unaccompanied into so rough a quarter. She felt completely at home and ignored both the lewd stares and the ribald invitations that followed her passage as she walked down toward the anchorage.

At the street's end she encountered a barricade manned by soldiery in dragon's hide armor, huddled about a brazier. The serask commanding them halted her with an upraised hand, his voice rough as he demanded to know what she did here.

Smiling, she answered, "The Tyrant's business," and drew the letter of marque from beneath her cloak. "You can read?"

"Aye," the serask grunted, granting her the courtesy of a "milady" as her brown eyes flashed anger. She watched him pore over the document, more sure of the seal than of the words. Then he asked, "What would you here, Lady?" as he returned the parchment.

"I've business with the vexillan, Quindar ek'Nyle," she replied, enjoying the exercise of authority. "Bring me to him."

The serask frowned, then shrugged, detailing a man to escort her through the barricade to the tower of the barbican overlooking the wharves. The soldier brought her to the gates, where more armored men stood watching, and explained her presence. The guards examined her with interested eyes as she tapped an impatient foot, and then one disappeared inside, returning moments later to announce the vexillan would see her.

Inside the barbican her nostrils pinched at the odor of stale sweat, leather, oiled metal, dragon hides, food, ale, and narcotic tobacco: if there was any disadvantage in what Anomius had made her, it lay in the animalistic heightening of her senses. She assumed a disapproving expression—a lady of high birth unaccustomed to such crude surroundings—and followed the plutarch who led her through the common rooms to the more comfortable chambers occupied by the vexillan.

Quindar ek'Nyle rose as she entered, a tall man, neither old nor young, his hair black and his bearing military. He wore loose breeks of scarlet cotton, folding over uniform boots, his shirt white, cinched by a leather belt from which hung a dagger. His eyes were frankly admiring as he motioned for the plutarch to leave them. He bowed and said, "Greetings, Lady. I understand you carry a letter?"

"Indeed."

Cennaire offered her credential, removing her cap and casually shaking loose her hair as the vexillan perused the document. He folded it carefully and returned it, gesturing to a chair.

"Please, be seated. You'll take wine with me?"

It was a matter of indifference to Cennaire, but she nodded, favoring him with a smile, surveying the chamber as he turned to a table on which stood a decanter and several glasses. It was a room neither better or worse than many she had known while servicing soldiers in Nhur-jabal, comfortable enough in a masculine way, the chair she occupied set across from another, logs burning in the hearth between them, a shuttered window defensively narrow above the table, the floor cold stone, a second door suggesting ek'Nyle's bedchamber lay beyond. It smelled of woodsmoke and metal, but as the vexillan turned back toward her those odors were surmounted by the scent of his mounting arousal. She took the glass he offered, concealing her amusement. She had ever enjoyed men's reactions to her physical charms, but now that pleasure was increased by the sense of superiority her new being afforded: to smell their thoughts was vastly amusing. She set her glass down and unclasped her cloak, sliding it from her shoulders. Ek'Nyle's scent grew stronger.

"So how may I serve you, Lady Cennaire?" he asked, gallantly raising his glass in a toast.

"I seek information." She sipped the wine, her eyes intent on his face. He was not unhandsome, in a pompous, martial way, and his desire was obvious; even without the guidance of her nose, it would be easy to manipulate him. "Information concerning travelers whose presence threatens the Tyrant."

The odor of ek'Nyle's arousal faded somewhat as

she described Calandryll and Bracht, replaced by the scent of tension, a wafting of alarm. Her interest was immediate, though she curbed herself, awaiting his response, sipping her wine.

Ek'Nyle sought to hide his alarm, smoothing his oiled beard as he mustered his thoughts. "I have seen them," he said with the merest hesitation. "They came on a black warboat filled with Vanu folk, a woman of that land with them."

Anomius had said nothing of a woman or a warboat, or Vanu folk: she filed that information and asked, "And where are they now?"

Ek'Nyle heard the anticipation in her voice and essayed a regretful smile. "Gone," he said, "five days since."

"Gone?" Cennaire realized the glass was about to shatter in her hand and eased her grip. "Gone where?"

"To Lysse, they said."

"Lysse holds cities enough to hide in," came the response, the huge brown eyes sparking threateningly. "Where in Lysse?"

Ek'Nyle sensed something of the power in this beautiful woman then, something he could not define, feeling it with those senses that operate below the conscious. It was beyond the authority granted her by the letter of marque, though that alone was enough to blight his career should he be held to blame. He swallowed hard, his skin prickling uncomfortably, and sought to divert both the responsibility and her clearly mounting anger.

"I suspected them," he said quickly. "I seized their cargo of dragons' hides and took them prisoner, but Menelian—the sorcerer appointed to defend Vishat'yi—examined them and declared them honest. They offered no danger to Kandahar, he said, and advised me to free them. More—he took them into his home like old friends. The men and the woman."

His fear hung in the air, a heady scent. Cennaire savored it. She nodded coldly and demanded, "Where is this Menelian?"

"Most likely at his villa." Ek'Nyle smiled nervously, not sure why he experienced so chill a sensation of apprehension as he met her gaze. "A house in the upper city."

"Take me there."

It was a command the vexillan obeyed with alacrity. This woman lacked the authority to so order him and he would usually have objected, but thoughts of dissent never entered his mind: for all her beauty he no longer contemplated her seduction, wanting for reasons he could not define, to be rid of her as quickly as possible. He nodded his agreement and rose to his feet.

"Do you give me a moment."

Without awaiting her reply he went into his bed-chamber, hurriedly tugging on a jerkin and his swordbelt, draping his scarlet cloak about his shoulders. It was a measure of his discomfort that he came close to forgetting his plumed helm. When he returned to the outer room she was standing, dressed, her lovely face set in austere lines.

"Please," he opened the door, bowing her through, "I'll summon an escort. It's not too far."

He heard himself stumbling, seeking to retrieve his dignity as he bellowed for a squad to form. Cennaire stilled her smile as she drank in his confusion, waiting as grumbling soldiers quit their dice and hurried to snatch up cloaks and weapons. At the entrance ek'Nyle offered his arm—a motion born of habit— then began to draw it back. Enjoying herself, Cennaire denied him the chance, setting her hand firmly upon his forearm before he could hide it beneath his cloak. "Describe this Vanu woman," she demanded as the uncomfortable vexillan escorted her toward the barricade.

Ek'Nyle complied, telling her of Katya and of Tekkan as they passed into the streets of the city and began to climb toward Menelian's residence. Cennaire listened in silence, knowing that she must relay word of these new players to Anomius even as she contemplated her forthcoming encounter with the sorcerer.

Best met, she decided, without witnesses. Should the mage detect what she now was he would likely denounce her, and while the letter she carried invested her with such authority that she might easily command the temporal forces, Anomius had warned her against revealing her true nature: such necromancy, he had explained, was frowned upon and would certainly turn all against her. It was unlikely these weak men could harm her, but they might well hamper her mission. She would, therefore, seek solitary audience with the sorcerer.

She nodded as ek'Nyle indicated the walls surrounding Menelian's villa and removed her hand from his arm. His relief was palpable, rendering her suggestion more easily accepted.

"You need not linger, vexillan. No doubt you've duties to attend, and this may take a while."

Ek'Nyle offered no argument, only nodded and sounded the bell that brought a servant to the gate. "The Lady Cennaire would speak with Menelian," he announced. "Bring her to him."

Without further ado, he saluted and spun about, beckoning for his men to follow. Cennaire ignored his departure as the gateman bowed and ushered her respectfully into the courtyard.

"My lady." He closed the gate and led her toward the house. "Do you wait here and I'll alert my master."

Cennaire waved dismissal and he left her in the vestibule. She glanced around, at the mosaic patterning the floor and the image of Burash standing in its niche. Then the far door opened and she was escorted deeper into the villa, to a chamber of rosewood panels that glowed warmly, reflecting the radiance of the fire and the single chandelier suspended above a table littered with scrolls and parchments. The servant bowed and departed as a man rose from behind the table.

"Lady Cennaire? I am Menelian."

His voice was light, a soft tenor, and he was younger than she had expected, rather handsome, his jaw shaved clean, his hair a dark reddish-brown, his eyes a surprising violet color. He wore a loose robe of black, woven with occult symbols, open over a white shirt and nigrescent breeks tucked into short, soft boots. His gaze was curious, but when she tested the air she sensed no alarm, only calm confidence overlaid with intrigue. She smiled, curtsying, and said, "Forgive me for so late an intrusion."

"There is nothing to forgive," he replied as he gestured at a chair. "Will you sit? Shall I send for wine?"

"Thank you."

She removed her cap and cloak, taking the offered seat and the opportunity to study him further as he went to the door, calling for a servant to bring wine. She thought perhaps he employed his art to mask himself, for on him she detected no scent of desire, only that cool curiosity. She adjusted her tunic, drawing it down from her slender neck, tauter over her breasts; no longer properly human, she yet retained the habits of her previous life.

Menelian returned with a salver and filled two goblets, smiling as he settled across from her. She saw his eyes stray to her neckline and felt the satisfaction of briefly scented desire. He asked, "What brings you here, Lady?"

"Please," she replied, "call me Cennaire."

"A pleasant name—Cennaire it shall be." He sipped, watching her face over the goblet's rim. Then: "And your business in Vishat'yi, Cennaire?"

"I come from Nhur-jabal," she answered, "on Tyrant's business."

Menelian nodded as if unsurprised, his expression unfathomable. Cennaire experienced a momentary confusion. Accustomed, even in life, to more positive male reactions, she found his apparent indifference to her charms somewhat disconcerting, even irritating. Save for that transient waft of unhidden lust he evinced no sign of attraction. Long-practiced artifice prompted her to lean forward, allowing her tunic to fall lower from her breasts as she reached beneath the silk to extract the letter of marque. She passed it to him, suspicious now that he used his magic to conceal his desire; that suspicion furthering another—that if he hid his true feelings, perhaps he hid more. Perhaps his own suspicion. She watched him glance carelessly at the letter, nod, and hand it back.

"You bear impressive credentials, Cennaire."

Did he play with words? She was uncertain: she smiled and said, "I am entrusted with such agency as may be vital to the Tyrant's cause."

"You speak of the rebels?" Menelian returned her smile. "We've seen none here."

"I speak of traitors," she said, "and alien spies."

Menelian's brows arched. "None here," he murmured, "as best I know—and I should, were there any."

Cennaire wondered if he warned her: this one was far harder to read than Quindar ek'Nyle. He concealed himself, hid his true feelings; and still she could not decide if that was through the use of magic, neither if it was instinctive nor deliberate. She eased back, settling an arm carelessly across the chair, deliberately emphasizing the thrust of her bosom, setting down her goblet to push long strands of glossy black hair from the pale oval of her face.

Still there was no discernible reaction. She assumed a serious expression and said, "Mayhap no longer here but recently present."

"Ah!" Menelian nodded as if at last understanding; as if she had been needlessly obscure. "You speak of Calandryll den Karynth and Bracht ni Errhyn."

Cennaire was startled by his honesty. Eyes widening in surprise, she murmured an affirmative.

"This is common enough knowledge," Menelian said calmly, his expression inscrutable. "Quindar ek'Nyle and most of the garrison know of it, and doubtless our good vexillan has already advised you of their arrival and departure."

It was difficult now to conceal her confusion, and she felt a hint of alarm. That Menelian knew she had spoken with ek'Nyle was likely due only to the report of his gatekeeper, but his cheerful admission ran against the grain of her presence in his home: unless he knew she was sent by Anomius—and how could that be?—he must surely believe she was come on Tyrant's business alone, and therefore the mere asking of such questions about travelers and traitors should alert him to potential danger. She could not assume him so great a fool as to casually dismiss Nhur-jabal's interest, so something else must lie behind his calm. Did he then suspect what she was? Holding her own face bland, she nodded.

"And no doubt he also told you they came on board a Vanu warboat mastered by Tekkan, with a woman named Katya."

Cennaire murmured agreement, suddenly aware of a subtle shifting in the sorcerer's attitude. Neither his expression nor his stance had altered, but on mention of the woman's name his guard had dropped a fraction. She realized that his desire for her was muted by a greater attraction, an overwhelming desire for this Katya. She was surprised to find herself jealous, jealous and increasingly angry.

"And that I examined them and commanded they be set free," she heard him add, "with all assistance given to the repairing of their vessel, which quit Vishat'yi some five days ago."

His expression remained imperturbable. Cennaire's lips pursed as her mind raced, increasingly convinced that he hid more than he revealed, that certainty disturbing. "They are proscribed by Tyrant's edict," she said sharply, seeking to gain advantage, to ruffle his implacable calm. "Deemed enemies of Kandahar."

"I met them, as you know," he returned, "and I found in them nothing to suggest they are our enemies. Rather, friends."

"Mayhap," she said, carefully now, "they employed sorcery to disguise their true natures."

"Impossible." Menelian shook his head, though his eyes never left her face. "Had that been so, I should have known it."

"Can you be certain?"

"Absolutely." He ducked his head confidently. "More wine?"

"Thank you, no."

She could not prevent the frown that creased her brow as Menelian stretched out a hand and crooked his fingers, that simple gesture bringing the decanter floating from the table, whatever scent he gave off masked by the smell of almonds. Was that demonstration a warning? Did he toy with her? She transformed frown to smile: one servant of Xenomenus to another.

"Where did they go?"

The sorcerer poured red wine and sent the decanter back to the table, sipping before he spoke.

"To Lysse, as Quindar doubtless told you. Specifically, to Aldarin."

"To Aldarin." It was another piece in the jigsaw of her hunt. "Yet Calandryll den Karynth hails from Secca."

"Indeed," the wizard murmured, "but it was to Aldarin they sailed."

"Why?" she asked.

"They've business there—money owed, a debtor to confront."

Cennaire wondered if this smile mocked her. "Nhur-jabal would sooner they had remained here," she said, "as prisoners."

"On what charge?" Menelian demanded. "They broke no laws, nor are they enemies. Why hold them, then?"

"I do not question the Tyrant's wishes," she answered, "only obey the orders given me."

"You bear a letter of marque," he returned, "but you've shown me no script bearing their names."

Cennaire was taken aback an instant. Then: "No, my instruction was verbal."

"Odd," Menelian said softly. "Were they truly enemies of Kandahar I'd assume their proscription would be written down, authorized with the seal of Nhurjabal. Who issued this instruction?"

Now faint scent reached Cennaire's attuned nostrils, though she found it difficult to read. Curiosity remained, but also definite suspicion, and—perhaps—hostility. Because, she wondered, he sought to protect this Vanu woman? Or for some other reason? His blunt question seemed a test: she said coldly, "The Tyrant Xenomenus."

"Xenomenus himself?" Menelian set his goblet aside; Cennaire sensed his suspicion mount. "The Tyrant concerns himself with this affair?"

Cennaire nodded.

"Such matters would more usually be within the province of his sorcerers," the mage said slowly. "Or Attam ek'Talus."

His violet eyes fastened on her face then, intense, and in her expression he must have read doubt, for he added by way of explanation, "The commander of the army."

"Of course." She forced a wan smile, seeking to cover herself. "Attam ek'Talus."

"Whose name you appear to find unfamiliar."

His voice changed tone, edged now with the steel of mounting certainty. Cennaire held her features still as she shrugged, affecting irritation that was not altogether feigned: the sorcerer's confidence began to anger her. "Do you question my authority?" she snapped.

Menelian spread his hands, a gesture that could be interpreted as either apology or unconcern. "Kandahar is reft with civil war, Cennaire, and you come hunting folk who are our friends—without written authority. I suggest you return to Nhur-jabal and tell them there that I have examined these men and vouch for

their probity. I think you'll find my word holds sway
with both the Tyrant's sorcerers and Attam ek'Talus."

Her anger grew: she sensed a trap laid and sprung.
"You take much upon yourself," she said.

"I am one of the Tyrant's sorcerers," he replied. "It
is my sworn duty to defend this city and my talent is
easily capable of discerning enmity. From whatever
source."

Sharp white teeth closed on her lower lip as she
contemplated his face and his words. Those last had
the ring of a direct challenge and all the instincts of
her newly undead being urged her to spring at him, to
attack and rend him as she felt sure she could, be he
sorcerer or no. She curbed the impulse, retaining her
role as agent of Nhur-jabal, a high-born lady come on
Tyrant's mission. Her huge eyes narrowed, she said,
"You defy the orders of the Tyrant?"

"I have seen no such orders," came the cool response, "only heard you tell me they exist. In turn, I
have advised you these folk you seek are not enemies
of Kandahar, and that on my word they were let go.
Should I be required to explain myself in Nhur-jabal,
then I shall go there. When—and if!—I receive written
instructions to that effect."

Diplomatically it was an impasse, and Cennaire
had no choice but to accept that. She had, perhaps,
learned as much as she could, and as much as
Anomius would demand of her, but this man irked
her—she would have more of him. She allowed her
anger to show, rising as if propelled by irritation at his
refusal to recognize her authority.

"You say they sailed for Aldarin five days gone?"

Menelian nodded.

"To seek some debtor—his name?"

"Varent den Tarl."

It was another piece in the puzzle, another clue:
she likely had sufficient that she could find them. Either find them in Aldarin or pick up their trail.
Anomius would surely be content with that and perhaps it were better she go to him with the informa-

tion, leave now; but she could not, for her own sake: she was anchored by her annoyance.

"You appear undecided." Menelian's voice intruded on her thoughts and she stared at him with unconcealed dislike. His next words struck sharp as a blade: "Mayhap you wonder what to tell your master."

"My master?"

Her eyes slitted. Through anger and surprise she caught a fresh scent, neither knowing nor caring whether the sorcerer dispensed with camouflaging magic or if his emotions grew too strong to hide any longer. She scented open hostility, suspicion becoming conviction. Danger!

"Is Anomius not your master?" Menelian rose to face her. "Or had I better name him your creator?"

Slitted eyes opened wide. "What do you say?" she hissed.

"That you are a creation of foulest necromancy," he answered. "A revenant! And that I shall not permit you to return to your maker."

Cennaire tensed. Menelian laughed, a single, humorless bark of sound. "Did you think to deceive me? I am a mage, revenant."

His loathing hung musky on the air, and with it confidence. He murmured, the words too low to catch, and again the almond scent came pungent to her nostrils. She experienced a momentary doubt: this man had known that he could best her and destroy her. "Yet still you welcomed me to your home," she said, her voice harsh now.

Menelian's lips curved in a thin line. "I'd a wish to learn how much you knew," he said. "And I do not believe you can best me."

"Mayhap not," she allowed, unsure what gramaryes he might employ to protect himself; certain that she must, at very least, endeavor to slay him now. "How know you my master's name?"

"Not all in Nhur-jabal favor his insane purpose," came the answer: that admission open proof of the wizard's confidence. "And some there are who would see it halted."

"For a stripling out of Lysse and a freesword Kern? Or is it for the woman's sake?" Now she laughed as his face registered shock. "Oh, Menelian, sorcerer you may be, but still a man. Your lust for her oozes from you at mention of her name. So, know this—that when I find them I shall slay her, too."

"You shall not!" he cried, and Cennaire had the satisfaction of scenting his sudden alarm.

Her smile was mocking as she said, "I shall. You cannot destroy me, but I shall take this woman you'd protect and tear out her heart. Think on that as you die, sorcerer!"

She sprang forward as she spoke, swift as a stooping falcon, hands raised and hooked like a harpy's talons, her face no longer lovely but transformed, like a window to her soul, into a mask of bestial fury. Menelian shouted a single word and the air was abruptly thick with the perfume of almonds. Cennaire felt the force of his spell wash over her, and knew that any living creature must surely be consumed by that occult power. Had she been a living creature, she would have died on the instant, but she was not: she was undead. Anomius had explained this to her—that the greater part of the glamours wrought by sorcerers were designed to work against the living, for it was usually against the living that they were needed. Undead, she was unaffected by such spells. She snarled laughter as she fell upon Menelian and saw the realization in his eyes.

Even then he was not entirely defenseless; the spells that invested her with the semblance of life were not entirely unaffected. Her furious attack was slowed and though she caught his shoulders in her hands, those mechanisms possessed of a strength that could crush flesh and snap bone, he fought against her, resisting her terrible fury. He raised his own hands, seizing her wrists as she sought to clutch his throat, and spat arcane syllables into her face.

She recognized that his sorcery depended, to at least some extent, on vocalization: she halted the forming spell by the simple expedient of driving a knee upward into his groin. From time to time she had employed the same action against some overly enthusiastic client and it worked as well against a sorcerer as any normal man. Menelian's words became a shriek of pain. His hold on her wrists loosened and she snatched her arms away as, helplessly, he was bent by the agony flaring in his belly. Cennaire chuckled—it sounded like a snarl of triumph—and locked a hand about his windpipe. Her fingers gouged deep, closing his throat, as with her other hand she slashed red lines across his face.

The violet eyes bulged, his skin suffused with crimson as blood vessels burst, that coloration rapidly lost beneath the welling that came from the cuts. Less powerfully now he battered at her arms and face and she held him off, not sure what damage he might inflict, but her vanity prompting her to avoid the risk of unsightly bruising.

"You were too confident," she rasped, and laughed once. "Men are always too confident."

She tightened her hold and his fists ceased their pounding. She clutched a wrist for fear he might yet employ a gramarye that needed no words, exulting in her strength as she forced him to his knees. He bowed before her, his eyes staring wide and horrified at her naked form, empty of any lust, but filled instead with fear. She savored the odor, aware that their struggle had disturbed lanterns, burning oil taking hold on the chamber, layering the room with smoke. She felt the magically induced strength begin to go out of him as his body strained to inhale the air denied by her grip and with an almost casual motion broke the wrist she held. He seemed not to notice the pain; nor when she took the other and snapped that, leaving both his hands limp and useless.

"What price your magicks now, sorcerer?" she demanded.

And with a single tightening of her fingers tore out his throat.

Menelian loosed an awful sigh through the ragged opening of his windpipe and fell forward against her knees. She stepped away from the corpse, breathing fast and deep, not from her exertions, for she felt no toll from those, but from the sheer excitement of what she had done. She had bested a mage! Bested one of the Tyrant's sorcerers! What might she not achieve?

She started as fists pounded wood, reminding her that smoke must now trickle beneath the door, Menelian's servants come to investigate. In confirmation she heard a nervous shout—"Master? Is all well, master?"—and looked about. The chamber was dense with smoke now and flame blazed all around her. She stood in the midst of the conflagration, not feeling the heat, but neither sure whether, or not, the flames could harm her. And threatened with exposure, without convenient excuse for the body at her feet. It would be easy to open the door and force a way through the servants—none there could halt her!—but that would beg questions, the answers perhaps leading back to Nhur-jabal and Anomius. Her creator had allowed her free rein, even warning her that she might find it necessary to slay Menelian, but he had also suggested that tact was preferable. And the dead man had spoken of sorcerers plotting against her master; men who might, did they learn what she had done, unite to destroy her. Singly, she believed she could defeat them, but not together. Should sufficient move en masse against her, then likely she would perish. Best then that she flee, leaving a mystery behind her that with any luck would not reach Nhur-jabal before she quit the city again in pursuit of her prey.

She favored the wizard's corpse with a last, scornful glance and promised, "All of them, fool. The men and the woman, too," then flung open a window and sprang through to the ground beyond.

Flames lit the night as she ran across a garden,

scaled the farther wall, and lost herself in the streets, the shouting of Menelian's servants fading behind her. With luck, she thought, it would be assumed her body was consumed in the conflagration. Without, well, she would be gone from Vishat'yi before any could come seeking her, thanks to her master.

She halted in a dark and silent square, composing herself as she concentrated on the spell Anomius had taught her. She visualized his chamber in Nhur-jabal, mouthing the arcane syllables he had impressed upon her, and smelled the scent of almonds thick on the cool, moist night air.

Anomius lounged upon a couch, propped against the silken cushions at his back, a disgusting epicure, seeming out of place in the luxurious surroundings of his chambers in the citadel, like a maggot in the clean, crisp flesh of a new-plucked apple. A decanter of crystal and silver stood beside a filled goblet on a low table of artfully worked copper at his elbow, his mottled hand delving in a bowl of sticky sweetmeats, their remnants already greasy on his jaw and clothing. Candlelight played on spilled sugar and the pale ivory of his hairless pate. He gulped down a tidbit as Cennaire materialized, his watery blue eyes registering no surprise, though his brows rose slightly, framing a question.

"It went well enough," she said, shaking out her own thick hair, and smoothing her tunic. "Though they were gone."

The wizard's eyes narrowed at this and he wiped a hand across his mouth, spilling crumbs of pastry and grains of sugar over the symbols embroidered on his robe. Irritably, he cleaned his hand on the hem, motioning with the other that she should explain.

She took a seat and succinctly advised him of all she had learned and done. When she was finished he nodded thoughtfully.

"So, I have enemies here." He plucked at the red-

veined bulb of his nose. "That my prowess gives rise
to envy is hardly surprising. They've laid glamours,
did you know?"

Cennaire shook her head.

"Oh, yes. These quarters"—his hands scattered
more crumbs as he gestured at the room—"these were
all set with gramaryes. Spells of observance, spells of
listening. They even tried to use a *quyvhal* to spy on
me. On me!"

He laughed, the sound an avian tittering that
flecked the detritus coating his robe with spittle.
Cennaire waited, studying his ugly face, wondering,
not for the first time since he had slain and resurrected her, if he was mad. It was of little moment: he
enjoyed a prominence in Nhur-jabal and a measure of
that status spilled over to her profit. She enjoyed that;
more, she enjoyed the power he had given her. And he
held her heart—held, therefore, the key to her existence.

"Fools," he muttered when his laughter ceased.
"Did they not think I'd know? And protect myself?
Their glamours are as naught compared with mine
and so, my lovely huntress, I am neither surprised nor
unduly alarmed that they plot against me—in time I
shall take my revenge. Meanwhile, when word comes
from Vishat'yi that Menelian is dead they'll have
some inkling of what they face."

Cennaire frowned at this, folding hands still
stained with the mage's blood on her thighs. "Might
they not then move against me?" she asked. "I was
able to defeat Menelian easily enough, but several,
acting in concert . . ."

"You shall be gone to Lysse." Anomius waved a casual hand, exposing discolored teeth in a smile she
supposed was intended to reassure. "Safe from their
magicks. Our quarry departed for Aldarin, you say?
And on a warboat out of Vanu?"

Cennaire nodded. "So Menelian claimed."

Sallow lips pursed thoughtfully as a grubby finger
dug at a nostril. "The man they seek is Varent den

Tarl," he said at last, flicking his finger. "The one who first employed them to find the grimoire. That much I knew, but this matter of the Vanu folk is interesting."

"Menelian said only that they sailed together," Cennaire offered, adding, "he lusted after the woman."

The wizard's watery blue gaze moved over her face and form appraisingly, the smile that accompanied his examination almost mocking. "But not after you," he whispered, "which, I sense, annoyed you."

Cennaire met his eyes unflinching. His smile grew broader, then faded. "No matter—do with her what you will. Only find Calandryll den Karynth and the Kern freesword."

"I shall," she promised.

"Aye," he murmured, less to her than himself, "though they travel to the edges of the world and beyond, I've no doubt you'll hunt them down. But even so . . ."

"What?" she asked, sensing for the first time an element of doubt behind his confidence.

"The Vanu folk," he replied, shrugging. "What part do they play? Those folk seldom venture farther south than Forshold, and that but rarely. From what you've learned it would seem this Katya—and Tekkan, was it?—have joined the game. If Calandryll and Bracht came to Vishat'yi on the Vanu boat with dragon hides to sell, then likely it was that craft brought them to Gessyth. Nothing was said of what they found there?"

"Nothing," Cennaire confirmed. "Menelian said only that they were friends to Kandahar."

Anomius grunted, digging again at a nostril. Cennaire, ladylike for all her past, looked away. Sorcerer though he was, and her maker, Anomius was a revolting man.

"Why should Vanu aid them?" he wondered, the question rhetorical. "To suppose their meeting depended only on chance is to accept too much. I know little enough of that land, but I've heard talk of shamans there with great powers—might they have arranged this joining of forces? And if they did, then why?"

"Mayhap they, too, seek the grimoire," Cennaire suggested.

"Mayhap." Anomius frowned, brow creasing in a myriad of lines as he pondered. "And if they do, it must truly be a tome of immense value. Perhaps even more than Calandryll believed, or"—his expression became menacing with anger—"more than he revealed."

"Could he have hidden that knowledge from you?"

Cennaire regretted the question as she saw his eyes grow cold with rage at the implied insult. This man had given her the life she now knew, and he could take it from her. Perhaps was the only man who surely could. Behind the fear his stare induced she felt a new thought take shape: perhaps someday she must destroy him to protect herself. But not yet; not until she had explored the limits of her newfound powers, not before she was confident of the victory. She smiled nervously, lowering her head in apology to watch him through the heavy curtain of her lashes, employing all the artistry of her old trade.

Anomius sniffed noisily, not deigning to answer the question. Instead, he said: "Do not slay them before you have the book. Do you understand? Until you have the grimoire safe, you shall not destroy them."

His voice was fierce and, dutifully, Cennaire nodded. In a subdued voice she asked, "And if they do not have it?"

He studied her a moment, his eyes speculative, and she feared she had gone too far. Then he smiled again, his expression unctuous as he said, "You think ahead, my pretty—aye, it may be they've delivered it to their employer and it rests now in the hands of Varent den Tarl. Be that so, you shall slay them—but only if you are certain beyond doubt of the grimoire's location.

Those two are subtle, their stratagems cunning, so be wary! If Varent den Tarl holds the book, then be sure you find him before you take my revenge. Above all I must have the book! Find that before you deal with them; after . . ."

His eyes roved her body, not with such lust as she was accustomed to seeing in men's eyes, but in contemplation of what she could, in her undead form, achieve, his tittering laughter finishing the sentence clearer than words might.

"So, your task is clear. Go now and bathe, sleep, and tomorrow we shall speak again; before you depart for Aldarin."

7

THE river valley that cradled Aldarin was gentler than the craggy heights surrounding Vishat'yi. Vineyards covered the slopes rising from the banks of the slow-moving Alda, the growths bare as yet, though budded with the promise of the bounty to come, and above them the grasslands of Lysse rustled in the breeze, checkered with the dark shapes of browsing cattle. Where the river met the Narrow Sea the city spanned the flow, all blue and gold in the lucid sunlight of the afternoon, its wall standing proud across the river's mouth, the ramparts extending in two sweeping horns to encompass the bay where ships bobbed on the tide. For all that blockhouses surmounted by the gantries of mangonels stood watch over the anchorage, and the great metal-barred gates looked sturdy enough to withstand the fiercest onslaught, it appeared a peaceful place, a merchant city going about its daily business.

Yet within those walls Calandryll hoped to find Rhythamun; hoped to confront the wizard and wrest from him the Arcanum. How—in a city that honored him as Varent den Tarl, and he possessed of awesome occult powers—Calandryll did not yet know. Only, as the warboat slowed its headlong rush, that he must; and that this felt like coming home.

He turned from his observation as he felt the vessel's passage ease, no longer propelled by the godly strength of Burash but now by the action of the sea alone, and looked to the waves. Beside him Bracht grunted as grey-green water swirled and the god rose up, wearing man's shape now, but nonetheless majestic, water running from huge shoulders, the mane of hair a glossy mantle as eyes like the depths of the ocean surveyed the watchers. Katya spoke softly in the Vanu tongue to her father, and Tekkan stared in awe as the great silent voice rang in their minds.

No farther shall I bring you, but go on alone with my blessing.

"Wait!" Calandryll shouted as a hand lifted in gesture of farewell. "We've need of you still. How shall we defeat Rhythamun? With all his power, do you not aid us?"

This is not within my aegis, returned the god, *you enter my sister Dera's wardship now. Do you need such aid as we may grant, then call on her.*

"And shall she answer?"

If so she chooses. But I may go no farther, lest I trespass upon her domain. Divine laughter echoed through their minds. *We gods are jealous of our realms.*

"But, Rhythamun . . ."

Calandryll's cry was silenced by the god's outthrust hand.

Is a man, for all his powers, no more than flesh laid upon the frame of his bones. All men may be defeated—to you comes the task of finding how.

At his side, Calandryll heard Bracht mutter, "Gods and sorcerers both, it seems, love riddles."

The Kern's presumption alarmed Calandryll and for a moment he feared Burash might take affront, turn all his oceanic wrath upon them. Instead he heard the laughter again, like waves booming in a sea cavern.

Though I be not your god, warrior, still you dare much to speak thus. Would you so dismiss Ahrd?

Bracht, unabashed, shrugged, grinning. "I'd ask of him plain advice," he answered.

I tell you what I may, Burash said. *Think you we gods are free of laws? No—different as we are to mortal men, so are our laws different. Might I bestride the land and take the Arcanum from Rhythamun's dead hands, do you not think I should take that course? I cannot; that is forbidden me.*

"Might Dera, then?" asked Calandryll.

No. Waves lashed as the god's great head shook. *Aid she may give you, if so she elects; but to put an end to Rhythamun . . . No.*

"Why not?" Bracht demanded bluntly, ignoring the warning hand Calandryll set upon his arm. "Does Rhythamun succeed, then she and you and Ahrd—all the Younger Gods!—stand threatened by Tharn."

You speak the truth, Bracht ni Errhyn. The soundless voice was solemn now, the huge head bowing a moment before rising to fasten the great green eyes on the Kern's defiant face. *Mayhap you three hold all our lives in your hands. But still we may not do that which destiny has given you for duty . . . it is forbidden us. This blasphemy Rhythamun would attempt is of man's making, and by man's hand it must be ended. Look to your own salvation, not to godly saviors—such aid as is ours to give shall be yours, but no more. Neither question me further, for I depart.*

Farewell.

Swift as he had appeared in the cavern, so Burash went, descending beneath the swell that roiled the sea where he had been. From the steering deck Calandryll and the others watched awhile, each locked in the lonely cell of their own thoughts, pondering the import of the god's words. It was Bracht who broke the silence: "So, we must go alone into the city."

"Aye." Calandryll turned his gaze landward. Sud-

denly Aldarin seemed less welcoming and his voice
faltered as he said, "We've no other choice."

"None." Bracht's voice was grim, the smile that
curved his lips no less so. "As we began, so we return."

"You forget," Katya said, "that we are three now.
With all my folk at our backs."

"You I'd not forget." Bracht shaped a gallant bow.
"But still . . ."

"We are scant few against a city that hails Varent
den Tarl," Calandryll finished for him. "Think you
we should find the Domm's ear if we bring him our
tale? More likely he'd laugh at us—before ordering us
imprisoned. And you've some inkling of the powers
Rhythamun wields. Likely he'll know we move
against him and employ sortilege to halt us."

"But still," Bracht repeated, "we go on."

His tone held neither doubt nor hesitation and
when Calandryll turned to study his face, it was set
in determined lines, as if the thought of surrender was
an alien thing.

"Mayhap to our deaths," he said.

Bracht chuckled at that, carelessly, his expression
transformed as he clapped Calandryll soundly on the
shoulder. "Mayhap," he agreed cheerfully, "but no
man lives forever, so shall that deter us?"

Calandryll stared at him awhile, then he, too, began to chuckle. "No," he declared. "Never!"

"Never!" echoed Katya, her smile encompassing
them both. "Tekkan! To Aldarin we go."

"And may all those gods we'd save go with us," the
helmsman murmured, then shouted in his own language, calling for his rested crew to take up the
sweeps and bring them in to harbor.

THE lean black warboat aroused an interest bordering
on consternation as it swept between the defensive
horns that encircled the anchorage. The mangonels
mounted on the blockhouses were visibly sighted in

as they approached, and long before Tekkan called for his oarsmen to slow their speed and let the craft drift in beside a wharf, archers were lined along the moles with bows drawn, pikemen standing at the ready behind them.

Calandryll, with Bracht and Katya, took position at the prow, holding firm to the arching neck of the dragonshead, shouting in Lyssian that they were come peacefully, with no intent to harm.

Into his ear, Bracht murmured, "Likely Rhythamun will hear of this ere long."

Calandryll nodded, looking to where the soldiery waited, wondering for a moment if he had been better advised to request of Burash that the god put them ashore in some bay farther up the coast, and they trek overland to the city. No, he decided, for if Rhythamun protected himself with gramaryes, then the sorcerer would learn of their arrival, however they chose to approach him. Their best hope—perhaps their only hope—lay in relying on the wizard's confidence, in trusting that he believed them entrapped deep in the wastes of Gessyth.

"Perhaps," he replied. "Or perhaps he believes us lost in Tezin-dar. Whichever, we are here now and can go only forward."

"Spoken like a warrior of Cuan na'For," Bracht complimented.

"But cautiously," Katya warned. "Does he believe us trapped in the lost city, then we hold an advantage we shall lose if we go headlong forward."

"Aye," Calandryll agreed, "we'd best disguise ourselves and scout the way before attempting to confront him."

Bracht shrugged, grinning wickedly. "There are more ways than one to advance into battle," he murmured, "and stealth is a warrior's friend."

So it was that they hung back, seeking to lose themselves among the crew as Tekkan spoke with the captain of the harbor guard, improvising a story that had the warboat roaming southward from Vanu for

reasons of trade and exploration, blown off course by
storms and wanting only to lay over in Aldarin awhile
to rest the crew before continuing home. Even in
Lysse's mild clime the changing season put a chill in
the air and the Vanu folk had donned cloaks of shaggy
fur and oiled cloth, so it was not difficult for the three
to go unnoticed as the helmsman spun his yarn. Con-
vincingly enough, it soon became apparent, that the
officer accepted they were neither corsairs nor some
raiding party out of Kandahar and granted they might
anchor there. Calandryll was somewhat surprised to
discover Tekkan so adept a liar, and delighted that his
glib tongue won them the freedom of the city without
further examination. Wrapped in his own cloak, he
huddled in the midst of the Vanu folk as they made
for a nearby tavern.

It was warm inside, a fire banked in the central
hearth, and at this hour the lamps went unlit, the low
ceiling and the supporting pillars that divided the
room providing a welcome half-light. They gathered
to the rear, where shadows hung deepest, ignoring the
curious stares of the few other drinkers as hoods were
thrown back and the pale blond hair characteristic
of the Vanu folk marked them as strangers. Enough
thronged between Calandryll and Bracht and the
other customers that any spies would have difficulty
identifying them, and Tekkan called for ale.

When all were served and the innkeeper's curiosity
satisfied, they settled to discussing their next move.

To go en masse to the palace Rhythamun occupied
in his guise as Varent den Tarl could only bring unwanted attention, Calandryll suggested; better to
reconnoiter cautiously and learn what they might before approaching the wizard. Bracht gave his support
to this, and it was agreed that they would all find
quarters in some suitable hostelry before proceeding
further.

"Should we not seek Dera's aid?" Katya wondered.

Calandryll thought a moment before replying, then
shook his head. "Perhaps not," he murmured. "At

least not yet. Varent den Tarl is a noble of this place and might well have ears even in the temples."

"Why should we need a temple?" the woman queried. "Burash came in answer to your call—shall Dera not?"

This was a matter he had pondered at length as the god drove them across the Narrow Sea, without reaching any real conclusions: again he shook his head.

"I cannot say, neither if Dera would hear me or how I summoned Burash. I know only that I drowned"—he grimaced at that unpleasant memory—"and that I believed I was doomed. That we all should die there. What summons I sent—what cry I made, or how—I know no better than you."

"But Menelian spoke of power in you," she urged, "and Burash, too."

He shrugged helplessly. "But could not, as I told you, define it. Nor can I—it remains a mystery. I can offer my private prayers to the goddess, but whether or not they will be heard, I cannot say."

"Try that," said Bracht. "That we should avoid the temples I agree, but we know something of Rhythamun's abilities and I'd have whatever aid we can muster when we go against him."

Calandryll bowed his head in agreement, wishing that Burash had spoken clearer. In this he found himself in concert with the freesword: it seemed that the gods did, indeed, speak in riddles. He felt the resolve that had come with Burash's intervention waver and he found himself wondering if their quest was foredoomed. The auguries he had heard, the scrying of the spaewives in Secca and Kharasul, the words of the Guardians in Tezin-dar, all spoke of three—Katya, Bracht, and he. But they were merely three mortal folk and now they had come back to Aldarin the quest once more seemed formidable. He was, for all Menelian had said, no sorcerer: he had no magic to use against Rhythamun, and he could not believe that blades were enough to defeat the mage. Neither cunning, for Rhythamun was protected as well by his status in the city as by his occult power. It remained to the elected three to find some way to wrest the Arcanum from the wizard, but he could see no clear path to success in that.

"Do what you can," he heard Bracht murmur, and realized that he brooded. "No man may do more."

He essayed a smile in answer to the Kern and said, "Aye. We've come too far to falter now."

Bracht nodded and Calandryll realized that he had unwittingly spoken the truth: to concede the game had not occurred to him; only that they might not win. His smile grew stronger and he raised his pot, draining the ale.

It was a stouter brew than the somewhat thin Kandaharian beer and he felt it fill his belly with memories. He was back in Lysse and to the east lay Secca—he wondered what transpired in his home. Tobias would by now be wed to Nadama: did they reside there, or might his brother be in the shipyards of Eryn, overseeing the construction of the promised warships? Did he believe his brother dead, slain by the Chaipaku? Or might he have received word from the assassins that Calandryll lived, their hands stayed by the god they worshipped? He chuckled at that thought, grimly wishing that he might see Tobias's face at the moment he got such alarming news. Someday—did he survive—he would likely face his brother, and what shock that must surely be. Doubtless Tobias remembered the youth who had lost himself in the palace libraries, thinking him still a bookish stripling. What would he think now of the hardened swordsman who downed his ale with such relish, contemplating attack on a wizard of proven power? Melancholy left him suddenly as it had come and he banged down his pot, calling for more ale.

"Your spirits lift," Katya observed, studying his smile, and he grinned at her, nodding: "Aye."

He offered no further explanation, though she continued to watch him, as if confused by his abruptly changing moods. He had become, he realized, increasingly like Bracht, accepting the moment for what it was, without undue brooding on where it might lead. That part of him that yet retained the vestiges of what he had been still brought him into melancholy contemplation from time to time, but those pessimistic humors were discarded with ever-increasing rapidity, lost under the tide of his resolve. He knew not where their quest would lead them, nor—if he was honest with himself—if they had any real hope of victory, but to quit was unthinkable: the only direction was forward. He found his tankard refilled and drank with renewed relish.

Beside him Bracht grinned and said, "You take your ale better now."

"It tastes better now," he returned, smile widening as he recalled their first meeting, "and I know my limits better now."

The freesword's grin remained, but in his eyes there was a hint of conjecture, as if he doubted the cheerful statement. Not, Calandryll recognized, where ale was concerned, but in other matters; and in those he, too, remained unsure. No matter, he decided, he would press onward, trusting in the gods and fate.

The landlord produced food then, great salvers of sausages and smoked meats, vegetables pickled in brine and vinegar, loaves of bread and thick wedges of milky cheese, and any questions Bracht or Katya might have pressed on him went unasked as they fell eagerly on the meal.

When they were finished they drained another mug and quit the tavern, choosing to divide their numbers among several hostelries in hopes of confusing potential observers. They were not aware of being followed or watched, but still it seemed the wisest course to separate, trusting that their disguising cloaks would render it impossible for any spies to decide which among the small groups finding lodgings in the Har-

bor Quarter were the three Rhythamun might seek
and which only crew.

Calandryll, Bracht, and Katya, accompanied by
Tekkan, left the rest while some seventeen remained
to continue the false trail, securing rooms in a place
called The Eagle. It seemed anonymous enough, a typical lodging house, three stories high, surrounded by a
walled courtyard with stabling to the rear, the ground
level occupied by a kitchen and a common room
where meals might be had. The three men took one
sizable chamber on the second story and Katya—
smiling as she rejected Bracht's suggestion that they
had all, or at least he and she, better remain
together—a single adjoining room.

Chuckling at his own defeat, the freesword inspected the chamber with professional expertise. It
held little more than the three beds, a small armoire,
and a single washstand. The planks of the floor
creaked and plaster flaked from the walls. The door
granted egress to a landing that looked down onto the
common room, the stairs in clear view. He grunted
his satisfaction and crossed to the one window,
throwing open the shutters to check that exit, should
it be needed in a hurry. Peering over his shoulder,
Calandryll saw a modest drop to the courtyard, the
wall low enough to climb without undue difficulty,
and went to a bed, unlatching his swordbelt before
stretching out with a contented sigh. He felt calm
now, knowing that they were committed and that
what they must attempt was best done with aid of
darkness.

"At dusk then," Bracht said, his confirmation further sign of the increasing similarity of their thinking.

"Aye." Calandryll clasped hands behind his head.
The room was warm and his belly was full: he felt
drowsy. "At dusk."

The Kern, too, flung himself down, removing his
swordbelt and carefully placing the sheathed falchion
across his legs.

He came instantly upright as a light tapping

sounded against the door, blade flashing from the scabbard. An instant later, Calandryll was on his feet with the straightsword drawn and ready, not needing Bracht's gesture to station himself by the window as the Kern faced the door.

"It's Katya," Tekkan declared, favoring them both with an almost-disapproving glance as he swung the door open to confirm his guess. "Could even Rhythamun have found us so soon?"

Bracht shrugged unabashed, sheathing his blade. Calandryll said, "Perhaps. And I'd not take the chance."

"Likely he'd employ magicks," Katya remarked as she entered.

"There was no scent of almonds," Calandryll reminded her. "As well we remember that, for it's likely all the warning we shall have."

The warrior woman nodded, smiling as Bracht motioned for her to join him on the bed, but seating herself beside Tekkan. "Do we go at dusk?" she asked.

Calandryll and Bracht exchanged smiles and the Kern said, "We think alike. In most things, at least."

He ignored the admonitory look Tekkan gave him, beaming innocently at the woman, who hid her answering smile from her father and said, "We three alone?"

"Aye." Bracht raised a hand as Tekkan began to protest, his swarthy features earnest as he turned to the boatmaster. "This must be a thing of stealth."

"To take more can only arouse suspicion," Calandryll elaborated. "The palace lies in a residential quarter and a crowd would be unusual."

Tekkan's face grew somber and he drove a hand through the heavy thatch of his greyed hair. "But only three?" he argued. "Against a sorcerer whose power is so great?"

"It seems we three are elected to the task," Calandryll returned. "Why, I know not; only that all the portents have spoken of we three alone. Besides, I think Rhythamun's power is great enough that whether we go alone, or with all your folk at our backs, it will make no difference."

"And if we fail," Katya said slowly, "then you must take word back to our homeland."

"A few, at least," Tekkan pleaded.

Katya reached out to take his hand, her grey eyes solemn. "As Calandryll says," she murmured, "be we few or many, it will make no difference."

"Save to warn of our coming," Bracht added.

"And should it come down to battle, then best your crew not be involved." Calandryll lent his advice to the argument. "Should the city watch take part and find your people with us, likely you and your boat will be held, and you'll not have chance to take word back."

"No harm shall come to Katya while I live," Bracht vowed. "You've my word on that."

"I know it." Tekkan graced the Kern with a thin smile. "But shall any of you live?"

"That chance was accepted when first we sailed," Katya declared, squeezing her father's hand. "And you're no bladesman."

"No." It was the first time Calandryll had seen Tekkan express regret at his unwarlike nature. "But Quara and her archers . . ."

"Are stout enough in honest fight," Katya said, "but of little use against magic."

"And your swords are?" Tekkan gestured at the sheathed blades. "I cannot doubt your courage—but your wisdom?"

"The gods stand with us," she answered, "and we must trust in them. Did Burash not prove that?"

Tekkan stared awhile at the hand she held, then sighed resignedly. "You are decided," he muttered in a low, gruff voice.

"I think it has been decided for us," Katya returned.

"Then so be it," her father allowed reluctantly. "But, Calandryll—you'll offer prayers to Dera that she aid you?"

Calandryll nodded, meeting the older man's grim stare. Tekkan forced a smile, grasping Katya's hand in both of his, and asked, "Have I no part to play, save waiting?"

It was Bracht who answered: "Best that you pass word among your folk to stand ready. Gather them discreetly in some harbor tavern, prepared to sail do we need take flight."

"And how shall I know?" asked the helmsman.

The Kern thought a moment and then, with a questioning glance at Calandryll and Katya, said, "Gather them together in that tavern we visited. How was it called?"

"The Seagull," Calandryll supplied.

"In the Seagull then," Bracht continued. "Ready to fight or sail. Does it come to fighting, you'll know soon enough; if we do not return by dawn, then you sail."

"I'll stand off the coast," Tekkan said in a voice that brooked no argument, "and wait out the day."

Bracht ducked his head in agreement. "A day, but no more." He looked to Katya and then to Calandryll. "If we are not returned by then you need wait no longer."

"I can think of no better plan," Calandryll said.

"This is sound," said Katya, and smiled. "And if all goes well, then we shall drink together in the Seagull and celebrate our victory."

Tekkan's face showed that he recognized this as encouragement and nothing more, but he forbore to dissent further and nodded his agreement.

"Then let's rest," Bracht suggested. "This may be a long night."

"Aye." Katya rose; Tekkan released her hands with obvious reluctance. "And I shall lock my door, for fear of intruders."

She looked to Bracht as she spoke, laughter in her eyes, and he feigned resentment, shrugging. As she went through the door he said, "For such a woman a man would gladly die," his voice pitched deliberately loud enough that she would hear.

She paused, turning back just long enough to say, "I hope none shall."

"Amen," whispered Tekkan as the door thudded shut.

"The gods willing, it shall not come to that," Calandryll offered, knowing it was poor enough reassurance, but not what else to say.

"Pray so," came Tekkan's forlorn response, no more confident than Calandryll's weak words.

"We do what we must," said Bracht, blunt as ever, and settled himself once more on the bed.

His eyes closed and in a little while his breathing softened into sleep. Calandryll wondered at his ability to find that haven so easily when, were he honest with himself, he shared all Tekkan's doubts. He glanced at the boatmaster and saw that Tekkan stared blindly at the beamed ceiling, his gaze unsighted. He tried to find words confident enough to comfort the man, but none came and he left Tekkan to his private thoughts, folding his arms like a lover about his scabbard as he dropped his head to the pillow.

Then started as Rhythamun's face formed against a backcloth of darkness, smiling wickedly as his hands reached out to shape some malicious glamour. He could not make out the words of the spell, nor did he want to hear them; only to snatch out his sword and cut the warlock down. He could not, for powerful fingers locked about his wrist and a hand pressed him back against the bed as the words pierced his sleepy mind.

"Dusk draws nigh and I'd eat before we venture out."

He groaned, the dream dissolving as he recognized Bracht's face, and sighed his relief.

"I thought"—he shook the last remnants of sleep from his mind—"I dreamed of Rhythamun."

The Kern released his grip, smiling. "I guessed as

much. Indeed, I feared you'd cut me down." He motioned to the window. "The time nears."

"Aye." Calandryll saw the sky was gone dark blue, the crescent of a new-risen moon suspended over the city. From below came the smells of food cooking and a low murmur of conversation. He rose, going to the washstand to splash chill water over his fevered face, then belted on his sword. He crossed to the window as Bracht roused Tekkan, seeing the lights of Aldarin twinkling golden below. "Go down and order food," he asked. "I'd be alone to commune with Dera."

If I can, he added to himself as Tekkan performed his own ablutions. Then, aloud: "I'll not be long."

He felt Bracht's hand on his shoulder, comradely, and turned toward the Kern's grave face. "As best you can," the freesword said gently. "And if she does not answer, well"—gravity became the familiar grin as the hand dropped to touch the falchion's hilt—"we've still these, and they've served us well enough so far."

Calandryll nodded, waiting for them to be gone. He watched the door close and looked again at the night sky.

Try as he might, he could feel nothing in him that suggested any ability to communicate with the goddess. Nor, he was surprised to realize, was there any fear; rather, he felt a tremendous calm, as if, his feet now firmly set upon the path, he accepted whatever lay ahead. He thought perhaps he should kneel: after all, he came as a supplicant, even though Dera's own fate likely rested in the balance of this night's events. The boards creaked as he sank down, his arms spreading wide as he bowed his head and called to the deity.

In silence he sent out his voice, asking that she aid them, that she lend them her strength in battle with Rhythamun, who would see her and all her kindred gods ground down beneath the heel of Tharn, the Mad God. Could she watch that happen? he asked. Would she allow it? Could she forsake her unwitting worshippers, or stand with those who sought to defend them and her, and all the Younger Gods? *Help me*, he begged. *Show yourself to me as Burash, your brother god, did. Show me how to defeat Rhythamun. Give me that power.*

He heard no answer, nor inside himself felt any stirring. He lifted his head, seeing the sky before him, framed within the rectangle of the window, a cobweb traced by moonlight across one corner, the silver sickle a fraction farther westward along its implacable journey. The chamber felt cold now and he shivered, arms dropping to his sides, the left slapping the hardened leather of his scabbard. It seemed, as Bracht had said so cheerfully, that blades must be their only weapons, for he felt no godly touch, no presence come responding to his prayers.

"So be it," he said aloud as he rose. And sighed once; then laughed once. "We shall do what we can; and do we fail, it shall not be for want of trying."

He ran fingers through his long hair and smoothed his tunic, the leather cracked and weathered by now, more mercenary's garb than prince's, and crossed to the door, striding out onto the landing and down the stairs to where his comrades waited with expectant faces.

His own told them he had no answers.

"No matter." Bracht raised a pitcher of the rich red wine for which the Alda valley was famous, filling a glass. "You offered no prayers to Burash but still he came; mayhap Dera, too, shall come in time of need."

Calandryll smiled thanks for that encouragement and took the proffered cup, drinking deep. Katya pushed a bowl of thick fish stew toward him and he ladled a generous measure onto his plate. "How shall we approach this palace?" she asked.

"By coach, I think," he replied around a mouthful of the spiced stew. "A coach will hide us from prying eyes."

"But not conceal us from such glamours as he might set," she murmured.

Calandryll answered with a shrug: words seemed redundant, for Katya stated the obvious and if they approached in fear of magicks, to approach at all was pointless. They had no choice save to hope.

"Do we discern spell-making, then we run," said Bracht, adding with a wry grin, "if we can."

"And if all seems well?"

"Then we enter," the Kern said firmly. "I left a horse in Varent's stable and I'd take him back."

"And if Rhythamun is gone?" Tekkan demanded.

All three looked to the boatmaster at that and it occurred to Calandryll that they had all chosen to forget that possibility. This return to Aldarin had acquired the feeling of approaching confrontation, and the thought that Rhythamun might be already departed had not figured in their thinking. He broke bread from the loaf at his elbow and said, "Then we must seek information from whoever remains."

"What does that stone you wear tell you?" asked Bracht, head ducking to indicate the talisman hung about Katya's neck.

"That he is here," she replied.

The Kern nodded. Tekkan seemed almost disappointed. Calandryll felt nothing: he wiped his plate with a hunk of bread, not much interested in further talk. It seemed to him that they must proceed on the assumption that Rhythamun remained in Aldarin, in the body of Varent den Tarl, and that speculation concerning his possible moves was fruitless: the sorcerer led the game and they could only follow. Were he departed, they could only hope to discover his destination and continue after; if he remained they must attack as best they could. Suddenly he felt a great impatience. He swallowed the bread and pushed his plate aside; took up his glass and drained it. "Shall we find out?" he demanded.

Without awaiting a reply he shoved his chair back, rising and drawing his cloak about his shoulders. Bracht's grin was fierce as he followed suit, Katya a little slower, pausing to speak with her father in the Vanu tongue, her words eliciting a wan smile from Tekkan.

"Until later," Calandryll murmured. "In the Seagull."

Tekkan nodded and said, "Aye, until later. And may Dera and all her fellow gods go with you."

THE coach was such as gentlefolk favored, a phaeton drawn by two deep-chested horses, the cab secured against the elements with narrow doors and windows covered by curtains of thick felt. Katya and Bracht, the hoods of their cloaks concealing their faces, sat side by side, Calandryll on the other bench, where he might direct the driver. The vehicle swayed on its leather springs, bouncing as it carried them away from the Harbor Quarter into the bowels of the city. The night was yet young and for a while they traveled busy streets, along the course of the Alda, the river hidden by the buildings that stood along its banks, then they turned across one of the many bridges and the roadway grew smoother, confirmation that they entered a more salubrious quarter. Soon the streets grew empty, the taverns and emporiums and their concomitant crowds left behind, replaced by the walled mansions of the wealthy. Neither Calandryll nor Bracht recognized the avenue along which Varent den Tarl's palace was situated until the coachman slowed his team, studying the insignia that marked the stuccoed walls.

From the window, Calandryll saw a familiar gate, and frowned as something about it struck him amiss. At first he was not sure—or could not believe his eyes—for the avenue was shaded with winter-stripped trees and the new moon not so bright as to shed clear light. He called for the coachman to halt, staring in numbed silence at the long pennants of white silk hung from the arched gate-top. They stirred fitfully in the night wind, ghostly at his dawning suspicion: he groaned.

"What is it?" Bracht's whisper was loud in his ear

as the freesword peered at the gate. "What are those ribbons?"

Calandryll's teeth ground hard together as the coachman's voice came from the seat above: "Shall you be staying overnight, or would you have me wait while you pay your respects?"

"Funerary pennants!" His answer was harsh with conjecture. "Someone has died here. In Lysse it's the custom to hang such ribbons to announce a death."

"Rhythamun?" Bracht's reply was disbelieving.

"More likely Varent den Tarl." Calandryll shook his head, turning a face paled by moon's light and apprehension toward the Kern. "Know you what that means?"

"That Rhythamun has quit the body," Katya said softly, helplessly, "and now inhabits another."

Bracht mouthed a curse. From the seat the coachman asked again, "Do I await you, or go on?"

"Go on!"

Calandryll flung the door open, springing to the street and tossing coins to the driver. Bracht came behind, pausing only to hand Katya down. Calandryll eyed the white pennants with loathing and hammered on the gate, the need for caution replaced now by the fear they had come too late.

Dera, but if Varent den Tarl was dead and Rhythamun ensconced in the form of some fresh victim their task was become near impossible! Must they now hunt a stranger, the warlock masked in another's body, faceless? He felt his heart beat faster, drumming a rhythm of awful trepidation as he waited for the gate to open, his fingers tapping impatiently on the hilt of his sword. At his side he heard Bracht demand, "How can he be dead if your stone points us here?" and Katya answer simply, "I know not," that reply met with another curse from the Kern.

Then the gate was opened by a servant dressed in Varent's blue and gold livery, divided across the chest by the white sash of mourning, his face hollowed by the shadows his lantern threw. "Masters?" he asked. "What would you in this sad place?"

"The Lord Varent den Tarl," Calandryll extemporized, composing himself to some semblance of calm. "He is dead?"

"Aye." The servant nodded solemnly. "And lies now in his coffin."

"We'd pay our respects," Calandryll said quickly. "Only today did we arrive in Aldarin, and this news was unknown to us."

"You knew him?" The white-sashed man raised the lantern higher, studying the visitors with an element of suspicion, as if such latecomers could herald no good. "I had thought all who would offer their farewells were come. On the morrow he shall be entombed in his family's crypt."

"Lord Varent commissioned us to a duty," Calandryll said firmly. "Do you speak with"—he hesitated as he racked his memory for near-forgotten names—"his man Darth. Aye, Darth; or Symeon, who manages his accounts—either one will vouch for us."

The servant paused, clearly torn between offending this tall young man who spoke in the accents of the Lyssian nobility for all he wore the appearance of some itinerant freesword, and the dubious nature of his arrival at so late an hour. Bracht resolved the problem.

The Kern pushed past Calandryll, settling himself directly before the servant. "I gave a black stallion into Darth's care," he snapped, "and Symeon will, I trust, confirm that some two thousand five hundred varre are owed me. Now—do you bring us inside, or . . ."

He touched the falchion's hilt suggestively; the servant started back, mumbling reluctant agreement, and beckoned them after him.

The mansion's doors were draped, like the gates, with white and the interior was mostly unlit, though a single chandelier illuminated the vestibule to which he brought them. He sketched a bow and murmured that they should wait, his expression one of relief as Calandryll waved his dismissal and frowned nervously at Bracht.

"Tact might well serve us better now," he whispered. "If—as it seems—worst has come to worst, we must learn all we may from Varent's people, not antagonize them."

"I'd enough of his prevarication." The Kern gestured irritably, then as abruptly grinned. "And we are here, are we not?"

"Aye," Calandryll allowed. "For what good it does us."

"Mayhap we shall find some clue," Katya suggested. "Did you not say he had a library?"

Calandryll nodded curtly. "Though I doubt he's left us markers to follow. And if he's taken some other form, time is even more our enemy."

"We do what we can." Bracht's voice was hard, defensive of the woman. Calandryll sighed and said, "I fear he shall escape us."

The Kern smiled briefly then, mollified, and said, "At least we face no magicks here."

Calandryll began to reply, but the inner door swung open then, admitting Darth. Like the gateman he wore a sash of white silk to indicate his mourning, wound about his waist, the hilt of a long dagger protruding. Red wine colored his lips and his step appeared a trifle unsteady as he came toward them. He studied them a moment, squinting as his eyes took time to focus, then ducked his head and smiled in recognition, his tongue thick as he greeted them.

"So you return at last, and with a beauty." His gaze flickered blearily over Katya and he offered an unstable bow before murmuring lewdly to Bracht, "Rytha will be disappointed."

Had he been less concerned with the enormity of events, Calandryll would have been amused by the reddening of the Kern's cheeks as Katya fixed him with a speculative glance, offsetting the anger sparked by Darth's drunken admiration. He cleared his throat and said, "Rytha? I had forgotten Rytha."

Darth shrugged carelessly and asked, "You've come for your horse? He's been well tended."

"And the money owed me," Bracht said, indicating Calandryll with a callused thumb, playing the part of mercenary bodyguard. "Two thousand five hundred varre were promised did I bring my charge back safe from Gessyth—which you can see I've done."

"Dera's love!" Darth shook his head in exaggerated censure. "Lord Varent lies scarce cold in his coffin and you talk of debts. Have you no respect, man?"

"Life goes on," said Bracht bluntly.

Darth's flushed features grew darker and Calandryll feared he might eject them, but then the man's stained mouth curved in a smile and he began to chuckle. "That much is true," he agreed, "but Symeon is majordomo to this household and he must settle all such matters now. Come—I'll bring you to him."

Calandryll raised a hand, halting him as he beckoned them to follow. "The sum was, indeed, agreed," he said, "but before such mundane matters are discussed, I'd pay my respects to Lord Varent."

Darth appeared impressed by this observation of the proprieties and nodded, ushering them from the vestibule along a gallery lit at intervals by the soft yellow glow of candles to a door hung with a single unbroken sheet of white.

As was the custom in Lysse a room had been cleared and set aside, that the coffin might stand alone, awaiting those who would say their last farewells. Pristine curtains covered the windows and the only light came from tall candelabra standing at the head and foot of a catafalque draped with more silk. Upon that platform stood a sarcophagus of marble worked in Varent's colors, blue and gold. Calandryll gazed at the elaborate coffin, not sure whether he felt apprehension or hope, his thoughts in turmoil at this dramatic turn of events. His instinct was to hurry forward, but he curbed his haste, forcing himself to approach slowly, head bowed in apparent reverence. He realized that he held his breath as he looked down, half expecting Rhythamun to spring up, laughing in triumph. But in the coffin there was only a body, a husk with all the life gone out of it. It was swathed in white, the still face gleaming in the candlelight, its lifelike appearance testament to the embalmer's artifice. Calandryll stared at the familiar features, the dark eyes dull now, no longer animated by the bright spark of existence.

This was, beyond all doubt, Varent den Tarl, and he was truly dead: Calandryll heard his stifled breath come out in a slow sigh and turned away.

He looked to Darth as Bracht and Katya approached the bier, his mind racing, horribly aware that the sorcerer had escaped and that he must somehow find a way to pursue. "When did he die?" he asked.

Darth took his hollow tone for grief, which in a way it was, and answered, "As is our custom, he's lain in state these past three weeks. And now the house is to be sold and I've to find some other employment."

He glanced accusingly at the catafalque: Calandryll assumed a sympathetic smile and said, "My condolences. Shall you bring us to Symeon now?"

Symeon was huddled behind the same cluttered desk in the same wood-paneled chamber where last they had seen him, as if he had not moved from there in all the time they had been gone. The single high window was shuttered, candlelight glinting off his bald pate and the spectacles that magnified his short-sighted eyes. Those fixed on the trio as Darth ushered them in.

"Two thousand five hundred varre," he said by way of welcome. "Which you prefer be paid in decuris. Correct?"

Bracht nodded and the little man opened a leather-bound register, fastidiously annotated a column of figures, and set down his quill. He wiped his inky hands on his grubby tunic, succeeding in transferring a generous measure to the sash that spanned the mound of his belly, and rose without further ado to crouch before the metal door set in the wall behind him. Calandryll watched as he brought a key from his breeches and set it in the lock. He swung the door open with a great huffing and reached into a chest he hid with his body. Coins clinked as he counted them into a leather pouch, then he closed the chest, returned it to the wall, and carefully locked the door. Wheezing, he rose to his feet and set the pouch on the farther edge of the desk.

"We thought you dead," he murmured, eyes shifting from their faces to the promised commission, "but a contract is a contract."

"Indeed," said Bracht, taking the pouch and weighing it thoughtfully in his hand.

"It's all there," said Symeon.

Bracht inclined his head and said, "I've no doubt," as he tucked the pouch safely beneath his jerkin.

The fat little man nodded, fingers caressing his ledgers as if he deemed all their business done and longed to return to his books. When they failed to remove themselves he grunted somewhat irritably and demanded, "Have you other matters we need discuss? Lord Varent had no kin and it falls to me to set this house in order that his possessions may be auctioned off."

So brusque was his inquiry Calandryll came close to laughter that he knew would come out hysteric. *Other matters? Aye,* he thought, *I'd discuss the manner of your master's death and the fact that he sought—still seeks, likely in another's form!—to raise the Mad God.* He bit back the threatening laughter and said aloud, "Our contract with Lord Varent is ended with his death, though I'd fain see his library again. He had rare volumes there, such as are not found in lesser collections. And he promised me its run on my return."

Symeon's plump mouth pursed and he plucked at

his lower lip with ink-stained fingers, as if debating the matter.

"Mayhap I'd find volumes I might wish to purchase," Calandryll urged, "and thus render your accounting easier. Price is no object."

The majordomo smiled avariciously at that and said, "I see no reason why we should not negotiate a suitable price. Darth, do you take them there?"

Without further courtesies he bent his head once more to his desk, busily scribbling.

"Fat slug," Darth muttered when the door was closed, "coin is his only love."

He led them to the familiar room, producing a tinderbox that he set to the candles there. As he worked, still muttering to himself, Calandryll put his mouth close to Bracht's ear and whispered, "Get him away if you can, and learn what you may—I'll see what's to be found here."

It was not difficult: the hearth was cold and the chamber chill, Darth evincing no hesitation when Bracht clapped a companionable hand to his shoulder and suggested they leave Calandryll to inspect the shelves while they repaired to warmer quarters and sampled the wine doubtless remaining in the dead man's cellars. Katya smiled refusal of their invitation to join them, declaring herself more interested in the library, and instantly the door was closed Calandryll dropped the latch and set to examining the room.

It seemed unlikely the wizard would be so foolish as to leave behind him the means by which he might be found, but still Calandryll hoped some indication might be revealed. It was, he knew, a threadbare hope and his optimism faded swiftly: it was soon apparent there were no obvious clues to Rhythamun's destination. The library had been tidied, the table on which Calandryll had spent long hours tracing Orwen's charts was bare, the shelves neatly stacked with such a profusion of scrolls and parchments and manuscripts that it would take weeks to study them all, and that with no certain guarantee of success. In

mounting desperation he looked about him: it seemed
the shelves laughed back, mocking. And then he remembered the hidden compartment from which
Varent had taken the charts.

It was a straw he clutched at, but still it seemed his
blood ran afire in his veins as he removed books that
would once have engrossed him, occupying him for
hours, for days, but that now were only an encum-
brance to what he sought. He tossed them carelessly
aside, revealing the secret panel, turned the knob that
sprung the compartment open.

Whatever he had dared hope might be there—some
other map, some clue to where the wizard went—he
had not anticipated what he found. The compartment
was empty save for a dull red stone attached to a
leather thong: the talisman he had worn so long. The
key that had opened Rhythamun's way to Tezin-dar.
He snatched his hand back as though from a serpent's
fangs, snarling an ugly oath. Katya gasped, drawing
out her own periapt, her grey eyes wide and stormy as
she clutched the jewel and matched his curse with
one no weaker.

"Thus he led us here," she said hoarsely. "And now
eludes us."

"No!" Calandryll snarled unthinking refusal, his
voice steeled with a rage born of frustration. "He
shall not!"

Unthinking, he grasped the pendant stone and drew
it out, cursing Rhythamun all the while, the curses
halting as he felt the thing grow warm in his hand,
the faint, dull fire at its center becoming a flame that
spewed the scent of almonds like mocking laughter in
his dumbstruck face.

He flung the stone away, the straightsword drawn
in the same movement, instinctive, for all his intel-
lect told him the blade was useless against the glamour of the talisman. Wide-eyed, his scalp prickling
with horrid anticipation, he saw the flame jet upward,
the shape of a man forming within its dancing light.
He cursed anew as he recognized the features, star-

ing aghast at the face of Varent den Tarl. The ghostly figure smiled scornfully back, the dark eyes filled with contempt, the voice that whispered like crackling flame, urbane, underpinned with horrid amusement.

"So, Calandryll, you escaped from Tezin-dar, for only your hand could invigorate the stone that doubtless led you here. Mayhap I should congratulate you, for I'd thought you safely ensnared."

Katya's saber sliced the indistinct form: it wavered, like smoke disturbed by a random breeze, and the mocking voice went on.

"Well done, then—you demonstrate a swiftness of thought I'd not expected. No matter! You served your purpose well enough when you brought me to the city and put the Arcanum in my hands."

The apparition laughed: insult and assault, both. Calandryll stared, unaware that he snarled, a leashed hound thirsting to attack.

"And now the book is mine, and I need only go to where Tharn rests, need only work the gramaryes of unbinding to raise the god. What then shall not be mine for the asking? Such might as petty men dream of, but dare not take for their own! And it is to you I owe thanks for that unlocking—know you, Calandryll, that without your aid I might not have accomplished this."

The phantom bowed; Calandryll's teeth grated.

"Do you hail me? Or do you curse me? The latter, I'd suspect, for your innocence was a wonder to behold, and I think that such as you cannot aspire to the heights of my dreaming. Still, you served me well and mayhap when I come into my own I shall reward you . . . if you live still when great Tharn once more walks abroad. If not, count your life well spent for what you gave me.

"And now, farewell. This body you knew is quit and I go on. Shall I tell you where? Mayhap not—the path I tread is not for such as you. So farewell, my dupe; and once more, my thanks."

The hated figure bowed again, its laughter ringing loud and mad and mocking. The flame that held it died. The scent of almonds faded and the room fell silent. The red stone lay dull, its animating magic spent, no more now than a worthless bauble.

Straightsword and saber slid into scabbards and for long moments Calandryll and Katya said nothing. It was she who at last spoke, her voice muted, empty of hope.

"He is gone and our quest comes to naught."

8

"No!" Calandryll came close before her, taking
her arms, his grip harsh as the single word. He
felt none of the despair that had earlier afflicted him,
only a great rage now, as if Rhythamun's mockery had
burned away all pessimism, leaving behind only determination. "Did you not say the taking of another's
shape is arduous, a thing needing time?"

Katya nodded dumbly, her grey eyes clouded with
resignation.

"And where should he do that, save here? Where he
might work his filthy magic at his leisure."

Confusion took the place of resignation and she
shrugged helplessly. "Likely that was so, but what
good to us?"

Calandryll realized his fingers dug into the fine
mail of her tunic: he loosed his hold, his face still
close to hers, his voice fierce.

"Then it may well be the folk here saw his victim!"
Now hope flickered in the grey orbs. She nodded. "So
we must question them. Carefully! Come—we'll go to
Symeon."

It seemed at first that she was rooted by confusion
and he took her arm again, dragging her to the door,
throwing up the latch, and slamming the wood panel

back with such force it thudded against the outer wall. In the corridor beyond she regained some of her customary vigor and he let go her arm as she matched him stride for stride, close to running in their urgency, hurrying to where the little majordomo still sat.

Symeon's shortsighted eyes blinked as they burst in, an expression of mingled irritation at so dramatic an entry and greed at the prospect of reward upon his round face.

"Did you find such volumes as interest you?" he asked, setting down his quill.

Calandryll resisted the impulse to seize the man, to shake answers from him. He did not doubt their story, were he to blurt it out, would find little credence with the scribe. Symeon would most likely dismiss them as mad, perhaps call servants or even the watch to eject them, answerless. Tact was called for here, hard though it was to rein in his temper, he forced a smile and said, "So many I must think on the matter, decide which interest me the most."

"There will be many coming to examine so fine a library," Symeon warned, "I suggest you decide ere long."

"Indeed I shall, and likely return on the morrow." Calandryll assumed a mask of remorse. "Tell me, when did Lord Varent die?"

"Three weeks past," came the now somewhat sullen answer, as if the death were relegated to the distant past, replaced now with the more important matter of disposing of the household.

"How?"

The single word was sharp and Symeon frowned, favoring him with a curious look as he replied, "None could say. He was hale enough, it seemed. We found his body in the library . . ."

"The library?"

"He'd spent the night there." Symeon nodded. "Such had become his habit of late—to spend hours poring over his books to the exclusion of all else."

Calandryll's gaze remained steady on the portly man's ink-flushed face as he felt excitement swell, struggling to conceal his urgency, aware that the future of his world might rest upon the acuity of his questions.

"Was he alone?"

Symeon's irritation grew, his eyes narrowing in puzzlement. Calandryll essayed a smile he trusted was reassuring, resisting the temptation to take out his sword, prick faster answers from the man.

"No, he'd business with some trader in horse-flesh," Symeon said slowly, adding new stains to his sash as he absently wiped his fingers. " 'Twas him alerted the household. A dealer with the Kerns, I believe, out of Gannshold. Darth spent more time with him than I."

Calandryll nodded, deciding that more was to be learned from Darth than from the reticent majordomo. "A sad loss," he murmured.

"One that leaves me with much to do," said Symeon, with obvious impatience.

Calandryll took the cue to leave. He ducked his head, saying, "Then I'd find my bodyguard and be gone. My thanks for your help."

Symeon waved an inky hand, not looking up as they quit the chamber and went in search of Bracht.

The freesword was settled in a chamber off the kitchen that gave access to the rear courtyard and the stables. A low arch separated the room from the larger area, where others of the bereaved household sat, and as Calandryll strode toward the sound of the Kern's voice he noticed Rytha among them. The girl favored Katya with a speculative stare that went unnoticed by the Vanu woman. Beyond the arch Bracht sat facing Darth over a wine-ringed table, a flagon of red wine half drunk between them, the better part of it, so Calandryll judged, gone down Darth's throat.

The retainer greeted them with drunken cheerfulness, rising unsteadily to fetch more cups and a fresh flagon from the outer room. Once his back was turned, Bracht's eyes framed an unspoken question.

"Rhythamun spent time with a horse trader out of Gannshold," Calandryll murmured as the sound of breaking glass was echoed by a woman's complaint, that with Darth's careless dismissal. "This man was with him when 'Varent' died. Have you learned aught else?"

"No more than that as yet." Bracht lowered his voice, glancing warily at Katya. "Rytha was here—it took a while to shake her off."

Katya eyed him in a way that suggested he would have other questions to answer at some more appropriate time and he grinned nervously, clearly relieved when Darth came back and set the cups and flagon down. He filled them, beaming hugely at Katya.

Calandryll drank and said idly, "Lord Varent was dealing with a trader out of Gannshold, so Symeon told me."

"Aye," Darth agreed with owlish gravity. "He was thinking of buying fresh stock and this fellow claimed to have the best. He made an offer for that stallion of yours."

This came with a nod in Bracht's direction and the Kern took up the interrogation. "How was he named?" he asked. "Mayhap I know him."

"Daven Tyras, as I recall," Darth said. "He spoke with an accent like yours."

Calandryll felt his pulse quicken. He thought Darth must surely hear the furious beat of his heart, perceive the urgency in his eyes. He forced his racing mind to some measure of calm, knowing that he must think clearly—if Rhythamun had quit Varent's body while in company with another, then surely that man must be the new receptacle for the wizard's malign intelligence, and he must learn all he could of the stranger. From the corner of his eye he saw Bracht frown, and heard the freesword murmur, "Daven Tyras," as if struggling to identify the name.

"A fellow about your size," Darth offered, "though sandy-haired."

"An ugly man?" Bracht invented. "With a drunkard's nose?"

"No, a comely enough fellow." Darth shook his head and winked lewdly. "Rytha took a fancy to him."

Bracht made a noncommittal noise and asked, "Were his eyes blue and small?"

"Brown and large," said Darth. "And his nose was sound enough, save it had been broken and spread across his face."

"Not the one I'd thought of, then," said Bracht; and to Calandryll's relief added: "Though I'd lief meet with him—he may have news of Cuan na'For."

"Too late for that," said Darth, filling his cup, "for he was gone the next day. Back to Gannshold, he said."

Calandryll heard the Kern bite back a curse. "It seems we return too late," he murmured with feigned distress. "Poor Varent."

"Aye," Darth agreed, "and poor us—he left no kin behind and the house is to be sold off. I've fresh employment to find."

"We all suffer loss, it seems," Calandryll declared sententiously. "Were I able, I'd offer you a position."

Darth shrugged, helping himself to yet more wine, succeeding in spilling a generous measure over the table. He grinned foolishly, then frowned and slapped the heel of his hand to his forehead in mock admonishment. "I'd near forgot you hail from Secca," he declared. "You've family there?"

Calandryll nodded. That Secca was his home was common enough knowledge to those such as Darth who had formed Varent's retinue when, in that guise, Rhythamun had visited the city, but none knew he was second son to Secca's Domm.

"You've not heard the news?" asked the man.

Calandryll shook his head. His impulse was to leave, believing they had gleaned all they might from

Darth, but something in the retainer's tone stayed him.

"The Domm ... Bylath, was that his name? ... he's dead. His son Tobias holds the title now."

Calandryll felt his hand clutch tight about his cup. Carefully, he set it down, not sure what impact this information had on him, not sure of his own emotions. His father was dead—did he experience grief? It seemed an age ago that Bylath's unthinking blow had determined him to flee, to pursue the high adventure, the great quest, Rhythamun trailed before him, bait to the innocent youth the wizard sought to dupe. In all the time since then he had thought little of his father, save that what he did disproved Bylath's contempt for his weakling, bookish son; thinking vaguely that if he survived the quest he should return in triumph to confront his father with his achievement. But now Bylath was dead and he felt . . .

He could not name it. Grief, perhaps; or perhaps anger, as if somehow Bylath thwarted him, denied him even now the satisfaction he had craved while still his father lived and scorned him. There was a sense of loss, but of what nature he could not define and he pushed it ruthlessly aside: if there was grief, he would mourn later; for now it was more important he determine how this changed situation might affect him. Bylath was dead and Tobias raised up—his brother, who had made compact with the Chaipaku to slay him, was Domm. On command of Burash the Brotherhood of Assassins no longer threatened him, but with all of Secca's resources at his command what stratagems might Tobias now employ?

And Darth—indeed, none in Aldarin—knew he was the late Domm's outlawed son. Through the chaotic emotions he felt came a single certainty: that his parentage was best kept secret.

"How did he die?" he asked in a voice he trusted was sufficiently indifferent no suspicion should be aroused. "When last I was . . ." he almost said, "in the palace," but caught himself, ". . . was in Secca he seemed hearty enough."

"A wasting sickness, so it's said," Darth expounded, "but there're rumors. I saw him, you know—when I was there with Lord Varent—and as you say, he looked in rude health." He tapped his nose in conspiratorial gesture, warming to his theme. "It's said Tobias couldn't wait to claim the throne and helped his father along. There's talk of poison. Not openly, mind you, but it's what folk say and it wouldn't be the first time some ambitious son decided he couldn't wait, eh?"

He chuckled, shaking his head in contemplation of the devious ways of the aristocracy. Calandryll brought his cup to his lips, drinking deep, less in need of the wine than the pause it gave him to think. This news could not—must not!—affect his pursuit of Rhythamun, but if Darth's gossip was true perhaps it was further indication that the Mad God stirred in sleep and, dreaming of release, even now cast his malign influence over the world. Civil war gripped Kandahar; Bylath was likely poisoned. Could Tharn somehow sense that Rhythamun moved toward his raising? More immediately, how might Tobias's ascencion affect the quest?

His expression must have reflected his interest, for Darth continued: "It's caused a stir, I'll tell you. Aldarin and Secca made pact to found a navy—that was why Lord Varent went there—to fight the corsairs. Now Tobias is talking about using it to attack Kandahar. You know there's war there? Well, it seems like Tobias wants to form alliance with the other cities and attack the Kands while they're fighting among themselves." He broke off to empty his cup, chuckling again as he refilled the mug. "Mayhap I'll find employment there, eh?"

"Aldarin agrees with this?" asked Calandryll, pale-faced. Surely such a design must mean Tharn stirred! "The other cities?"

"Not yet." Darth wiped his mouth, shrugging.

"Our Domm wavers. Tobias came avisiting a while back, though, and spent a good deal of time with Lord Varent. From what I overheard, Lord Varent favored the notion, but now he's dead"—this with exaggerated grief and a cup raised in mournful toast—"well, Daric relied on Lord Varent for sound advice. Tobias went on, him and his new bride, to Wessyl. A ceremonial progress they called it, to assure the cities of Secca's good intent, but those of us close to such matters know he's looking to persuade all Lysse to war."

That Tobias had claimed Nadama for his wife was no surprise to Calandryll; that he felt no pain was a pleasing shock. It seemed as if another had loved Nadama, some earlier incarnation now passed beyond that youthful passion. He murmured an inarticulate response and said, "I'd heard talk of a younger brother . . . some family dispute?"

"Aye," said Darth, and laughed loud, stabbing a finger in Calandryll's direction. "Dera, but I'd forgotten! You share his name, no? Calandryll?"

Calandryll smiled and nodded.

Darth said, "That's right. He fled the city round when we left it, I recall. Just why I don't know, but Tobias had him posted outlaw with a reward of ten thousand varre on his head. Some say 'twas him poisoned Bylath, but that doesn't make much sense to me. If he was plotting against his father, why'd he not poison his brother, too? And why run away if he was after the throne?"

"Why indeed?" murmured Calandryll blandly.

"Still," said Darth, "ten thousand varre's a handsome reward, eh? I'd not mind getting my hands on him for so much."

"Nor I." Bracht rejoined the conversation, his dark face a mask as he looked to the topic of the discussion. "But where might he be?"

"Who knows?" Darth returned. "Hiding somewhere, I'd guess. Unless he's dead—I heard a rumor Tobias set the Chaipaku on his tail."

"The Brotherhood of Assassins?" Bracht nodded solemnly. "Likely dead, then."

"With them after him, aye," Darth agreed, squinting as he turned his glazed eyes in Calandryll's direction, their focus hard to find. "I'll tell you something funny, though—Tobias had his likeness posted and there's some resemblance to you. You'd best be careful, eh?"

"I shall," Calandryll promised, forcing humorless laughter.

"Of course," Darth went on, "it's not much of a similarity. Calandryll den Karynth looks a fop. As if he never set foot outside the palace; not like you, my friend."

"Even so, I'll heed your warning," Calandryll averred sincerely. "And look to avoid Tobias."

"In that case you'd best not visit Wessyl." Darth giggled. "Or Eryn or Gannshold, for he was northward bound. And come to think of it, his progress was to take him along the Gann Peaks to Forshold before returning south by way of Hyme. In fact, you'd best stay clear of all the cities, for it was his intent to visit every one!"

This struck him as mightily amusing and he began to rock unsteadily in his chair, spluttering wine as he laughed. Calandryll stretched his own lips in approximation of a smile, catching Bracht's eye and motioning toward the outer door. The Kern nodded, glancing at Katya, who stared in barely concealed disgust at the drunken Darth. She in turn took the hint, leaning back to vent a huge yawn.

"Best we depart," the freesword suggested.

"The night's young yet," Darth slurred, "and there's wine aplenty to be drunk."

"Even so." Bracht smiled, looking again to Katya.

Darth's unfocused eyes followed his gaze and he raised a knowing finger: "The night's young and you'd not waste it, eh? Were I in your boots I'd feel the same. Rytha'll be upset, though."

"I'll take my horse," Bracht said quickly, his smile

faltering as Katya's eyes flashed a stormy warning of explanations to come. "My gear is in the tack room?"

"It is. I'll show you."

Darth attempted to rise. Unsuccessfully: halfway to his feet he toppled backward, sending his chair tumbling as he sprawled full length on the floor.

"Mayhap you'd best remain," Bracht murmured.

"Mayhap," agreed Darth cheerfully, and promptly closed his eyes, commencing a stentorian snoring.

"Darth needs help to his bed," Calandryll called into the outer room, answered by a chorus of dismissive laughter.

A fat woman replied, "Let him lie, the drunken sot," and Calandryll shrugged, following Bracht and Katya out into the courtyard.

The moon stood high by now, close to midnight, and they hurried to the stables. The stalls were built along the outer wall, half gated, with the upper sections folded back. Calandryll thought they must check each one, but Bracht paused, emitting a low, keening cry that was answered with an eager snicker as a glossy black head emerged, loosing a loud whinny as the stallion recognized his master.

"So, you remember me still." The Kern fondled the great head, gently as if he caressed a woman. "Come then."

He swung the lower half of the gate open and the stallion pranced out, nudging the freesword with such rough affection that Bracht was sent staggering backward. He flung his arms around the neck, rubbing the stallion's cheek with his own as he crooned softly in the language of Cuan na'For.

"Tekkan awaits," Katya warned, "and while I'd not spoil a second reunion . . ."

"Aye." Bracht took a handful of nigrescent mane and led the horse to where the household stored its harness. A solitary lantern hung by the door and Calandryll snatched it from its hook, holding it aloft as they entered. Bracht found his tackle and swiftly saddled the horse, leading it back to the gates. A few pale faces watched them from the kitchen, but no keeper waited at the egress and only a simple bolt secured the panels: in moments they stood in the avenue.

Farther along the broad roadway a carriage deposited folk outside a mansion where lights blazed and Calandryll hailed the driver, instructing him to bring them with all haste to the Seagull tavern. Bracht declined to take the coach, preferring to reacquaint himself with his mount, and so Calandryll found himself riding alone with Katya.

For some time they traveled in silence, contemplating the events of the night and the information they had won, their thoughts accompanied by the clatter of shod hooves on flagstones and the steady creaking of the coach. Then, as they crossed a bridge spanning the Alda, Katya said gently, "I am sorry for your father's death."

Calandryll shrugged: he had thought not of that, but of Daven Tyras and the likelihood of overtaking the man, the likelihood of even finding him. Her well-meant words served as a reminder, but still he found it difficult to assess his feelings. It was as though, like Nadama, Bylath had become a shadowy figure from his past, sufficiently obscured by time that his demise held no real impact. The pursuit of Rhythamun outweighed, it seemed, such personal loss; or he was hardened even sterner than he had thought.

He did not know how to respond, so he said, "Tobias is a dangerous enemy. If he posts my likeness across Lysse . . ."

"Darth failed to recognize you," she returned.

"He was drunk." Calandryll turned from her compassionate gaze to the window, where Bracht paced the carriage, teeth flashing in a smile of pure enjoyment. "Someone more sober might."

"How, if we travel by sea?" she demanded.

He turned from studying the joyful Kern to face her again, directing a thumb toward the horseman. "I doubt Bracht will relinquish his stallion now they've found one another once more. And if Daven Tyras came from Gannshold and is returned there . . ." He frowned, shaking his head. "No, I suspect we must travel overland."

"Then we must travel carefully," she murmured, her own eyes shifting to observe the Kern, pausing a moment before she added in a deliberately casual tone, "Who is Rytha?"

"One of Varent's women," Calandryll replied, unthinking; more concerned with the dangers imposed by his proscription than Bracht's amorous adventures. "Bracht"—he caught himself, suddenly embarrassed— "knew her. When Rhythamun first brought us to Aldarin."

"How well?" Katya demanded.

Calandryll shrugged awkwardly. "We were not here long."

"Long enough, I think." The interior of the coach was shadowy enough he could not read her expression, but her voice was edged. "Is she pretty?"

Helplessly, he said, "I suppose so. I barely remember her. Nor, I think, does Bracht."

"But she remembers him."

"Would you not?" He wondered at her irritation, thinking that such jealousy as he heard in her voice might well jeopardize their alliance, just as the Kern's possessive protection did. He was surprised to hear her answer come soft with doubt, as if he had caught her in some transgression, confused by her own responses.

"Aye. I would and always shall. But I had not thought . . ." She hesitated, shaking her head, moonlight dancing briefly silver on her long hair as they crossed a plaza where no buildings intervened to obscure the crescent. "But I have never . . . In Vanu it is different . . . We . . ."

Her voice trailed off and Calandryll saw that she was both confused and embarrassed. It came to him that he still knew little enough of her homeland or the ways of its people. Nor had he seen this warrior woman so unsure of herself: it was as though, in the gaps between those uncertain words, she showed a part of herself previously hidden, a part more vulnerable than he had ever thought. Earnestly, he said, "Bracht loves you. There is no doubting that; and since he first set eyes on you, he's not looked at another."

"He's had little chance," she returned, but just before they left the plaza and plunged again into shadows Calandryll saw her smile and heard reassurance in her voice. He smiled back and said, "It would make no difference—he pledged his word, and you've mine that he does not renege on that. Nor, where you are concerned, does he want to."

He saw her smile grow wider as she turned to look from the window, the lanterns strung along the road they followed revealing a fondness in her grey eyes as she studied the laughing rider. Bracht caught her glance and waved: Calandryll was pleased to see her wave back.

Soon after, the coach entered the Harbor Quarter and deposited them outside the Seagull. The clepsydra set above the long counter that spanned one wall of the tavern showed the hour a fraction past midnight as they entered. Tekkan sat with some dozen of his crew at the far end of the low-ceilinged tavern, his weather-beaten face lighting with relief as he saw them shoving through the crowd toward him. He cleared a space on the bench, sending one of his men sufficiently fluent in the Lyssian tongue to order ale and demanded they tell him everything.

His face darkened and he muttered an oath as Katya and Calandryll related their account of Rhythamun's magical appearance. Swiftly, they advised him of Daven Tyras and their belief that the sorcerer must have stolen the horse trader's body in which to continue his search for Tharn.

"But surely this means he's lost to us," he argued.

"What can we do, save go back to Vanu and seek the aid of our holy men?"

"No." Calandryll shook his head emphatically. "If Daven Tyras came from Gannshold, then likely he returns there."

"And Darth said he spoke in the accents of Cuan na'For," added Bracht, "so mayhap he's of the clans, or a half-blood."

"How does that help?" Tekkan shrugged.

"Think you the Mad God rests in Lysse?" asked Calandryll, and when the boatmaster shaped a negative: "Or in any of the lands where the Younger Gods hold sway? Were that so, they would surely league to thwart Rhythamun—no, Tharn must surely lie beyond all the lands men know."

"Beyond the Borrhun-maj?" Tekkan ran fingers through his beard, nervously. "Then we've lost him."

"He's gained a start, but all Cuan na'For, all the Jesseryn Plain, lie betwixt here and the Borrhun-maj," Bracht said. "And in Cuan na'For I yet have friends." He grinned a moment, thoughtfully. "Enemies, too, but that's another matter. If this Daven Tyras seeks to cross my homeland, then likely I can discover where he goes."

Tekkan saw the direction of their thinking and began to argue anew. "You'd pursue a man you know only by some drunkard's description? A warlock who may take another's body at will? This is madness!" He pounded fist to tabletop. "I say we sail for Vanu, to consult the holy men."

"The taking is not so easy," Katya said, using the common tongue that Bracht and Calandryll might understand. "There's scant chance he'll take another while that of Daven Tyras serves him well enough. Why should he, when he believes us likely trapped in Tezin-dar?"

"Why then quit that of Varent den Tarl?" demanded Tekkan.

"Because Varent den Tarl was a noble of this city," Calandryll said patiently, "a counsellor to the Domm,

Daric. Such a man could not readily leave Aldarin to wander the world."

"While a horse trader is expected to travel," said Bracht.

"And if we sail for Vanu we likely shall lose him," said Katya.

Tekkan frowned, gesturing at the Vanu folk. "And these? Shall I leave my vessel here in Aldarin harbor?"

Calandryll looked to Bracht, to Katya, and in their eyes saw confirmation of that same decision he had, unwittingly, reached. Katya laid hand to her father's arm, speaking softly.

"You shall not accompany us where we go. Better that you return to Vanu and tell the holy men what we do. Mayhap they shall contrive some design to aid us, but now we three must travel overland."

"On horseback," said Bracht with unfeigned enthusiasm.

Tekkan studied them one by one, seeing determination writ vivid on their faces. His own darkened and he sighed, head falling awhile, then lifting, resignation in his pale eyes.

"I'd lief dissuade you," he said slowly, "but I see I cannot. Hard though it be, I can find no argument. So it shall be as you say—you overland and I back to Vanu."

"Remember this." Katya touched her chest, where the talisman hung suspended. "While I wear the stone, the holy men shall always know where I am, and can perhaps find some way to reach me through its agency."

"Aye, there's that." Tekkan nodded sadly. "Shall you leave now?"

"On the morrow," Bracht answered. "We've two mounts to buy yet."

"Two?"

They told him of Bracht's stallion. Calandryll thought of mentioning his proscription, but decided against such increment of the man's worries; neither did his daughter nor Bracht see fit to raise the matter.

"So be it then," Tekkan agreed with obvious reluctance, and fixed Bracht and Calandryll with a stern eye. "Heed me now—I place Katya in your charge. Does aught untoward occur, you shall answer to me."

Calandryll bowed his head, understanding the man's meaning and acknowledging the charge. Bracht's comprehension was slower; he said, "You've already my word no harm shall come to her while I live."

"I do not speak of sword-harm," Tekkan replied, "save from that sword all men wear."

Beside him, Katya blushed. The Kern frowned, as if startled by the outspoken warning. Calandryll saw his tanned face darken, the blue eyes narrowing dangerously. He took affront, Calandryll realized, tensing in anticipation of violent reaction, prepared to intervene. But then Bracht straightened on the bench, returning Tekkan stare for stare, his face no less grave than the boatmaster's.

"When first we sailed for Gessyth," he declared in formal tones, "I pledged your daughter and you that I should abide by those strictures she laid upon me— that I should hold tight rein on what I feel for her, and not address that matter until the Arcanum be destroyed and she home safe in Vanu. I do not forget my word!"

So fierce did that last sentence come that Tekkan started back, his own lined features suffused now with the blood that rushed to his cheeks. He ducked his head in apology, expression softening as he said, "Forgive me, Bracht ni Errhyn. Fatherly concern renders my tongue clumsy."

Bracht gestured his acceptance, speaking gentler: "Think you I'd lay hand on her, save she said me aye, Tekkan?"

"No." The older man shook his head, regaining his composure as he studied the freesword's face. "I do not."

"Then the matter's settled," Bracht said, "and I suggest we drink this ale and find our beds, for we've animals to purchase and likely hard riding ahead if we're to snare our quarry."

"Aye." Tekkan raised his mug to each in turn. "To success and a safe homecoming."

They drained the ale and quit the tavern, the Vanu folk dispersing to their individual lodgings with instructions to meet Tekkan at the warboat on the next day's second tide while the four started back for their own hostelry. Father and daughter walked ahead, engaged in earnest conversation, Calandryll falling into step alongside Bracht. Cloud rafted the sky now, laying streamers across the moon, the led stallion snorting vapor into the chilly night. Bracht slowed deliberately, letting Katya and Tekkan move a little distance apart, and turned an inquisitive face to Calandryll.

"I had thought to answer questions regarding Rytha," he murmured.

"You need not worry." Calandryll chuckled softly. "Katya asked me about your . . . relationship . . . and I told her you had known Rytha, but now have eyes only for her."

"Which, Ahrd knows is true enough." The Kern studied the cloak-swathed figure before them appreciatively. "My thanks for your diplomacy, my friend."

"We shall likely need more than diplomacy in the days to come," Calandryll responded. "Rhythamun's far enough ahead of us, and my outlawry may present us with problems."

"Aye, ten thousand varre's enough to uncloud any man's sight"—Bracht grinned—"but mayhap we can disguise you somewhat."

"Save by such magicks as Rhythamun used to bring me out of Secca I cannot see how," Calandryll muttered. "And if we're to hold his trail we must surely pass through the northern cities."

"I'd not use magic," said Bracht. "The less of that

I encounter, the better. No, we'll find simpler means."

"How?" Calandryll demanded, but the Kern merely chuckled and refused to elaborate further.

THE morning dawned bright, the sun a brilliant disc shining from a steely sky empty of cloud save where vagabond billows clustered far off over the Narrow Sea. Frost rimed the windowpanes and the cobbles of the hostelry's courtyard, and from the kitchen came the welcome smell of porridge and frying bacon. Calandryll was not surprised to find Bracht already abroad, guessing that the Kern would be found in the stable with his beloved horse. He left Tekkan to his ablutions and went down to the common room, ordering a generous breakfast and succeeding in consuming at least half before the others joined him. Bracht was in excellent spirits, enthused by the prospect of leaving the sea behind and continuing on horseback; Katya and Tekkan, aware that this day was likely the last they would be together, were more subdued, and in this Bracht demonstrated a somewhat unusual tact.

"We need but two animals until we reach Cuan na'For," he declared. "To cross the grass we'll require a packhorse, but that may be purchased in Gannshold. Calandryll and I can buy the mounts we need now without your aid. Let us meet here at noon."

Katya flashed him a grateful smile that he answered with a bow; Tekkan murmured his thanks and Bracht rose grinning, beckoning Calandryll to join him.

They secured directions to the Equestrian Quarter and quit the hostelry, setting off on foot. By day's light Aldarin was a bustling city, the streets and plazas crowded, filled with the sounds and scents of the multitude of folk who sold and bought, or merely gazed and strolled the promenades. In one of those great squares lined with eating houses and taverns there was a pillar, similar to those employed in Secca for the posting of such notices as were deemed of public import: official pronouncements, edicts, new laws, and news of laws broken. Calandryll urged his companion to halt a moment, studying the column. On it he saw his likeness and the announcement of Tobias's promised reward. It was, as Darth had unknowingly suggested, not a very good likeness: the face he saw was that of a youth, carefree and bland, somewhat soft of feature, with neat-cut hair and rather vague eyes. It had been copied, he realized, from a portrait that hung in his father's—now his brother's!—palace, one painted some years ago. It announced him outlawed for crimes against Secca, ten thousand varre promised for his apprehension or delivery of his recognizable head.

He cursed as he read his brother's treachery, thankful that the chilly morning allowed him to wear a concealing cloak but still, unthinkingly, drawing the hood farther over his face.

"A poor enough likeness," Bracht murmured. "What do the words say?"

Calandryll had forgotten the Kern could neither read nor write and in a low, angry voice recited the legend. Bracht nodded grimly and said, "I think that when our quest is ended there should be an accounting with your brother. A wise man leaves no enemies at his back."

Calandryll shrugged, moving away from the pillar, wondering if the eyes he felt fastened upon him were real, or existed only in his imagination. "Did you not leave enemies in Cuan na'For?" he demanded.

"Aye." He heard some hesitation in the Kern's reply. "But that was a different matter."

He turned his head to study Bracht, finding the freesword's features set impassively, his expression suggesting he did not wish to discuss the affair: he wondered what his comrade held back.

"Come," Bracht said, seeking somewhat obviously

to change the subject, "we've horses to buy and that trade takes time."

One day, Calandryll decided, he must press the Kern to explain what secret lay in his past that had driven him from his homeland. But not now: he knew Bracht well enough that he could accept such things would be revealed in time, and now more urgent matters were to hand.

They left the plaza and made their way along streets and alleys to a quarter set hard against the northern section of the wall, the odors of cooking food and wine, of ale and people, replaced by the strengthening scent of horseflesh, dung, and hay. It lent a spring to Bracht's step, his stride quickening as they drew steadily closer, his head thrown back to savor the pungent smells as if they were choice perfumes.

He chuckled gleefully as they passed beneath a high arch into a great square filled with a milling mass of animals and men. Set into the city wall facing them was a gate, out of which the horses might be taken to graze on the upland meadows, and to either side spacious stables and barns thrust out, interspersed with saddleries and a few ale shops, the whole encircling the central area, which divided into corrals and pens with avenues between where the beasts might be put through their paces for prospective buyers.

Bracht paused a moment beneath the arch, studying the scene with delighted eyes, then nodded, smiling broadly. "Mayhap we can learn more of Daven Tyras here," he murmured, and plunged into the midst of the activity.

At first it seemed to Calandryll chaotic, the morning loud with the whinnying of horses, the drumming of their hooves, and the shouts of men, the flagstones slippery with the dung that flavored the cold air, mingling with the sweeter scent of stored hay and astringent urine, the plunging equines and their handlers seeming to pass at random, forcing the unwary to rapidly seek the safety of the fences. Gradually, under Bracht's experienced tutelage, he saw a pattern was imposed. There, dray horses were to be found; here, palfreys suitable for gentlewomen; close on the gate the pens held ponies, small enough that children might comfortably handle them; to one side were carriage horses; on another, pack animals. The riding horses occupied the center, though even here subtle divisions existed, Bracht pointing out those fit for the hunt and those more suited to bearing an armored man, those bred for racing and those hardier beasts capable of both speed and endurance. It was to the area containing these latter mounts that they gravitated.

At first they wandered, seemingly idly, among the corrals, pausing here and there to make a closer examination of the stock. The traders recognized Bracht immediately for a Kern, his long ponytail and dark, hawkish features marking him clearly as a clansman from the north, and he took advantage of this to inquire about Daven Tyras.

Several of the dealers knew the man, confirming the description they had from Darth and adding a few details Varent's servant had failed to notice. A tooth, they learned, was missing from his upper jaw, lending his voice a slight sibilance, and the thumb of his left hand was cocked from an old break. He was known to come from Gannshold and—as Bracht had suggested—was a half-blood, his father of Lyssian descent, his mother of the Lykard clan. Such visits as he made to Aldarin were infrequent, his most recent ended now, as best the dealers knew, for he had not been seen these last few weeks.

It was little enough information on which to chase a man across the world but, Calandryll trusted, sufficient that they might pick up his trail. How they would deal with him he put aside for now; just as he put aside the difficulties posed by the sorcerer's head start. At least it seemed the wizard had made no real attempt to cover his trail, which likely meant he assumed them trapped in Tezin-dar, the apparition left behind in the magical stone no more than vanity, a last insult thrown by a man confident of victory: overconfident, Calandryll hoped.

Agreeing they had gleaned all they might and should now depart the city swiftly as possible, they concentrated on selecting horses.

This Calandryll left entirely to Bracht, bowing to the Kern's superior knowledge of the animals and his obvious experience of horse trading. It took some time, and Calandryll found his patience tried as his comrade haggled enthusiastically, but finally two beasts were purchased from the array of saddle stock. For Katya, Bracht picked a grey, for Calandryll a slightly taller chestnut. Both were geldings, deep-chested and rangy, capable, both Kern and dealer promised, of combining speed with staying power. They led the beasts away to a saddlery, where full harness was bought, and then, with noon approaching, started back to the lodging house.

Along the way Bracht halted, dismounting and tossing Calandryll his reins, ignoring the question that followed him into the emporium he entered. Calandryll was left with no choice save to wait, wondering what his comrade sought in an establishment devoted to the sale of cosmetics and perfumes. Nor did Bracht offer any explanation when he emerged, and Calandryll concluded that he had purchased some gift for Katya, unlikely as that seemed, for the warrior woman needed no artificial aids to enhance her beauty and wore no perfume that he had ever smelled. Still, Bracht appeared mightily satisfied as he swung astride the grey horse and continued on their way.

Katya and Tekkan awaited them in the common room and they ate a somber meal, the boatmaster rising immediately he was done to announce his imminent departure. The outgoing tide was shortly due and he wished to inspect the warboat before clearing the anchorage. "Best you leave as soon as you may," he told them, taking their hands and indicating his daughter with a turn of his head. "Our farewells are said and I'd not prolong the moment. May all the gods go with you, and from Vanu the holy men will send whatever aid they can. May victory be yours!"

It seemed to Calandryll that his eyes were moist, but his spine was straight as he spun about and marched from the common room and he did not look back.

Katya watched him leave, her lovely face sad, and her voice low as she said, "He speaks the truth. Best we go."

"Aye." Bracht's gaze was solicitous as he answered her, but an element of amusement sounded as he gestured at Calandryll. "But first there's the matter of this outlaw's appearance."

He whispered in her ear and she nodded, going toward the kitchen. Bracht beckoned, grinning wide, and Calandryll followed dutifully to their chamber, wondering how the Kern intended to disguise him. His skin was by now tanned near as dark as Bracht's, and his features had lost all softness, the gentle contours of his face hardened and thinned. His eyes were no longer wide, but narrowed by the days of staring over the ocean. His shoulders had broadened and he stood taller, his bearing not that of some bookish princeling but a swordsman's. Equally, the worn leather of his breeks and tunic suggested some itinerant freesword, that impression accentuated by the blade he carried. He was sufficiently altered that he might deceive the cursory examination of one such as Darth, but keener eyes would likely see the similarities with the face depicted on the bill of outlawry, and his sun-bleached hair was clearly that of a Lyssian, like enough to the luxuriant manes of his father and brother as to attract attention.

Bracht echoed his thought: "That pale hair marks you," the freesword murmured. "Save for that you could pass as a clansman. So . . ."

With a flourish he produced his purchase, not a gift for Katya but a small gallipot that, with its lid removed, revealed a thick black paste. Calandryll recognized it as a dye, such as women—and a few vain men—were wont to use to mask the grey age put in their hair.

Katya entered then, carrying a steaming ewer. "Here," Bracht instructed, indicating that Calandryll should seat himself by the washstand, "the merchant who sold me this assured me it will darken the greyest head."

Katya poured hot water over his long hair and the Kern applied the paste, fetching a comb from his saddlebags to work the stuff evenly through the wet locks. Done, he threw Calandryll a towel, and when his hair was roughly dried, he combed it again, drawing it back from his face and binding it with a length of rawhide in a tail akin to his own. He found a little mirror of polished metal in his gear and held it up to Calandryll's face: a jet-haired Kern looked back.

"If you can, put an accent on your speech," he advised, "and should any doubt, tell them you're of halfblood stock—your mother came from Lysse and your father was of the clan Asyth."

It seemed ironic to assume a background so similar to that of Daven Tyras, and at the same time fitting to turn Rhythamun's fell trickery to such advantage: Calandryll voiced his agreement, doing his best to emulate the nuances of Cuan na'For.

"You'll do," Bracht said. "You'll pass readily enough as a freesword. Besides, your proscription makes no mention of your traveling with companions." He turned to Katya, indicating his handiwork. "How say you?"

Katya nodded. "I'd take you both for bladesmen, never princes."

"Which we are." Bracht grinned. "And with yet another advantage—few men will look at us while you are present."

The smile with which she answered his sally was brief and Calandryll saw that she regretted Tekkan's leaving deeper than she admitted. It occurred to him that she had been seldom—indeed, perhaps never—far from her father's side.

"So," he said briskly, "I am now become a half-blood out of Cuan na'For. Do we ride toward that land?"

"Aye!"

Bracht snatched up his gear, tossed Calandryll's to him, and took Katya's arm, steering her from the chamber. Her own saddlebags were packed and ready, and without further delay they settled their account and mounted the waiting horses.

Before the sun was passed much farther across the wintry sky they passed out of Aldarin's northern gate, seeming to any who observed them three footloose mercenaries, likely traveling in search of employment in the border reaches.

9

Northward from Aldarin the road followed the coastline to Wessyl, on to Eryn with its shipyards, and thence to the fortress of Gannshold. Eastward, it connected Aldarin with Secca and that city with Hyme and Gannshold's sister, Forshold, its circumnavigation of Lysse completed by the section winding through the foothills of the Gann Peaks to link the border cities. It was the land's chief artery, a great channel along which ran the blood of trade, a post road, and—on occasion—the route of marching armies. It was a well-built road, raised up for most of its length on earthworks, drained, and paved with great wide slabs into whose surfaces countless wagons and carts and carriages had worn grooves, the shallowness of which attested to the immutable solidity of the stone. Such repair as was, from time to time, needed was carried out by that city whose aegis lay closest to the damage. The farthest boundaries of each city were indicated by marker stones, the land between those milliary columns claimed by none, save through economic influence, for there lay the farms and steadings that found a market in the cities for their produce and, in turn, relied upon the manufactories resting safe within the city walls for such items as they could not themselves work.

It was along this road that the three questers traveled, for it was the swiftest way to Gannshold and while the route necessitated their passing through the cities where Calandryll's outlawry might well occasion difficulty, they deemed speed the more urgent consideration and trusted in Bracht's disguising to bring them safely to their destination.

They rode hard, the Kern's great stallion setting the pace, the chestnut and the grey proving his judgment of horseflesh as they matched the black in its mile-eating stride. Long before the sun drew close to the western horizon they had left Aldarin far behind, the road running straight through sere meadows where cattle foraged for what little browsing the departing winter allowed them beneath its scattering of thin snow, the vineyards of the river valley a memory as the sky darkened and the wind strengthened off the Narrow Sea. Beside the road, orchards were planted, their trees stark now, thrusting out bare limbs as if in supplication to the risen moon, and far off, as the shadows lengthened, they saw the lights of a farmhouse twinkling. Ahead, Calandryll knew, a caravanserai would be found, set beside the road, about a day's wagon journey clear of the city; at their pace they would reach it before full dark: they decided to avail themselves of its facilities.

"Tobias will have come this way," Calandryll warned, shouting over the thunder of hoofbeats, not yet fully confident of his disguise, "and he'll doubtless have posted my likeness there."

"That of Calandryll den Karnyth," Bracht yelled back, pausing a moment to think, then grinning as he found a name. "Not Calan of the clan Asyth. Aye, Calan—there's a ring to it."

Calandryll nodded acceptance of his new name, but some doubt must have remained on his face for Bracht added, "Ahrd, man! There's no one will recognize you now. Save, mayhap, those who knew you before, and them only do they look close. How say you, Katya?"

He looked across to the woman and she shouted agreement, though her face remained unsmiling and once more Calandryll thought how hard she found this parting from her own folk. In time, he supposed, she would come to accept it: he had, albeit the circumstances of his departure from the familiar confines of Secca and his family had been somewhat different. He smiled at her, seeking to cheer her, but she offered no response beyond a faint twitching of her lips that soon faded back into an expression of grim resolve so that he concluded it were better to leave her be, to let her come to terms with her loss in her own time.

Whether Bracht had earlier reached that same conclusion, or was merely too enthused to find himself once more ahorse to notice her distress, he was not sure. The former, he suspected, for while the Kern showed no great display of sympathy, but treated her as he had always done, that was likely, he decided after a moment's thought, the best course. Katya was not the kind to welcome excessive commiseration.

Indeed, he felt other, more physically pressing concerns. He had been long enough on shipboard that he had come close to forgetting what it was to sit a horse, especially at the pace Bracht set, and now he was reminded that the equestrian mode of travel made demands utterly different to any other. He found himself anticipating their arrival at the caravanserai with increasing eagerness, confident that it would offer baths and soft beds, as his muscles ached dully from the steady pounding of seat against saddle that somehow succeeded in radiating throughout his entire body.

He was thankful when light showed through the gloom and the Kern eased the stallion down to a walk, instinctively cautious of approaching without first surveying their destination.

The way station was set a little distance off from

the road, surrounded by a chest-high wall of sturdy blocks, its gate standing open, announced by a single large lantern hung from the apex of a vaulting arch. Beyond, the windows were honestly lit, revealing a square building rising two stories to a flat, walled roof, stables and a barn behind. As they entered the courtyard two barefoot boys came running toward them, promising to tend the animals. Calandryll was unsurprised when Bracht insisted on inspecting the stabling himself, though when the Kern suggested he take Katya's mount while she make herself comfortable within he could not help smiling his approval of the simple courtesy.

Katya accepted the offer, walking a trifle stiff-legged toward the inn, and Calandryll, feeling himself more than a little abused by his saddle, passed his reins to a boy and limped to the stables.

They met with Bracht's acceptance and once the beasts were unsaddled and the children paid to rub them down and see to their feeding, the two men followed Katya into the caravanserai.

The larger part of the lower floor was occupied by a single chamber, divided into an area at the rear set aside for eating and the rest devoted to casual drinking. A generous fire blazed in a spacious hearth, its heat trapped by the shuttered windows, and several patrons were already settled to their dinners, others seated in the drinking area with mugs of foaming ale or flasks of wine before them. They looked up as Calandryll and Bracht came in, but none paid them more attention than newcomers might usually find, subjecting them to a cursory examination before returning to their own conversations. Of Katya there was no sign and they approached the counter, where a plump, red-cheeked man with pale, fine hair arranged in thin strands across his balding pate greeted them cheerfully. At his back, pinned to a shelf holding earthenware mugs, was notice of Calandryll's proscription; he started at the sight, drawing his cloak

tighter about him to conceal the hand that moved to
his sword's hilt.

Bracht envinced no such hesitation, but called for
ale like any thirsty wayfarer and inquired as to
Katya's whereabouts.

"Gone to bathe," the innkeeper replied as he
tapped a barrel. "She said you'd be wanting two
rooms."

"Aye," said Bracht, "and baths ourselves."

"Soon as the lady's done." The man set mugs before them, studying their faces with unconcealed interest. "Kerns, are you? Long way from home, eh?
Freeswords?"

Bracht nodded; Calandryll found it difficult to take
his eyes from the poster. The balding man saw his interest and grinned. "Ten thousand varre, eh? Handsome reward that. Wonder what he did?" He turned
as he spoke, regarding the likeness, then moved to
face them again. "The Domm Tobias stayed here, you
know. Him and his lady. On a progress, they were,
and he had that put up."

There was no suspicion in either his gaze or his
voice and Calandryll felt himself begin to relax. At
his elbow Bracht drank with relish and stared openly
at the bill.

"Aye, it's a handsome reward," he murmured, wiping a mustache of foam from his mouth. "I'd not object to earning that, did I encounter him."

The innkeeper rested the expanse of his stomach
against the counter and shrugged. "Rumor is he's fled
to Kandahar," he declared as if imparting some secret
knowledge. "They say he poisoned his father and
tried to murder his brother—the Domm, now, who
stayed here—but that failed and he looked for refuge
with the Kand rebels. You heard about that?"

Bracht nodded again, solemnly.

"So where are you bound?" asked the garrulous in-
keeper. "Back home, eh? I'm called Portus, by the
way."

"Bracht," said the Kern, and indicated Calandryll with his mug. "This is Calan."

"Welcome to you both," said Portus. "Escorting the lady, are you? Not that she need fear many, from the way she bears herself."

"No," Bracht agreed.

Portus seemed more interested in his own questions than their answers, the flow of his conversation continuing unabated as he turned to draw himself a mug.

"So you're northbound, eh? We don't see too many Kerns around here. Some freeswords like you every once in a while; maybe the odd horse trader looking to cut himself a better deal than he'd find in Gannshold."

Confident now that his disguise was effective, Calandryll chose to take a part. Thickening his voice in what he trusted was a fair approximation of Bracht's accent, he said, "We heard of one but recently. A man named Daven Tyras?"

"Was a half-blood passed through some while past," Portus returned. "A closemouthed man, he was; but that, as I recall, was the name he gave."

"A man with sandy hair and a broken nose?" Calandryll asked.

"That's him," Portus agreed. "A friend of yours, is he?"

"We know him," Calandryll said, grateful for this confirmation: for all they were some weeks behind Rhythamun, at least they were on the right trail. "He trades in horses, out of Gannshold."

"Never said where he was going." Portus shrugged. "In fact, he hardly said a thing. A surly fellow, I thought. No offense to Kerns."

"There's none taken," said Bracht.

Portus nodded and, seeing their mugs emptied, scooped them up and filled them unasked. "Didn't drink much either"—he beamed—"and that, from what I've seen, is unlike a Kern. Fond of your ale, you fellows."

"Of good ale," Bracht said.

"You'll taste none better." The fat man tilted his own mug, setting it down with an enthusiastic smacking of his plump lips. "The Alda valley may be famous for its wine, but I reckon we brew some of the best ale, too."

He appeared set to engage them in idle talk all evening and Calandryll, feeling his legs and shoulders stiffening, began to wonder how they might escape his loquacity. He was saved from excuses by the woman who stuck her head past a half-opened door to call that the lady was done with her bathing and anyone else requiring a tub should speak up now.

"These two," Portus shouted back. Then softer to them, "You'll not object to sharing a tub, I trust?"

"So long as it's hot," Calandryll declared.

"You could boil lobsters in it," said the innkeeper. "Talking of which, shall I have the kitchen prepare your dinner? We keep a fixed menu here, but I can promise you it's good."

"As soon we're done," Bracht agreed.

"A boy'll bring you to your room after," Portus promised. "Key's in the door and dinner'll be waiting."

The Kern nodded his thanks and downed his ale. Calandryll followed suit, a trifle slower, and they hefted their saddlebags and walked toward the inner door. There, a corridor revealed a narrow staircase leading to the upper level and the kitchen, from which came appetizing smells to confirm Portus's boast, the woman who had called beckoning them to an open doorway that emitted clouds of steam. "It's all set out," she said, lifting her apron to wipe at her sweat-beaded face. "Shout when you're ready."

They went into the bathroom, finding a massive wooden tub awash with near-boiling water, coarse soap and rough towels laid out on a table beside two buckets of cold water. Without further ado they stripped and lowered themselves into the bath. Both set their sheated swords upright against the tub.

"So we follow his trail," Bracht murmured, scrubbing vigorously at his scarred chest.

"But weeks behind." Calandryll felt the aches begin to ease from his body, sighing contentedly. For all the urgency of their quest, at this moment he wanted nothing more than to lay back in the hot water, letting it work its simple magic.

"He makes no effort to conceal himself," Bracht said, "and mayhap travels in no great haste—if we ride hard . . ."

"Aye." Calandryll sank deeper, the water lapping against his chin, the heat rendering him drowsy. To think of Rhythamun was difficult as he relaxed; to contemplate what they should do if—when!—they caught up harder: he forced his drooping eyes open, his mind to concentrate. "But what then?"

"Then"—Bracht shrugged, grinning fiercely—"what happens happens. Some godly intervention, perhaps."

Calandryll grunted vague agreement, less confident than the Kern. It was Bracht's way to take each day as it came, his still to worry, to ponder the outcome of events. He was not, despite the intervention of Burash in Kandahar, certain that they could rely on the Younger Gods coming to their aid; yet without such assistance he could envisage no means by which they might overcome the warlock. They, after all, were no more than human, frail as all mortal flesh, while Rhythamun had at his command all the powers of the occult. Blades were of no account against that strength, yet steel and cunning were all they had, save hope. Perhaps, he mused, it was better to adopt Bracht's pragmatism; and hope the gods would play a part.

He pushed doubt away and himself upright, applying soap with a determination that sent water slopping over the edges of the tub.

When they both were done, doused with cold water and toweled dry, dressed again, they quit the bath chamber and called for someone to bring them to their room. One of the stable boys came running, leading them up the stairs to a chamber overlooking the courtyard, two beds against the wall, the bulk of a chimney between imparting a cozy warmth.

"The lady awaits you downstairs," the child advised them, staring with wide-eyed curiosity. "Are you really Kern freeswords?"

"Aye," Bracht replied, and to Calandryll when the gaping child was gone, "It seems my guising is effective."

"Indeed." Calandryll adjusted his scabbard, grinning ruefully. "While I remain on foot. Ahorse my body must yet remember how hard a saddle is."

Bracht chuckled. "A few days on the road will bring that back."

"Aye," Calandryll groaned, "a few hard days."

Still chuckling, Bracht motioned him through the door and they went down to the common room to find Katya.

She sat alone to the rear of the dining area, a mug of ale untouched before her, her face somber, ignoring the curious stares that came her way. The smile she offered them was brief and her grey eyes were cloudy with some indefinable emotion. They took places to either side as Portus bustled up with brimming mugs in hand, announcing the imminent arrival of their dinner.

"The grey suits you?" asked Bracht.

"You chose well."

Her voice was dull and Calandryll saw a flicker of concern spark in Bracht's eyes. He sought to divert her by telling her what they had learned of Daven Tyras, but still she remained introverted, only nodding in response, unlike her usual self.

"Do we set a hard pace, and he not hurry," Bracht said with a sidelong glance at Calandryll, "we may yet overtake him ere we reach Gannshold."

"Aye," was all she said to that and Calandryll saw Bracht frown, his own face registering doubt at this uncharacteristic dullness.

Soup was set before them then and they ate awhile in a silence broken at last by the woman.

"I had not thought it would feel like this," she murmured, pushing her bowl away still half full. "I feel . . . alone."

"We are with you," Bracht said gently.

"Aye." She favored them each with a wan smile. "And I thank you for that, but still . . ." She shook her head, eyes lowered as the bowls were removed and platters of roasted meat set in their places. "Forgive me."

It came as a shock to Calandryll to see tears glisten in the corners of her eyes, moist announcement of a vulnerability he had not seen in her before, nor suspected. He saw Bracht take her hand, holding it gently, his voice low as he bent toward her. What the Kern said he could not hear, but Katya brightened a little and ducked her head once, straightening on the bench and flexing her shoulders as if she sought to shuck off the melancholy that gripped her.

"I have never before been apart from my folk," she said quietly. "I had not thought we should be separated; nor, when we parted, that I should feel it so. It will pass, I suppose."

This was said fiercer, as if she endeavored to convince herself, and Bracht said earnestly, "It will, my word on it."

"And your word is good," she said as softly as before.

Bracht nodded. "I know what it is to leave your homeland and your people, to go among strangers," he said. "Calandryll, too. Three wanderers, we are, but while we are together we are, in a fashion, among our own folk."

Katya smiled again at that reassurance, but there remained about her still that air of loss, as if she wanted to accept his words but could not, entirely, believe in them.

"Time heals the wounds of parting," Calandryll offered, and would have said more had Portus not joined them, settling himself across the table with genial insensitivity. He inquired how they liked their dinner, blithely ignorant of Bracht's hostile glare, remarking on Katya's lack of appetite as if he feared his cuisine failed to meet with their approval.

"The meal is excellent," Calandryll said tactfully, "but we rode hard today and the lady is tired."

Katya flashed him a grateful glance for that and soon after excused herself.

"We leave at first light," Bracht called as she moved away, answered with a wave.

Portus watched her depart, his eyes admiring. "A handsome woman," he murmured. "Not like any Kern I've seen."

Both men ignored the question implicit in his voice, though he seemed neither to notice or take offense, but promptly engaged them in another somewhat one-sided conversation. They ate as he talked, content to listen and pick up what news they might, learning that Tobias had passed a night in the caravanserai several weeks ago; that the word out of Kandahar was of a land divided, Sathoman ek'Hennem holding all the eastern coast as the Tyrant massed an army to confront the rebels; that all trade with the war-torn kingdom had ceased. It was mostly gossip and among it all there was little of interest or advantage, save that Daven Tyras rode a piebald horse and traveled alone. They let him prattle on until his attention was diverted by other patrons demanding service and took that opportunity to find their beds.

They were, as Calandryll had anticipated, soft, and he sank rapidly into a dreamless sleep, emerging reluctantly as Bracht shook his shoulder, bidding him rise.

He clambered from the warmth of the bed, shivering as he dressed, remembering to draw his hair back and bind it in the fashion of Cuan na'For. As an afterthought, he checked his pillow, pleased to find no trace of black on the linen: the dye the Kern had used seemed most effective. Then, carrying their cloaks and saddlebags, they went together to Katya's chamber. She was clad and seemed anxious to depart, though no more cheerful than the night before. Calandryll thought she likely sought the occupation of travel as a palliative and certainly she ate her breakfast with better appetite, or at least speedily, as though it represented an unwanted delay.

They settled their account, Portus markedly less garrulous in the cold light of morning, and fetched their animals from the stables.

The sun was barely above the horizon, a sullen disc of dull gold that cast unwelcoming light over the frost riming the cobbles, their breath steaming as they cinched harness and swung astride the horses. None others were about so early, save the inn's folk, and they clattered out onto the road as if they were the only three in all the world. To the north, long banks of livid cloud, lit yellow along their undersides, hung low in the sky, presaging an unseasonal snowfall, as though the elements themselves were disarrayed. The wind was off the sea, tangy with ocean scent, but as they cantered northward it swung around, driving the cloud banks steadily closer. By midmorning snow skirled from a sky gone entirely grey, melting in great droplets on their cloaks and the hides of the sweating horses, layering the countryside with a mantle of white. By noon it was falling harder, gathering on the road so that the packed dirt grew treacherous and they were forced to proceed slower, wary of the horses stumbling. Even so, they held a fast enough pace that by midafternoon they had reached the second caravanserai.

They halted there only long enough to rest the animals and drink mulled wine, purchasing sufficient food to see them through the night and the next day, continuing on against the advice of the innkeeper, who promised them more snow would fall, likely through what remained of the day and all the night.

His warning proved correct for the snow fell steadily thicker, a curtain of drifting whiteness as impene-

trable as the dark, bringing an early twilight that
found them on a stretch of road running lonely
through woodland where great trees arched denuded
limbs over their heads, the trunks offering the only
likely shelter.

Bracht called a halt, Calandryll willing enough in
this inhospitable landscape to concede him leadership
and Katya still sunk in despondency, and took them a
little way off the road. He appeared unperturbed by
their situation, walking the stallion deeper among the
trees until he found a glade where cypress and cedars
grew close enough together their branches met to
form a threadbare semblance of a roof. He dismounted
there, setting Calandryll and Katya to gathering wood
for a fire while he rubbed down the horses and man-
tled them with saddle blankets.

Calandryll had thought himself capable by now of
surviving in the wild, but to his embarrassment he
found it impossible to light the pile of branches, the
sparks he struck from his tinderbox spluttering and
dying amid the kindling without hint of flame. Furiously he drove flint against striker, with no better results, expressing his frustration with curses as he was
forced to recognize his inexperience. He started as a
hand touched his shoulder, face reddening as he
turned from his task to find Katya standing close.

"Like this," she advised with a quick, apologetic
smile, stooping to add moss to his construction, taking the tinderbox from him and succeeding at her first
attempt to raise a flame. "It takes practice."

"Which our outlaw prince lacks," Bracht observed,
grinning.

Once, in another life, Calandryll might have resented the Kern's cheerful gibe, but now he only
shrugged, returning Bracht's grin.

"My time with you is a constant education," he
said, chuckling.

"Another lesson, then," Bracht declared. "I shall
teach you how to make a bedchamber."

He took Calandryll off into the wood as Katya blew

the fire to life, indicating the fallen branches that might be used to form a crude sleeping platform and those that would provide shelter overhead. Under his instruction Calandryll built a rough lean-to, the Kern more rapidly setting up two others.

"It will do for now," he remarked, "but in Wessyl, if not before, we must kit ourselves against this weather."

"We should have thought to bring canvas from the warboat," Katya murmured, the brief display of good humor she had evinced at Calandryll's fruitless attempt at fire lighting dissolving like the snow that drifted through the branches.

"I'd not thought to find snow so far south," Bracht said.

Katya nodded without speaking again, crouching with her hands thrust out to the rising flames, her head lowered as if she sought consolation in the blaze.

"Still, we shall be comfortable enough." Bracht spoke to her back; Calandryll thought he would reach out, touch her, but he seemed to think better of it and made no move, only adding, "We shall sleep dry tonight, and we've food."

He got no answer, and with a troubled glance in her direction set a kettle filled with snow to boil, adding to it what they had purchased earlier so that soon a savory stew simmered.

They ate, the ride and the cold edging their appetites, the stew welcome insulation against the pervading chill. Bracht made some attempt at cheerful conversation, but Katya remained silent save when directly addressed, her mood serving to emphasize the bleakness of their surroundings, and in time the Kern gave up, suggesting they take to their makeshift beds. He banked the fire so that it should last through the night and they each climbed into their respective shelters.

Calandryll stretched out on a layer of springy branches, sweet-scented and comfortable enough,

those above and his cloak holding off the snow if not
the cold that seemed to creep inexorably through his
body. The fire warmed one side of him, but the other,
no matter how tight he wrapped himself in the cloak,
remained chilled and he turned constantly, wondering
how his companions fared. Both, it seemed, were
more accustomed to such hardship, for as he lay shivering restlessly he heard no sounds from their lean-
tos, only the crackle of smoldering branches and the
sizzling of melted snow, the shuffling and blowing of
the horses. He had thought himself inured to discomfort, but this was very different to sleeping rough in
Kandahar or the nights spent in the sticky heat of
Gessyth, and he began to wonder how he might cope
on the plains of Cuan na'For should they need to enter that land. He would, he supposed, adapt in
time—he had already adjusted to so many changes—
but for now, he decided, he had never felt less comfortable. He yawned hugely and closed his eyes,
willing himself to ignore the cold.

It seemed an impossible task and he was surprised,
when he opened his eyes again, to realize that the
light was changed, the snow no longer drifting canescent from the darkness but paled and glittering
against a brightening sky: dawn was come and he had
slept. His teeth started promptly to chattering again
and he crawled from the piney shelter to add fresh
branches to the fire, groaning as stiffened limbs protested the movement. He huddled awhile by the
blaze, luxuriating in its warmth, watching the eastern
sky fade from salmon pink to a blue the color of slate,
decorated with shafts of gold by the rising sun. Birds
began to sing and he hoped that presaged an end to
the snowfall as he pushed upright and went to where
the patient horses waited.

They appeared to have suffered no ill effects; indeed, they seemed to have spent a more comfortable
night than he, clustering close together to share their
body warmth, greeting him with soft snickers and a
shaking of heads that sent flakes tumbling in kaleido-

scope colors from their manes. He doled them each a
measure of oats and returned to the fire, filling the
kettle with fresh snow as Bracht emerged.

The Kern was as little inconvenienced as the animals, stretching as though risen from a bed of duck
down, his dark face split by a sizable grin as he saw
Calandryll's expression. He looked toward the animals and Calandryll said, "They're fed," the announcement greeted with a nod of approval. He
scooped up a handful of snow, rubbing it over his face
in lieu of washing, and walked off into the trees.

While he attended to his personal needs Katya rose,
no less lithe, as if such nights were usual in Vanu. She
glanced at the sky and murmured, "The snow will
stop soon," then she, too, disappeared among the timber. Calandryll spilled tea into the kettle, his companions' cheerful hardiness serving only to remind him of
his own discomfort. Morosely he stirred the brew.

"Your bed was not to your liking?"

He looked up as Bracht came out of the trees, his
downturned mouth all the answer the Kern needed.
Bracht chuckled and began to rummage through the
saddlebags in search of breakfast. Calandryll said,
"Katya claims the snow will stop soon."

Bracht looked up and nodded. "Soon enough, but
still it will slow us. The road will likely be hard going." He turned as snow crunched under Katya's
boots. "How say you?"

The woman shrugged and Calandryll thought she
seemed no more cheerful. She said, "Today. Come tomorrow's dawn it will be melting."

Calandryll bowed to their superior weather lore,
content for now to allow the fire to restore warmth to
blood and joints and muscles.

"The inns along this road," Katya asked, "are they
all so close?"

"For travelers in wagons," he replied, mildly
pleased that in this at least he knew more than they.
"For traders and the like, who move slower than we."

Katya grunted a curse. Bracht said, "Then we use

them only when we must," and chuckled as Calandryll groaned. "We'll purchase tents when we can—a good tent is shelter enough."

Calandryll could think of no suitable answer: speed was of the essence, its price, it seemed, discomfort.

Hot tea and breakfast, for all it consisted of no more than dried beef and hard biscuits, cheered him a little and he felt somewhat happier as they mounted and returned to the road.

It was, as Bracht had warned, difficult to negotiate. The snow eased off as the morning grew older, the sky no longer banked with grey nimbus but brightened to a hard and cloudless azure, the sun striking brilliant sparks from the great drifts that lay across their way, the horses plunging sometimes chest-deep, Bracht's powerful stallion breaking them a trail, the geldings content enough to follow in his path. They made the best time they could, but even so dusk fell before they came in sight of the next caravanserai and—the decision eliciting a sigh of relief from Calandryll—chose to spend the night there.

The place was twin to Portus's establishment, if more crowded with itinerants who had opted to wait out the blizzard. They learned that Daven Tyras had passed through, but now, thanks to the storm, had gained a day or more. This news was taken with phlegmatic acceptance by Bracht, less stoically by Calandryll, while Katya, who had lost some of her gloom during the day, fell once more into brooding. Nonetheless, to bathe in hot water and eat well before retiring to comfortable beds were luxuries that cheered them all and they departed the next morning in better spirits.

The day, too, cheered them, the sun establishing itself early in a sky free of cloud, warming the air so that what snow yet remained began, just as Katya had promised, to melt rapidly, their pace increasing steadily as they cantered northward, hooves splashing rainbows from the puddles that now spread across their way.

That night they once again found shelter in a caravanserai, though for the next three they slept in the
open, Calandryll finding, to his delight, that he grew
increasingly accustomed to such rude accommoda-
tions, even that, under Bracht's tutelage, he mastered
the art of the campfire. Within a day or two, he estimated, they would reach Wessyl, and with that calcu-
lation came the sudden realization that the days
lengthened, spring, for all this inclement weather, advancing steadily.

He had kept no calendar—it seemed a pointless exercise where they had gone, save perhaps to count off
the days to the Mad God's raising—and it was a shock
that the winter solstice had gone unnoticed for it was
celebrated in Secca with feasting and revelries, a great
masked ball in the palace, and when last he had par-
ticipated he had sat at his father's side, his eyes seeking Nadama among the crowd, jealous of her
attention, alarmed when she danced with Tobias.
This year the festival had gone unnoticed, his attention occupied entirely by the quest. Indeed, he had
forgotten to observe any of the festivals since departing Secca—the days devoted to the gods, his own
birthday, all had passed unheeded. He was a year
older—it seemed far more and soon it would be a full
year since he had fled his home. He smiled thoughtfully as the weight of time sank in: it seemed so long,
and yet no time at all, as if his journeying with Bracht
and Katya were a thing entire unto itself, unending.
Perhaps, he thought, *it is; Menelian had suggested
that Tharn must lie beyond the limits of the world
and perhaps we must journey beyond the limits of
time to thwart Rhythamun.* That alone felt solid, a
fact infrangible: that Rhythamun must be thwarted;
though still he was not sure how, only that the pursuit must continue.

That night he offered a prayer to Dera, asking the
goddess's forgiveness for his omissions and her aid in
the successful conclusion of the quest. If she heard,
she returned no sign, and he fell asleep wondering if

perhaps she turned away her face, consigning the folk
of Lysse to the awful fate threatened by the Mad God.
It seemed to him a terrible carelessness if it were so,
but he could not shake off the doubt and in the
morning his mood was akin to Katya's: one of somber
reflection.

He cursed himself for such pessimism, but it remained with him as they galloped northward through
a day turned squally, rafts of serried grey cloud blowing constantly off the Narrow Sea to send rain drumming in fierce outbursts, as if in confirmation of his
fears.

They traversed moor and marshland now, ahead
only a dull landscape of undulating hills and tussocky
grass, colorless beneath the neutral sky. The road
wound around the hillocks, weaving among them as if
to tantalize with its promise of swift passage, the land
to either side bare and windswept, scattered with
reedy ponds and little rivulets that filled the ancient
road with puddles, or, where the way dipped lowest,
overran the dirt in muddy streams. It was a bleak terrain that seemed populated by nothing save curlews
and honking geese, devoid of farmsteads or other
travelers, the last caravanserai passed that morning,
the next, save they be delayed, certainly found too
soon to merit halting, leaving the prospect of a damp
and miserable night.

It was a surprise to come upon the crone in such a
place.

At first, as they rounded the shoulder of a drumlin
shadowed by the westering sun, it seemed a great
bundle of reeds was somehow animated, proceeding
along the road of its own volition. Only when the
heap wavered and fell, sheaves scattering, did they see
the woman beneath, her threadbare gown a fusty
green of a shade so similar to her burden as to merge,
indistinguishable, with the rushes she stooped to
gather. Calandryll slowed his horse as they approached, seeing a face scoured by age and wind turn
toward him, a hand rising to brush meager strands of

ivory hair from a forehead webbed with wrinkles,
eyes a dulled and hopeless blue observing him dispas-
sionately. The ancient made neither sound nor movement, seeming not to anticipate help or sympathy,
but only to wait, silently watchful. Unthinking, he
brought the chestnut to a halt. Bracht turned the
black stallion to the side as if to ride around the old
woman, then thought better of it and reined in. To
the rear, Katya followed suit.

"Shall I help you, mother?"

Calandryll swung down as he spoke. Bracht said,
"We've leagues to cover yet," and Calandryll gestured
at the crone, bending to loop rein about fetlock, saying, "Would you leave her unaided?"

Impatience flashed briefly in the Kern's blue eyes,
but he shook his head and answered, "No," as he dismounted.

Katya studied them a moment, her expression unfathomable, then she, too, sprang down, hobbling her
grey and moving to join them.

It took little enough time to gather up the fallen
reeds and rebuild the stook, but when that was done
the bundle seemed greater than before and far larger
than so frail a woman might carry. She stood staring
at it, as though assembling her strength. Her shoulders were narrow and bowed, the wrists that pro-
truded from her sleeves thin, sticklike; Calandryll
saw that her feet were bare and muddied from her labors; her gown seemed far too worn to hold out the
wind. He spoke without thought: "Where do you live,
mother? We can use my horse to carry this."

At his side Bracht let out a short, sharp breath, indicative of his impatience; Calandryll ignored him.
The crone said, "Not far," and waved a withered hand
in the general direction of the marshes.

Calandryll nodded and bent to lift the stook: it was
more than he could raise alone and he looked to
Bracht for help. The Kern sighed, shrugged, and lent
his strength to the task. Together, they maneuvered

the bundle onto the chestnut's saddle and lashed it in place.

"Should we ignore her?" Calandryll met Bracht's accusing stare. "We ask the aid of gods—why should they aid us if we ignore her need?"

He thought to receive some angry retort in answer, but instead the Kern shrugged again and ducked his head.

"Aye." He grinned, bowing in the crone's direction. "Forgive me, mother; in my haste I forget my manners."

"You find them, and my thanks." The old woman's voice was reedy as her load, barely discernible over the wind. "This way."

She turned, starting away, halting when Katya stepped forward, a hand upon her arm.

"Would you take my horse? You've likely walked enough."

"You are kind."

The crone nodded and allowed the warrior woman to lift her up astride the grey, where she perched like some windblown scarecrow, her seat precarious, her legs too short to reach the stirrups.

"Take the saddle horn," Katya advised. "You're safe enough."

The old woman obeyed, exposing yellow gatepost teeth in a smile of gratitude, her hands locked about the saddle horn as Katya took up the reins and began to walk. Calandryll and Bracht fell into step behind; a curious procession as they moved slowly along the road.

They descended the drumlin and went a little way farther before the old woman indicated they should turn off, between two low monticules where a stream gurgled, their approach startling a heron that rose on ponderous wings, croaking its annoyance. The ground was boggy, the marsh grass bedewed by rainfall, their boots and the horses' hooves sinking in to draw loose with sticky, sucking sounds. It seemed a wonder to Calandryll that anyone should choose to live in so forlorn a place, and then that perhaps the old woman had no choice. He watched her, toylike on Katya's saddle, and thought what a miserable existence she must have out here in this desolate landscape. Perhaps in summer it was more cheerful, but now, with the sky looming obdurate and grey overhead, the wind rustling like eerie laughter, it was a place he had sooner left behind. Still, it was unthinkable that they should have ignored the old woman's plight: his words to Bracht had come out instinctively—how should those seeking help go on heedless of those in need?

Beyond the close-spaced monticules the land broadened in a shallow depression, filled along its center with a stinking marsh set round with blackened reed mace. They skirted the quagmire, crossing the rivulet that fed the slough to climb the farther slope. Beyond that the land dipped again and then rose once more onto firmer footing, no longer soggy, sere grass spreading over a low plateau. The wind, its passage uncontested by hillocks, blew stronger here, salty and rank with the perfume of the surrounding bogland. The horizon was lost in lowering cloud and as they continued across the plateau more rain lashed down. Calandryll wondered where the crone sited her dwelling, for in all that mournful wasteland he could see no sign of habitation.

Then, where wind-tortured stands of broom thrust tangled limbs from the dank sward, a cut showed.

It fell down narrow and steep to a bowl sheltered by encircling hillocks. A spring babbled from among blue-black stones, birthing a stream of clear water that meandered across a little meadow of healthier grass. Beside the spring stood a lopsided hut, its walls haphazard, constructed of random planks and undressed branches, stone blocks that might have come from some earlier building long since tumbled down, its roof a wild thatching of reed. A little distance separate stood a no less ramshackle structure suggestive of a barn fallen long ago into disrepair. They halted

there and Katya lifted the crone down as Calandryll
and Bracht lowered the stook. From the entrance of
the hovel came a black cat that studied them with
suspicious yellow eyes, let loose a piercing shriek,
and ran as if terrified across the meadow to disappear
over the farther ridge.

"He seeks his dinner," the old woman explained,
"and I would offer you the same."

"We'd not impose upon you." Calandryll smiled,
thinking that likely it were better they offered to
share the contents of their saddlebags than take what
little she might have.

"Nor should we delay," Bracht added, but kindly.
"We've yet a way to travel."

"A storm builds," answered the crone, beckoning
with crooked fingers. "Come."

Bracht smiled rejection, taking up his reins as if to
mount. Calandryll, for no reason he could understand,
paused, then asked, "Where would you have your
reeds, mother?"

"There." The crone pointed to the ruin of the barn.
"And put up your horses, too."

"We cannot linger," Bracht said. "We'll stow your
reeds and be on our way."

"Into the storm?" Yellow teeth flashed dully in an
ugly smile. "You'll not travel far, warrior."

As if in confirmation, a peel of thunder crashed and
lightning stabbed jagged fingers toward the earth. The
rain strengthened, heavy droplets splashing into the
stream; the thunder dinned again, like some great
drum beaten against the skin of the livid sky.
Calandryll wiped his face, motioning for Bracht to
take up one end of the bundled reeds, and they hauled
the stook across to the barn.

Inside, the place was oddly dry, the roof, for all it
consisted only of a patchwork thatch, holding out the
downpour that now beat a savage whiplash across the
meadow. Clean straw was spread over a floor of aged
stone, a rusted manger holding an amplitude of
sweetly scented hay, a trough filled with potable wa-

ter. Calandryll caught Bracht's eye and frowned, seeing curiosity on the Kern's face.

"There is something strange about all this," he murmured.

"Aye." Bracht kicked the stook. "You and I together found this hard enough to lift, and she's frail as one of her own reeds."

"And this"—Calandryll indicated the barn—"Sound as any stable. With hay and water . . . as if visitors are expected."

The Kern nodded, his eyes become troubled, fingers toying with the hilt of his falchion. "This place has the dimensions of witchcraft," he murmured. "Is she some harpy, luring us here?"

"I think not." Calandryll shook his head, possessed of a certainty he could not explain. "I believe her honest."

Bracht's answering gaze expressed doubt. He said, "No matter, we're best on our way."

For reasons he could understand no better than his certainty the crone presented no threat, Calandryll hesitated to agree, though still he moved with Bracht to the open door. And halted as Katya came out of an afternoon gone midnight black save where lightning's silver shafted down, leading the three horses, her face glistening wet, and somber, but not, he thought, with that depression that had gripped her. It seemed rather, as he studied her grey eyes, a kind of introspection that had little to do with nostalgia for her kinfolk. He stood back as she brought the animals inside.

"I thought," she said slowly, seeming unsure of both her words and motive, "that it were better we accept her hospitality."

"Aye." He ducked his head in agreement, taking the chestnut's reins. "In this storm . . ."

"We can still ride," Bracht interrupted. "Better a dousing than . . ."

He broke off, shaking his head as if the thread of his warning were lost, puzzlement mapped by the creasing of his forehead, the doubt in his eyes.

"Bracht fears a harpy lures us to her lair," Calandryll explained. "Or a marsh witch exercises her glamours."

"An old woman offers us shelter." Katya set to unbuckling her saddle. "Only that—a lonely old woman."

Bracht stared at her, dubious. "You know this?" he challenged.

"I believe it." Katya tugged her saddle from the grey's back, set it aside. "I trust her."

She began to rub down the gelding. Outside, rain and thunder increased, the one a steady drumbeat, like myriad fingers tapping above their heads, though still no drops passed through the thatch, the other a great, fierce clashing that rolled and echoed like the angry roaring of some immense, invisible beast. Lightning bleached all their faces, painted silver over Katya's hair. Calandryll loosened the chestnut's harness.

"I cannot understand this," Bracht said, shouting over the bombardment of exterior sound. "Are you possessed by some glamour?"

Katya laughed for the first time in days, tossing back her hair as she faced the Kern across her horse's flanks.

"What is there to understand?" she asked. "How far might we travel in this storm, in this sorry countryside? A glamour? No—save that the offer of shelter and hot food enchant me."

"We'd need camp soon enough," Calandryll added. "Why not here? At least we shall have a roof above us."

"I . . ." Bracht shook his head, shrugged. "Very well, it shall be as you wish."

Calandryll was not sure whether the Kern acceded from a desire to please Katya or because Bracht began to feel the same pervading confidence that convinced him the crone offered no harm. He smiled as he saw the stallion unsaddled, Bracht scrubbing at the glossy hide with a vigor designed to conceal his doubt.

The animals tended and settled, they drew on their

cloaks and ran through pelting rain to the hovel, light showing now about its drooping door and irregular windows. Inside, the single room was dry and warm, perfumed with the herbs that hung in bunches from the rafters, a fire blazing merrily in a stone hearth, a blackened cookpot suspended over the flames, stirred by the crone. She greeted them with a nod and a gap-toothed smile, gesturing at the rough chairs set about a precarious table. A clay jug stood upon the table, beside it four cups of the same material. At the old woman's feet the cat glanced idly up from its delicate toilet. Calandryll saw blood about its muzzle.

"He found his dinner," the crone said, "and soon yours shall be ready. For now—I've wine to offer."

She rose from her stool, hobbling to the table to pour the wine, pass them each a cup, smiling as Bracht hesitated.

"Neither bane nor cantrip, warrior. Only wine." She raised her own mug, drinking deep. "And a toast to those who aid a helpless woman."

Katya was the first to sip, then Calandryll, Bracht a little slower, not yet entirely convinced. The wine was good, smooth on the tongue and rich, subtly flavored. Calandryll drank again and said, "We've food we might add to your pot, mother."

"No, no." She shook her head. "Your offer is kindly taken, but I've fare aplenty. One thing, however—I'd have your names."

He was close to blurting out his true identity, but a warning glance from Bracht reminded him and he said, "I am Calan; this, Katya; he is Bracht."

It seemed some hint of amusement sparkled in her dull eyes as he said the false name, or perhaps it was merely the reflection of the rush lights, for she only nodded and returned, "And I am Edra," setting down her cup and going back to the fire.

"How do you live here, Edra?" asked Katya. "It seems a lonely place."

"Well enough," the crone replied enigmatically, "I find what company I need."

Calandryll looked around. The place was simple, crude even, but surprisingly comfortable. The floor was solid stone—the foundation of an earlier building, he supposed—strewn with mats of woven rush, and clean. Against the rear wall stood a low pallet, piled with sheepskins, close by a chest, beside the hearth was a cupboard from which Edra now took bowls and platters of the same rough pottery as the cups and jug. Unthinking, he rose to help her, aware as he took the platters that, like the barn, this hovel was free of drafts for all the wind howled outside. Indeed, the fury of the storm dimmed in here, shut out by the gapped walls.

"You are kind," she murmured as he set the platters down, favoring him with an oddly speculative look. "Where do you go?"

"To Gannshold," he answered, thinking that it could do no harm to tell this lonely ancient their destination.

"You've business there?"

She spoke as she stooped to lift the pot; he took it from her, their fingers touching an instant, and said, "We seek a man named Daven Tyras. A trader in horses. A half-blood Kern with sandy hair and a broken nose. Mayhap you've seen him go by."

"Few travel the north road in this season." She began to dole out the contents of the pot. "And that one I've not seen, though he may have passed. Why do you seek him?"

"He stole a thing," Bracht intervened, speaking quickly, before Calandryll had chance to answer. "We—Calan and I—were hired to find it, but he stole it from us and we'd have it back."

"Ah, so you are freeswords." Edra nodded, glancing from one to the other, her wrinkled face impossible to read. "It must be a thing of some value, that you chase this man across Lysse so hard."

"How can you know that?" Bracht demanded suspiciously. "That we chase him across Lysse?"

Edra shrugged, thin shoulders stretching worn

gown. "You ride for Gannshold," she said, "and there's little enough betwixt here and Aldarin. Are you not come from there?"

Bracht nodded, abashed: it was an obvious enough explanation.

"And you, Katya," the crone asked, "are you a freesword, too?"

"We ride together," Katya replied.

"But I think you are not of Lysse. You've the look of the north about you, of some far land."

She spooned up stew as she said it, face bent to the table. Katya said, "I am Vanu born."

"Ah, Vanu." Edra nodded over her bowl. "That is very far away. Close on the Borrhun-maj, which folk say boundaries the world itself. Do you not miss your homeland, Katya? Your kinfolk?"

"Aye." For a moment Katya's eyes clouded and the corners of her wide mouth turned down, her voice soft as she murmured, "I do."

"But likely when you have found this thing you seek you will return there, no?"

Katya hesitated and Bracht said firmly, "Aye. We shall go there together."

"And you, Calan? Shall you go home then?"

Calandryll lowered his spoon, taken aback by the question, unsure of his answer: where was his home now? Surely not in Secca. Home was become an amorphous thing, a concept vague as the beliefs, the hopes, he had forsaken when he fled. He pursed his lips and said softly, "Perhaps. Or perhaps I shall go to Vanu, too."

"Not Cuan na'For, then?"

Again he wondered if he saw amusement in the faded gaze, or only a trick of the flickering light. He smiled indefinitely, shrugging. Edra smiled back and said, "Forgive my questions. I keep you from your dinner, but such fine company is rare and my tongue runs away."

He smiled, not speaking, feeling that she somehow saw through his disguise and knew him for who and what he was. But still he felt no fear, no belief that she was a witch or harpy. He tasted the stew and his smile grew wider: it was excellent; hare, he decided, spiced with herbs, the broth thick with vegetables, and filling. Across the table he saw Bracht eating as eagerly, his suspicions seemingly forgotten, or set aside.

He would have forborn to take a second platter but Edra urged it on him, assuring him that she had food aplenty, and when all was consumed they finished the jug of wine, speaking of their journey northward and of Aldarin, relaxing.

The storm still raged outside when Edra suggested they sleep, finding sheepskins and rugs that she spread before the hearth, apologizing that she could offer no better beds.

"Better than the roadside on such a night," Katya declared. "Our thanks for this, and an excellent meal."

"It is deserved," Edra replied, smiling as Bracht glanced at her and adding, "Did you not come to my aid?"

She went to her own bed then and they settled by the fire. Bracht slept, as ever, with the falchion cradled like a lover in his arms, but both Calandryll and Katya set their blades by their sides, trusting, though they knew not why, in the old woman; sure that they slept safe this night.

And Calandryll dreamed. Or believed it was a dream: later, he decided it was an answer to forgotten prayers.

10

H E woke—or dreamed he woke—to the touch of
Edra's hand upon his cheek. He opened his eyes
and saw her crouching beside him, a shapeless figure
limned in moonlight, beckoning him to rise. Without
question or conscious thought, he obeyed, instantly
alert, moving silently after her. Neither Katya nor
Bracht stirred, and that was strange for the Kern slept
cat-cautious, his senses, even in the depths of slumber, seemingly attuned to his surroundings. Now
though he lay beneath the piled sheepskins, feet toward the fire, a beatific smile curving his lips, one
hand loose about the falchion's hilt. Calandryll wondered how that could be and decided it was because
he dreamed, no matter that he had felt the crone's fingers dry on his skin, could hear the murmur of the
banked fire, the sound of thunder a low grumbling far
off to the south. He crossed the little room and followed Edra to the door, remembering that before it
had creaked on rusted hinges, aware that now it
opened silently and closed with no more noise. He
stepped outside into the night.

The air smelled fresh, as if invigorated by the
storm, no longer rank with marsh gasses, but perfumed with the scent of night-blooming flowers, and

balmy as a summer afternoon. This was, he thought,
a most interesting dream, with nothing in it of threat
but, rather, a sense of peace and promise. Over his
head the sky spread wide and clear, stars sparkling,
points of brilliance pricked through the velvet blue
canopy, like distant torches or the running lights of
ships, the moon distended, close to full, the radiance
it cast gentle as a caress. A breeze stirred, setting the
grass that filled the little meadow to rustling, the babble of the spring-fed stream a musical counterpoint,
silvery cymbals to the fluting of the wind. He looked
down as the black cat insinuated itself between his
legs, purring, moving fluidly off into the darkness.
Edra beckoned again and he stepped away from the
hut, thinking that this was a remarkably vivid dream,
not thinking to question it as he went after the crone
across the grass to the crown of a hillock.

The wind blew stronger there—he felt it on his
face, felt it shift his hair—and Edra halted, looking
back toward the hovel. Calandryll followed her gaze:
the hut was unchanged in its physical aspect, but now
it seemed not a sorry little construction of ramshackle bits and pieces, but a place of refuge, a safe haven
from storm and peril, for an instant a palace filled
with light.

"You might remain here. This is not so bad a
place."

He stared about and knew that it was so—night
spread a magical mantle over the bogland and he saw
how it might be when spring came, how summer
would transform the sloughs and quagmires.

"I cannot," he said.

"You should be safe here." Her voice was different,
no longer a reedy whisper but deeper, mellifluous, and
very confident. He shook his head and said again, "I
cannot."

"Why not?"

"Because then Rhythamun should use the Arcanum to find Tharn and raise the Mad God. That must
not be."

It did not occur to him to conceal his purpose: at a level below the conscious he knew that this dream was spun from the fabric of honesty, and that to prevaricate was to unravel it.

"Rhythamun?"

"He has the shape of Daven Tyras now; before, he was Varent den Tarl, but still he is Rhythamun."

"Ah, I see—a shape-changer."

"Aye, and mad as the god he'd return to life."

"And you would prevent him."

"I and Bracht and Katya—we must, lest all the world go down into chaos."

"You three wear the trappings of mortality—how shall you prevent him?"

"I do not know. Only that we must attempt it."

She nodded, her lined face approving, and when he looked closer at her he saw that she was changed. She was no longer a crone but a woman in the prime of her life, dressed in a gown that caught the soft effulgence of the gibbous moon and trapped it in folds of luminance so that she stood wreathed in light. Great waves of golden hair fell free to her shoulders, flowing about a face that was simultaneously unique and that of every woman he had known with love; that of his mother, and Katya, Nadama, Reba the spaewife: all became one in that visage, and as he stared in wonderment at eyes blue as the midsummer sky he knew—or dreamed he knew—that he looked upon the face of the goddess.

"Dera," he whispered, falling to his knees.

She reached down, lifting him, saying, "You need not offer me obeisance; rather, it is I should kneel to you."

He shook his head no.

"Aye," she said, "for do you not quest in my name? Do you—and your comrades—not ride to battle in my defense? Should we Younger Gods not offer you thanks for that?"

"What else should we do?" he asked.

She smiled then and it seemed the night was banished and he stood beneath the sun, but she gave no direct answer, saying instead, "Not all men think as you. In Kandahar there are mages know something of the Arcanum and what it means, but they do not go out seeking Rhythamun. Those of Vanu who name themselves sages are all aware of the book's import, but still they send Katya in their place."

"They are peaceful folk," he said, "and in Kandahar the sorcerers are bound to the Tyrant, bound to fight his war."

"Yet for all the blood spilled there, still that war should seem petty set beside what Tharn would visit on men."

"I think perhaps they do not understand."

He shrugged and the goddess asked, "Do you?"

"I know that Tharn is named the Mad God," he replied, "and I believe that to attempt his awakening is insane. I'd not see chaos visited on the world."

"Is the world so important then? Has it treated you so kindly?"

He frowned, surprised by the question. It seemed at such variance to all he believed, to all he knew, that he could not find a ready answer. At length he said, "Does Rhythamun succeed and Tharn awake, surely you should be destroyed."

"All things end." She gestured at the moon, past its zenith now, its descent to the western horizon begun. "As surely as night must."

Again he frowned. "Do you tell me to forsake this quest?"

"No." She smiled again and shook her head, brilliance coruscating from her hair. "I say only that you have options."

"Not in this," he said.

"You found the Arcanum. It might well be that Tharn would thank you for that. You might find favor in his eyes."

He shuddered, dismissing the notion, saying "No!" in a tone of utter rejection.

His response seemed to please her, but still she

touched a hand to his arm and said, "It might well be your quest cannot succeed."

"Is that a reason to give it up?" He shook his head, answering himself: "No!"

"You might well die in the attempt."

"Aye." Now he nodded. "But still we must try."

For long moments she studied his face, then smiled anew and said, "You are brave."

He felt such pleasure at that encomium his cheeks reddened. Like some embarrassed boy he shuffled his feet, his eyes lowered as he murmured, "Am I?"

"You chase a wizard," she said softly, "a sorcerer of terrible power, whose fell subtleties you already know. Has he not tricked you before? Do you not think he will trick others to his cause?"

It seemed irrelevant that she so obviously saw through his disguise, knowing who he truly was and of his dealing with the warlock—she was, after all, a goddess, and this was but a dream.

"Even so." He shrugged.

"Even so," she returned. "Though it likely be impossible; though you shall undoubtedly earn Tharn's enmity does Rhythamun succeed; though you may well die before that day comes—even so, you'd go on?"

"Even so," he said, firmly now.

"There are few left of your mettle, Calandryll."

Her voice was almost wistful; he shrugged again and said, "I am not alone. Katya and Bracht are of the same stamp. More . . ."

"In their ways," she said, "aye. And for that they, too, have my thanks. But there's iron of a different kind in you."

He smiled, dismissing that compliment, his mind fixed on what she said of gratitude, wondering if he dare voice the thought that came. Why not? This was a dream, was it not? And in dreams all things are possible.

"I'd ask more of you than thanks," he said.

He thought perhaps he ventured too audacious on

capricious ground, for it seemed a shadow passed across her face, like cloud drifting over the moon. "What would you ask of me?" she wondered.

"Help," he said. "We are—as you say—only mortal and we hunt an enemy impervious to honest steel. Aid us! I know not how, but give us the means by which we may defeat Rhythamun."

Her face was solemn as she looked into his eyes and he feared he had gone too far. But then she said, "Has my brother Burash not come to your aid? And so, too, shall I—so far as I may. But we Younger Gods are not of such stuff as Tharn and Balatur, just as they are lesser creatures than Yl and Kyta, and my power is limited, as is that of Burash. I've no sway beyond Lysse."

She paused, her lovely face thoughtful. Calandryll said urgently, "Whatever aid you can. Anything."

"We Younger Gods are not omnipotent. Principles beyond your easy understanding govern us, surely as time governs mortal men." Again she paused; Calandryll waited, breath held. "But this I tell you, though you'll not yet understand me, nor, I suspect, believe me—that which you need to defeat Rhythamun you have already."

"I do not understand," he agreed. "Do you say it in words I may comprehend?"

"I cannot," she told him gravely, "lest there be disturbed a balance complex beyond your knowing. Only that you may succeed."

He opened his mouth to voice protest, reminded of Bracht's blunt pronouncements on the circuitous natures of gods and wizards, but her hand rose, silencing him. "Hold to your belief," she advised, "and remember my words. Beyond that I may say no more, save"—her face clouded again, briefly, her lips pursing as if she deliberated within herself—"that you shall ride safe in Lysse, for all your brother seeks you. That gift is mine to give, and one more—give me your sword."

He had not known he wore the blade. Indeed was

sure that when he rose he had not brought it with him, though now, unquestioning, he drew it and passed it to her.

She took it by the hilt and ran one hand down the length of the blade before returning the weapon. "Doubtless you shall face magicks along your way, such as can defeat plain steel," she advised. "Know then, that this blade carries my blessing and shall cut magicks as it cuts flesh. Now, enough—come, sleep before day finds us and you must be on your way."

She spoke gently enough, but still her tone brooked no refusal and he bowed his head, accepting, following her down from the hillock and back toward the hut, aware that she changed along the way, becoming once more the crone, Edra. She closed the door—silently as before—and went to her pallet. Calandryll resumed his place by the hearth, sure now that he dreamed, for still Bracht and Katya slept on, and in moments he joined them.

He woke greatly refreshed, the strange events of the night blurring in the light of a new day, becoming, as is the way with dreams, steadily less distinct as he rose and stretched and went out to the spring to bathe. Bracht came with him and when they were done and Katya took her turn, they went to the barn to check the animals, who seemed content enough. The storm was long spent now, the sky still hoary, but brightened by the sun that hung hazy behind the curtaining grey, cheering the hollow with the promise of the turning season. Dew shone on the grass and birds sang, flashes of color on the surrounding hillocks.

"I was wrong, it seems," Bracht admitted, elaborating when Calandryll expressed his incomprehension, "about Edra. If she be a marsh witch, she's a kindly nature."

Calandryll nodded, something tugging at his memory, insubstantial, so that he could not quite pin it

down. Indeed, it seemed to him that he had forgotten
something important until they were once more on
the road, breakfasted on griddle cakes and cheese,
their farewells said and Edra's hovel left behind. The
crone guided them to the highway, standing beside a
hillock as they set heels to their mounts and cantered
northward.

He looked back then, raising a hand in salute, and
saw a single shaft of sunlight glance down, illuminat-
ing the old woman. In that moment she became again
the goddess, radiant, her own hand lifted in benedic-
tion. He gasped, the night in all its details flooding
back, knowing that it had not been a dream. Beside
him he heard Katya's startled cry, looking toward her
and seeing on her face an expression he knew must be
the mirror of his own. When he looked again to where
Dera stood, she was gone.

"What's amiss?" Bracht stared from one to the
other, frowning. "Your faces tell me you look on
ghosts."

"Not ghosts." Calandryll shook his head, a smile
shaping, tentative, through burgeoning certitude. "A
goddess."

"I thought I dreamed," Katya murmured. "I had
forgotten it until I looked back and saw her."

"I, too," said Calandryll.

"I looked back," said Bracht, "and all I saw was an
old woman."

"Not Dera?" asked Katya.

The Kern shook his head, frown deepening. "The
goddess? No—I saw only Edra." He turned in his saddle, eyeing Calandryll with an expression close to suspicion. "You, too, saw Dera?"

Calandryll nodded. "For a moment, when the sun
shone down." His smile grew wider, no longer tentative. "And last night she spoke with me. In a dream,
I thought; but now . . ."

"Tell me," Bracht urged.

Calandryll outlined all that had been said.

"So—if your . . . dream . . . was true—you've a useful blade." Bracht's face was thoughtful now. "And you, Katya, what did she tell you?"

The warrior woman spoke over the pounding of the hooves, her eyes alight with excitement and, Calandryll realized, something else. It seemed as though a weight were lifted from her, the depression that had assailed her since parting from Tekkan and the Vanu folk banished, her familiar spirit restored in full measure.

"Edra woke me," she told them, "and asked me to walk a while with her. I did—it did not occur to me to refuse and I thought I must tread the paths of sleep, dreaming, though it was a most realistic dream. Like Calandryll, I had forgotten it until I saw her then, but now . . ." She smiled as though savoring the memory, brilliantly. "We walked across a meadow akin to the high grasslands of Vanu, under the moon, though I felt no chill, nor any fear. She told me—still Edra, then—that I need not go on, but might be restored to my own folk, brought safe home to Vanu. I . . ." She looked away a moment and Calandryll thought he saw her blush as she glanced sidelong at Bracht. "I said I could not leave you; that we are sworn to hunt Rhythamun, no matter where he goes or what dangers we face. She became Dera then and told me to hold faith, that although they are bound by laws above man's understanding, the Younger Gods aid us as they can. And that I should not mourn the parting from my people, but take joy in what stands clear before me, offered."

She broke off then, her cheeks darkened beneath their tan, and Calandryll was sure she blushed as Bracht demanded bluntly, "What is that?"

"Love," she said, low-voiced. "Such love as is rare, and to be treasured greatly."

Now—much to Calandryll's surprise—it was the Kern's face that reddened. He shifted uncomfortably in his saddle, staring fixedly ahead awhile, then shrugged and grinned like a boy caught out in some

prank. "You know that I love you," he said, no louder
than she had spoken. "Have I not made that clear?"

"Aye." Katya nodded solemnly, gravity disappearing as she smiled again. "But now our love is blessed,
and I see that I was wrong to grieve so for what must
be. That parting from my people is necessary to our
quest, and that we shall meet again."

Calandryll saw Bracht catch that "our," his face
lighting from within. He thought that were it possible
he should fade discreetly into the background, to
leave these two alone; but that was not possible and
he contented himself with holding silent, a hoofbeat
behind.

"That is good," Bracht said, louder now and
gravely. "And I am pleased you mourn no longer."

"The promise made remains," said Katya. "Not until we bring the Arcanum safe to Vanu and it is
destroyed . . ."

"I know," Bracht said, "and I accept."

"I hope," Katya said, "that it is not too long."

Bracht's laughter rang out at that, startling a flock
of geese that browsed a little distance from the road,
sending the birds skyward on thundering wings,
honking. The skein circled overhead, wary until the
three riders had moved on, then settling back to the
dank grasses.

"One thing in all this troubles me," Bracht announced after a while. "Why did I not see Dera?"

Calandryll pondered a moment, then suggested:
"Mayhap because you are the only one of us without
doubt. When I saw how Rhythamun had used me, I
grew uncertain, I felt his treachery hard; Katya was
saddened by parting. But you, you've never faltered—
mayhap you had no need of Dera's succor."

"Mayhap," the Kern allowed.

"I think it must be that," Katya agreed. "Only you
have never questioned where we go, or what we face."

Bracht nodded without speaking further and
Calandryll wondered at his expression. The Kern's
dark features were set in impassive lines, but in his

eyes there was a clouding, as if he felt less certain. "There are some I'd lief not face again," he murmured lowly, the words not meant to be overheard, but carried back on the wind so that Calandryll caught them. Katya, a little ahead now, did not hear and Calandryll decided against questioning Bracht. Instead, he heeled the chestnut gelding alongside, matching the black stallion's stride, and they spoke no more, only rode, hard, for the north.

THE weather harshened as they came to Wessyl, a wind howling in off the Narrow Sea, herding lowering black billows of threatening cloud across the sky, laden with rain that fell in fierce flurries, the droplets often enough freezing so that they arrived as hail, bouncing off the road and stinging exposed flesh with their insensate attack. The land, too, was bleak, no longer quaggy but rising in great sweeps of desolate heath, scattered with stands of wind-wracked trees and outcrops of the hard grey stone from which the city was built.

It was a forbidding place, unyielding in the dimming light of the rainswept afternoon, set atop a headland that stood guardian over the bight of Eryn, its harbor below, almost a separate town, connected by a long walled avenue to the larger structure above. Sundry vessels lay at anchor, tossed on a choppy sea, lateen-rigged caravels and fishing craft for the most part, but among them the bulkier shapes of single-masted nefs and lean, low warboats. The shipyards of Eryn, Calandryll saw, had been busy, that realization prompting him to wonder how far ahead Tobias might be. The thought was alarming: a progress such as his brother made did not travel fast. The new-hailed Domm and his bride would be feasted by their peers in each town they visited, gifts would be exchanged, treaties renewed, and fresh agreements reached. For all he knew, Tobias might be here in Wessyl. Surely the city would be posted with his likeness, and he wondered, despite Dera's assurance of safe passage through Lysse, how well his disguise would stand up.

He could not help but feel tension grip him as they approached the city gates and he was grateful for the rain and lengthening shadows that allowed him to huddle within his cloak, the cowl drawn forward to conceal his features. It abated somewhat as the guards, deterred from close examination by rain and wind, waved them through with only the briefest admonishment that they entered a peaceful and law-abiding town and had best curb their Kernish ways while sojourning within the walls. Then, as he saw a pillar plastered with an assortment of notices, his proscription among them, the tension returned and he rode again uneasy past rain-washed buildings that seemed to press in suspiciously, their glistening granite walls reminiscent of jail's confines.

He expressed his fears to Bracht and the freesword laughed, assuring him that none should take him for more than a wandering Kern, a mercenary returning home to Cuan na'For. He felt less confident, thinking that Bracht yet rode on the surge of good humor Katya's revelation had launched, but it seemed his comrade was correct, for they found lodgings in a tavern close by the walls and none there paid him especial attention.

"Even so," he declared as they brought their horses into the stable, "I'd not linger here."

"But the one night," Bracht promised, "and so long as it takes us to purchase tents. Beyond that we've no cause to remain."

Calandryll nodded, allowing himself to be mollified by the assurance. "Is this what it feels like to be an outlaw?" he murmured ruefully.

"Within a city's walls, aye." Bracht grinned, and added thoughtfully, "In Cuan na'For it's easier."

Something in his tone prompted Katya to look up from her grooming. "Someday you must tell me about your outlawry," she said, smiling.

Bracht nodded, though his face remained thoughtful, masking some hidden doubt as he replied with, Calandryll thought, a forced lightness, "Someday. Though soon enough I think we shall be in Cuan na'For."

"Shall we?" Katya paused in her currying. "Are you so sure now we'll not find him in Gannshold?"

"Save he delay for some reason, I think not." Bracht shook his head. "Can Tharn lie there? I think not—I think the Mad God rests, as all have said, beyond the world's boundaries, and Rhythamun will not linger along the way but make all haste to his destination."

"But still we might catch up," suggested Calandryll. "If he believes us entrapped in Tezin-dar it might be that he feels no great need of haste."

Bracht shrugged and said, "I think that such as Rhythamun learn little of patience no matter how long they live. I think he'll not remain in Gannshold longer than he must."

"You'd thought to perhaps overtake him," Katya said. "What prompts this change of tune?"

"Dera promised Calandryll safe passage through Lysse," the Kern replied slowly, "yet seemed unaware of Rhythamun's location. Surely she'd know, were he in Gannshold, and have said as much. I fear he's passed on, into Cuan na'For."

"Perhaps," Katya allowed, the admission reluctant. "But still he may linger there."

It came to Calandryll then that she spoke more in hope than true belief, and it dawned upon him that those words she had spoken on the road had held a meaning—a confession, perhaps—that he had not until now fully recognized. She hoped, he felt, that their quest be soon ended as much now from the desire to realize the consummation of the promises exchanged with Bracht as for the reasons that had brought her questing out from Vanu. He did not—could not!— doubt her commitment to the hunt, but now that devotion was lent a greater urgency by the commoner emotion of love. It was hard for them, he realized, to hold such feelings bound by the vows they had made. To ride so long together unable, thanks to those vows, to indulge, physically, the desire they felt, forbidden by their honor. Honor, he thought, was a strange thing, and hard-won, hard to hold; and both these comrades were honorable. Once more, he felt like an intruder, busying himself with his horse as Bracht said softly, "If Ahrd wills it, so shall it be. But still I think we must go farther."

"To the Borrhun-maj and beyond?" said Katya, question and resignation mingled in her voice.

"Where we must," said Bracht.

Katya ducked her head, torchlight striking silver sparks from her flaxen hair.

"So let's be done here," Bracht said firmly, "and eat and find our beds. And be soonest gone from this dismal city."

"Aye!" Katya smiled across the horses. "As soon we may."

By common accord they finished grooming the animals, saw them fed, and went into the tavern.

Calandryll's fears proved groundless: they attracted no more attention than any other patrons, finding a table, as had become their habit, to the rear of the common room where they ordered a meal and mugs of ale. The folk of Wessyl were, it seemed, largely uncommunicative, for neither the landlord nor any of the guests attempted to engage them in conversation as the southerly folk had done. Instead, they were served mostly in silence and what questions they ventured answered curtly, as if folk in Wessyl kept themselves to themselves and met the inquiries of strangers with a grim and taciturn courtesy. Of Daven Tyras they learned nothing, which was not particularly surprising: it was far easier for a traveler to slip unnoticed through a city than to escape attention in the caravanserais along the road. That they gained on Tobias and his retinue was more disturbing, and Calandryll thought they should perhaps avoid Eryn and travel overland to Gannshold in hopes his brother lingered at the shipyards. He felt more confident now that he could pass for a Kern among strangers, but should Tobias lay eyes on him . . . Surely his own sibling must see through his disguise. Him, or Nadama, or any number of the retainers who had known the young prince Calandryll den Karynth in Secca.

He voiced his thoughts to Bracht and Katya as they ate grilled fish, and they agreed that they should quit the road where it curved around the bight into Eryn to travel cross-country to the Gann Peaks.

"But Gannshold we cannot avoid," Katya warned. "Even though Rhythamun be gone, still we must learn what we may there."

"I doubt a half-blood trader in horses and the Domm of Secca hold common company," Bracht reassured, "and mayhap your brother is already departed. Even be he there, we'll not be invited to sup at the same table."

"But if he sees me in the streets . . ." Calandryll argued.

"He'll see a freesword Kern all swathed in cloak against the cold"—Bracht grinned—"not his runaway brother. Rest easy, Calan."

"Nadama would know me," Calandryll muttered in reply, "I think."

"You made so great an impression, eh?" Bracht chuckled wickedly. "Even wed to your brother, she holds your handsome face locked forever in her memory?"

Calandryll grinned back, a trifle shamefaced: his own memories of Nadama were dulled and dimmed by time—would she truly remember him so well? Likely, he decided, Bracht was right and he could pass by them all as invisible as he had departing Secca. He shrugged, setting aside his doubts, and emptied his mug.

Soon after they found their rooms, the tavern not so popular that they need share, but each given their own chamber. Calandryll's stood at the building's corner, affording him two windows overlooking Wessyl.

One faced across the steepled rooftops of the upper
city, the other down toward the mouth of the bight,
and for a while he leaned his elbows on the stone of
the sill, peering out. The night was dark, the filled
moon obscured by cloud, the wind gusting lonely
through streets that held no people. Lanterns flickered there and he could make out the twin lines indicating the avenue running down to the harbor. The
sea was an oily wash, booming distantly on moles and
breakwaters, the ships moored there indistinct, blending into the darkness. He thought of the bellicose vessels he had seen and wondered if in them he discerned
some design of his brother's beyond the mere defense
of Lysse's sea-lanes. The rumors heard along the road
to Wessyl had spoken of Tobias calling for war with
Kandahar and those nefs, with their high castles for
archers and arbalests, were not such craft as would
ride guardian to merchantmen. That duty was for the
sleek, fast-moving warboats: the nefs were designed
to carry soldiery, to attack landward and deposit their
troops to storm shore defenses.

Did Tobias truly intend war, then? Was the reason
for his progress to persuade his fellow Domms to that
cause? He had spoken for that in Secca, when Varent
den Tarl had first come, and Bylath had spoken him
down. But now Bylath was dead and Tobias ruled—
perhaps the clouds of war did gather. Calandryll shuddered, thinking that if that was so it must surely be
sign that Tharn even now wielded some influence,
that even dreaming the Mad God reached out to sully
the world.

And opposed against his chaotic purpose there were
but three.

It was a disconcerting thought, no matter that he
had the assurance of a goddess he held the means of
Rhythamun's defeat within him. He could not see it,
and on so gloomy a night it was hard to find the
surety that had filled him as Dera spoke her enigmatic promise. Easier, as he stared out, rain splashing
against his face, to slip back into the mood of doubt,

the grim despondency, that had gripped him before. In the eye of his mind he conjured once more that dreamlike conversation and, to his pleasant surprise, the looming doubt dissolved; in its place he felt an abstruse confidence, as if the goddess, with words and touch, had imbued him with a conviction beyond his understanding. He could not define it, nor put a shape to it, but still it was there: he knew. And that, of itself, was a gift. Reassured, he drew the shutters closed and turned to his bed.

Sleep came easily, sound and empty of dreams, disturbed finally by the insistent tapping that intruded on his slumber. He opened his eyes to darkness, yawning, a hand reaching instinctively for the straightsword set on the counterpane beside him. Left hand about the scabbard, right on the sword's hilt, he padded shivering to the door. The chamber was cold and the bare stones of the floor struck chill against his feet. It seemed the innkeepers of Wessyl were as sparing of heat as they were of conversation. Sleepily, he demanded who woke him and from the corridor outside came Bracht's voice: he slipped the latch.

"An early start, we said," the grinning Kern declared, striding past Calandryll to throw back the shutters. "Put up your sword and put on your clothes."

His good humor was answered with a grunt, through teeth clenched against the cold. His fortitude, Calandryll decided, had its drawbacks, but he tossed the sheathed sword to the bed and went to the washstand, not particularly surprised to find a thin coating of ice riming the ewer. He gasped as he bathed his face and chest, hurriedly drying himself and tugging on his clothing.

Through the window he saw milky fog enveloping the city, all hung with glittering ice crystals, dulling what little sound there was at so early an hour. The harbor was lost in the brume; indeed, it was impossible to see farther than the nearest buildings. It reminded him of Vishat'yi and he wondered briefly how

Menelian fared as he laced his tunic and belted his sword to his waist.

"So, breakfast, tents, and we depart," Bracht said cheerfully. "Come—Katya will join us at table."

Calandryll hung his cloak about his shoulders, grateful for its warmth, and picked up his saddlebags, following Kern out and down a flight of stone stairs to the common room.

That was little warmer than the upper level, a sleepy-eyed drudge with soot-smeared cheeks and sacklike gown feeding fresh logs to the fire, the innkeeper yawning hugely as he emerged from the kitchen, seemingly surprised to find any guests about so early. Scratching his head he grumpily advised them that his kitchen folk were barely awake and the best he could offer was porridge and yesterday's bread, his ovens not yet fired.

"Then that must do," Bracht said, his good cheer unaffected by the man's poor humor. "And information—where might we purchase tents?"

"Sailmakers Gate."

The innkeeper sniffed and turned to leave, halted by Bracht's raised hand. "And where is that found? Mayhap you've not noticed we're strangers here."

The man favored the Kern with a sour look and began to mumble something about freeswords, thinking better of it as Bracht casually fingered the hilt of his dirk, still smiling with his mouth. Instead he gave them directions, scowling as he was dismissed with a careless wave.

"Unfriendly folk," Bracht murmured.

"Aye."

Calandryll was not yet disposed to conversation, but when Katya joined them moments later she and Bracht made up for his silence. She greeted them with a smile, enthusiastically spooning the porridge delivered to their table, talking cheerfully of their departure, and before long Calandryll shook off his sleepiness, his comrades' vitality awakening his own spirits. It was, indeed, heartening to think that soon they would put this grey and gloomy city behind them.

Their bellies filled, they settled their account with Rhythamun's coin and fetched their horses from the stable. The fog still hung thick upon the upper city, but as they descended the long avenue leading to the waterfront a breeze got up, blowing in off the Narrow Sea to tatter the mist and send it skirling in heavy tendrils about the streets. They found the Sailmakers Gate and negotiated the purchase of three small tents, fashioned of stout canvas, with sturdy groundsheets, that they lashed behind their saddles. Then, with no further reason to remain in Wessyl, they rode back up the avenue and found the same gate through which they had entered. None looked back as they trotted northward through the fog.

THE moorland remained enshrouded throughout the day, slowing their progress so that they elected to pass the night in the caravanserai they encountered a little while before sunset. They found a better welcome there, the landlord willing enough to talk, and from him they discovered that a man answering to their description of Daven Tryas had passed by some time before, also that Tobias and his retinue were now not long ahead. They quit the hostelry at dawn, the fog dissipated during the night and the day coming clear and cold, the sky a pale blue save where the sun bathed the welkin with gold. They made better time, passing the night in the tents and the next day drawing close to Eryn.

The road curved to the northwest here, following the coastline around the innermost recess of the great bight to enter the shipyard city. From there it ran due north to Gannshold and Calandryll, drawing on his memories of books and maps long studied in Secca, calculated they should find it again several leagues inland. Of the country they must cross he knew little, beyond that it climbed over stony moors to the Gann

Peaks, a lonely and largely unpeopled terrain, the domain of isolated wildfowlers and huntsmen, where
hospitality would be hard found.

"Likely swift as the road," Bracht declared as they
turned off the raised flagstones onto a sweep of coarse
grass dotted with stunted heather. "And an unlikely
place to encounter your brother."

Calandryll agreed, heeling the chestnut gelding to
match pace with the Kern's stallion as Bracht gave the
big horse his head.

They thundered over the grass, hooves leaving a
trail of divots, the moorland spreading wide before
them, a harlequin pattern of green brightened by the
blue of heather and the gold of broom, silver where
little streams bisected the moss and grass. Curlews
sang their bubbling song and snipe chippered; lap-
wings and redshanks scattered at their passage, and
overhead buzzards and peregrines circled hopefully. It
felt good to gallop through so free a landscape and
Calandryll gave himself over to the exhilaration of
the ride.

When all three animals had had their fill of running they slowed to a steady canter, halting when the
watery sun reached its zenith to rest awhile and eat
before proceeding on until twilight. They camped
then, in the fold of a low hill that broke the cooling
assault of the wind, a stream tinkling by its foot, their
fire cheerful as night fell, the horses hobbled and
cropping contentedly on the sturdy grass. Bracht produced snares from his saddlebags and set them out on
the far side of the hill, promising they should eat hare
or rabbit on the morrow, and Calandryll thought that
he could live happily in such a way forever, the comforts he had taken for granted in his father's palace
seeming now like some dream. He chuckled as he
stretched out in his tent, listening to the wind, wondering where Tobias slept this night and what his
brother might think of him now.

Probably that he was a greater threat than ever, he
decided, for he felt now that he could defeat Tobias in

honest fight, thinking then of what Bracht had said, that likely someday there must come an accounting. Perhaps, he mused as sleep weighted his eyes, but on some other day, when matters of far greater importance were settled. Save that he represented a dangerous hindrance to their quest, Tobias seemed of little moment now, a problem to be confronted at need, not dwelt upon. His ambition seemed petty in light of the threat facing all the world, and even the knowledge that he had commissioned the assassination of their father failed to stir in Calandryll any very fierce response. He wondered if he should feel some deeper emotion about that slaying, but could not: it was as though Bylath, on that far-off day when he had struck his younger son and so clearly demonstrated his contempt, had severed all ties between them, electing his own fate. Perhaps someday he would confront Tobias with that crime and demand he answer, but for now matters of far greater weight occupied him and he set such thoughts aside. He became with each passing day, it occurred to him as he folded his cloak warmer about his chin, more like the pragmatic Kern who had befriended him a year ago. It felt far longer—as if he had known Bracht all his life—and on that thought he slept.

Morning saw the Kern's promise fulfilled and they breakfasted on two plump hares before continuing on across the empty landscape toward Gannshold. Neither fog nor rain conspired to hinder them and they made good time over the moors, the ground rising steadily as they drew ever closer to the mountains ahead, the gorse and heather interspersed now with stands of scrubby, windswept juniper and cottonwood. They encountered no one save a distant figure that watched them from a ridge, wary, as though suspicious of interlopers, and in two more days they came to the road again.

It was late in the morning, the sun close to its midmost point, shining out of a sky the color of a duck's egg and streaked with long mare's-tails of cirrus blown out by the high north wind. They cantered at a steady pace, thinking that soon they should halt to eat and rest the animals, Gannshold now only a few days distant. Bracht was a little way ahead, topping a low rise, when he slowed the stallion to a walk, lifting a hand in warning. Calandryll and Katya reined in, coming alongside the Kern, who indicated with a nod the sight that had prompted his caution.

The road dipped before them, running straight across a shallow valley, a stream at its center spanned by a small bridge. The approach to the bridge was lined on either side with a procession of colorful wagons and carriages, their teams set out on picket lines to graze, as on the grass beside the water servants bustled about a pavilion of black and green stripes under the laughing eyes of women in luxurious traveling gowns and men in light armor.

From the carts and the poles set about the pavilion fluttered pennants in the same colors, black and green: those of Secca.

Calandryll gasped, scanning the crowd, recognizing the insignia that decorated the silver breastplates and halfhelms of the soldiers, the livery of the servitors. In a low voice, as if afraid he might be overheard, he said, "Tobias."

Bracht nodded. "Nor any way to go save forward."

"Can we not ride around?"

Calandryll looked inland, thinking that they could quit the road here and cross the stream farther up the valley; knowing even as he said it that so obvious a detour must surely arouse suspicion.

Katya confirmed his doubt with a gesture at the archers set about the perimeter of the gathering, who even now nocked their bows, staring at the three riders. "They see us," she remarked coolly. "Do we seek to avoid them, they'll likely seek to know why."

"And look to run us down," Bracht added, his eyes moving to the mail-clad lancers standing to the rear of the bowmen. "Taking us for scouts for some robber band."

Calandryll mouthed a curse as a sergeant shouted something, pointing toward them, his words relayed so that a familiar figure detached itself from the throng around the tent, striding proudly to the fore of the crowd.

Sunlight sparkled on polished armor as the man raised a hand to shade his eyes, peering toward the low ridge. His head was bare, the leonine mass of his reddish-brown hair tousled by the wind, and despite the distance between them, sufficient that individual features were blurred, Calandryll knew that he looked on his brother. He felt cold fingers of anticipation scratch his spine, convinced that at any moment Tobias must recognize him and send the lancers of the Palace Guard galloping to attack, that the bows must be drawn to shower arrows on him. He licked lips gone dry as Tobias turned to speak with those closest to him, and saw a woman move to his side, her auburn hair gathered in a snood. His brother draped an arm about her shoulders, saying something that brought a smile to her full lips and a flurry of laughter from the attendant entourage. Calandryll recognized Nadama, and in some part of his mind not numbed by dread saw that she was still lovely. He was absently pleased to find that sight of her brought no pang of loss, but perhaps that was simply because fear of recognition outweighed all else.

"Best we proceed," Bracht decided.

"He'll surely know me," Calandryll objected.

The Kern glanced at him, appraisingly. "Shall the Domm of Secca pay so much attention to a wandering freesword?" He shook his head, answering his own question. "Come—they've seen us now and to avoid them must surely bring them after us. If worst arrives at worst, we ride through."

Confidently, he heeled the stallion up to a trot, leaving Calandryll no choice but to follow, down the slope toward the bridge. Toward the brother who sought his death.

As a drowning man clutches at the merest straw,

so he sought the talisman of Dera's promise, but still
he felt his heart beat faster as they drew nearer the
watching crowd. It seemed his skin prickled as he saw
the half-drawn bows, thinking that it needed but a
word from Tobias to lift him, pincushioned with
shafts, from the saddle; that his horse was wearied by
the morning's ride while the chargers of the Palace
Guard were rested, fresh.

From the corner of his mouth Bracht said, "You are
Calan, a warrior of Cuan na'For. Remember only
that."

Calandryll's own mouth was too dry to venture a
response. Silently, he cursed the arrogance that left
the road so narrowed by his brother's train: the vehi-
cles occupied sufficient space that he could not even
find refuge between his companions, but must fall
into single file to pass between the blockage. That
was typical of Tobias, he thought, to assume owner-
ship where he had no right. Anger rose to join his
trepidation.

"Better," Bracht murmured. "Hold that prideful expression."

Ahead the bowmen clustered in a watchful knot.
From beside the stream servants called, announcing
the readiness of the midday meal.

If the lancers of the Palace Guard come out,
Calandryll thought, *they will surely know me. If To-*
bias or Nadama see me close, they will surely know
me. He clenched his teeth, heart drumming madly
against his ribs; faster, it seemed, than the hooves of
his mount clattered on the flags of the road, and
louder. He did his best to stare ahead, to act the part
assigned him, only to find his eyes drawn irresistibly
toward the onlookers, as if some psychic magnet
tugged his gaze toward Tobias. His brother had aged,
he saw, his handsome face harder, lines etched about
his patrician mouth, his eyes containing something
more than his remembered arrogance, something cold
and implacable.

They were almost level with the archers now and

Bracht slowed again as the soldiers pressed in on the road, soothing the big stallion as he snorted and pranced, sensing his rider's tension. Katya's grey caught the mood and curvetted nervously: Calandryll held his chestnut on a tight rein as the gelding whickered, stamping. The sergeant who had first warned of their approach stepped forward, a hand casual upon his sword's hilt. Behind him his men waited. Behind them Tobias stared hard at the three riders. For a moment his eyes met Calandryll's and the younger brother thought that surely his time had come, that the order must be given to attack and he must fall here, on this stretch of lonely road, his quest undone, the way left clear for Rhythamun. Then Tobias's haughty gaze passed over him, and the Domm leaned closer to Nadama, spoke into her ear. She laughed again, teeth bright between the red of her lips. Calandryll felt sure the comment was about him: he tensed, thinking that if one bow lifted toward him he would draw sword and put heel to horse.

Instead, Tobias turned away, drawing Nadama with him as they moved toward the pavilion: three itinerant Kerns of only transitory interest to the Domm of Secca.

"Careful, lest he bite. Armed men make him nervous."

Bracht favored the sergeant with an easy smile, loosing just enough rein that the stallion could turn his head and bare yellow teeth at the soldier. The man stepped out of his path, eyeing the Kern and his comrades with the dispassionate suspicion of the professional soldier.

"You've a fine animal." His eyes traveled leisurely over the black horse, on to the grey and the chestnut. "All of you."

"Aye," Bracht agreed, "we prize our beasts in Cuan na'For."

The sergeant nodded and motioned for his men to clear the road. Calandryll rode past him, certain that at any moment recognition must dawn, the prickling

that had afflicted his chest reasserting itself across his
back as he went by the archers. He saw Tobias and
Nadama disappear inside the pavilion. Then he was
past the last of the bowmen and clattering onto the
bridge, lifting the chestnut to a canter as, ahead,
Bracht gathered speed, conscious of sweat cold on face
and ribs.

Katya moved to his side as they crossed the valley,
smiling. "You can let out your breath now," she advised.

He had not known he held it until he heard himself
sigh, and then he shuddered, breathing deep, sucking
in great lungfuls of air as the road rose again, climbing
the farther slope over the ridge that cut off sight of
the pavilion and the clustered wagons and all the folk
who might have known him. He shook his head, not
yet ready to speak, confused by the emotions that
racked him. Fear had been there, that he could readily
admit, but fear was no longer unfamiliar and he had
learned to control it, and knew that what he felt was
more than fear. It was, perhaps, the presence, the
sight, of his brother—the knowledge that had Tobias
recognized him, he would not have hesitated to order
his execution—forcing upon him the stark realization
that he no longer had home or family in a manner no
longer abstract but immediate and physical. Perhaps
equally the sight of Tobias and Nadama together, the
real and physical reminder that the woman he had
once loved now chose his brother. It had been easy
enough to accept those facts distanced by geography
and time, but to see them—to know them—for reality
was to confront their immediacy. He shook his head
again, suddenly aware that his eyes blurred tearily,
and raised a hand to wipe the moisture from his
cheeks. Not speaking, Katya reached across to touch
his shoulder and he smiled thinly, grateful for her
silent sympathy.

Bracht grinned and said, "I disguised you well—
they saw only a warrior of Cuan na'For," then gestured that they speed their pace.

"Or Dera blinded them," Calandryll murmured, feeling guilt now, that he had doubted the promise of the goddess. He heeled the chestnut to a gallop, giving himself over to the act of riding as he sought to match the longer stride of the Kern's stallion, letting the wind blow away his confusion.

They rode thus until the horses began to tire and then halted to eat, confident that Tobias and his retinue lay leagues behind them. From the size of the Seccan party and its leisurely manner it was obvious they would reach Gannshold long before the city could be posted with Calandryll's likeness, and that was a comfort that cheered him: by the time night descended on the moorlands and they made camp he had put away his disharmony and once more found calm, consigning both his brother and the woman he had once thought he loved to the hindmost part of his memory.

THE next day the Gann Peaks loomed dark across the horizon, and in another the moors gave sway to foothills, all dotted with thickening pine and larch that spread a patterned canopy of myriad greens, all glossy with the promise of spring, over the slopes. The road rose steadily through the timber, climbing ever upward toward the beckoning mountains, built through deep cuts walled with blue-grey granite and across arching bridges over couloirs where streams foamed fierce, curving in serpentine terraces up slopes where pines grew precarious and along valleys bright with flowers. By day raptors hung in the sky above and at night owls hooted. On the third day they came to the gates of Gannshold.

11

*K*ESHAM-VAJ still smoldered, the sky lit red by the fires that still burned, the night still redolent of almonds and the carrion stench of corpses. Inside the Tyrant's great pavilion censers filled the air with the sweeter odor of incense and roasting meat was only a little tainted by the malodorous aftermath of battle. Xenomenus, by habit fastidious, waved a perfumed handkerchief about his face, beaming hugely as his captains reported the great victory.

The rebel forces withdrew in disarray, scurrying like rats desperate to abandon a sinking ship from the plateau. They retreated eastward, into the Fayne, likely to group on Sathoman ek'Hennem's keep, looking to establish a defensive line between the Tyrant's armies and the coastal cities they still held. Cavalry and mounted archers harried them, and the Fayne Lord still lived, still lofted the banner of rebellion, but this day's victory belonged to Xenomenus and ere long blockaded Mhazomul and Mherut-yi must fall. It was a question of pressing onward, of cutting supply lines to isolate the coastal settlements totally, starve out the defenders. It would not be done overnight; indeed, it might not be done inside this year's ending, even—this with wary, sidelong glances at the black-robed sorcerers who stood behind the Tyrant—with the aid Xenomenus commanded. It was a beginning, a glorious beginning, with the summer to march and fight, that progress inevitably slowed by winter, but come the next year's spring—summer at the latest— and all Kandahar should once more bow to its rightful ruler and Sathoman ek'Hennem's head decorate the walls of Nhur-jabal.

"Quite. Well done." Xenomenus pressed the hand-kerchief to his nose—Burash, but these soldiers smelled of sweat and blood and steel, of dragon-hide armor worn too long!—his smile unwavering, for this was, truly, a mighty victory, a vindication of his belief. "Let all the companies celebrate. Wine shall be sent them."

"And the war?" his commanders asked. "When do we march on?"

"Word shall be sent you," Xenomenus promised. "That decision I shall take on the morrow. For now, I'd take my ease."

A languid hand dismissed the officers and they quit the pavilion, not complaining overmuch, for they were, largely, plain soldiers, their faith put more in steel than sorcery, and what they had witnessed in the taking of this town raised memories of the Sorcerers' War, which most had sooner forgotten. But still none spoke against the aid they had, for Kesham-vaj had been horribly defended and without the cabal might never have been taken.

His captains gone, Xenomenus beckoned his sorcerers closer, Anomius stepping closest of all.

"Was I not correct?" he asked, anticipating only agreement. "Some among you, I know, would have left this man forgotten in the dungeons. Now see— has he not given us Kesham-vaj? Given us our first triumph?"

Anomius simpered, bowing and beaming. Lykander said, "Indeed, Lord Xenomenus. There was great wisdom in that decision."

He ducked his head, hands folding across the swell

of his belly, accepting the wave of acknowledgment the Tyrant granted him, not seeing the contemptuous glance Anomius flung his way.

"Aye," said Xenomenus complacently. "There was, and now Kesham-vaj is mine again and Sathoman ek'Hennem in retreat. But"—his weak face assumed an expression he believed stern—"the war is not yet over. We've work yet to do. And this news out of Lysse disturbs me."

"I think you've little need to worry on that score," Lykander said. "That land is poor in thaumaturgists, and what there are scarce able to stand against us."

"Mayhap," Xenomenus allowed, "but still my spies tell me there's a navy founded. War craft already anchored off Eryn and Wessyl—should Lysse decide to take a hand . . ."

He paused, handkerchief fluttering, and Lykander said, "They've not the time, Lord Tyrant. Before that fleet may sail we'll once more hold the coastal cities, and still our navy is the greater, even now."

Xenomenus pursed his lips. "Would that Bylath yet ruled in Secca," he murmured. "That son of his— Tobias, may Burash rot his eyes!—looks to command the Narrow Sea, I think. There's ambition in that whelp and I'd not be surprised did he look to make himself Tyrant of Lysse."

"Surely not, Lord," murmured Caranthus, his voice soft, his smile deliberately reassuring. "Were that his aim, he must conquer all the cities; and the cities of Lysse are renowned for their independence. Were that his aim, why—he must fight a war over all Lysse before he might think of assaulting Kandahar."

"There's that," said Xenomenus. "But what if he persuaded the Domms of Lysse to offer alliance with ek'Hennem? What then, eh?"

"He's still to see the navy built," said Lemomal, "and to convince his fellow Domms to his cause. If that be his intention."

"Before he can hope to do that," said Lykander, "you shall have your victory over the rebels."

"Shall I?" the Tyrant asked, the question directed at Anomius.

"You shall," said the little man, his parchment pale scalp shining as he ducked his head. "My word on it."

Xenomenus brought the handkerchief closer to his nose: for all that he was useful, still Anomius carried about him an odor most offensive, as if things rotted in his mouth, or some internal decay corrupted his flesh, loosing foulness where he went. Indeed, had he not proven his worth—and still promised success to come—Xenomenus would have ordered his sorcerers to unleash the gramaryes they assured him pertained and had Anomius destroyed. His smile was hard to retain, this close to the mage, and he leaned back in his great chair.

"I trust so," he murmured.

"It shall be so," said Anomius with utter confidence. "You shall see Sathoman driven from all your cities, back to Fayne Keep. And then that stronghold shall be razed. I promise it."

He flourished a bow that was somewhat spoilt by the drip it loosed from his bulbous nose, falling to join whatever else decorated the frontage of his robe. Xenomenus preferred not to contemplate what those smears and stains might be; indeed, he preferred to avoid Anomius altogether. Had the ugly little man not been so valuable . . . He pushed the thought away, not entirely certain the wizard did not read his mind.

"I shall hold you to that," he said. Then, softer, "But I wonder if something should not be done about Tobias den Karynth."

"He can be slain," said Anomius, eager as a fighting dog that scents blood. "There are ways, Lord, be I allowed."

He raised his arms, the soiled cuffs of his robe falling back to expose the bracelets bound about his wrists, the gesture deliberately significant. At his back, Cenobar and Rassuman fixed warning eyes on the Tyrant; Andrycus shook his head vigorously.

Xenomenus's smile thinned as he, too, shook his

head, his response carefully ambiguous. "Not yet, I think," he said. "I'd not have Kandahar accused of interference in the affairs of Lysse . . . not yet, at least."

Anomius shrugged, letting his sleeves drop back, covering the magical bonds. *The puppy weakens,* he thought, *he learns a need of me and in time he'll order me freed. And then I shall teach these Tyrant's sorcerers what real magic is. For now, though, I've enough—Cennaire in Lysse; the puppy learning trust. I've time. Oh, certainly I have time.* He twisted fleshy lips in semblance of a humble smile, his watery blue eyes hooded.

"For now," he heard Xenomenus announce, "we've sufficient. This Lyssian navy, this ambitious Domm: both problems for another day. I grow weary, gentlemen—do you leave me now."

The sorcerers bowed and departed the pavilion for their own subfusc canopy as servants began to lay a table before the Tyrant and musicians commenced a soothing tune. Cenobar looked toward the ravaged town and shaped a small gesture intended for Rassuman's eyes alone. Those, for all their age, caught it and answered, catching Andrycus's attention, he nodding slightly. *Later,* the signals said, *in privacy.*

THE very air shimmered with the force of the spell the three cast, as if fire, cold and unseen, burned about them, securing the hut from unwanted observation both physical and occult. It lay outside the ravaged walls of Kesham-vaj, and some distance from the tents of Tyrant and sorcerers and commanders, likely once some herdsman's hut, now, for all its frugal comforts, the site of conspiracy. They sat upon rough stools about a crude table, their faces illuminated by a light invisible beyond the bare stone walls, grave with the import—the inherent danger—of what they discussed.

"He waxes stronger," Cenobar said, "and for all

he's the look of a grave-worm about him, his tongue is subtle."

"Aye, and the taking of this place elevates him," said Andrycus, stroking absently at a hand smooth-fleshed and pink as a babe's. "Ere long he'll have Xenomenus's trust."

"I think," said Rassuman, older than his companions and calmer, "you misjudge our Tyrant there. I think he's little enough love for Anomius, save as a tool. Do we bring Sathoman ek'Hennem down and then, I suspect, Xenomenus will order him slain."

"If he may be, then," said Cenobar gloomily. "There's greater occult power in that one than I'd suspected."

"You think he may find a way to break his bonds?" asked Andrycus.

Cenobar shrugged, leaving Rassuman to answer: "Not yet. In time, perhaps, were our vigilance relaxed. Or he found allies."

"Lykander?" Andrycus demanded. "Surely not even he . . ."

"As Cenobar points out, he's a subtle tongue," said Rassuman, "and our plump colleague was never immune to flattery. Nor lacking in his own ambition."

"What should Anomius promise him?" Andrycus asked. "What could he promise him?"

"Power unlimited." The older sorcerer's voice was soft with warning. "Power undreamed of."

"The Arcanum?" Andrycus shook his head vigorously. "Surely Lykander must denounce him, did he make so insane an offer."

"How should he know?" asked Cenobar. "He believes Calandryll and the others chase a grimoire, not that fell tome."

"Do you forget Menelian?" Rassuman said, somber now. "Of all the lesser wizards he was the strongest— but still he died."

Cenobar ducked his head, in both agreement and mourning. "But Menelian told the revenant nothing.

Surely Anomius still believes he sends her after a grimoire?"

"He sent her to Lysse," returned Rassuman, "and does she succeed—does she catch up with them— what shall she then learn? Surely that the object of their quest is no mere grimoire, but the Arcanum itself."

"Even then," Cenobar said slowly, assembling his thoughts, "they do not have the book. Poor Menelian told us that much—that this Rhythamun took it from them—so, though she may well take revenge on Anomius's behalf, still she'll not have the book."

Rassuman nodded, his patrician features solemn. "I'd lief they escape her attentions," he murmured, "but do they not, then surely she must learn the true nature of their quest and report that knowledge to Anomius. And once he knows . . . shall he prove so different to Rhythamun?"

"Would even he?" gasped Andrycus.

"I believe he would," said Rassuman. "Cenobar?"

The younger sorcerer nodded. "I believe him mad," he said. "I believe that if he learned of the Arcanum he'd vie with Rhythamun to have it for himself."

"Then we must destroy him!" Andrycus cried. "Him and the revenant's heart, both!"

"He's protected too well," returned Rassuman, his voice edged harsh with chagrin. "By his own gramaryes now, and by Lykander."

"Surely if we told Lykander, told the others, what we know," said Andrycus, "then they'd side with us. Given that knowledge, even Xenomenus must surely grant permission to slay him."

"I think our Tyrant might well find a way to delay any such decision," Rassuman said. "For all he's a weaker man than his father—and he weaker than Dyomanus—still he's no fool. None can deny the Fayne Lord is the greatest threat Kandahar has known, and until that temporal danger is ended, I think Xenomenus will keep Anomius alive; no matter what arguments we lay before him.

"More—Lykander and the rest saw the same disturbance in the occult fundus we discerned, but chose to ignore it. Shall they of a sudden shift their beliefs? We voiced our concerns before: with little enough effect, and I doubt they'll change their minds now."

"And their magic protects him," added Cenobar. "No less than his own. We three, alone, could not destroy him."

"Mayhap we cannot convince Lykander," Andrycus argued, "but what of Caranthus? Lemomal and Padruar?"

"Lemomal allies with Lykander," Rassuman said, "seeing him chief among our circle. Caranthus is blind in his allegiance to the office of Tyrant. Padruar, perhaps, might be persuaded; but Padruar is a great sitter on fences and I suspect that did we approach him, he might well look to balance our arguments against those of Lykander—which would almost certainly prove a roundabout way of telling Anomius all we know."

"Still I cannot believe Lykander would lend himself to Tharn's raising," Andrycus said.

"Nor I," Rassuman agreed. "Caranthus, Lemomal, Padruar even less. But neither can I believe they would agree to destroy Anomius. At least, not until his purpose is served."

"When he may prove too strong to destroy," said Cenobar.

"Perhaps," said Rassuman. "But we of the inner circle, together—then I think it could be done."

"You say we must wait?" asked Andrycus. "Until the rebellion is quelled? What then of this Lyssian navy? This Domm of Secca? Might Xenomenus not then find further use for Anomius?"

"Those things the inner circle and our own soldiery can defeat," said Rassuman. "Should worse come to worst, then it may be we take Anomius's course and slay this Tobias den Karynth. But until the rebels are defeated, I think Anomius stands inviolate."

"Burash!" cried Andrycus. "He'll find a place among us at this rate."

"Has he not already?" asked Cenobar sourly. "More to the point—what are we to do? If we cannot convince Lykander and the others he should be slain— and I agree that's an unlikely optimism—then his foul revenant continues to roam free, and does she find her prey . . ."

"Then Anomius must learn of the Arcanum," Andrycus finished.

"Worse than that," said Rassuman.

"Worse?" Andrycus stared in horror at the older man. "What could be worse?"

"That she slay them," came the grim answer. "That she slay them and leave the field to Rhythamun, or Anomius. That she leave the way open to the resurrection of the Mad God."

Andrycus groaned, hands—natural and new-grown—rising to brush helplessly at his long hair. Cenobar asked, "What of Vanu? Calandryll and Bracht came to Vishat-yi on a Vanu warboat, with Vanu folk, Menelian said. The woman, Katya, was sent by the holy men of that land. And all our scrying told of three questers. What part is taken by the holy men?"

"I know not." Rassuman shrugged. "Only what Menelian told us—that the holy men of Vanu would have the book to destroy it."

"Better it had remained in Tezin-dar," Andrycus muttered.

"Undoubtedly," said Rassuman. "But it did not. And had it, still I think there would have come another Rhythamun. So the world turns, my friend, and until the Arcanum is destroyed the threat of Tharn's raising remains with us."

"We should have seen it clearer," said Andrycus. "We should have acted sooner."

"Best we forget such should haves, such mayhaps," said Rassuman, stern enough the younger man was shaken from his gloom. "Better we turn our eyes forward, to what we can do, not waste our time looking back at what we might have done."

"What can we do?" asked Cenobar. "It would seem our hands are tied: Anomius is a danger we cannot as yet eliminate, and Rhythamun goes free—to Tharn's resting place, we must assume—while those who might halt him are stalked by Anomius's revenant. We cannot even rely on the aid of our fellow sorcerers."

"Might we not slay the revenant?" wondered Andrycus. "End that threat, at the least."

"Save we secure her heart, no," said Rassuman.

"Then let us attempt that," urged Andrycus.

"Of that we thought, "Cenobar said, "but Anomius binds it with gramaryes. Whether he carries it with him, or it rests in Nhur-jabal, we cannot know. Only that did we destroy it, he should know on the instant. Even did we draw close, he should know."

"Let him know!" Andrycus rasped, extending his healed hand: a challenge. "This cost me pain and even did the destroying anger him, I'd willingly match my magic against his."

"Again?" asked Rassuman, the mild question edged. "When we faced him before the cost was your hand and Zytharan's life. He was powerful then; and now . . . now he's stronger."

"Thanks to Lykander," grunted Andrycus. "But even so, prepared, we three in concert . . ."

"Should earn Xenomenus's displeasure," Cenobar interrupted. "Burash knows, Andrycus, that I mourn Zytharan—Menelian, too—and no less your pain, but the little worm's seduced our Tyrant and Lykander, too. Remember his promise, when we brought him from the oubliette—that the revenant was the price of his aid."

"Aye," said Rassuman solemnly, "and he's crazed enough with lust for vengeance that he'd hold that promise. Did we destroy the woman's heart, then I think he'd sooner die than aid us in this war."

"And Xenomenus looks to end it swift," said

Cenobar. "And without Anomius to undo those gramaryes he cast, it must be a long and costly campaign.
Ergo, while the Tyrant needs him he stands inviolate. Him and his revenant, both."

"Then we can do nothing!" moaned Andrycus.
"Save stand by and watch the world brought down in
chaos."

"Courage!" Rassuman advised, his voice stern.
"For now I think we can only watch and wait—but as
the hunter watches: patiently, biding our time, ready
to strike. We must be subtle, and look to more than
magic to further our cause. Certainly, Anomius's ability to undo those gramaryes of protection that defend
the rebel's holdings endow him with importance, but
still our skills are needed. Xenomenus must not be allowed to forget that—that while Anomius is valuable,
still we are needed. Neither that Anomius served
ek'Hennem and turned his coat—that he may look to
turn again."

"And Lykander," Cenobar murmured thoughtfully.
"We might well remind him that as Anomius's star
burns brighter, so is he overshadowed."

"You see the gist of it." Rassuman smiled. "Our
tongues may do what spells cannot. We must look to
undermine this upstart where we can."

"But still there's the revenant," said Andrycus.

"Whom as yet we cannot touch," said Rassuman.
"But do we watch . . . carefully, patiently . . . then
mayhap we shall find a chink in his armor."

"Caranthus might be easily convinced," Cenobar
suggested, raising a hand as Rassuman's brows lifted
in warning. "Oh, not with direct warnings, nor blandishments, but—as you say—subtly, that Anomius
must be, ultimately, a threat to Xenomenus. And did
Lykander perceive him a threat to his own prominence, then Lemomal would surely follow his lead."

"And then Padruar would likely climb down from
his fence." Rassuman nodded. "On our side."

"All this," said Andrycus, "must take time. What
if the revenant finds the three meanwhile?"

"She's not omnipotent, and their finding may take her time," Rassuman answered, slowly and carefully, brow wrinkling as he pondered his words, "I think that she must report to her master then, and that when—if!—she does, then Anomius must find one desire balanced against another. Listen—he lusts for vengeance and for power in equal measure, no?" He waited as, in turn, Cenobar and Andrycus voiced their agreement. "And sooner or later the revenant will likely learn the grimoire is merely a fiction, that the quest is for the Arcanum; and that the Arcanum is held by Rhythamun. She will tell Anomius this and he must then make his choice: shall he bid his creature slay the questers, or look to use them for his own ends? Lust for power balanced against lust for vengeance."

"Surely he'll bid her slay them"—Andrycus frowned—"and send her on in pursuit of Rhythamun."

"Mayhap," Rassuman allowed, "and mayhap not. There's a design in this, albeit too complex for our discerning, and perhaps Anomius will sense that. Once already those three came close—they went where none have gone, did they not? Into fabled Tezin-dar; and came out alive to continue their hunt—and our scrying suggests there must be three to end Tharn's threat. So: might it not be that Anomius bids the creature let them live? Until, at least, they've found the book."

"That's a slender hope," Andrycus said.

"But all we have," said Rassuman. "Save some agency beyond our comprehension intervene on their behalf."

"Could we but send our magicks to aid them," whispered Andrycus.

"We cannot." Rassuman smiled wanly. "Only our prayers; and whatever undermining of Anomius we may contrive. Beyond that they have only their own skills."

"May Burash and all his kindred gods be with

them," Cenobar intoned. "For such aid they'll surely need."

"Aye," said Rassuman, "but meanwhile, we shall do what little we can. Subtlety, my friends! Let our tongues be cunning and our eyes keen."

"And should that be not enough?" demanded Andrycus. "Should the revenant somehow bring the book to Anomius? What then?"

"Then," said Rassuman, his voice resolute, "we make that sacrifice Menelian made—no matter the cost, we seek to destroy Anomius."

"Amen," said Cenobar as Andrycus ducked his head in grim agreement.

ALDARIN was, Cennaire thought, a city in which her former trade might have been plied with considerable profit. There was wealth here, and distributed more evenly than in Nhur-jabal, and for all the Seaman's Gate and the Courtesans Quarter had their share of handsome women, still she was an exotic among these fair-skinned Lyssians, and it became rapidly obvious she might take her pick from the menfolk. It amused her—it always had—how easily men's heads might be turned by an artful glance, a discreetly revealed portion of flesh. A skirt flared to show an ankle, a movement, seemingly careless, that exposed a little of her swelling bosom, and men became inflamed. A lowering of her lashes, a tongue drawn in demure promise over her lips, and they were hers to command: it was an additional pleasure that now she recognized their desire with senses infinitely more subtle, could smell it on them, see it like a flame burning behind their eyes. Were she not pressed by the urgency of her master's business she might well have dallied, intoxicated by that power. But she had a task to perform, and that was paramount—her heart lay with Anomius, and whatever power she now exercised, that which he held over her was the greater. It was the power of life after death, the ultimate power, and she looked to do his bidding in this strange land.

She went first to the mansion of Varent den Tarl, and found it empty save for a handful of servants retained to keep the palatial building in good order. Their master, she learned at the gate, was dead, which gave her pause until she explained—concealing the amusement this truth afforded her—that she sought not Lord Varent den Tarl, but three acquaintances of his: a Lyssian named Calandryll, a Kern by the name of Bracht, and a woman named Katya. That and the assumption of a forlorn expression, a fluttering of her lashes, won her audience with an ugly little bald man, so immersed in his accounts, so dried up and withered, he evinced only the slightest reaction to her artifice. Symeon, he was called, and his lack of interest piqued her, though she hid that, concentrating on learning what she might.

"They were here," he told her, oblivious to both the thrusting of her breasts and the ink he smudged upon his cheek. "They went. Find Darth. Ask him—he knew them better than I, and I've much work to do."

Cennaire ignored the obvious dismissal, smiling demurely as she inquired where Darth might be found and how she might know him.

"He was paid off," said Symeon. "He's likely drinking his bounty away. Try the Mercenaries Quarter, or the docks."

Cennaire thought perhaps he was unmanned, so faint was the anticipated odor, weaker than the musty smell of his books and the ink liberally spattered over his robe and skin, and it crossed her mind to slay him, for no reason other than his disinterest. That temptation she resisted, knowing it must endanger her hunt, and instead thanked him and went seeking Darth.

Tall and brown-haired, Symeon had said, with an ale flush in his cheeks, his family name Cobal. It was little enough and it took her several days to find him, her inquires leaving three men, overeager in their de-

sire to have her dally with them awhile, with broken
bones. A fourth, more pressing than the rest, she slew,
but all were in the rougher quarters of the city and
she doubted the venting of her anger would arouse
undue suspicions. Indeed, save she be brought for examination before a mage, she did not think the city
authorities would believe so slender a mere woman
capable of inflicting such injuries. Darth she found in
a tavern frequented by freeswords, the Bladesman.

He was settled beneath a window that cast warm
sunlight over his face, emphasizing the mottling of
his cheeks and the blood that shot his eyes, those taking a moment to focus as she took a chair across the
table from him and favored him with a seductive
smile.

"I am called Cennaire," she said. "You are Darth
Cobal, no?"

"My name," he agreed, gaping.

His voice was somewhat slurred and she thought
the flagon of red wine at his elbow was not the first
he had drunk that day, but his eyes narrowed as he
looked at her and through the wine vapors she
smelled his instant desire. This was no Symeon: this
one she could manipulate easily. She touched tongue
to lips, hand to hair, arranged her skirts. Darth
shouted for a fresh cup and another flagon of Alda red,
making a show of the purse he carried, still heavy
with coin.

"Symeon said I might find you here."

She turned her head as if to survey the tavern,
granting him her profile, knowing the movement
drew her gown taut across her bosom, not needing the
smell of him to advertise the effect because she heard
it in the sharp intake of his breath.

Darth licked his lips, torn between curiosity and
lust, the latter—Cennaire savored the musky scent—
stronger, the wine leeching his common sense, vinous
overconfidence in its place. He said, "Symeon? That
dried-out little toad? What business had you with
him?"

"I sought you."

His odor grew heady in Cennaire's nostrils; she held her smile as he straightened his back, flattered, taking the cup the serving wench brought and filling it unasked, pushing it toward her with a clumsy attempt at a courtly bow.

"Me? Dera, but my luck changes then." It was an afterthought to ask, "Why?"

"Might we speak in private?" she returned, her voice husky, conspiratorial. "Somewhere alone?"

It seemed not to occur to Darth that it was improbable such a woman would seek him out with amorous intent: the smell of his desire became almost overwhelming as he nodded.

"There're rooms above. We could go there."

Cennaire frowned prettily and shook her head. Too many had seen her enter here, and taken notice of their conversation; more precisely, of her. It might be that she must slay this drunken sot, and did it come to that she preferred it be in some location his corpse would attract less attention, somewhere she'd not be linked to the killing.

"A private house?" she murmured, thinking that if they left together folk might well assume she hired him as a freesword. Surely none could believe she looked to bed him?

Darth nodded again, vigorously. "Drink up," he urged.

Cennaire drained her cup and rose. Darth followed, less steadily, beaming as he tossed coins on the table.

He offered her his arm, but she pretended not to see, walking ahead of him, acting the part of some highborn lady come ahiring as they quit the tavern and went out into the afternoon sunlight. Darth paused a moment then, blinking and shaking his head, grinning foolishly before indicating a narrow street that ran down toward the harbor.

"There're houses there." His voice was lewd, his gaze no less innocent. "We can get a room."

"Excellent," she declared, old practice imbuing the single word with the promise of pleasure.

Darth's smile grew wider and he stepped gallantly ahead, swaggering as he strode between the buildings. Cennaire studied his back, noting the long sword he wore, the dirk. His shoulders were broad, muscular, and she suspected that sober he might well be a useful fighter. Neither his likely strength nor his weapons gave her cause for worry: she knew herself the stronger, and blades offered her no threat, even did it come to that. She followed him, skirts raised daintily clear of the feculent cobbles.

He halted where the street disgorged on a quiet square, the houses seemingly innocent lodging places; he flourished a bow, a little more successful this time, and flung out an arm.

"Milady Cennaire, do you choose one?"

Cennaire glanced round, selecting a house on the farther side, and said, "Do you obtain us a room, Darth, and I'll follow you."

He was far too intoxicated with desire for her to think other than that some highborn lady chose to dally with him, and nodded, moving almost at a trot to the building she chose. Cennaire waited in the shadow of a balcony, and walked quickly across the square when he appeared again, beckoning.

Discreetly, no concierge observed their entry and Darth led her to a room on the first floor, a plain chamber, furnished with a sizable bed, a washstand, and an armoire. He had already drawn the shutters closed, dust drifting lazily in the bands of sunlight that filtered through the wood. He latched the door and turned toward her, his eyes roaming her body as he loosed his swordbelt and tossed it aside. Cennaire granted him a smile, removing her light cloak, folding it over the armoire. She smelled him come closer and turned to place hands against his chest, pushing him gently back, his breath wine-sour on her face.

"A moment," she murmured. "To talk."

"Talk?" His advance was halted by that unexpected

suggestion rather than the pressure of her hands. "About what?"

"Calandryll," she said, "and Bracht. A Vanu woman named Katya."

"Them?" The odors of wine and lust were joined by the scent of confusion. "What about them?"

"They came seeking your master, no? To discuss some . . . affair . . . with Lord Varent den Tarl? A matter of a book."

Darth frowned, head cocked, wiping his mouth. Cennaire noticed that his hands were callused, the nails dirty. "What's that to you?" he asked. "Surely we're not come here to talk of them."

"They came," she said. "No? And found Lord Varent dead. Tell me what they said, what they asked."

"Milady . . . Cennaire." Darth took a step toward her. "Do you toy with me? We've the chamber you requested, a bed. Let's not waste it."

He took another step. His hands were on her shoulders, drawing her close against his chest, his mouth descending toward her face. For an instant she thought perhaps she might grant him his wish, secure the information once he was sated: it could not take long and he was no worse than many of the clients she had entertained, better than some. But that was before—when she was no more than a pretty girl, with no more than her beauty and her wits to secure her way in life. Now she was more than that, and she need no longer bow to the whims of wine-soaked men; now there were other ways.

Darth was not sure how he came to find himself on the floor. He did not think he had drunk so much, nor did the bare boards have any carpet on which he might have tripped. He grinned, a trifle embarrassed, and began to rise. Then gasped as he was lifted, flung backward to land sprawling on the bed. He was shocked to realize Cennaire knelt above him; frightened as it dawned that she had thrown him, that she now clutched his shirt in one slender hand, the other cupped about his jaw, and that her eyes no longer held promise of anything save suffering. Abruptly, driven out by the intensity of her gaze, the heady effects of a morning's drinking quit him. He had rather he was still numbed by the wine as he felt her fingers tighten and thought his jaw must crumble under the pressure.

Cennaire studied him a moment, drinking in his odor, savoring the terror that brightened his bloodshot eyes. The smell of lust was satisfying, amusing, but this was intoxicating. She checked herself before she crushed his jaw—he would need to speak.

"Tell me," she commanded.

He clutched her wrists, the tendons in his own bulging as he fought to break her hold. He could not, and struck at her face; she caught his fist and squeezed, a hand silencing his scream as the bones in his fingers broke. He began to choke, tears in his eyes. When she took her hand from his mouth he asked, "What are you?" in a voice that creaked with fear.

"I am Cennaire," she said, "and if you fail to tell me what you know of them I shall kill you, slowly."

Acceptance of that promise shone in his eyes, in the suddenly sharper reek that came. She thought he might faint then and slapped him, once, rocking his head to the side. Blood trickled from the corner of his mouth, where cheek and teeth had met.

"Tell me," she repeated. "Everything."

Darth told her, holding nothing back, racking his fear-fuddled mind for every memory, speaking fast, the words a defense against the implacable pressure he knew could squeeze out his life.

When he was finished Cennaire released her grip and he made a terrible mistake: his last. He lunged from the bed, oblivious of the pain as his broken hand struck the floor, and snatched at his sword. Before the blade cleared the scabbard, Cennaire fell on him and broke his neck.

She rose then, no longer interested in the corpse, delicately straightening rumpled clothes, arranging tousled hair, and concentrated her mind on her own room. That was in a lodging house on the far side of Aldarin, in a more salubrious quarter, where visiting gentlefolk might find comfortable accommodation, and she had memorized every detail.

She mouthed the words Anomius had taught her and smelled the scent of almonds on the air. For an instant there was a sense of unbeing, of a void about her, terrifying, for it seemed a place in which she might be lost, condemned to exist there forever, heartless and consequently denied the release of death, save her master destroy her heart . . .

For an instant only . . . and then she stood in familiar surroundings, smiling again as confidence returned.

The sun as yet stood high in the sky and she luxuriated in a bath, for appearance sake ate dinner, biding her time until the hour came to report. Then, secure behind a locked door, she fetched a mirror from her baggage and placed it carefully on the dressing table, settling before the glass. For a while she admired her reflection, then spoke the second gramarye taught her. Once more the pungency of almonds wafted and her image wavered, the glass darkening, swirling misty, the darkness there becoming a whirlpool of colors that resolved into Anomius's sallow features.

"What have you learned?"

His voice was faint, a whisper almost, but urgent: Cennaire leaned closer, her answer barely louder: "I found a man who knew them . . ."

"Knew them? Where are they?" She saw his watery blue eyes narrow, perspective distorting as he bent closer, his bulbous nose occupying the larger part of the glass.

"Gone from Aldarin."

"What? Gone where?"

"North, I think."

"You think? Do you not know?"

"Let me explain . . ."

"Aye, you'd best. I'm but a thought from Nhurjabal, and your heart lies there."

The threat implicit in his words was needless—did she not serve him loyally?—and Cennaire resented it. Even so, she thought, it told her things that might, someday, prove useful. He was at Kesham-vaj, the box in Nhur-jabal: his magic, certainly, could bring him there on the instant. But without the Tyrant's sorcerers' knowledge? She thought not; nor that the black-robed wizards, or the Tyrant himself, would agree to his departure. Courtesan she had been, but that did not mean her mind was slow; rather, the opposite, no less that she looked to the future, to her own safety.

The crossing to Lysse had afforded her time to consider her situation and already it had occurred to her that once her task was dispensed, Anomius might find no further use for her. And she knew his necromancy was frowned on by his fellow mages. Did he secure his grimoire—rather, did she secure it for him—would he, or they, permit her to exist still? A further thought: *Once Anomius had delivered the Fayne Lord to Xenomenus, might the Tyrant's sorcerers not destroy Anomius himself? Or try, at least.* They resented him, she knew, and did they succeed, then surely her existence would be ended with his. Her only sure guarantee of safety, she had decided, lay in securing for herself the box that held her heart.

These rebellious thoughts flashed swift through her mind, finding no expression in eyes or gesture: for now Anomius was, truly, her master. She smiled an apology and said, "Varent den Tarl is dead."

"What?" The wizard's response was a whiplash.

Cennaire flinched and said swiftly, "They came here and found his body; they asked questions. They appeared interested in a man called Daven Tyras."

In the mirror, Anomius's image frowned; a finger, ragged-nailed, rubbed at his nose. Then he showed yellow teeth in an expression more snarl than smile and said, "Go on."

"Daven Tyras is a trader in horses out of Gannshold, a half-blood Kern. He spent some time with Varent den Tarl—the last to see him alive—and is gone now. I questioned one of Varent's household, but he could not say where this Daven Tyras went, only that once the three had that knowledge they left."

"Varent dead, eh?" Anomius nodded thoughtfully. "And our quarry asking questions about a horse trader? I think Varent must shift his shape. Aye! For reasons I've yet to comprehend, he takes the body of Daven Tyras."

"I've his description," Cennaire said.

Anomius ducked his head. "Good. And the grimoire?"

"None I've spoken with know anything of that. Only that Calandryll and Bracht were employed by Varent to find some book."

"That much I knew—it was the grimoire. But why should Varent shift his shape? Why take the body of this Daven Tyras?"

Cennaire shrugged.

"There's more to this than I first thought," Anomius murmured. "Our quarry league with Vanu folk; Varent takes another's form; and it would seem now they must go north, to Gannshold. Why?"

Having no answer, Cennaire said nothing, only waited.

After a while Anomius said, "You've done well enough. Now go to Gannshold—find Daven Tyras. Find the grimoire."

"And the three?" asked Cennaire.

"Find the one and you'll find them," Anomius told her. "But the grimoire first! Secure that and then slay them."

Dutifully, Cennaire nodded. The image in the mirror faded, and then the glass was no more than that: a glass such as ladies use, innocent. She used it to tidy her hair and then went to inquire where and how she might arrange sea passage to Gannshold.

12

O F all the cities of Lysse, Gannshold was acknowledged the oldest, and that venerability
was chronicled clear in the lines of the ancient walls,
like the rings that chart the age of trees. First built
when Lysse and Cuan na'For both were young, and
quarrelsome in the way of youthful rivalry, the city's
core was the great citadel that sprawled across the
egress of the pass through the western edge of the
Gann Peaks, its ramparts climbing the stone to either
side, machicolated and teethed with bartizans that
still, in these more peaceful times, bore mangonels
and heavy arbalests in memory of the days when the
horse clans ventured bellicose to the south. Below
that grim reminder lay the buildings of the earliest
settlement, themselves protected by a vaulting,
betowered wall, and beyond that another, lower, more
houses between the two. The approach to this final
outer wall was itself defended naturally by the terrain, the road running up straight across a wide, bare
slope flanked to either side by craggy outthrusts of
the mountains, ending on a glacis overlooked by twin
watchtowers. Gannshold was said to be inpregnable
and, indeed, the city had never been conquered, stand-

ing now, by custom and common consent, aloof from the internecine struggles that sometimes racked the land it warded.

Viewed from the open space of the glacis, it presented a solemn face to the three riders as they drew nearer the gates.

The sun was a little way past its zenith, on a day clear-skied and warm, bathing the sprawling city in light that softened the harsh outlines of the fortifications, spilling over walls and rooftops to brighten the hard, blue-tinted granite and the darker slate, etching stark the outlines of the siege engines and the high columns of the towers and bartizans. The gates themselves stood open, massive structures banded with age-blackened metal that granted ingress down a short tunnel to a plaza from which but one avenue gave exit, that and the opening of the passage guarded by soldiery in the blue and black of the hold. They were efficient in their examination of the newcomers, and briskly courteous, demanding their names and the nature of their business, which Bracht—elected spokesman—explained was personal, a return to Cuan na'For after time spent wandering Lysse. The captain of the watch accepted this readily, accustomed to the peregrinations of Kern mercenaries, and waved them on to the inner city with no more than a casual reminder that they yet remained on Lyssian soil and were, consequently, subject to Lyssian laws.

Bracht voiced acknowledgment and led the way from the plaza, along the avenue to a network of wider, bisecting streets set out, Calandryll realized as they progressed deeper into Gannshold, on a grid pattern occasioned by the embrace of the mountains. What he knew of this vast guardian city came solely from books and he stared about as the Kern, familiar with the place, steered them onward. The buildings, denied lateral expansion, grew upward, rising far higher than the structures of Secca or Aldarin, climbing five, even six, stories, so that it seemed they rode down canyons, overshadowed, those not lit by the sun

pooled with darkness even this close to noon.
Balconies jutted above, adding their own weight to
the sense of enclosure, and what open spaces there
were, were jammed with stalls and thronging crowds,
as many dark-haired Kerns visible as there were the
fairer folk of Lysse. There seemed to be no parks or
gardens and before long he experienced a mild claus-
trophobia, realizing how attuned he had grown to the
open spaces they had traveled. It dampened his natural curiosity, and he wondered how long they should
remain here.

Long enough, he supposed, to ascertain whether
Daven Tyras yet lingered, or—the more likely, it
seemed—their quarry had departed. Had he gone, then
they must learn what they might of his going—
whether he traveled with companions, and in which
direction if he had spoken of a destination; some clue
to guide them across the prairies beyond the mountains. If he remained—Calandryll was not sure; a confrontation, he supposed, though how that might end
he could not guess, despite Dera's assurance that he
contained within himself the means to defeat the
warlock. That promise was a mystery, for while it
seemed he did possess the ability to summon the
Younger Gods—for all he knew not how—their words
were enigmatic, leaving him unenlightened. Perhaps,
he thought, that revelation would come at need, as
magic he understood no better than the godly promises had aided him before. He could only hope, and
press on, holding as firm he could to that faith.

He was brought from his reverie by the shadow of
the inner wall, falling on his face as he approached so
that he looked out again, seeing the rampart stretch
out across their path to meet a narrowing of the surrounding cliffs: the true mouth of the pass into Cuan
na'For.

Like its predecessor, this barrier was crenellated
and surmounted with bartizans, but unmanned and
constructed of older stone, the hard granite enlivened
by ivy that clambered in great masses over the blocks.

Once it had been faced with an open area, a killing ground for the defenders, but now, between the wall and the closest buildings, that space was filled with impermanent structures, rickety constructions of wood and jumbled stone erected against the solidity of the wall. It smelled of unwashed bodies and waste, as if the detritus of Gannshold, both human and organic, were deposited here.

"The Beggars Gate," Bracht said, lifting the pace a little as ragged folk pressed in with outthrust hands and pleas for coin. "We'll find lodgings beyond."

"Beyond," Calandryll saw, meant the inner city, for between two ramshackle hutments stood an open gate and another short tunnel gave access to a wide avenue flanked by older houses, overlooked by the massive bulk of the citadel. That loomed, like an ancient but still watchful sentinel, over all the surrounding buildings, austere despite the sunlight that bathed its ramparts, glittering on the helms and pikestaffs of the soldiery patrolling its towering walls. For all that ominous presence, this part of Gannshold was brighter, more airy, than the outer sections. The streets were wider, the buildings lower, as if the original inhabitants had enjoyed more room, or been fewer in number, than those come later, crowding their dwelling places into what space was left. Soldiers manned the end of the tunnel, but idly, offering Calandryll and his companions no interruption: they were there, he guessed, to deny the beggars entrance.

Certainly, they entered a more salubrious section, some houses even boasting tiny gardens, though Bracht brought them swiftly past these to a quarter filled with taverns and lodging houses, where Kerns outnumbered Lyssians and the smell of horses was strong. He eased his stallion to the side of a square occupied entirely by drinking houses, clear of the traffic, and reined in.

"The Equestrian Quarter lies there." He pointed toward an avenue whose ending seemed to devolve on open space, the breeze wafting from it redolent of dung and horse sweat. "And likely Daven Tyras is known there, and in these taverns."

"But you think him gone."

Katya looked toward the avenue, her grey eyes narrowed; Bracht nodded and said, "Aye. I cannot believe he lingers here."

"We've but the one way to find out," Calandryll said.

"And two to approach him if he does remain—head on, or cautiously." Bracht's face was solemn as he eyed his companions. "Do we take counsel?"

Calandryll returned the Kern's stare no less earnestly. His impulse, come this far, was to press on as swift they might to a conclusion. If Rhythamun yet dwelt, in Daven Tyras's form, in Gannshold it seemed the better course to seek him out, to trust the gods and look to slay the man before he had opportunity to proceed. No less, were he departed as Bracht suspected, to go after him. But hard-learned caution bade him be wary where Rhythamun was concerned, and he paused before replying, aware that Bracht and Katya, both, waited on his word. It seemed the decision was passed to him, as if the telling of Dera's promise had elected him leader in the final confrontation. He sighed; like the Kern, he doubted Rhythamun remained still in Gannshold, but if he did . . . He frowned, unable to decide the better course. To learn what they could of the man whose form the warlock had stolen before seeking him out? Or go now, hoping that the element of surprise—and the unknown power the gods had promised—would win them the day? He looked up, as if seeking an answer from the sky. It stood high and blue above, the black shapes of choughs wheeling about the peaks and the towers of the citadel, none offering answer.

"We're weeks behind him," he said slowly, knowing that he prevaricated, "and likely you're right—he's gone north."

"But if not . . ." Katya murmured.

"He'll not likely expect to see us," Bracht finished for her.

Calandryll nodded, sucking in a deep breath, seeing his comrades' eyes upon him, waiting. Briefly, resentment flared that the decision should rest with him. In so much else he deferred to Bracht, and Katya's pursuit had been the longer—why should they now lay this burden on him? *Because,* said a voice inside his mind, *the gods say you hold the means of Rhythamun's defeat. Shall you falter now?* He licked his lips, the stirring in his belly akin to that preceding battle: they had ridden hard and far to this place, to this potential conflict.

"Aye," he said at last, "let's seek him now."

Bracht's response was a fierce, tight grin, a single grunt of acceptance. Katya said, "So be it," and loosened her saber.

"Then this way," the Kern said, turning his mount back into the press of traffic, leading them toward the avenue.

They passed into shadow, then into sunlight again as the road ended at a great square filled with the clamor and the odors of horses and men. Calandryll was reminded of the Equestrian Quarter in Aldarin, but this was far larger, the smell of it heady, the noise deafening, flies rising in buzzing black clouds from the dung underfoot, the traders here nearly all Kerns or half-bloods, the corrals a sea of tossing equine heads. To find a single man in so much confusion seemed an impossible task.

"The season aids us," Bracht shouted over the din, gesturing at the apparent chaos. "So early, there are fewer traders. Come foaling time . . ."

What else he said was lost under the clatter of hooves as two Kerns drove a bunch of horses past. Calandryll nodded, leaning across to put his mouth close to Bracht's ear.

"Where do we begin?"

"With men I can trust," the Kern answered. "But

leave that part to me—there are ways these things are done."

Calandryll frowned and would have questioned his companion further, but Bracht gave him no choice, heeling the black stallion into the maelstrom of men and beasts. Calandryll and Katya followed close behind, dispute—or conversation—denied by the sheer volume of sound. It seemed the Kern rode directionless, merely wandering among the pens, but his eyes roved constantly over the crowd, as if he sought in the teeming throng some particular person. Did he, Calandryll wondered, discarding the thought with a puzzled shake of his head, hope to spot Daven Tyras in all this confusion? No, he realized, as Bracht glanced back, beckoning, and led them toward a stockade built out from the wall of the citadel itself.

On the fence two men sat watching a herd of yearlings. Neither were young, their sleek, dark hair streaked with grey, their faces weathered as much by the years as the seasons. Both wore the leather breeks, the high boots and tunics common to the folk of Cuan na'For, and from their belts hung swords and dirks. Their eyes, as they turned to study the approaching trio, were set in nests of wrinkles, but clear and of the same startling blue as Bracht's.

The Kern reined in, his right hand lifted, palm outward and with the fingers spread. Calandryll remembered that he had offered a similar greeting to the great oak that had disgorged the *byah* with its warning of Rhythamun's treachery. He saw the salute returned, both men swinging to face Bracht, their eyes traveling from him to Calandryll, on to Katya. It was the most cursory of examinations and yet Calandryll felt he had been studied and judged in the moment: he was abruptly aware of his disguise, convinced these two saw past the black-dyed hair to his Lyssian origins.

Bracht confirmed his belief.

"I am Bracht ni Errhyn of the clan Asyth," the Kern announced ceremoniously. "This, Katya,

Tekkan's daughter, of Vanu; this, Calandryll den Karynth of Lysse."

"I know you, Bracht ni Errhyn," returned the older of the pair no less formally, addressing himself as much to Calandryll and Katya. "I am Gart ni Morrhyn of the Asyth, and this"—he indicated his fellow with a sideways nod—"is Kythan ni Morrhyn, my brother. We give you greeting."

"And we you," Bracht said, his face grave as he added, "I am pleased to find you in good health."

"Innocence and honest natures are our allies," said Gart with patently assumed gravity, "and we anticipate a lengthy old age."

Bracht smiled, chuckling at that and shaking his head. Calandryll watched them, listening carefully, familiar enough with the tongue of Cuan na'For that he could follow most of what they said, what he understood intriguing. He saw some protocol was followed, ritual greetings giving way to banter, and that these two brothers were no strangers to Bracht. For the moment he and Katya were excluded from the conversation, Kern addressing Kern, Gart and Kythan not realizing, he suspected, that he understood what they said.

"Have you come looking for more Lykard horses, Bracht ni Errhyn?" asked Kythan with a solemnity that was belied by the twinkle in his eye. "Or perhaps to pay werecoin?"

Bracht's answering smile was brief and taut. "I have werecoin aplenty," he said, "and I hope to settle that matter; but later, have I the chance."

"I do not believe Jehenne ni Larrhyn is very interested in werecoin," Kythan said, no longer attempting solemnity, his grin open now, "but in some more . . . personal . . . restitution."

"The Lykard were ever vengeful." Gart nodded.

"I had thought that affair might be forgotten," Bracht said, "and Jehenne with another." The sentence elicited a chuckling and an enthusiastic shaking of heads, as if this were a matter of great amusement.

"The memory of the clan Lykard is long," said Gart.

"And Jehenne ni Larrhyn's a prodigious thing," added Kythan. "Were you contemplating a ride northward I should ride hard, were I in your saddle. You and your stranger comrades, all."

His eyes moved to Katya as he spoke, framing a silent question.

Bracht shook his head once and said, "Jehenne need find no quarrel with her."

Gart shrugged. "She rides with you and she is beautiful. Do you tell me you have not . . ."

"No," Bracht said quickly, turning a troubled glance Katya's way, for all she sat her horse in silence, unaware of what was said. Calandryll, sensing a pattern emergent, wondered what the Kern might tell her; for his own part fascinated by the exchange.

Gart's brows rose; Kythan said, "Does your blood thin in this southern clime, then?"

"I have taken a vow," Bracht answered. "There is an understanding between us."

"Were I in your saddle"—Kythan grinned—"I'd welcome an understanding with one such as she."

Calandryll saw Bracht's mouth tighten a fraction at the sally, but the Kern held his temper in check and forced a smile. It seemed he accepted such ribaldry better from his own kind than from others. "That blade she wears, she can use," he said. "While yours, save I miss my guess, is rusty and likely worn from excessive misuse."

Both older men laughed uproariously at this and Gart nodded eagerly, slapping his chortling brother so hard upon the back that Kythan was almost dislodged from his perch. "I trust your blade's as sharp as your tongue," he stuttered through his laughter, "for do you encounter any of the ni Larrhyn family you'll need a keen edge."

"Or a fast horse," said Kythan. "That black's still sound?"

"I ride the wind," Bracht declared, "and do the

Lykard but give me opportunity, I've werecoin enough to assuage even Jehenne's temper."

"Do they give you the opportunity," said Gart, more seriously, "which is a gamble I'd think on long before casting those particular dice. But come—we sit here agossiping when we might better loosen our tongues with ale. You've varre, you say? Then I say we match you coin for coin and cup for cup. I'd hear of your adventuring, and what—save madness—brings you back to Lykard territory."

Calandryll understood sufficient of the conversation he was able to recognize that no mention was yet made of Daven Tyras; equally, from the energetic way both older men sprang from the fence, that little choice was left save to drink with them. He curbed his impatience, forgetting that not long ago he had delayed, following Bracht's example as the Kern dismounted.

"What do they say?" demanded Katya, frowning as Kythan swung back a gate, advising them that their mounts should be safe inside the corral.

"That we should leave our animals here awhile," Calandryll explained, "and drink ale with them."

"Ale?" The flaxen head swung in irritation. "Do we not seek Rhythamun? Shall we waste time in some tavern?"

"Trust me." Bracht led his stallion into the corral. "We'll have answers soon enough."

The warrior woman's frown deepened a moment and her grey eyes flashed dangerously, as though a storm gathered in the orbs, but then she muttered something in her own language and dropped limber from the gelding, leading the horse after Calandryll's chestnut into the corral.

Gart and Kythan studied both animals as they waited by the gate, nodding their approval. Gart asked, "Where did you find them?"

"In Aldarin," Bracht replied.

"But out of Cuan na'For lest I misjudge them," said Kythan. "Their cost?"

Bracht named the sum and Kythan grinned. "You'd pay less here," he advised.

"We found ourselves in Aldarin," Bracht said, shrugging. "In need of mounts."

"There's the cost of herding them so far south," said Gart.

"The herdsmen to pay." Kythan nodded.

"The journey back," said Gart.

"Too far," Kythan observed.

"Not worth the trouble," Gart agreed, "no matter the price."

Their pecuniary discussion continued as they closed the gate and led the way along the wall to an open-fronted tavern; Calandryll wondered if all Kerns suffered avarice. Certainly it had seemed when Bracht first agreed to escort him to Gessyth that coin had been the freesword's chief consideration and he recalled how he had accused Bracht of greed. Indeed, when they had returned to Aldarin, his comrade had shown concern for his promised reward, reminding Calandryll of his mercenary leanings. But now . . . this talk of—how was she called?—Jehenne ni Larrhyn, of werecoin to be paid in settlement of some dispute, appeared to set a different stamp on Bracht's intentions. Perhaps, he thought, he would learn now why the Kern had fled his homeland. And, he trusted, of Daven Tyras.

It seemed the taverns of the quarter were divided in some clannish configuration, the patrons of this one cut from similar stamp to Bracht and the two older men, while in others Calandryll saw differences of clothing and coloration suggestive of different origins. Here, he guessed, the Asyth held sway, for around them sat men mostly dressed in breeks and tunics of black leather, blue of eye, their hair dark and gathered in loose tails like Bracht's and, he remembered, his. Some called greetings, but softly, as if wary that unfriendly ears—on Lykard heads? Calandryll wondered—might overhear, and when Bracht answered them, he made a warning gesture so that none approached, leaving the three alone with the two brothers. They found a table and called for ale.

"What news?" Bracht indicated the north with a glance toward the bulk of the citadel.

"Your father, your mother—both thrive." Gart drank deep, smacking his lips in appreciation. "Mykah offered the ni Larrhyn horses in compensation, but they were refused."

"Jehenne would still sooner have you, it would seem," said Kythan with a sly grin. "The answer she returned was that you and two strong nails alone would suffice."

He paused to drink, carefully dramatic. Gart nodded and explained: "You because it was agreed, the nails to crucify you."

"Do you truly intend to go home, you'd as well delay awhile," Kythan advised, serious now. "Once our stock is sold we shall go back, and some others of the clan—you'd find safety in numbers."

"Or take the Lyssian road to Forshold." Gart nodded. "For the Lykard rove more easterly of late."

Bracht's eyes spoke a question at that and Gart shrugged, saying, "The creatures of Hell Mouth stir, it seems, and neither the drachomannii nor blades hold them to the pass."

"They venture out?"

Calandryll heard surprise in Bracht's voice, perusing his memory for what he knew of Hell Mouth. It was the name the folk of Cuan na'For gave the Geff Pass, he recalled, and when he had suggested they might depart Gessyth by that route Bracht had warned against such a direction, speaking of strangeling creatures therein. And now they stirred? What, he wondered, did that portend—some further indication that the Mad God sent out his malign influence? He saw Gart duck his head in confirmation and concentrated his attention on the Kern's words.

"It would seem so, from what we've heard. Though as yet the Asyth lands go untouched, the Lykard speak of horses taken, and men; they ride well clear these days. Closer to the Asyth grazing."

"No matter." Bracht shaped a dismissive gesture. "We must go on, and without delay, save we find the man we seek."

"Ah," said Kythan, "I sense a tale unfolding here. Wait . . ."

He drained his mug, Gart swiftly following suit, and shouted for more ale. When it was brought, both brothers drank and leaned forward, their eyes intent on Bracht's face, clearly eager to hear his story. How much, Calandryll wondered, would his comrade reveal? How much should be told? So far it had seemed the wiser course to hold their knowledge of Rhythamun and his fell purpose to themselves; neither had the occasion arisen when revelation seemed profitable. But now? He was not sure.

"A man named Daven Tyras," Bracht said.

Recognition showed on both faces. Kythan nodded; Gart said, "A half-blood trader in poor horses?"

Bracht grunted agreement. Kythan said, "His mother of Lykard stock, his father out of Lysse?"

"He's here?" demanded Bracht, his voice harsh.

Whatever protocol governed these matters, it appeared Bracht had broken it by so direct a question: the brothers seemed momentarily taken aback, as if the correct approach was to skirt around the subject, to come gradually upon it.

Even so—perhaps impressed by Bracht's fierce look—the two Kerns shook their heads and Gart said, "No. He passed through Gannshold some weeks ago. Three? Four?"

"Four," said Kythan. "We'd just sold that roan stallion."

"Aye—four, then," Gart agreed.

Bracht cursed, for all it was what he had expected. Calandryll felt a hand upon his arm and turned to find Katya frowning curiously, clearly frustrated by her lack of understanding. "I heard the name," she said. "What news?"

"That he went north four weeks ago," Calandryll explained, and heard the warrior woman curse in her own language.

Bracht said, "Wait," and returned his attention to the brothers.

"Tell me what you know of him."

Gart and Kythan exchanged a look as if confirming their shared memories, then Gart said, "You know his face?"

Succinctly, Bracht repeated Darth's description of Daven Tyras, and what else they had learned on the way northward. Gart nodded agreement, drank, wiped foam from his lips, and said, "He still rides the piebald gelding, but he left Gannshold in company with some Lykard of his mother's family—the ni Brhyn—more than that, we cannot tell you."

He shrugged, aped by Kythan, who asked, "You have some quarrel with the half-blood?"

Bracht paused an instant, then ducked his head, saying, "He stole a thing."

"A thing," Kythan murmured, "that brings you north with a warrior woman out of Vanu and a Lyssian disguised as a clansman, eh? This must be a very important thing . . ."

The question was indirect, but nonetheless there; Bracht nodded, smiling briefly, and with scant humor. "It is a book," he said. "We . . ."

His words were drowned by the spluttering of the brothers. Gart coughed ale, choking, and Kythan pounded him vigorously on the back, his own chin wet with the ale that dribbled from his gaping mouth.

"A book?" It seemed a matter of utter incredulity. "You'd risk Jehenne ni Larrhyn's vengeance for a book?"

"What use have you for a book?" Gart's expression suggested such a thing was beyond comprehension. He wiped at his ale-soaked shirt, sipped again, as if that action would restore normality. "Have you learned to read while you sojourned in Lysse?"

"No," Bracht said, "but I took payment to find it. And I am vowed to bring it safe to Vanu."

"You find employment with her?"

Katya frowned afresh as the brothers turned toward her, fidgeting impatiently. Calandryll motioned her to silence as Bracht said, "No. She is bound by the same vow—that we bring the book to her land."

"This has the makings of a tale to fill the winter nights," Kythan remarked. "Such a tale as the bards unfold—Bracht ni Errhyn rides in search of a . . . book . . . in company with Katya of Vanu and a guised Lyssian."

His eyes moved to Calandryll, once more asking an unspoken question. Bracht grinned conspiratorially, answering: "In a while Tobias den Karynth, now Domm of Secca, will come to Gannshold. He will post Calandryll outlaw, claiming him a father-slayer."

The brothers' eyes narrowed at this and Bracht quickly added, "He is not! Tobias employed the Chaipaku to poison his father and set the blame at Calandryll's feet while Calandryll rode with me."

"A father-slayer is . . ." Gart used a word Calandryll did not understand, though the expression of disgust that contorted his weather-beaten features suggested clear enough its meaning.

"Aye," said Bracht, "and as we've traveled the length of Lysse, it was needful to employ this masquerade."

"Which you'd prefer we keep to ourselves," said Gart.

"In pursuit of a book," said Kythan.

"Aye," said Bracht, answering both men.

"The Chaipaku," said Gart; a trifle nervously, Calandryll thought. "Does the Brotherhood, too, seek you?"

"No longer," Bracht said.

"No longer?" Now Kythan forgot the indirection seemingly demanded by Kernish protocol. "Northward, Jehenne ni Larrhyn would see you crucified; you ride with a man hunted by the Domm of Secca;

and you tell us the Chaipaku, too, have sought you? You've a talent for enemies, Bracht."

Calandryll saw his comrade shrug, grinning as if his fellow Kern lavished praise upon him. "The tale is lengthy," he said, "and for another time. For now, it's the thing that we find Daven Tyras."

"Gone through the pass these four weeks hence," said Gart, "as we told you. Now? Likely he's with the ni Brhyn."

"Can Daven Tyras read?" Kythan asked wonderingly.

Bracht nodded. Gart said, "This book must be a thing of great value. The length of Lysse, you say? And northward into the arms of the Lykard? And all that you may bring this book to Vanu, where no clansman has gone before?"

Again Bracht nodded, not answering the question that danced in Gart's eyes. Instead he asked, "Are there folk of the ni Larrhyn here who might carry promise of werecoin to Jehenne?"

The brothers grunted agreement, heads turning toward a tavern some distance away along the wall. Calandryll followed their gaze and saw the drinkers there were lighter of hair, which they wore in two long plaits dangling either side of their heads.

"Ni Larrhyn and ni Brhyn, both," said Gart. "Among other families—and all likely to seek your life should they learn you're here."

"Jehenne has made it known that should it prove overly difficult to deliver you alive, your head will suffice," Kythan amplified. "Providing it is preserved well enough she can recognize you. Though her preference is that she see you nailed to a tree."

Calandryll started at this news; it began to seem they rode headlong into dangers more immediate than confrontation with Rhythamun, his trail hedged with obstacles. Fate seemed to weight the dice of fortune against them. In his ear Katya hissed, "What is it? What is said?" and he gestured her to silence again as

Bracht smiled coldly and said, "Is Gannshold no longer neutral? Does the covenant no longer hold?"

"In most things," said Gart, and shrugged elaborately. "But in this? Jehenne is powerful now, and very angry. It is not impossible some of the hotter-headed warriors could forget the covenant."

"Chador died while you've been awandering," said Kythan, "and Jehenne leads the ni Larrhyn now. She has promised much to the warrior who delivers her you. Or your head."

"I had not thought her affections so fierce." Bracht's expression grew sour as he looked to where the fairer-haired men sat. "Even so, I have werecoin aplenty—nigh on five thousand varre."

"That much?" Gart's mouth gaped open.

"Ahrd!" gasped a wide-eyed Kythan.

"An approach might be made?" Bracht asked.

"For so much it might," Gart said slowly.

"That's more werecoin than was ever offered," said Kythan.

"But still, perhaps, not enough." Gart's wrinkles deepened. "Jehenne's anger runs hot. Your father offered the forty horses you took, and then forty more of her own choosing, with saddles and bridles for each, but still she refused. You and two nails, she said, save that Mykah himself deliver her your head."

"How did he reply?" wondered Bracht.

"That should you return she might come aseeking," said Gart. "But that she had best ride in company with all her clan, for should she look to take you by force every warrior of the Asyth would stand against her."

Bracht grinned hugely at that, slapping his thigh and saying, "The fire burns hot in my father still."

"He'd not give you over to the ni Larrhyn," Gart said, "even does it come to clan war."

"I'd not see that." Bracht's grin faded. "Daven Tyras is my quarry . . . the book he holds."

He shook his head, lips thinning as he thought a

moment, then turned to Calandryll, speaking in Lyssian.

"How much of this do you understand?"

"Most, I think," Calandryll replied.

"And Katya?"

"None," she snapped. "I hear the name, Daven Tyras, but what you say . . ." She shook an angry wave of flaxen hair, like sunlight dancing over the stormy grey of her eyes.

"I ask that you be patient." Bracht touched her hand an instant. "After, I'll explain all." He turned again to Calandryll. "I think perhaps we must tell them."

He waited on an answer as Calandryll paused. Need they keep their quest secret from the brothers? Did Gart and Kythan understand the import of their quest, then likely they would lend what aid they could. They seemed stout-hearted enough, and if Bracht trusted them . . . He ducked his head: "Do you think it needful."

"I think it might well smooth our passage," Bracht said.

"Then, aye," Calandryll agreed.

The brothers understood the exchange, he guessed, for their eyes switched back and forth as he and Bracht spoke, curiosity writ clear on their faces, that expression transforming to expectancy on his agreement.

Bracht turned to them and said, "What I tell you is for your ears alone. Do you give your word on that?"

Solemnly they nodded, each in turn raising a hand in the splay-fingered gesture, then clenching a fist. "In Ahrd's holy name," said Gart, echoed by Kythan.

"Then listen well," said Bracht. "The book I seek is called the Arcanum. It was fashioned by the First Gods and lost in Tezin-dar . . ."

"Tezin-dar?" Kythan frowned. "Where is Tezin-dar?"

"The whole of this story is longer than I've time

for now," Bracht said. "Do you hear me out and I'll tell you what's needful."

"A half-told tale is kin to a three-legged horse," Kythan complained. Then shrugged as Bracht sighed. "Even so, I'll curb my tongue and hear you out—for promise of a full account later."

"You'll have it," Bracht promised, "do I live to tell it. Now—Tezin-dar is a city ages old, in Gessyth, warded by magic. The book—the Arcanum—was hidden there by Yl and Kyta, after the godwars." He ignored the grunts of surprise—or disbelief?—the brothers vented, motioning them to remain silent. "When the First Gods sent their sons down into limbo they left behind this book, which reveals the resting places of Tharn and Balatur. It was taken from Tezin-dar by a mage, Rhythamun, who wore another's form and who would use the book to raise the Mad God."

Again he paused as Gart and Kythan gaped and grunted in wonderment, continuing: "Fate—or the Younger Gods, I know not which for sure—brought we three together, bound to hunt Rhythamun and take the book from him, to deliver it to Vanu that the holy men of that place may destroy it. Rhythamun wore the body of a lord of Aldarin then, and we followed him there, where we learned of his taking another—Daven Tyras!"

"A gharan-evur," Gart said softly, disgust in his voice.

"Aye, such he is," Bracht said, "and we have hunted him across Lysse, and now it seems we must go into Cuan na'For, Jehenne ni Larrhyn or no. Does Daven Tyras—Rhythamun!—succeed, then Tharn shall rise and all the world, all the Younger Gods, go down into chaos."

He broke off, sipping ale. For long moments the brothers stared at him, as if he were mad, then Gart said, "Did any other tell me this tale, I'd name him crazed."

Kythan said, "Surely the Mad God does not rest in Cuan na'For."

"I—we—think not," Bracht answered. "Likely Rythamun must only cross Cuan na'For to some farther place. Mayhap beyond the Borrhun-maj. Wherever—we must go after him."

"You three alone?" asked Gart dubiously.

"So it was scried." Bracht nodded.

"And if he succeeds, he will raise the Mad God?" The older man shook his head, puzzled. "By Ahrd, he must be crazed."

"He is," Bracht said.

"He would destroy Ahrd?" asked Kythan softly, aghast at thought of such blasphemy. "How shall we aid you?"

"Aye," said Gart. "How?"

Whatever reservations they had entertained were banished, doubt converted to awestruck certainty. From their eyes, their faces—over which flitted expressions both horrified and resolute—Calandryll saw that they accepted the truth. Where they had previously doubted the wisdom of risking encounter with Jehenne ni Larrhyn, of even alerting the Lykard to Bracht's presence in Gannshold, there was now the realization that those chances must be taken, lest Rhythamun succeed; lest their god and all his kin fall to Tharn's madness.

"We cannot delay here." Bracht indicated Gannshold with a sweeping hand. "Each day brings Rhythamun closer to his goal—we must go on, swift as we may."

"The Lykard will not believe this," murmured Gart. "Do we bring them this tale, they will claim it a coward's imagining, to buy you free of Jehenne's wrath."

"Do you believe me?" Bracht demanded.

Gart and Kythan looked long at each other, then, in unison, nodded. The elder brother said, "Aye. You were never a tale-spinner."

"Nor a coward," added Kythan. "But still—what shall we do?"

"Say nothing to them of this quest, but take my offer of werecoin to them." Bracht looked toward the other tavern. "Mediate on my behalf as best you can. Do the Lykard halt us, then they leave Rhythamun free to bring down the world."

"Even do they accept"—Gart stabbed a thumb in the direction of the Lykard—"still word must go to Jehenne, and she make the decision. Save she know your story, I do not think she will agree; save the drachomannii see this warlock for what he is, he'll find sanctuary with the ni Brhyn."

"He's cunning," Bracht said, "and a sorcerer of great power. He might well hide himself from even the drachomannii. I say again—take my offer of werecoin to the Lykard; offer four thousand for Jehenne, the rest to buy me safe passage. Do enough headmen agree, then Jehenne must accept."

"It may be enough," Gart allowed cautiously. "But in the doing we must reveal your presence here. If they refuse . . ."

"I'll take the chance," Bracht said, "and trust the covenant holds. If not . . . we must go north, no matter."

"Likely to ride into Jehenne's arms," Gart said, his dark face dour. "And die."

Bracht only shrugged.

"Send word ahead," Kythan suggested. "Send a messenger—I'll go, do you ask it—to tell Jehenne your story. Mayhap she'll believe it and have her own drachomannii assess the man."

"Or laugh at the telling, as Gart says." Bracht shook his head. "No, I do not think that is the way. And such an envoy might well warn Rhythamun of our coming—afford him chance to flee."

Kythan sighed, accepting; Gart said, "This is no easy thing. It seems the scales stand weighted against you, danger to both sides. Even do you escape Jehenne's wrath, the ni Brhyn will not likely hand you this man, not thinking him one of theirs by blood."

"Send word to the ni Errhyn," said Kythan, "to Mykah—that he send a raiding party to snatch the man."

"Who is a sorcerer of great power," Bracht repeated, "and likely capable of slaughtering the raiders before he flees. No, it is we three who must go against him and we three alone. So was it scried—that none others may do this thing."

Kythan grunted, frustrated, and scratched his head. Beside him, his brother drank ale and absently called for more. When it was brought he supped deep and said, "So you would have us act as intermediaries, with no word of what you attempt."

Bracht ducked his head and said, "I can think of no better plan."

"And do the Lykard agree," said Gart somberly, "you ride against a mage protected by both his thaumaturgy and the ni Brhyn. I do not see how you can win this."

"Nor I," said Bracht cheerfully, "but still it is written that we must attempt it. Listen—we have spoken with gods on this quest and they have promised us what aid is theirs to give. When the time comes . . ."

He shrugged as the brothers gaped afresh. "You have spoken with gods?" Kythan mumbled.

"Ahrd sent a *byah* to warn of Rhythamun's treachery," Bracht said, "and in Kandahar, Burash saved us from the Chaipaku; on the road here Dera appeared to Calandryll and Katya. She said"—he turned his head to indicate Calandryll—"that he holds the means of Rhythamun's defeat."

"He's a thaumaturge?" asked Gart suspiciously, and Bracht shook his head. "No. There's power in him, but neither he nor we understand its nature. Only that the goddess promised it may defeat Rhythamun—to which end we must confront the mage."

"This is the stuff of legend," whispered Kythan. "The bards will tell this ages hence."

"If we succeed," Bracht said. "And to succeed, we must find Daven Tyras; we must go into Cuan na'For."

"And we've a part to play." Kythan grinned proudly, clapping Gart enthusiastically on the shoulder. "Well, brother, do we go to the Lykard with Bracht's offer?"

"Aye"—Gart nodded, more cautious—"but softly. Do they refuse us, then there remains the matter of these three departing Gannshold unhindered. Let's think on that awhile."

Kythan sobered, his smile fading. Gart stroked his chin, then nodded as if some decision were reached. "Do they accept, all is well," he said carefully. "There are sufficient here Jehenne must stand bound by clan decision. At least that you have safe passage outside the ni Larrhyn lands. If not, then you must look to go out unnoticed. Those mounts you ride look sound enough and a night's rest should see them ready to run should flight be needful, so—do you rest yourselves, Kythan and I will take the offer to the Lykard and bring you word of what they say. Be it nay, then you go out at dawn, when the north gates open, and I'll find warriors of the Asyth to guard your backs, to delay pursuit or troublesome messengers."

"I'd not see you break the covenant," Bracht said.

"We'll not." Gart smiled wolfishly. "Does it come to that, you'll go out with a party—the covenant holds no sway beyond the gates and we can set an ambush, that you may ride free."

"We've lodgings nearby," offered Kythan, "and you can find rooms there. Wait for us there."

Bracht looked to Calandryll, brows raised in question. He thought a moment but could find neither a better plan nor fault with this: he nodded his acceptance and Bracht said, "So be it."

"Then let's fetch your animals and bring you to the inn," said Gart. "Then we'll beard the Lykard."

"Ahrd grant they agree," declared Kythan fervently.

They drained their mugs and Bracht tossed coin to the table, waving away the brothers' offer of payment. The sun was moved across the sky by now, the afternoon darkening toward twilight with rafts of heavy grey cloud blown southward on a wind that whispered chill from the mountains, slapping at the pennants along the walls of the citadel. Lanterns were already lit in several of the taverns and most had emptied as they spoke, the bustle of the Equestrian Quarter diminished, the haggling of the traders outweighed by the sound of horses as business wound down. Calandryll stared warily about as they passed close by the tavern favored by the Lykard, but none there paid them especial attention and they came unopposed to the brothers' corral. The yearlings there were grouped toward one end, nervously eyeing Bracht's stallion, who stood as if on guard, the two geldings in attendance, snickering a greeting as he saw his master. They fetched the three horses out and followed Gart and Kythan back across the great yard, along an avenue to an inn surrounded by a high wall. Over the gate hung a sign, its faded paint depicting a prancing horse, beneath the equine figure the name: The Horseman's Rest.

"The stables are good," Gart said, "and mostly Asyth find lodgings here—you'll sleep safe enough."

"You've our thanks for this," Bracht said.

"What else should we do?" Gart smiled. "Come, let's find the landlord and see you settled."

"I'll see to your horses," Kythan offered, and somewhat to Calandryll's surprise, Bracht agreed: it appeared a fellow Kern might be entrusted with the task.

This early in the year there were rooms aplenty and they were quickly ensconced in three adjoining chambers, the brothers leaving them with promises that they would return immediately they had some response from the Lykard. No sooner were they gone than Katya presented herself in Bracht's room, shouting for Calandryll to join them. Her voice, he thought, sounded stormy as her eyes had been while she sat unknowing what was said throughout the afternoon: he hurried to obey her summons.

She stood with her back to the window, resting against the sill, arms crossed over her chest; Bracht stood facing her, his expression apologetic. Calandryll closed the door and found a place on the single bed.

"So, I've sat listening without understanding, patiently." Her voice was carefully measured, as if she held temper in check. "Do you now tell me what you discussed? Is Daven Tyras gone on?"

"Gone on," Bracht said, and outlined the gist of his discussion with the two Kerns.

When he was finished Katya nodded, fixing him with an unfathomable stare. "So we must go into Cuan na'For," she murmured, "and whether that be hard or easy hangs on the Lykards' decision."

Bracht nodded, and in a colder voice Katya asked, "And this Jehenne ni Larrhyn? Who is she? Why does she seek your death?"

Calandryll, no less curious, turned eagerly to Bracht, awaiting his response. Perhaps now he would learn what mystery lay in the freesword's past that had driven him outlawed from Cuan na'For, the bits and pieces of the afternoon's conversation knitting into some comprehensible whole. He saw Bracht swallow, ill at ease, eyes falling a moment from Katya's demanding gaze. Then the Kern shrugged, cleared his throat, and began to speak.

"Jehenne ni Larrhyn is the daughter of Chador, a ketoman—headman—of the Lykard," he said slowly, raising his eyes to meet Katya's, his expression that of a man who pleads for understanding, or forgiveness. "My father is Mykah, ketoman of the ni Errhyn family. Our grazing grounds adjoin, and down the years our clans have feuded. My father sought to forge a lasting peace and sent a matchmaker to the ni Larrhyn, to arrange a marriage that should bind our families—mine to Jehenne."

Katya's tanned face paled, save where a flush suffused her cheeks, as if they had been struck. Her eyes, stormy until now, grew icy and when she spoke her voice held a hollow chill.

"You are wed?"

"No!" Bracht shook his head vigorously, a hand chopping the air in dismissive gesture. "Ahrd, no!"

"Then what?"

Calandryll was unsure whether Katya's tone was cold with anger or fear. He saw her folded arms tighten, fingers clutching at the fine links of her hauberk, tight against the emotion that played in her eyes.

"The arrangement was made by our fathers," Bracht said, squaring his shoulders. "I met Jehenne and . . . she was attractive. I agreed to think on the union . . . She was a prize . . ." His voice faltered and he licked his lips as if fear of Katya's reaction dried his mouth. "Her father sent forty horses for pledge price, thinking the affair agreed. I . . ."

He shrugged, raising his hands, dropping them, the left clutching the hilt of his falchion as if seeking strength in that contact, the right opening helplessly. Calandryll had never seen his friend so ill at ease.

"Go on," said Katya in a tone cooler than the wind that now rattled about the shutters.

"Jehenne favored the match," Bracht said, "Chador and my father favored it—all thought it pleased me." He paused again, sighed, and went on in a low voice. "At first it did . . . the preparations were begun, but then I saw Jehenne's temper. We courted—we were riding together when her mount faltered, threw her. It was no great fall, but she was enraged—she used a whip on the horse, cut the beast bloody."

He shrugged and said, "I could not troth myself to a woman who beats horses."

Katya's fingers loosed their grip on her shirt, the wintry storm departing her eyes, replaced with puzzlement. In a softer voice she said, "And?"

"I told my father. He told me the matter was too

far advanced—that did I withdraw I should offer insult
to all the ni Larrhyn and likely spark clan war. But I
could not wed a woman who strikes her horse! I fled
into Lysse. With"—this with a grin part shamefaced,
part triumphant—"the forty ni Larrhyn animals."

"So you are not wed?" said Katya. "Nor ever
were?"

Bracht shook his head. Calandryll looked from one
to the other, not sure whether he felt amused or
shocked, awaiting Katya's response.

"Merely a horse thief."

"They were ni Larrhyn horses."

The Kern's tone was defensive, as if the origin of
the animals justified and explained his action. Katya
said, "And now this Jehenne ni Larrhyn would see
you dead."

"She's a fierce temper." Bracht nodded.

"And you spurned her because she beat a horse."

"She used a quirt," Bracht said, his tone outraged,
as if such action were unthinkable.

For long moments Katya stared at him and he
stood silent, a man awaiting judgment. Then, like
winter's ice melting in the heat of a fire, the grey eyes
warmed, the full lips curved in a smile. She moved
from the window, a pace forward, a second, arms unfolding, rising to strike balled fists against Bracht's
chest as she laughed, loud and long. The Kern, surprised, staggered back. His legs met the bed and
Calandryll flung himself clear as Bracht toppled,
sprawling full length. He rose on his elbows, staring
up as Katya faced him, hands on hips now, shaking
her head. Calandryll saw him flinch as the warrior
woman abruptly leaned forward, kneeling above him,
hands reaching for his head.

No blow landed, but instead Katya cupped his face
in both her hands, stooping to kiss him, briefly, but
nonetheless soundly, full on the lips. As suddenly, she
withdrew, chuckling as she returned to the window.

"You're not angry?" Bracht asked.

"That you're not wed?" The flaxen mane tumbled

as she shook her head. "No! That this woman threatens our quest? Aye."

"Mayhap my offer of werecoin shall settle that," Bracht said, easing upright. "It's a greater price than any has offered before."

Their eyes locked, feasting on each other's faces, hot with this clearing of doubt. Bracht rose, pacing a single step toward Katya, halting, right hand reaching out to touch her cheek, the callused fingers gentle as they stroked a swift caress. In his own language he whispered, "This vow is hard." In Lyssian he said, "That was why I took Varent's coin—to end the matter."

Calandryll saw Katya shudder at the touch, heard the sharp intake of her breath, her eyes closing a moment, still smiling. Bracht lowered his hand and she asked, "And if it does not?"

"It may, at least, buy us passage over those lands not claimed by the ni Larrhyn," Bracht said. "To the ni Brhyn grazing, where Rhythamun has likely gone."

"And if not that?"

"Then we ride wary."

"Through a land filled with enemies."

"Aye, but together."

"Aye," she said softly, her gaze like fire on his face. "Together. I'd have it no other way."

13

"RHYTHAMUN would seem to be moving northward, if he travels with the ni Brhyn." Bracht pushed aside the detritus of their evening meal, drawing his dirk and using the point to scratch a crude map into the wood of the tabletop. "The Lykard grazing lies to the west, from Hell Mouth to the opening of the Gannshold pass. The ni Larrhyn lands are here, the ni Brhyn here."

Calandryll watched as the blade charted the grasslands of Cuan na'For. The territory claimed by the ni Larrhyn lay hard against the Gann Peaks, its easternmost boundary touching the egress of the canyon guarded by the great citadel, extending toward the central mass of the Cuan na'Dru. The ni Brhyn occupied an area to the north, about the edgewoods of the great forest.

"We thought as much," he said, and tapped a fingertip to the splintered circle indicating the Cuan na'Dru. "But will he go through the forest or around it?"

"Around. The Cuan na'Dru is guarded by the Gruagach, and I wonder if even Rhythamun's magic could stand against them." Bracht glanced at Gart and Kythan, who nodded emphatically. "They're an older folk than men and possessed of older powers. More, Ahrd's strength is greatest in the forest—which Rhythamun must surely know—and I do not think the god would allow him passage. No, I think he'll go around."

"Then"—Calandryll traced a line from Gannshold to the ni Brhyn grazing, around the Cuan na'Dru—"does Ahrd favor us, we've the opportunity to get ahead of him."

"Dera promised we should have help of her kindred gods," Katya murmured. "Perhaps this is our chance."

Bracht nodded, once, doubt cloudy in his eyes. "Even so," he murmured, "we must cross the eastern portion of the Lykard grazing. And for days we must travel over ni Larrhyn territory."

His smile was grim as the news Gart and Kythan had brought back from their attempt to mediate with the Lykard: the representatives of the ni Larrhyn had refused point-blank to accept offer of werecoin. The others, cynically, had agreed that in return for one thousand varre Bracht should have free passage over their grass and—rejecting the advice of the brothers—he had decided to pay that sum.

"Ahrd, man!" Gart had protested. "Why waste the coin? You'll not reach their grazing save you escape the ni Larrhyn."

He had not needed to add he thought this unlikely, but still Bracht had shrugged and asked him to return with the payment, pointing out that did they survive the crossing of the ni Larrhyn territory they would still ride within the aegis of the Lykard, and the pursuit of Rhythamun would be the easier without hostile families opposing their passage. Grumbling, but nonetheless obedient, the brothers had gone back to their negotiations, returning to the Horseman's Rest with the tokens of safe conduct. Those talismans—small sticks of oakwood inscribed with clan marks and tied with colored feathers—now rested in Bracht's saddlebags as he outlined the path they must soon take.

"The covenant ends beyond the walls of Gannshold," he continued, "and while the pass is claimed by none, the ni Larrhyn may look to attack us there."

"We've a score of warriors to thwart ambush," Gart said. "They'll meet us at the gate, at dawn."

"And halt any ni Larrhyn messengers," added Kythan.

"But still you've Jehenne to fear," said Gart.

They spoke in Lyssian now, that Katya might understand, and she nodded, staring at the lines etched across the table.

"How many days?" she asked.

"While the ni Larrhyn might halt us?" Bracht thought a moment, glancing to Gart and Kythan for confirmation. "Twenty if we ride hard and fast, without delay. If we must hide or fight . . ."

He shrugged and Gart said, "What little is left of your life," in a low voice.

"Skirt round," urged Kythan, tracing a path east of the Lykard lands. "Go through the pass and cut eastward into Asyth grazing, then ride north. Cut back westward into the ni Brhyn's territory."

"Too long." Bracht shook his head. "Each day brings Rhythamun closer to his goal."

"Ahrd!" Gart grunted. "You've not the least idea where he goes, save that it's likely beyond the edges of the world, beyond even the Borrhun-maj."

"Aye"—Bracht nodded—"and so we must look to find him, or find his trail, soon as we may."

"Shall you hunt him ghostly?" argued the older man. "For does Jehenne find you, it shall be your spirits that are left to quest—your bodies will hang on a tree."

"We've no choice," Bracht said.

"And godly promises to aid us," said Katya.

Gart shook his head at that and said, "Ahrd holds sway in Cuan na'For, and to reach his domain you must still cross ni Larrhyn land."

Bracht toyed with his dirk, turning the blade be-

tween his hands, then looked in turn at Katya and
Calandryll. "There's much in what they say," he murmured, "and hazard aplenty on the faster path.
Jehenne's quarrel is with me, not you, though if she
finds you in my company you'll likely suffer the same
fate. Would you then ride east, find the safer way?"

"And risk losing Rhythamun's trail?" Katya shook
her head, her face empty of any doubt. "We've faced
hazard ere now and likely shall again. I say we put our
trust in the gods and our blades and ride the swifter
way."

She and Bracht looked to Calandryll for an answer
and he ran a finger along the scratch indicating the
Gann Peaks, the boundaries of the clan territories, up
and across to the Cuan na'Dru.

"To reach the Asyth lands, what? Three days, four?
Then northward before we may go west again—
fourteen, fifteen days?" Like Katya he shook his head.
"We're far enough behind already—I say we take the
chance."

Bracht's smile was fierce, approving as he ducked
his head and grunted what might have been a laugh,
fixing Gart and Kythan with a stare both kindly and
determined.

"You see? I ride with warriors!" He sheathed his
dirk, leaning forward across the table. "We chase the
world's ending and none shall stand in our way."

Gart sighed; Kythan shrugged. "Then we'll come
for you at first light," said the older brother.

"There's more I'd ask of you," Bracht said. "I'd purchase a packhorse for our gear. We've tents and blankets, but I'd lief carry sufficient food we need not
hunt. And bows might well prove useful."

"You'll have them," promised Gart.

"How long shall we hold the pass?" asked Kythan.

"Three days," Bracht said. "Longer if you can."

Kythan nodded. "You shall have it."

Gart said, "You're set on this course?" and Bracht
answered, "Aye, we've no other choice save to concede the game."

"Then may Ahrd favor you," Gart returned solemnly, beckoning to his brother. "Come—we've a horse to find, provisions to purchase."

The two men rose, bowed formally to Katya, and said their farewells.

"Until first light," Bracht said as they quit the common room.

When they were gone he called for more ale, his dark face pensive. He appeared momentarily lost in thought and Calandryll, himself musing on what lay ahead, felt no great inclination to speak. He had not thought their pursuit of Rhythamun would be easy, but neither had he anticipated the enmity of an entire Kernish family. The odds, it seemed, stood heavy against them and he wondered pessimistically if their quest should end in Cuan na'For, thwarted by a vengeful woman. But there was, as Bracht had said, little enough choice in the matter, save to give up, and that was an alternative none could countenance. They must, he decided, thinking on what Katya had said, place their trust in the Younger Gods—to rely on blades alone seemed foolish optimism.

He was brought from his contemplation by Katya's voice. She alone appeared undeterred by the prospect of Jehenne ni Larrhyn's wrath, and he wondered if this stemmed from her encounter with Dera, or Bracht's revelation of his past, the dissolution of that sudden, unexpected doubt seeming to firm the bond between them, to infuse her with renewed determination. It was almost, he thought, as if she regarded Jehenne as a challenge.

"Why did you not warn us of this?" she asked. "Of your enemies in Cuan na'For?"

Her tone was mild but still Bracht grew somewhat shamefaced as he replied, "I had hoped there would be no need. I had hoped the affair would be forgotten—or that the coin I took from Rhythamun would settle it."

He held his mug a moment, swirling the dark ale,

then added: "I went against my father's will, and that
is not a thing I am proud of."

"But she beat her horse," said Katya lightly.

"Aye," Bracht agreed with a tight grin, "but even
so . . . What I did was like to spark clan war. Mayhap
I should not have taken the horses."

"Perhaps you should have followed your father's
wishes," said Katya, "and wed this Jehenne. Horse
beater though she be."

She teased him, Calandryll saw, and that Bracht
mistook her bantering tone. The Kern's look darkened, his eyes opening blue and wide, the expression
on his face intent as he stared at the warrior woman.

"Then I should not have met you," he said.

"No," Katya said, and smiled.

"Perhaps there was always some design," offered
Calandryll. "That we three should meet."

Katya nodded slowly. "I think it must be so," she
murmured. "And if it be so, then surely we are fated
to find Rhythamun, no matter what stands in our
way."

"Ahrd grant you're right," Bracht said fervently.
"But once through the pass we must ride wary."

"Then let's to bed," Katya suggested. "I'd enjoy one
last night's safe sleep."

It seemed sound advice and they emptied their
mugs, settling their account with the landlord before
retiring, adding a few extra coins that he warn them
should any hot-headed Lykard come seeking them,
and keep his mouth closed concerning their departure. Bracht paused a moment when they reached the
stairs, bidding the others go on as he went to the
kitchen. Calandryll thought perhaps he looked to arrange them breakfast and in his own chamber lit the
single candle and voiced a prayer to Dera that she
grant them what aid she might, even though they
traveled beyond the boundaries of her aegis. That devotion attended, he settled to honing his sword and
dirk, his mind too occupied with all he had learned

that day to yet find sleep. He was interrupted by a
knocking, Bracht's soft voice calling for entry.

He set his weapons aside and unlatched the door to
see the Kern standing with a steaming bucket in his
hand.

"Your hair," Bracht said in explanation. "Do we encounter the Lykard, they'll take unkindlier to one disguised as an Asyth. Should worst come to worst, they
might hesitate to crucify a Lyssian."

Calandryll's hands clenched involuntarily at the
thought and he motioned the Kern into the room.
Bracht set down the bucket and brought a gallipot
from inside his tunic, tossing the small container to
Calandryll.

"This, so I was told, will wash out the dye."

Calandryll nodded, murmuring thanks, and Bracht
bade him good night, leaving him alone again.

He latched the door once more and stripped off his
shirt, shivering in the chilly night air as he spilled hot
water into the basin surmounting the solitary washstand. He undid his ponytail and doused his head,
opening the gallipot to scoop out thick paste, a
creamy white and smelling faintly of roses, that he
worked into his long hair. The water in the basin
turned a dull grey, then black. He emptied the contents out the window and repeated the process until
all the cream was gone: it was difficult to be sure by
candlelight, but when he studied his appearance in
the little metal mirror, it seemed he was once again
fair-haired. It occurred to him then that their early departure would likely be marked, and that if Tobias
questioned the soldiers of Gannshold closely enough
his brother would learn that he had passed through
the city ahead of the ceremonial procession. Might
Tobias then recall the Kern he had seen on the road?
The thought prompted Calandryll to chuckle as he
contemplated his brother's frustration and, still grinning, he finished the edging of his blades and climbed
beneath the sheets.

The bed was pleasantly warm, soft, and comforting

after the nights spent in the open—and the nights to come, when, he surmised, they must sleep light, with one of their party likely on guard. Even so, he could not at first sleep, for it seemed they passed from one chapter of their quest into another, and that set in an unknown land where a jealous woman threatened to halt their endeavor. And did they succeed in avoiding Jehenne ni Larrhyn, still they must find Rhythamun among the ni Brhyn, or pick up his trail, which, in the vastness of Cuan na'For, could surely be no easy task. Somehow, he told himself as moonlight filtered pale through the shutters, layering thin bands of wan radiance across his pillows, they would; they must, lest Rhythamun triumph and the Mad God rise. And should the warlock succeed, then he and Bracht and Katya, surely, would be dead, for in the midst of all the uncertainties fate set before them there remained a single constant thing, the one immutable fact—that whatever hazards faced them, whatever obstacles they might encounter, they would go on, unto death if needs be.

There existed no doubt of that and it was a strangely comforting thought: one that, finally, lulled him into dreamless slumber.

DAWN, he saw when Bracht's knocking woke him, came late to Gannshold. The walls of the pass held off the early sun and the sky above the city only hinted at the approaching day, night still clinging tenebrous against the roseate wash that outlined the eastern rimrock. He sprang from the warmth of the bed cursing the chill that gritted his teeth, and flung the door open with a mumbled greeting. Bracht entered, dressed for departure and cheerful, watching as Calandryll lit the candle and swiftly performed his morning toilet.

"It worked well." The Kern gestured at Calandryll's hair as he bound it back in the tail that now felt natural. "You look yourself again."

Calandryll grunted an inarticulate reply, shrugging into his tunic. He belted on his sword and flung his cloak about his shoulders, taking up his saddlebags, hoping they might find time for breakfast.

Bracht quashed such optimism. "Gart awaits us below," he said. "Come, Katya should be dressed by now."

She was, and they went together from the inn, out to the courtyard where Gart waited with six or seven sturdy Kerns, watching the silent street. "Kythan waits with the rest by the gate," he announced as they saddled their animals. "The packhorse is there, with bows, shafts, and sufficient food to last you a goodly while."

"And you came unseen?"

Bracht's question was answered with a brief smile, Gart's teeth white in the gloom, wolfish.

"There were two of the ni Larrhyn set to follow us." He chuckled, low. "They'll have sore heads when they awake."

"Again you've our thanks," Bracht said, and Gart shrugged, shaping a dismissive gesture. "Swift now," he advised. "The ni Larrhyn may well anticipate this and look to find us at the gate."

They heeded his words, cinching girths tight, and mounted and rode out, onto a cobbled street that sent the clatter of their hooves ringing off the surrounding buildings. Like a clarion, Calandryll thought, announcing their furtive departure. He peered about, right hand light upon the straightsword's hilt, his desire for breakfast forgotten now, anticipation filling the hollowness in his belly, but in the darkness that still filled the alleyways and avenues there was no sign of ambush; nor any sound other than that made by their horses, and the barking of dogs disturbed by such early travelers. Kerns came out of the shadows to either end of the street, whispering assurances that they were not followed, and Gart led the way toward the north gate. Above, the sky began to pale, the dull grey brightening as the rising sun began its contest with night's rear guard, an opalescent glow extending westward. Birds set to singing, and where the massive bulk of the central fortress rose over the city, the black shapes of choughs and ravens launched themselves, swirling raucous about the heights.

They reached the gate just as the line of light along the rimrock became a reddish-gold and a horn sounded from the ramparts, announcing the commencement of a new day. Shadow still clustered dark about the foot of the great wall, filled with the protesting rumble of the opening portals and the shouts of the soldiery as watches were exchanged. Mounted men came toward them, Kythan calling soft greeting, his fellow riders gathering protective around the three.

"No trouble?" asked Gart, and his brother shook his head, saying, "None."

"Then come."

Gart took the lead as they moved across the square confronting the gates. Overhead, red gave way to gold, pushing across the mountaintops, driving a wide band of brightening blue across the sky. Calandryll looked to where the gates stood open on the pass and saw the way as yet still shadowed by the walls. He saw Gart halt as soldiers came out, exchanging a few words: the soldiers fell back, watching as the column went by.

Stygian darkness descended once more while they traversed the tunnel through the walls, briefly as horses were lifted to a canter, giving way to steadily increasing brightness as they emerged into the pass. Gart speeded their pace to a gallop, the canyon ringing with the magnified thunder of hoofbeats, and as if approving of their venture, the sun rose over the heights, spilling golden light down the length of the cleft.

There was no formal road here, but rather a natural path of time-smoothed stone, wide and flat, bordered on either side by the near-vertical slopes of the Gann Peaks. Scrub clung tenacious along the edges, and higher up Calandryll saw pines thrusting out from the cliffs, a stream tumbling silvery over the rock. The air grew warmer, bird song louder, the blue band of sky streaked with tails of white cirrus. They rode hard along the flat, looking to put distance and time at their backs, defense against pursuit.

The canyon began to rise, climbing toward an apparently blank wall of sun-washed blue-grey granite. It was the foot of a lesser peak, and about the apex, snow shone brilliant. Their way curved around the base, still rising, narrowed between steep faces of naked stone. It was a long climb and after a while the horses began to blow, affected by the altitude, and Calandryll experienced a mild dizziness, squinting as the snowed caps of the higher mountains wavered and shimmered, as if seen through water. They slowed on Gart's command, cantering the last league to a place where the road widened again, the pass opening out into a broad bowl, its width grassy and ringed with larches, a shallow stream splashing along the perimeter. The wind whistled a chilly tune through the branches, and where they shaded the ground most deeply, Calandryll saw patches of half-melted, icy snow. He was surprised to see the sun risen halfway to its zenith. Gart reined in, beckoning them forward.

"This will make a comfortable enough camp." He turned in his saddle, surveying the mountain meadow, grinning ferociously as he added, "And a good place to fight, do the ni Larrhyn come after you."

Bracht nodded and they clasped hands. Kythan approached, leading a dappled horse, its back bulky with gear.

"All you'll need," he said. "The bows topmost. Ahrd be with you."

"And with you," Bracht returned, taking the rope Kythan offered and looping it about his saddle horn. "All of you."

Kythan smiled, no less fierce than his brother. "It's been a while since I've enjoyed a good fight. And do they give chase, we'll earn a place in the tale the bards make."

"Ahrd willing," said Bracht gravely, and took Kythan's hand.

In turn, the brothers clasped hands with Calandryll and Katya, bidding them good fortune. "Come," Bracht said, and they followed him across the meadow. Behind, the assembled men of the clan Asyth set to building their camp, setting watch over the egress of the road where it emerged onto the grass.

"Do the ni Larrhyn look to chase us," Bracht murmured, "or send word to Jehenne, they'll have a hard time of it."

His voice was proud and Calandryll nodded, thinking that it was heartening to find such stout friends among so many enemies.

Across the meadow Bracht ignored the wider way, leading them instead to a narrow gorge that ran level awhile before rising again, and they allowed the horses to find their own pace, moving at a walk up a goat trail that meandered about great sweeping flanks of rock, often enough shadowed by the overhang of ledges and walls that jutted like broken dragons' teeth against the cloud-streamered brightness of the sky. The air was thin and they spoke little, concentrating on the slow, steady ascent. They must, Calandryll thought, climb over the backbone of the Gann Peaks, and how long before they descended into warmer, more breathable air, he was not sure. Soon, he hoped, for this was a high, cold place, lonely and oddly depressing, the sheer weight of stone and sky all round serving to emphasize that they were but three, setting out for hostile ground.

They halted at noon, sheltering from the wind in the lee of jumbled slabs fallen down from the peaks above, opening the dappled horse's pack to find oats for the animals, dried meat and hard biscuit for themselves. After they had eaten, Bracht inspected the bows Kythan had secured, and the arrows, distributing the weapons with a grunt of approval.

They were of a type favored by the Kerns, wood reinforced with bone, much shorter than the yew longbows common to Lysse, and curved deeper: more effective from horseback. Calandryll tested his, grateful for the hours spent practicing on the warboat, for the shortbow was no easy thing to draw, the plating of bone lending it a power its lesser size might otherwise have denied. Satisfied, he unstrung the weapon and stowed it alongside the quiver, in a case of soft hide against the elements, beside his saddle.

"How long before we reach Cuan na'For?" Katya asked as they prepared to leave.

"This is Cuan na'For," Bracht answered. "Though no clan lays claim to these highlands."

"Why not?" The warrior woman frowned her surprise as she looked about. "These little hills remind me of Vanu."

"Ahrd!" Bracht shivered, grimacing his distaste. "Little hills? These are mountains."

"In Vanu we'd name them hills." Katya smiled.

"And I'm vowed to go there," said Bracht, grinning ruefully.

"Shall you change your mind then?"

Katya's smile became challenging; Bracht shook his head vigorously. "No," he said, laughing. "Though I must climb the clouds, still I'll climb them with you—for you."

Calandryll wondered if wind and cold reddened Katya's cheeks, but she said nothing more, only shook her own head, chuckling as she swung astride the grey gelding.

"Why do none claim them?" Calandryll wondered.

Bracht waved a dismissive hand. "Do you see grazing up here? For goats, perhaps; but for horses? No! This is no-man's-land—the grass is our domain."

"Then I ask—how long before we reach the grass?" Katya said.

"Two days." Bracht looked skyward. "Spring's well

enough advanced we'll not find rain or snow to hinder us."

"Only Jehenne ni Larrhyn."

"Aye." Bracht replied, sobering. "Only Jehenne. Or any other of her family."

"I think she'll not halt us."

Katya's voice was fierce, her grey eyes resolute. Bracht's, Calandryll saw, were less confident. He looked at his hands, gloved, and thought that beneath the leather he felt his palms prickle with unpleasant contemplation. "Would she truly crucify you?" he asked. "Crucify all of us?"

"Me, certainly." Bracht nodded grimly. "Katya and you . . . perhaps; because you ride with me. The Lykard favor that punishment—they'd nail me to an oak and leave my fate to Ahrd."

"To Ahrd?" Calandryll gasped. "How should Ahrd decide the fate of a man with nails through his hands?"

Bracht shrugged and said, "They claim that should the punishment be unjust Ahrd's oak will reject the nails." Calandryll watched aghast as he snorted cynical laughter, spat, and added, "As best I know, Ahrd has found none innocent yet."

It was a daunting thought and Calandryll sought comfort in the reminder that they had faced like dangers and survived—they had escaped Anomius, defeated the cannibals of Gash, won through the perils of Gessyth's dreadful swamps, found safety from the Chaipaku. They must, he told himself, trust in the benign assistance of the Younger Gods, that and their own skills. Surely they must elude Jehenne ni Larrhyn's vengeance. But still he could not resist clenching his hands: crucifixion seemed somehow a worse death. He wondered if his companions felt the same trepidation. If so, they gave no sign, Bracht taking the lead as the trail wound through a stand of wind-twisted pines, Katya behind him, looking about as eagerly as though they embarked on some pleasur-

able jaunt. He elected to hold his own counsel and endeavor to hide his sudden anxiety.

Past the pines the trail rose up a wide slope, curving around a sweeping shoulder of bare rock to enter
a couloir that ran down steep enough his mind became entirely concentrated on the descent. Snowmelt
rendered the footing treacherous, the gulley smooth-
floored and high-sided, shadowy as the day passed
into afternoon. They emerged onto a plateau where
more trees grew, bent like old, rheumatic men by the
wind. Birds wheeled overhead—more choughs, ravens,
sometimes an eagle, proud above the lesser avians.
Pine martens darted through the timber at their approach and farther up the slopes ibex and huge-horned
sheep grazed the crannies. The sun shone bright, but
the air was cold and thin, their progress slow, retarded
by altitude, the level ground of the plateau a welcome
interruption of the seesaw climb that seemed to answer each descent with a longer upward slope.

At such a height the day lingered, as if they clambered closer to the sun, and Calandryll was thankful
when Bracht called a halt where a pocket of grass
grew, surrounded on three sides by walls of stone. It
seemed they sat atop the peaks, for few now rose
above them and the egress from the pocket afforded a
view of lower elevations, jagged stone spreading to
north and east and west. They pitched their tents and
got a fire started, blankets spread over the horses
against the cold that grew as the sun fell toward the
horizon. The sky in that direction burned fiery, defying the blue darkness that spread inexorably from the
east, like a cloak trailed behind the risen crescent of
the new moon. Stars pricked through the velvet panoply and the wind dropped, tricksy, before blowing
again, fiercer and colder. The fire fluttered, sparks
streaming into the night, and from the lower slopes
wolves howled, setting the horses to snickering and
stamping, the black stallion screaming a challenge.
Bracht set meat to roasting and they huddled in their
cloaks, savoring the smell, their appetites sharpened.

"Is Vanu truly so"—the Kern gestured at their surroundings—"bleak as this?"

"Bleak?" Katya pushed a strand of flaxen hair back from her face, her expression quizzical. "This is not very bleak. In Vanu, now, the mountains will be still snow-covered. These are just a little cold."

Bracht grunted noncommittally; Calandryll frowned, thinking that these seemed to him mightily chill. Vanu, he decided, must be a hard land if Katya dismissed these mountains so casually.

"Do we need to cross the Borrhun-maj . . ." She shrugged expressively, firelight emphasizing the mischievous smile that curved her full mouth. "Then you shall see real mountains."

"Ahrd grant we may seize the Arcanum in Cuan na'For then," said Bracht, "for these are high enough for me."

That reminder of their purpose drove the smile from Katya's face and she nodded soberly, reaching out to turn a piece of meat. "I wonder where Tekkan is now," she murmured.

"Likely closing on Vanu," Bracht said firmly, "to alert your holy men to what we do."

Katya nodded, her smile a little restored by that reassurance. Calandryll said, "And Menelian. I wonder how he fares?"

"Aye." Now the Kern's face grew somber. "Has he found the means of halting Anomius's revenant?"

Calandryll had near forgotten that threat: of the sorcerer's creation there had been no sign, and all that had passed since they quit Kandahar had served to drive that hazard from his mind. He shrugged and said, "Likely he has, else surely the creature would have found us."

Bracht ducked his head. "I know little enough of revenants, but soon we'll be in Cuan na'For, where the finding of us will be harder."

"That's a bone to gnaw on when it comes," said Katya. "We've enough ahead to think on without our looking back."

Mention of bone appeared to remind Calandryll's stomach that it was still empty, for it promptly vented a prodigious rumbling; Katya and Bracht began to laugh. "I think"—the Kern chuckled—"that perhaps this meat is ready."

"Roasted or raw"—Calandryll rubbed his complaining belly—"I'm ready for it."

Still chuckling, Bracht fetched the strips from the fire and they ate. For all that blood dripped when his teeth broke the charred skin, it seemed to Calandryll a banquet, and he gorged, lying back when he was done with a sigh of pure contentment.

"These little mountains," Bracht said with a grin in Katya's direction, "would seem to edge our comrade's appetite."

"And render him somewhat barbarous," she returned, dabbing fastidiously at her mouth.

Unconcerned, Calandryll licked blood from his lips, wiped grease away with a careless hand. "Dera," he remarked cheerfully, "I think I've never been so hungry."

"You'll find it so awhile," Bracht told him, "until we reach the lower slopes."

"When shall that be?" Calandryll lifted on his elbows, deciding his feet could remain a little longer by the fire.

"We climb no higher." Bracht tossed a fresh branch into the flames. "From here, the way runs down. Two days will see us on the grass."

"And those wolves?" Calandryll cocked his head, listening to the eerie howling. "Shall the horses be safe, or must we mount a guard?"

"No need." Bracht shook his head. "They're below us yet—where the hunting's better—and the fire will hold them off. That and my horse: he's match for any wolf."

Calandryll nodded and yawned. With his hunger satisfied he realized he was mightily tired. Idly he murmured, "Did your Lykard friends pursue us? I wonder."

"No friends of mine." Bracht's voice grew harsh. "And if they did, they'll have a hard time of it."

"Gart and Kythan proved true friends," Calandryll murmured.

"They're Asyth," Bracht said, as if that were all the explanation necessary.

"True friends," repeated Calandryll drowsily.

"Clan," Bracht said. "That bond runs strong."

"And the tokens you bought?" asked Katya. "Shall they prove as sound?"

"Aye." Bracht used his dirk to return a fallen log to the fire. "Once given, they may not be reclaimed. With those, we've safe conduct over all save the ni Larrhyn grazing."

Katya nodded, her face thoughtful. "Even the ni Brhyn?"

"Even the ni Brhyn," Bracht confirmed.

"Then the Lykard cannot know that Daven Tyras is Rhythamun," the woman murmured.

"I doubt even the Lykard"—Calandryll heard contempt in Bracht's voice—"would give Rhythamun aid. Did you think it so?"

Katya shrugged a vague negative. "I know as little of Cuan na'For as you know of Vanu," she said pensively, "but it would seem that if Rhythamun hides his identity, he must travel slower—at whatever pace the ni Brhyn set. Also, he cannot suspect we chase him—if he did, surely he'd have fabricated some tale, that the Lykard hold us back."

"Likely," Bracht agreed.

"Then I believe we've a better chance than any yet of halting him." Her tone was enthusiastic enough; Calandryll shrugged off his weariness, concentrating on her words. "We're agreed he'll not risk facing Ahrd in the Cuan na'Dru—that he will look to go around the forest?"

Bracht nodded; Calandryll waited.

"And Ahrd lives in every tree?"

"The forests and woodlands are his," Bracht said. "The oaks more than the rest."

"Then shall Ahrd not know where he goes?"

Again Bracht nodded.

"While the ni Brhyn are unlikely to give him up, save he reveal himself for what he is."

"Even the ni Brhyn despise a gharan-evur," Bracht said.

"Then I think that if we've Ahrd's help we can find him, away from the ni Brhyn. When he travels on—around the Cuan na'Dru."

Bracht frowned as realization dawned, doubt—and perhaps, Calandryll thought, a measure of fear, too—in his eyes. "You'd go through the Cuan na'Dru?" he asked.

Katya nodded: "Did Ahrd permit, then we'd likely emerge ahead, with the god to tell us where we might cross Rhythamun's path."

"Did Ahrd permit," Bracht said slowly. "And the Gruagach."

"Burash aided us," Katya reminded the Kern, "and Dera. Why not Ahrd? And these Gruagach?"

"The Gruagach are strangeling creatures." Bracht's voice was wary. "No man has seen them and lived. They guard the Cuan na'Dru fiercely. I'd not count on their permitting it."

Katya shrugged. "I say only it is a way. Mayhap the best way."

"I'd sooner face him among the ni Brhyn."

The Kern spoke low, clearly troubled by the thought of encountering the mysterious Gruagach. It came to Calandryll that it was the first time he had seen hint of fear in Bracht. "You spoke of drachomannii recognizing him," he offered. "What are they? Would they aid us?"

"Did they recognize him," Bracht said, "but they are not sorcerers. The word means ghost-talkers— you'd name them shamans, I think. They guide the clans, speak with the spirits, make the offerings to Ahrd. They might discern what Rhythamun is and cast him out, but more than that . . ." He gestured helplessly. "No, I think we must rely on that power in you to win this fight."

"And in the Younger Gods," Katya insisted. "In Ahrd."

"Aye," Bracht allowed, somewhat reluctantly. "But still I'd not go among the Gruagach, save we've no other choice left us."

He was obviously discomforted by the thought, rising to check the horses as if he sought those few moments alone, forcing an end to further discussion of the prospect.

"At least," Katya murmured as she watched him, "we've the advantage of surprise. Rhythamun must surely believe us trapped in Tezin-dar, and thinking that will leave no ambush behind."

Calandryll grunted sleepy agreement, neither then knowing Katya was wrong.

MORNING found the wind dropped away and the grass frost-rimed, glittering silvery under the harsh blue of a cloudless sky. The sun was a hazy disc far off to the east, hurling long shadows from the peaks and crags, outlining soaring birds stark against the azure. Breath steamed, and Calandryll hurried to build the fire as Bracht tended the horses and Katya retreated behind the privacy of the rocks to attend her toilet. They boiled tea and ate more of the dried meat, crouching, wrapped in their cloaks, about the fire as the sun climbed a little farther up the sky, then kicked the smoldering logs submissive and saddled the animals, riding out of the hollow's shelter onto a trail that slanted precipitously down across a face of smooth stone.

As Bracht had promised, they had crested the backbone of the mountains now and their way was a steady descent, though still by no means easy. Lesser tors lay below them, cordillera that ran like telluric waves washing against the distant blue-green mistiness that was the flatland of Cuan na'For, and the trail wound a tortuous way down shale-strewn gradients, along gullies, cliff faces, and couloirs. The few level places they crossed were a welcome relief, the gradients they climbed fewer and less steep, the road mostly finding a way around the heights, or between them. Timber grew thicker, spruce and hemlock and cedar spreading over the slopes, and they rode over more mountain meadows, an ever-increasing number of streams running cold and silver toward the foothills, like pointers to their destination. Squirrels chattered at their passing and the birds of the high mountains were gradually replaced with crows and kestrels, peregrines and buzzards. The air warmed and they shed their cloaks as the sun approached its zenith, donning them again as the day aged, the sun westering, allowing the new moon's sickle dominance of the heavens. That night owls hooted in the trees sheltering their camp, pine needles affording a springy mattress, the fire giving off the sweet scent of cedar as it crackled cheerfully, coruscating sparks toward the overhanging canopy of branches. The moon hymn of the wolves sounded closer and Calandryll fingered his bow, wondering aloud if they need mount a guard.

"No." Bracht shook his head, tossing a flesh-stripped bone onto the fire. "They'll not trouble us."

"But they hunt nearby," Calandryll protested.

"But not us," said the Kern easily. "What do you know of wolves?"

"Not much," Calandryll admitted. "That shepherds hate them, and farmers . . . In Lysse they're sometimes hunted. Folk say they'll attack unwary travelers, be the pack large enough."

Bracht laughed. "Shepherds hate wolves because they threaten the flocks," he said, "and so they weave tales of their ferocity. But never have I known a pack—no matter how large—attack a man. Rather, they avoid men, and men's fires. They might, were they hungry enough and in sufficient number, try for a horse, but I think we're safe enough."

"And the horses?" Calandryll frowned, still toying nervously with his bow. "Shall they be safe?"

"This close to us and our fire," Bracht answered, "aye. Those wolves you hear can fill their bellies readily enough on the game in these hills. And as I said before—my stallion is match for any wolf."

Calandryll bowed to the Kern's greater knowledge. His own experience of the lupine predators was, he allowed, limited mostly to folklore. In Secca he had taken little enough pleasure in hunting, preferring his books, his scholarly pursuits, to the chase, and had largely refused the invitations extended by his father and brother to join them on their forays, from which they would sometimes return with the carcass of a wolf, and lurid tales of the dead creature's ferocity. Bracht must know, he thought; but still, as he lay in his tent, he found sleep hard to find while the pack chorused, and kept both blade and bow to hand.

The dawn reinforced Bracht's assurance, for neither had the horses suffered attack nor could any sign of wolf spoor be found nearby; there was, Calandryll thought not for the first time, learning to be gleaned outside the books he had loved so well, in the observation of things beyond the confines of the palace library or the dissertation of scholars. It came to him then, as he squatted among the trees, that he had not held a book—save for that cursory examination of Varent den Tarl's library—in over a year now. Nor— this to his surprise—much missed the lack. A year ago he would have believed that unthinkable, but now the tomes over which he had doted, the scrolls and parchments and leather-bound volumes that had comprised the major and undoubtedly most important part of his life, seemed little more than a nebulous memory of a life left behind, like Secca's walls and Nadama, Tobias's scorn and his father's contempt. He rose, smiling and stretching, listening to the bird song in the surrounding trees, able now to identify far more than he had known that long-ago day when he had ridden out through Secca's gates to

find—he now recognized—a freedom he had not
known existed.

He was still smiling as he returned to the fire and
took the tea Bracht offered, savoring the brew as he
watched the light strengthen, filtering in shafts of
golden blue through the timber.

"You're mightily cheerful," Katya remarked, and
he nodded, beaming, answering "Aye," encompassing
their camp with a gesture. "This life is good."

"As well you think it so," said Bracht dryly, "for
there's much of it ahead. By nightfall we'll be on the
grass and in ni Larrhyn territory, and there we shall
need to mount a watch—against human wolves."

"Are the Lykard so fierce?" he asked, and Bracht
nodded.

"They are," he said. "And I think that with
Jehenne leading the ni Larrhyn now, that family will
be the fiercest."

Even that sobering warning failed to dampen
Calandryll's good humor and he hummed a half-
forgotten song as he struck his tent and stowed it
with the others on the packhorse, saddling his chestnut and taking the rearmost position as Bracht led
them onward through the timber.

They rode until midmorning through the trees,
then over more rock where only scrub grew, picking
up a stream and following its course down through
clefts and gorges to a wide cirque where a lake pooled
blue, reflecting the firs that ringed its circumference.
There they halted and ate, leaving the lake behind as
they climbed a narrow chine, seeing the final, lowest
stretch of cordillera ahead, beyond that, still misty,
the grass of the plains, an ax-sharp cut showing where
they should emerge onto the grassland.

Between the chine and the last line of hills the
trees grew thick, the trail patterned by the sunlight
that shone through the interwoven canopy of branches,
the air resinous and drowsy with the buzz of insects.
The hills ahead were lost behind the trunks and it was
a shock to find themselves in the mouth of the cut, the

timber ending dramatically on grey stone. The sun was moved toward its setting by now and Bracht announced that they would traverse the ravine and make camp at its farther end, heeling the black stallion into the defile.

The horse snickered nervously, tossing its head and stamping; behind, the packhorse whickered, plunging on the tether. Abruptly, Calandryll felt his chestnut quiver and curvet, threatening to unseat him. He heard Bracht curse and as his mount spun, prancing, he saw Katya's grey demonstrate the same reluctance to enter the cleft. It was all he could do to stay in the saddle, fighting the protesting animal to a standstill that left it with flattened ears and wildly rolling eyes, teeth champing against the bit. It pawed the rocky ground, snorting, and he backed it a little, feeling its protestations diminish as it moved farther from the ravine. Katya came back to join him, and her mount, likewise, calmed as it drew away from the shadowed stone. His eyes met the warrior woman's, hers clouded with a doubt he knew must be reflected in his own, and they both looked to where Bracht still fought the nervous stallion.

"Something must lie within," Calandryll shouted. "The horses sense it, or smell it."

"Come back," Katya called.

Cursing soundly, Bracht turned the stallion and trotted back to join them, the wild-eyed packhorse needing no encouragement, but matching the black stride for stride.

"What?" snapped the Kern, turning in his saddle to peer into the depths. "I saw nothing."

"It must lie farther in," Calandryll said. "Out of sight."

Bracht leaned forward to stroke the stallion's neck, soothing the great beast, and it tossed its head once and was still. The packhorse moved to the farthest extent of its tether, as far from the rock as it could get, seeking the proximity of the other animals, where it stood trembling.

"Something must be there," Katya said, fingering her saber.

Bracht grunted, eyeing the gloomy passage. "Save we spend two days or more riding these hills to the main pass, we've no choice but to enter." His voice, like his expression, was dour. "And the light will be gone ere long."

Calandryll looked skyward and saw the Kern was right: the sun lay close to the western peaks; soon the defile would lie in total darkness. He felt a great reluctance to attempt the passage by night.

"Perhaps we should camp here and go through when the sun stands high." He glanced at Bracht, at Katya, awaiting their response.

"Does anything malign lurk within, then likely it will emerge by darkness"—Bracht shook his head—"and here shall be no safer than there."

"And time is our enemy," Katya said, though with no great enthusiasm. "To find the other pass will delay us too long."

And perhaps the other pass is guarded, Calandryll thought, then promptly wondered why that word guarded sprang so readily to mind. Perhaps, he decided, because their way had been so far untroubled, unopposed. They had crossed Lysse without hindrance, quit Gannshold without obstruction. Perhaps it had been too easy. It was an uncomforting thought and he answered with a reluctant nod when Bracht said, "I think we have little choice."

"But wary," cautioned Katya.

"Aye," the Kern agreed, and turned to Calandryll again. "Do you sense aught of magic here?"

Calandryll sniffed the air. Horse sweat, pine scent, stone, and the mounting chill were all his nostrils found and he shook his head.

"Mayhap the Lykard slaughtered some beast," Bracht murmured, "and the smell of blood unnerves the horses."

"Your stallion, too?" asked Katya, and Bracht grunted a negative.

"We must lead them," he said, "and carry torches. If some beast haunts the way, flame will likely drive it off."

For no reason he could properly justify, Calandryll felt the certainty that whatever waited within the cleft was no mere beast to be frightened by flaming brands; but even so, it seemed, as Bracht had said, that little choice was left them: he joined the Kern in gathering branches, fashioning the sappy pine into stout flambeaux.

On Bracht's command they sacrificed a blanket to the making of blindfolds, that they secured over the horses' eyes. The reins were given into Katya's hands, her protests overridden by the Kern, who pointed out that of them all, he was the most adept with a blade, and that Calandryll's sword was blessed by Dera, and thus—were the unknown obstacle of sorcerous origin—likely their most effective weapon.

So it was that the two men went first into the defile, falchion and straightsword unsheathed, torches flaming in their left hands, Katya following some little way behind, cursing softly in the Vanu tongue as she struggled with the still-unwilling animals.

The air inside the cut was cold, the walls high and smooth, cutting off the sun even though the sky above remained blue. Calandryll realized he sweated as moisture chilled on his face and chest. He thought the beating of his heart must surely pound loud enough to be heard over the sputtering of the torches; his mouth was dry, and on the nape of his neck he felt the short hairs prickle. He held his torch forward, his sword at the ready, eyes probing the gloom ahead.

It seemed little affected by the light of the flambeaux, as if unnatural darkness held sway between the confining walls, and he was grateful for Bracht's presence. The Kern stepped resolutely out, his hawkish features lit red by the flames, his eyes narrowed in a grim visage, frowning as his nostrils flared, like a cautious animal testing the air. He glanced briefly at Calandryll, raised brows framing a silent question, and Calandryll nodded: through the piny odor of the torches he caught the scent of almonds.

Then that brief warning was overcome with another, a foul, charnel-house reek, as if flesh corrupted, its decay wafting thick along the cut, rotten and ripe so that he gagged, spitting.

"Magic!" he heard Bracht shout, what confirming answer he might have given stilled in his throat by the dreadful roar that gusted out on the Kern's cry.

It bellowed, echoing deafeningly off the stone, dinning ferociously against their eardrums, drowning the screaming of the blindfolded horses, Katya's yell. The sound of it seemed to magnify the darkness so that they stood lost in a fell night, swathed in a blackness so dense the torches were only pinprick lights, dulled by the stygian gloom and fetid stench that washed all around.

Faintly, near lost in that awful roaring, he heard Bracht shout, "Ahrd stand with us now!" and, unsure whether he voiced a prayer or a battle cry, answered, "Dera defend us!"

It seemed then that the roaring became a terrible choking growl, or laughter, and the darkness swirled, like mist shifted by the rushing passage of some great body, a mass so large it pushed aside the gloom. Through it—from it—charged a thing he could not at first define, only start back, sword defensive before him as corpse breath blew against his face and he stared in horror at the apparition crouching to spring.

It wore the body of a wolf, but no wolf known to man. It was huge, its jaws mantraps edged with dagger teeth, its eyes red and lit with a malignant intelligence. Its pelt was grey and ragged, torn, with yellow bone visible through the cuts, sinews exposed along its bunched legs, bone and raw muscle about the jaws. It looked a thing resurrected, some atavism, a dire-wolf long dead but now invested with a kind of life that it might halt them. It sprang.

Calandryll screamed a helpless challenge, raising his blade even as he knew the creature must over-

whelm him with its bulk alone, that those horrendous jaws must fasten on his head and crush his
skull. He was only dimly aware of Bracht thrusting
from the side, the falchion slashing viciously at flesh
that parted to spill out writhing maggots, the torch in
the Kern's left hand scorching hair that lent its own
rank stink to the fetid reek of the monster's rotting
body. It was pure instinct that bent Calandryll's
knees, dropping him below the snapping jaws, turning
him to the side, away from the dead thing's charge as
he drove the straightsword into a shoulder that
flapped tatters of unsavory skin, wounds that should
have bled but did not.

He heard the beast's growl change then, and Bracht
shout, "Ware Katya! Ware the horses!"

The Kern darted back, interposing himself between
the wolf-thing and the woman, but the creature ignored him, spinning to face Calandryll again, as if
whatever intelligence animated its defunct body fixed
on him alone. He crouched, torch and sword ready, no
longer afraid—too invigorated by fear to recognize its
presence—seeing the exposed muscles bunch anew.
Bracht struck again, from the creature's rear, carving
bloodless wounds over the hindquarters, hacking with
the falchion, driving the torch hard against the rump.
Uselessly: claws long as a man's fingers scrabbled on
stone as the beast launched itself once more at
Calandryll, and he flung himself aside, letting it go
past now, so that he and Bracht again stood between
it and Katya. The horses screamed, fighting her hold
on the reins, plunging so that she was lifted off her
feet, swinging helplessly as she sought to prevent
them fleeing wild back into the hills.

Calandryll saw sudden advantage in the confines of
the ravine as the monstrous dire-wolf landed; its bulk
was great enough it faced a moment northward, unable to turn as he sprang forward, driving his sword
hard and deep between two bare ribs. It howled then,
in pain as much as rage, and he turned the blade sav-

agely, dragging it corkscrewed out to strike again as
the thing turned, slashing across a shoulder.

The massive jaws snapped shut and he thrust his
torch at the face. The jaws opened, closing on the
flambeaux, snatching it from his hand. Smoke gusted
between the teeth, the monster's throat lit red as its
eyes, flames darting through the holes in its corrupted
flesh. It dropped the torch, the brand guttering and
dying, and the growling seemed again to become
laughter, the eyes fixing—contemptuous, he
thought—on his face. Certain now that he would die,
uncaring now, he slashed the straightsword in an arc
across the grim muzzle. The creature howled, and in
its scream he heard more pain than rage. At his side
he heard Bracht yell, "Your blade! Dera's magic works
against it!" and cut again, once, twice, carving lines
that should have bled, had life and not magic animated the thing, over the snarling face.

The dire-wolf faltered, crouching, but this time not
springing to the attack; almost, it seemed, cowering.
Calandryll danced a step toward it, thrusting, and saw
it retreat. He laughed, a cry near wild as the beast's
howling, and feinted at the muzzle. The head turned,
jaws snapping, and he rode his blow in beneath the
great maw, into the throat, carving a hole there,
snatching back his arm as the thing flinched and
twisted, threatening to tear his blade from his grip.
He backed away, motioning for Bracht to leave him
room and waited as the monster poised to spring.

He saw the huge body tense. He saw the great dead
legs straighten, propelling the creature forward and
up, the red eyes hidden by the parted jaws. And
dropped to a crouch, ignoring Bracht's cry as the
gloom grew darker, the air above him filled with the
hurtling body. He rammed the straightsword upward,
into the chest, rising with the blade, all his strength,
all his weight, all his trust in the goddess, behind the
blow.

The sword drove quillons-deep into the wolf-corpse
and the defile filled with its awful howl. Then silence

as its bulk bore him down and he was crushed beneath the stinking fur, struggling, close to panic, to escape the weight, choking on the stench. He could not breathe, nor fight clear. His head swam; his stomach rebelled, and he thought that he must vomit, drown in his own bile. He was unaware of Bracht's hands on his flailing wrist, dragging him from the writhing, still howling beast until his lungs were filled with cleaner air and his vision cleared enough that he could see the carrion creature's death throes.

He saw then that he had guessed aright: that the edge cuts delivered served only to irritate the beast; that the implantation of the goddess-favored sword destroyed it. He watched as the jaws stretched back from the fangs, agonized, and the red light in the eyes dulled, the great legs kicking ever feebler.

Then gasped, starting a horrified pace backward as the twice-dead thing spoke.

"So, again you survive. My congratulations—you prove more tenacious than I had anticipated, but no matter. I know now that you pursue me and so can leave further obstacles in your way. And worse than this, I promise. Better that you concede me the game, for you cannot win and only death awaits you do you continue. Go back now, fools! Go back while you still have your petty lives. Enjoy what time you have left, for now I wax wrathful and when Tharn rises you shall be called to account."

The voice was Rhythamun's.

14

RHYTHAMUN's voice faded; the corpse-wolf decayed, hide shriveling over bones and maggot-
infested organs that crumbled into dust; the carrion
stench dissipated. Calandryll snatched up his sword
from the powdery relict, passing the blade through
the flame of Bracht's torch: an act of cauterization, of
cleansing. Both stood staring at the dessicated remains, startled from their distasteful observation by
Katya's shout.

"Now that's done, do you help me with these
horses before they run free?"

So pragmatic was her demand that Calandryll
found himself laughing as he turned, running with
Bracht to where the warrior woman still fought the
still terrified animals. They each seized reins, calming
the beasts as best they could and leading them at a
trot past the remnants, the hooves scattering the dust,
leaving no trace behind. The sky yet held a little of
the day's light and farther along the defile they removed the blindfolds, mounting and riding hard, in silence, to where the gulley opened on the grass of
Cuan na'For.

By then the sun was gone and twilight descended
over the prairie, the cordillera ending as abruptly as

they had begun, cedar and cypress covering the gentle slope that ran down to the edge of the great grass sea. They made camp among the timber, by mutual assent riding out some distance from the pass to find a place where a narrow stream offered clean water and the dense clustering of trunks would conceal their fire. Calandryll plunged his face into the water, grateful for its cleansing cold, rinsing a mouth in which he could still taste the filth of the wolf-thing. Even then he thought he still smelled the creature's rank scent on his tunic and breeks, and would have stripped them off and washed them had they the time. But that commodity—the more so now!—was short-supplied: Rhythamun knew they lived and came after him, and now, more than ever, they must be on their guard. He cursed himself as he dried his face, that glum as he walked to the fire and squatted close to its flames, letting the sweet-scented smoke drift about clothing that held too near a memory of the fight with the resurrected dire-wolf.

"You slew the thing." Bracht turned spitted meat in the cheerful flames. "Why brood on it?"

"I should have guessed," he returned, inwardly directed anger rendering his answer curt. "In Aldarin I should have guessed, when Rhythamun spoke through the stone."

"Guessed what?" Bracht asked.

"That he would never leave the way so open."

"He thought us lost in Tezin-dar," Katya said. "Trapped there by the closing gates."

"He thinks farther ahead, more subtly."

Calandryll scowled into the fire; Bracht said gently, "Do you explain?"

"He hoped we should be lost in Tezin-dar." Calandryll reached out, passing a hand through the flames. "Perhaps even thought we were, but still that would never be enough for him. He had to know—and so he left the stone, imbued with his magic. I was a fool to touch it. I should have known."

"We deal with sorcery," Bracht said, "and that is ever devious."

"Still I should have known—that more than vanity, pride, whatever reasons I ascribed, lay behind that manifestation. Do you not see?"

Bracht shook his head; Katya studied Calandryll's face, her eyes intent. He continued: "The talisman was linked with me; connected by his magic. In my hand it came to life, he appeared before us"—this with a glance at Katya, who ducked her head in agreement—"and then I thought mere pride governed his sortilege, that he worked his magicks solely to mock us. But he planned deeper—when I touched the stone, I told him we survived; that we were come back to Aldarin. And in telling him, I warned him—he must then consider the likelihood of our pursuing him, and consequently devise stratagems against us."

"He changed his shape," Bracht said. "He took the form of Daven Tyras—surely he thought to deceive us thus, to escape us."

"Surely he hoped to thus deceive us," retorted Calandryll, anger still in his voice, on his face. "Surely he hoped that in another's body he would leave us behind, lose himself in Cuan na'For. But the prize he seeks is dreadful enough he'll not take chances. No, he looks to halt even the possibility of pursuit. Hence that wolf-beast."

Bracht glanced skyward at that, scanning the heavens and the trees, perhaps remembering the *quyvhal* Anomius had sent to watch them in Kandahar. When his eyes returned to Calandryll's face they were troubled and he asked, "How could he know we should take the lesser trail?"

"Likely," Calandryll replied, "there's some similar monstrosity left to guard the larger pass. Likely there's some occult beast that wards every entrance into Cuan na'For."

"But still you slew it," said the Kern.

"Aye." Calandryll nodded, once and sourly. "And

in so doing, told him where we are. Likely he's sent Lykard riding to apprehend us even now."

"I think not," Katya said, and he spun toward her, frowning.

"No? Then what shall he do? Grant us free passage? Set his token with those others Bracht bought?"

She ignored the bitterness in his voice, fixing him with a grey-eyed stare as she said, "How should he tell the Lykard of us, save he reveals himself for a warlock? Bracht, did you not say even the Lykard would turn against him were he revealed?"

"Aye," Bracht answered. "Did he show himself— did the ghost-talkers scry him true—even the Lykard would surely join against him."

"Then what he does, he must do in secret. I think he'll not look to hinder his own passage by arousing enmity among those he looks to for aid. I think what spells he works must be done clandestine, hidden from the ghost-talkers lest he lose the support of the ni Brhyn. They surely believe him Daven Tyras, no? And so, Daven Tyras he must be—a half-blood and nothing more. I do not think he'll send out warriors to block our way."

She fell silent, awaiting a response. Bracht nodded, grunting approval of her logic. Calandryll paused, thinking on her words, finding them convincing— there was much sense in them—but not yet quite ready to give up his anger, for all it was directed at himself.

"Even so," he muttered, "you heard him speak—he promised further obstacles in our path. Already we face the wrath of Jehenne ni Larrhyn, and now it seems we must anticipate thaumaturgy besides. Shall we fight our way across all Cuan na'For?"

"If we must," Bracht said. "Ahrd, Calandryll! Today we faced a creation of nightmare and you slew it! You wear a blade blessed by a goddess—and that's proven true. Whatever gramaryes he weaves to halt us, we face them as they come. We've the Younger Gods as allies and Rhythamun shall not escape us!"

"Save we die in the chase."

"There's that," Bracht agreed casually. "But is that
reason to concede the field?"

"No." Calandryll shook his head, beginning to
smile. "But still I wish we'd not forewarned him."

Bracht shrugged, reaching out to remove meat that
threatened to burn forgotten, passing them each a
spitted piece.

"I think," said Katya slowly, holding the meat in
both her hands, "that Cuan na'For is likely too great
he may watch it all. Likely he knows of the ni
Larrhyn's enmity and looks to that to . . . delay . . . us.
Likely he'll loose those occult creations he threatened, but still they must find us; or be left like markers along his trail. And as Bracht says—the first is
already slain, so why not the next? I think time our
greatest enemy now."

She paused, nibbling daintily, wiping grease from
her chin.

"Say on," urged Calandryll, cheering now, his anger
fading, intrigued by the direction her thinking took.

"He rides with the ni Brhyn," she went on, "northward. Likely, are we not agreed, toward the Borrhun-
maj?"

"It seems the most probable course," Calandryll
allowed.

"And while he remains ahead, he's the advantage of
us."

"With Jehenne ni Larrhyn and whatever else he's
magicked twixt us and him, aye."

"Then could we overtake him, or get ahead of him,
we'd deny him that advantage."

Calandryll said, "Aye, that's true."

Bracht said, "I do not think I like the direction of
this."

Katya chuckled. Calandryll nodded slowly: "You
say we should ride for the Cuan na'Dru, directly."

The woman, in turn, nodded. "As I said before—
trusting in Ahrd."

"Ahrd I trust," Bracht said, low. "The Gruagach . . ."

He left the sentence hanging: unspoken threat. "Can they be so dangerous?" Katya said, not really asking a question. "You say they guard your tree god, and once already Ahrd has sent you help. Burash promised that Calandryll would be heard, should he cry for aid; Dera told us her kin will give what assistance they may. So—shall Ahrd permit his guardians to harm us?"

Bracht shrugged, not speaking, doubt hooding his eyes.

"What else is there?" Katya pressed. "We've Jehenne to avoid, and Rhythamun's creations; he's likely with the ni Brhyn now, or gone on. Toward the Kess Imbrun and the Jesseryn Plain, perhaps. Shall we skirt round the forest?"

"I think he will," said Bracht.

"Then, even though he knows we come after him, he must take that time to avoid Ahrd's domain. Do we cross it, we may come out ahead of him. May well learn from Ahrd where he is."

"Do the Gruagach grant us that passage," Bracht said.

"Gods!" Katya shook her head, her expression pitched somewhere between amusement and frustration. "You'll take the chance of Jehenne ni Larrhyn nailing you to a tree, you'll charge bare-blade against a dead thing made by foul necromancy, but these Gruagach . . . What are they, that they set such doubt in you?"

"The forest guardians," Bracht said, a trifle sullenly, as if he thought his courage questioned—which in a way, Calandryll supposed, it was. "I know no more of them than that. Save that through the edgewoods of the Cuan na'Dru lie the moldering bones of men who have seen them."

"Men who've spoken with gods?" asked Katya, her voice gentle now, reassuring. "Men promised godly aid?"

Bracht shrugged again, tossing the stick he held
into the fire. Grease sizzled briefly, spitting in the
flames. Bracht wiped his hands on grass, staring
moodily into the darkness.

"I think," Calandryll offered tentatively, troubled
by the Kern's obvious reservations, "that we may
have no other choice."

"Mayhap he does not go north," Bracht said, but
with no great conviction.

"Where then?" Katya demanded. "Not east, for
that way he'd have found easier—swifter—passage by
boat, out of Aldarin. West? Back into Gessyth? Why
leave the swamps, then? Why go back to Aldarin at
all?"

"He goes north," Bracht admitted.

"And ahead of us," said Katya. "Far enough ahead
he's opportunity to elude us. Do you know the
Jesseryn Plain?"

"No." Bracht waved a negative hand.

"Nor I, or Calandryll," she said. "But while he remains in Cuan na'For we at least know he takes the
shape of Daven Tyras, and you know this land. What
if he goes across the Kess Imbrun and steals the body
of some Jesseryte? Then it may be we must pursue a
stranger in a strange land. I say our best chance of victory is here, now—and therefore speed is of the essence."

Bracht sighed, studying her earnest face; turned
worried eyes to Calandryll, who was not sure what
the Kern wanted of him, but could only duck his head
in agreement and say, "I think Katya's right."

"Ahrd is not our enemy," she murmured, "so how
shall his guardians be?"

"We might approach the edgewoods," Calandryll
said. "Cautiously, and do the Gruagach deny us entry,
then we ride around."

Bracht's lips narrowed, pressing together, and for a
moment Calandryll thought he would argue for the
more circuitous route, but then he grunted, nodded,
and said, "So be it—we attempt the Cuan na'Dru."

Katya smiled, but it went unnoticed by the Kern, for he rose and walked over to the horses, as if to hide his doubts, or to reassure himself with the proximity of the familiar animals. Calandryll watched as he stroked the stallion's muscular neck, the black head rising to nuzzle his face, a snicker of pleasure gusting from the beast's nostrils.

"You think me right?" asked Katya softly, so that Bracht should not hear.

Calandryll turned toward her. In the firelight her hair shone like red-gold, the flames playing shadow games across her face. He wondered if she doubted as he nodded. "You've logic," he agreed. "It seems our swiftest course."

It was, he knew, a somewhat equivocal answer, but there was that in Bracht's reaction that aroused his own doubts. The Kern's initial hesitation to enter Cuan na'For at all had been explained, and once it became obvious they must come here, he had agreed, despite the threat of crucifixion—which, it seemed to Calandryll, was a threat unpleasant enough to give any man pause—but this was something else, something deeper. Bracht's courage was proven—beyond his own, he thought—and so this reluctance to venture even close to the Gruagach must be a thing set deeper in the Kern than any fear of physical hazard, something that appeared to strike into the roots of his soul. And if his doubts were soundly based—if the mysterious Gruagach should deny them entrance, or look to slay them—then it must be the longer way.

"He's no coward," he heard Katya murmur, as if echoing his own thoughts, "I wonder what they are, these Gruagach?"

"I expect," he answered slowly, as if Bracht's doubts infected his own mind, "that we shall find out."

Katya nodded and he saw a measure of reservation in her eyes.

"But still it's the logical thing," he said, not sure if he sought to instill confidence in her or himself, "and as you say—Ahrd must surely be our friend and let us safely through."

"Aye." She smiled. "But I'd lief Bracht believed that a little stronger."

Whether he did or not, Bracht gave no sign when he came back to the fire, though he seemed resolute enough, as if, committed now, he allowed himself no more room for doubt. Or hid it, resuming his more customary manner as he outlined what lay ahead and how they should commence their journey across the grass.

With spring come, he explained, the horse herds would be foaling and the clans largely occupied with that, tending and guarding their animals, rather than roaming the prairie. That would limit the activities of potential enemies, affording a better chance of reaching the Cuan na'Dru unhindered. Nor would they ride land quite so open as Calandryll had anticipated, for while the central forest was by far the largest spread of woodland, it was not the only one, the grass between them and it scattered with lesser hursts, and broken by combes and straths. They would, inevitably, cross open terrain, but with luck and Bracht's knowledge of the Lykard grazing, they had fair enough chance of escaping detection.

"Gart and Kythan spoke of them massing eastward," Katya said, "because the creatures of Hell Mouth stir."

"We ride the very edge of their grazing," Bracht replied. "The line betwixt theirs and my own clan's— even with Hell Mouth spilling out its strangeling things, they'll not risk war with the Asyth while their mares drop foals."

"And if Rhythamun is still with the ni Brhyn?" Calandryll asked. "What then?"

"We've the tokens to bring us safe over their territory," Bracht answered. "We confront him—challenge him. With such a charge against him, the drachomannii must scry him and he'll be exposed for what he is."

"A sorcerer of proven power," Calandryll grunted.

"Aye, of that there's no doubt," Bracht said, and grinned, his old self again. "And then—well, you tell me to trust in the Younger Gods, so surely you must trust in Dera's promise that you've the power in you to defeat him."

Calandryll grinned back, caught in the trap: so it was—he must trust the goddess, even though he felt no inkling of that promised ability. In the final analysis they had, all of them, only faith to sustain them; but that so far, he reminded himself, had served well enough. He chuckled, that becoming a yawn, and Bracht suggested they bed down.

THE new morning spread mist through the timber, drifting down from the hills to wreathe the trees in ethereal grey, moisture sparkling on grass and branches and horse hide as the sun shone pale in the east and the fattening moon lingered reluctant at the westernmost limit of the sky. Calandryll rebuilt the fire as Bracht checked the horses and Katya prepared their breakfast, and when they had eaten they prepared to mount.

"String your bows," Bracht advised, "and ride ready to use them. If fight we must, it's likely to be off horseback."

They obeyed, latching the quivers forward of their saddles and fixing the bows inside the containers. Calandryll, for all his practice, wondered how well he might flight a shaft from the back of a running horse, thinking that that was a very different proposition to firing from the ground, or the deck of a warboat. *Faith*, he told himself, *have faith. With any luck we'll pass unchallenged.*

He held that thought as he swung astride the chestnut gelding and followed Bracht down the slope, leaving the spread of timber behind, cedar and cypress thinning until before them lay a vast spread of grass. Bracht reined in there, all the doubts of the last night

seemingly forgotten as he beamed, rising in his stirrups to encompass the panorama with a sweeping gesture. "Cuan na'For," he said, reverence in his tone,
delight shining in his blue eyes.

Calandryll stared round, for a moment daunted by
the vastness of the prairie stretching before them. The
sun was risen higher and the sky grown purest blue,
high banks of cumulus building white as snow across
the eastern horizon, ribbons of cirrus streamered high
overhead. A breeze set the grass to rippling and he
thought it was as though he looked upon a sea, a great
earthly ocean, its waters a myriad shifting shades of
green. Far off sunlight sparkled on a river, and scattered over the enormous expanse of verdant land
there were darker patches, like cloud shadows—the
woodlands Bracht had promised. The air was fresh,
clean, and scented with the smell of the grass, of
springtime growth. He thought no land could be
larger, and then that the finding of Rhythamun in
such an enormity must surely be impossible; which,
in turn, convinced him that Katya had been right and
they must look to Ahrd for help.

"Come," he heard Bracht say, and heeled the chestnut to a canter, going down the last of the gradient
onto flatter ground, where the grass grew high and
rustled in the wind like some half-heard song, a wistful melody counterpointed by the trilling and chir-
ruping of the little birds that fluttered, bright-plumed,
among the verdancy.

They held a steady pace until they came to the
river, its banks marked by willows, steep where the
grass ended, with benches of yellow sand from which
ducks and wagtails fled at their arrival. Bracht bade
them wait awhile as he rode a way along the bank, in
both directions, his eyes intent upon the sand, returning to inform them he found no sign of hoofprints to
indicate the presence of Lykard, and they splashed
across the shallow water and continued on.

At noon they halted to rest the animals and eat,
still without sight of other humans, though often

they saw scattered herds of wild horses grazing the lush prairie, the king stallions whickering a challenge that was answered by Bracht's mount.

They cantered on, Calandryll realizing how deceptive the terrain was, for what had seemed from that morning's vantage point flat grassland rolled and folded in distance-hidden hollows, shallow bowls, and occasionally sharp-flanked cuts. A squadron of horsemen might wait hidden in those undulations, unseen until a careless rider came down on them, or they on him, and he grew more wary, scanning their surroundings as Bracht did. But still no riders were met, although toward the midmost hour of the afternoon they saw, off to the west, plumes of smoke drifting up, marking the position of some Lykard encampment. They speeded their pace then, leaving the smoke behind as they drew nearer a hurst.

As with the land itself, the perspectives of the wood were deceptive. It seemed at first of no great size, but as they closed on it, it seemed to grow, to expand to east and west, far larger than Calandryll had judged. Silver-barked birches were lit by the descending sun, spread like some natural pallisade about the perimeter of the woodland, giving way to hornbeams deeper in, those rising high, to spread their limbs over ground barely grassed and still thick with a crisp layering of fallen leaves. Bracht led them in until the prairie was lost to sight, their path shadowy and loud with bird song, riding steadily deeper until alders showed where a spring gurgled up to form a small pond. They halted there, gathering the makings of a fire but not setting spark to the tinder until dusk fell and the sky grew dark, concealing the smoke. Then, confident that the density of surrounding trunks would hide the glow, they prepared a meal and pitched their tents. Remembering the smoke from the Lykard fires they decided to mount a guard that night, and Calandryll was shaken awake by Katya, the middle watch falling to him.

He wrapped his cloak about his shoulders, the

nights being still chilly, and slung his quiver across
his back, taking up his bow as he paced a dutiful
round. The moon thickened, lancing pale light over
the woodland floor, and through the overhang of
branches he saw a vista of stars twinkling. The horses
snuffled and snorted, making those sounds horses
make in sleep; nightjars sang their strident song and
owls their softer calls; earthbound predators hunted
the darkness, their presence announced only by the
dying cries of their prey. But he felt no threat, for all
he held an arrow nocked, as if the wood breathed
peace, telling him in its dendroid way that no harm
should come while they remained within its boundaries. He thought perhaps this was some silent message sent by Ahrd, so firm was the conviction, though
this particular woodland seemed not to contain any
oaks. His watch was uneventful and he woke Bracht
at the agreed hour to find his bed and fall calmly into
a dreamless sleep.

The next morning dawned bright, and after eating
they started off again through the timber, Bracht once
more in the lead. The narrow trail they took slowed
them and it was close on noon before they left the
wood, emerging on the open ground with no sign of
further welcome cover ahead. Still, they encountered
no ni Larrhyn riders as they traversed the prairie, alternating between canter and walk, the sun warm on
their backs, the ever-present wind rustling the knee-
high grass. They saw more horses, and sometimes the
wild dogs Bracht explained were the chief predators of
the grasslands, though the canines stayed always, can-
nily, well beyond bowshot. They were ugly creatures,
blunt of muzzle and heavy-jawed, with long legs and
stubby tails, mottled of coat so that they blended
with the grass, appearing and disappearing like phantoms as they hunted. It was a profitable time for
them, when sickly foals might be easily taken, and
that culling, Bracht declared, ensured they offered no
danger—in leaner seasons they might, unlike the

wolves of the higher country, chance attacking a careless rider.

That night they camped in a shallow hollow, without a fire, aware of the smoke they had seen during the afternoon, closer than before, and started early, while the sun was barely over the eastern horizon. Bracht passed the packhorse into Calandryll's care, announcing his intention of scouting ahead, and kicked the black stallion to a gallop that carried him rapidly out of sight.

He returned around midmorning, riding fast, swinging the stallion alongside Katya's grey gelding as she and Calandryll waited nervously to learn what he had found.

"Ni Larrhyn horsemen," he declared, pointing directly ahead. "Moving across our path."

"Coming our way?" the warrior woman asked.

"Moving westward." Bracht shook his head. "But still they'll see us, save we're careful."

Calandryll stared round, seeing only the grass: no place to hide.

"Swift," Bracht snapped and he realized he had slowed instinctively, heeling the chestnut up to a canter on the Kern's urging, the packhorse whickering a protest as the tether was snatched tight. "Do we fight them?" he called.

"We hide from them," Bracht returned, leaving Calandryll no choice but to follow, confused.

It seemed they must ride head-on toward the ni Larrhyn, their paths intersecting, for if the riders crossed their way and they continued this northward progress he could see no other choice in it, nor refuge of any kind. *Bracht knows this country*, he told himself, *trust him*; but still he doubted, thinking that surely they must gallop into a battle.

They splashed across a stream, lined like the earlier river with willows and alders, and he realized the terrain sloped upward, and that Bracht made directly for the crest, where surely they must be outlined in all this flat country. But when he topped the ridge he saw no sign of horsemen and guessed the land folded, hiding them, confidence in the Kern's prairie lore growing then. Cheered, he urged the chestnut to a faster pace, thundering down the farther slope, over more flat, then down again, into a wide bowl, where Bracht reined in.

The Kern was out of his saddle in the same moment, the stallion curvetting as the reins snapped tight. Bracht reached down, seizing a fetlock and lifting as he shoved hard against the animal's shoulder, muttering urgently in his own language. The stallion snorted a protest, but it knelt, trained to the maneuver, and rolled onto its side. Bracht stroked the muzzle, briefly, still speaking, and dropped the reins across the glossy neck; the stallion remained supine as he darted back.

"Hold the packhorse," he commanded as he repeated the action, rougher with Calandryll's mount and Katya's. "And lie across their necks. Keep a hand on the muzzle; keep them down and silent."

Calandryll obeyed, twisting to watch as Bracht shouldered the packhorse down and followed his own instructions.

Then they could only wait, after a while aware of a vibration that drummed from the ground, telling them horses approached. Calandryll felt an insect land on his neck, treading delicately through the sweat there, its touch feather-light and mightily irritating. He held one hand clamped over the chestnut's nostrils, feeling the beast's neck strain against his weight, as he slapped with his other at the offending bug. It lifted clear, only to return once he removed his hand and he gave up the attempt, resigning himself to suffering its attentions as the vibration became sound, resolving into the steady pounding of hooves. They came closer, louder and louder, and he fastened his hand tighter on the chestnut as the gelding's eyes rolled and it struggled to rise. He felt the insect joined by another, teasing him, urging him to let go his hold on the horse and slap them away. He resisted the temptation, chancing a look round, seeing Katya sprawled across her grey, her tanned face slick with sweat, her eyes intent on the rim of the bowl. Bracht lay farther back, immobile over the packhorse. Calandryll saw that his bow and quiver lay before the animal and thought that he had not noticed the Kern take up the weapon. The black stallion lay utterly still.

The hoofbeats seemed overwhelming now, like sullen thunder, as if the riders came down into the hollow. Calandryll cursed silently, realizing that his own bow lay trapped beneath the bulk of the chestnut, then that the ni Larrhyn must surely be so close as to render the bow useless: when they saw the three intruders it must surely be swordwork that was needed. He wondered how many warriors there were.

Then, to his surprise, he sensed a difference in the sound, in the vibration. It lessened, the drumbeat pounding fading, growing indistinct until it was no more than a memory, an echo held by strained nerves. He started as a hand touched his shoulder and heard Bracht say cheerfully, "Save you develop some unnatural affection for that horse you can let it up."

He wriggled clear, the beast surging to its feet, shaking its head and blowing, eyes still rolling. He stroked it, soothing its nervousness until he felt sure the trembling in both of them was gone. Katya, likewise, gentled her mount, and Bracht the packhorse, calling softly to the stallion, which came upright of its own accord and stood silently surveying its master.

"I'd thought . . ." Calandryll paused, sighing gustily. "Dera, but I'd thought they must come on us then."

Bracht chuckled, motioning for him to mount. "There are places enough to hide"—he grinned—"do you know the land. You'll learn."

Calandryll nodded from his saddle. Bracht walked the packhorse closer to the stallion, mounted, and beckoned them after him, up out of the concealing bowl, but eastward now, circling north again across a swath cut through the grass.

"We need ride wary awhile," he warned, looking to the west. "Their camp will be close."

How close they saw as dusk came down, the twilight revealing stark the glow of campfires, less than a league distant.

"So," Bracht decided, "we'll rest a little and go on through the night—they'll be out after the wild foals again on the morrow. It may be we must travel by darkness a spell."

Neither Calandryll nor Katya found fault with his argument and they ate cold meat as full darkness spread over the prairie and the wind dropped away, the air growing colder.

"Shall they not find our trail?" asked Calandryll.

"They'll find a trail," Bracht agreed, "but Ahrd willing, they'll think it no more than wild horses."

"Then shall they not follow it?" Calandryll wondered. "If they hunt wild horses?"

"Four are scarce worth their time," Bracht assured him. "And they'll see there are no foals. No, I think we're safe enough, save they sight us."

Which, Calandryll thought, was all too easy if no convenient hollow or hurst presented itself.

That pessimism, though, he kept to himself as they mounted again and proceeded on their journey.

It was hardly slowed by the darkness, for the moon was filled enough now that the grassland shone silvery beneath its glow, that augmented by starlight, the sky stretching vast overhead, presenting myriad constellations to light their way. Calandryll thought that he had never seen so many stars, not even as they crossed the Narrow Sea or the interior of Lysse, as if the vast expanse of Cuan na'For was mirrored in the sky. They cantered like ghosts, league after league until the panoply above was dimmed by the approach of dawn. Bracht slowed then, as the star-pocked velvet became grey, the eastern horizon glowing with the flirtation of the false dawn. They found a stream and

paused on its bank to water their animals, not daring
to linger there, for fear of wild horses coming to
drink, their presence attracting the Lykard. Instead,
they rode on as the false dawn faded and the world
was blanketed in darkest grey obfuscation, Bracht finally calling a halt below the scarp of a low ridge, declaring that they might sleep awhile and go on once
he had scouted their surroundings.

Calandryll had the first watch and climbed to the
ridge's crest to see the sun come brilliant into the sky,
the world bathed in hues of fire that ran like liquid
flame against the last vestiges of night, birds rising
loud all about and the wind starting again, softly insistent. He heard the howling of the dog packs as they
commenced their day's hunting, and the whinnying of
the wild horses, the stallions screaming defiance at
the canines. Far off, close to the limits of his vision,
he saw a herd break from its grazing and begin to run,
coming south and west, toward the ridge. As the
horses drew closer, smaller shapes became visible,
loping behind, and he saw the herd was pursued, or
driven, by a fluid line of dogs. He watched as a dappled mare faltered, slowing, and three dogs ran close,
snapping at her legs. Two more moved to attack
from the front and a stallion turned from his headlong flight to charge back, his scream a challenge.
Calandryll watched, fascinated by the drama, as the
stallion plunged headlong at the dogs, bowling one
over, yelping, spinning to dash hooves down against
the tumbling predator. A second was sent flying by the
rear hooves and then the mare was running clear,
the stallion pausing a moment, plunging, pawing air,
the morning loud with his shrill whickering before
he, too, raced to rejoin the herd.

Calandryll followed their progress, seeing a group
of dogs break off the pursuit to fall upon a foundering
youngster, this one less fortunate than the mare, soon
hamstrung, soon after dead. He turned from the dog's
bloody gorging to watch the herd, seeing it turn from
the direction of the ridge to run westward, toward the

columns of windblown smoke that marked the ni
Larrhyn encampment. That was too far distant that
he could make out anything more than a vague
smudging on the grass, a hint of sizable tents, but in
time he saw horsemen coming out, presumably
alerted by the crying of the horses and the howling of
their pursuers. He crouched closer to the ground, confident that over such a distance he could not be seen,
but still urged by caution to avoid the chance.

Herd and horsemen came together, the one turning
northward, the riders going past, loosing arrows at the
dogs. Faintly now, Calandryll heard the yowling that
announced a hit, and then the pack was gone, faded
back into the grass, and the Lykard warriors turned after the herd. Where the foal had gone down birds circled, black against the early morning sky, waiting for
the dogs to finish their feasting that theirs might begin. Calandryll sighed, mourning the foal's demise
even as he acknowledged the inexorable cycle. He ran
his hands through the dew-wet grass and rubbed them
over his face, murmuring a prayer to Dera, and then,
for good measure, one to Ahrd, reminded by the
drama how close death stood in this wide and open
country.

When the sun had risen higher he woke Bracht,
pointing out the Lykard camp.

The Kern nodded, grunting, and said, "Best we
sleep the day out with them so close, and travel by
night again."

"Shall I unsaddle the horses?" Calandryll asked.

"I think not." Bracht stared to where the smoke
rose, his face solemn. "It might be we need to move
out fast."

Calandryll shrugged and left the Kern to his watch,
going down the slope to stretch out on his blanket,
tired now.

Warmed pleasantly by the sun he slept soon and
sound, waking slowly, at first not sure where he was,
then starting as he heard the sound of scraping on
steel. His right hand was locked firm about the hilt of

his sword before he recalled he lay on the ground below a ridge in Cuan na'For, a group of hostile ni
Larrhyn not far away. That remembrance brought the
straightsword smooth from the scabbard as he rolled,
coming to a crouch even as the remnants of sleep quit
his eyes. He saw Bracht grinning, looking up from the
honing of his falchion, and slid the blade home into
the sheath.

"All's well," Bracht said. "Katya holds the watch
and you've slept the better part of the day."

Calandryll peered skyward, seeing the sun moved
across the blue, closing on the western horizon. Katya
was squatted on the ridge crest, her bow across her
knees, and the horses grazed contentedly a little way
off. He found his water bottle and took a long drink,
then his stomach rumbled and Bracht chuckled,
pointing to the saddlebags lying nearby.

"Cold food again. And more until we find some
safer place."

It was sufficient for Calandryll: the dried meat and
hard biscuit seemed a luxury, eaten without immediate threat of belligerent interruption.

His hunger sated, he went in search of what privacy the terrain offered to attend another need, and
that done, returned to squat by Bracht, tending his
own blades with the whetstone.

"Shall we travel always by night?" he asked, answered with a shaking of Bracht's head.

"For a while, perhaps, but in a day or two we'll be
clear of this grazing and go by day again."

"Shall there not be more ni Larrhyn, then?" he
wondered.

"Not soon," Bracht said. "The families are scattered in spring—once we're clear of this group, our
way will be open awhile."

Calandryll nodded, thinking a moment, then: "Do
they not join?"

"Not yet," Bracht replied. "Not until the foaling is
done. Then they'll mass—at summer's start—close on
the Cuan na'Dru to thank Ahrd for his bounty and

ask his blessing. Again toward winter, but not yet: now they're spread thin. Luck was with us, that we came into Cuan na'For at this time of year."

"Luck?" Calandryll murmured. "Or some design?"

"Whichever." Bracht shrugged. "It's our good fortune."

"I wonder if the Younger Gods had a hand in it," Calandryll said thoughtfully. "Had Burash not carried us so swift over the Narrow Sea . . ."

Bracht grunted and said, "Perhaps. But then perhaps if the Chaipaku had not taken us, Burash would not have taken a hand. Did the Brotherhood then act their part?"

"Perhaps they did," Calandryll said. "Albeit unwittingly."

"Theirs was—is!—aid I'd do without." Bracht chuckled.

"Still." Calandryll shrugged, suddenly enjoying this enforced leisure that afforded him the time to muse on such philosophical considerations. "We've said before that it seems Tharn perhaps stirs in his limbo to affect the world. Why not Balatur, also? Perhaps he, too, plays some dreaming part."

"Perhaps," Bracht allowed, "or perhaps it was no more than chance that brought us back to Lysse, over the Gann Peaks, at a good time."

Calandryll nodded. "Or the Younger Gods, or Balatur even, lend us what aid they may."

"That so," Bracht said doubtfully, "why do they not halt Rhythamun themselves?"

"The design denies it." Calandryll shook his head. "Dera told us their aid is limited, that this is a thing of men—that men must play their part."

"She spoke to you and Katya," Bracht reminded him. "Not to me. If there's some design here, I cannot see it. I see only we three, in pursuit of Rhythamun; with little enough help save what we make for ourselves."

"I believe there's more," Calandryll declared firmly.

"Then pray Ahrd's planted some woods in our way," retorted Bracht, "for we'll encounter no Lykard there."

"Why not?"

The Kern frowned a moment, his expression suggesting Calandryll had asked a question so foolish he had no ready answer. Then he smiled, his dark features warming. "I forget you know so little of Cuan na'For," he said gently, friendship's patience in his voice and eyes. "Cuan na'For is a land of horses, of horsemen, no? And horses live on the grass." He gestured with the falchion, encompassing the prairie all around. "With so much, they've no taste for woodland—so animals and men, both, inhabit the open country, not the woods."

Calandryll nodded, understanding. "So in woodland, we are safe," he said.

"Aye," said Bracht.

"But surely you use wood?"

"That's true." Bracht used a thumb to test the falchion's edge, gingerly, grunting his satisfaction and sliding the blade home in its scabbard. "For the great carts, the lodge poles, saddles and such stuff ... but taken from those coppices Ahrd allows may be touched. And never oak!"

"How do you know," asked Calandryll, "which may be touched, and which not?"

"The drachomannii, the ghost-talkers, decide," Bracht said. "They speak with Ahrd and he advises them."

Again Calandryll nodded. "These ghost-talkers ..." he began to ask, silenced by the swift raising of Bracht's hand.

"Best not discuss them," the Kern said quickly. "There'll be one there." He stabbed a finger in the direction of the ni Larrhyn camp. "And they have long ears. Did he hear you ..."

He shrugged, leaving the sentence unfinished. Calandryll ducked his head, accepting, thinking that there was much to learn of Cuan na'For and its ways;

much that was not mentioned in the works of
Sarnium or Medith, or any of the scholars and histo-
rians he had once read so avidly. So long ago, it
seemed. Perhaps someday he would scribe it all, all he
learned on this quest . . . He smiled at the thought, reminded that it was one he had entertained before.
And that before such bookish matters might be in-
dulged, the quest must first be concluded; and suc-
cessfully, for otherwise he and Bracht and Katya must
surely all be fallen victim to Rhythamun's insane ambition.

He finished the edging of his own weapons, aware
that the sky darkened in the east and soon they would
be on their way again.

Indeed, as the sun fell below the rim of the world
and the sky to the west was banded with red light,
Bracht called Katya down from the ridge and they ate
a hurried meal, mounting as the last of the light faded
and the constellations spread thick above. Again the
night was bright with the light of moon and stars, and
they were able to proceed near as fast as if they rode
under the sun, the menacing glow of the ni Larrhyn
campfires disappearing behind them, the prairie
empty before.

Once, they came on a sleeping dog pack, lifting to
a gallop as the canines yelped and snapped in alarm at
the disturbance, but the beasts scattered rather than
attacking them, and soon their outraged snarling
faded into the silence of the night. Twice, they disturbed herds, though these did little more than
whicker and watch, the stallions prancing, offering no
more threat than the startled dogs. They forded a sizable river and rode through a coppice where hewn
trunks and pollarding showed Lykard usage, though
not, to judge by the fresh growth, of recent origin.
Close on dawn, as the sky once more brightened, they
halted, this time on flat country, devoid of ridges or
hollows, or any other cover.

"Should we not go on?" Calandryll asked.

"In a while," Bracht answered, dismounting. "The horses must rest, should they need to run."

"Shall the ni Larrhyn range this far?" asked Katya, that met with a grim smile and a nod.

"Ahrd willing, they'll not find us." Bracht unsaddled his stallion, removed the packhorse's load. "But if they do, we'll want rested animals—save you look to fight them."

"I'd sooner not," she replied, and set to rubbing down her mount. "But this is a very open place."

"A little while only," the Kern promised. "Until the horses have their wind. Then we'll go on. Until then, our watch had best be alert."

Calandryll had rather they continued, for this was—as Katya remarked—a mightily exposed spot, and though he followed Bracht's example, stripping off the chestnut's saddle and ministering to the beast, he felt very nervous. Too much so, he found, to sleep, for though Bracht took the first watch, advising his companions to rest themselves, when he stretched on his blanket and closed his eyes he could think of nothing save wandering Lykard happening upon them and his ears strained for sound of hoofbeats, cries of alarm. None came as the true dawn lit the sky, but still he could not sleep and after a while of tossing restlessly while Katya slumbered—seemingly able to relax at will, like Bracht—he gave up and rose, pacing to where the Kern squatted.

"I've not your knack for sleep," he murmured when Bracht glanced his way. "Shall I take the watch?"

"We'll share it."

Bracht grinned briefly, and Calandryll saw that his expression was somber, abruptly realizing that the Kern's apparent confidence was designed more to reassure, to grant his comrades a measure of rest, than from any genuine belief in their safety. "You think they'll find us," he said slowly.

"I think they may," Bracht returned. "But still the horses need rest."

"And if they do?"

"We run or fight; it depends."

"On what?"

"On how many there are. On how eager they are for battle."

Calandryll nodded, not much liking the options offered, accepting the impossibility of parley.

"They'll know me for Asyth," Bracht expanded, "and look to slay me for that alone—I trespass on their grazing. Do they recognize me . . . Well"—he chuckled, softly and sourly—"then they'll seek to bring me to Jehenne and her nails."

Calandryll shuddered at the thought. "But if we can outrun them," he said, "we'll do that, no?"

Bracht paused a moment before replying. Then: "I say this once, and once only, lest those ears we spoke of hear—do they see us and take back word, then the ghost-talkers have ways of communicating and will doubtless alert every camp 'twixt here and the Cuan na'Dru to our presence. If but a few find us, then our safest course is to slay them. Leave their bodies for the dogs and turn their horses loose to join the wild herds; thus we may escape detection longer."

"Even though they offer no fight?" Calandryll frowned. "Even if we may outrun them?"

"Even so," Bracht said. "Save you'd have all the ni Larrhyn come hunting us."

"And if they are many?" Calandryll demanded. "Too many to slay?"

"Then we run." Bracht shrugged. "And pray Ahrd sees us safe."

Calandryll sighed, staring into the brightening morning. It seemed likely his hands must be once more stained with innocent blood, albeit that of men who would halt their quest, but unknowing. It remained a dilemma for his conscience: still he could not accept that ends, no matter how lofty, justified means; but neither could he see any alternative, should it come to fighting. He could find no answer other than to say, "Ahrd grant we go unhindered."

"Aye," said Bracht, his voice flat.

They remained awhile longer and then the Kern declared the animals sufficiently rested. They woke Katya and readied the horses for departure, the sun a handspan now over the eastern skyline, cloud building there, dark, promising rain before nightfall. Still, the day was warm and bright, spring advancing steadily toward summer, and as they rode Calandryll began to hope his fears were unfounded, even though they crossed the widest expanse of flatland yet encountered.

By noon they had seen no one, only horses and wild dogs and birds, and they halted briefly to snatch hurried mouthfuls of food before continuing on, aware of the morning's cloud drifting steadily closer, hammerheads lofting now, from time to time lit by great flashes of lightning, rain curtains hung beneath. Bracht led them at a canter, halting every so often to stand in his stirrups, or even climb precariously onto his saddle to survey the terrain. Toward midafternoon he sprang down cursing, shouting for them to ride hard.

They obeyed on the instant, lifting their mounts to a gallop, on a line westward of their chosen direction, the drumming of the hooves an urgent accompaniment to the rumble of the still distant thunder.

"Seven riders," Bracht yelled over the pounding. "Ahead and to our right. Coming toward us!"

Calandryll looked to the east, willing the storm to come faster: rain and lightning would provide cover, perhaps enable them to avoid killing. Even as he thought it—prayed for it!—he knew that save for divine intervention it was a fruitless hope.

"Did they see us?" Katya shouted.

"Perhaps not yet," came Bracht's answer. "But likely soon enough."

"Can we not hide?" asked Calandryll. "As we did before?"

"Not here." Bracht flung an angry hand at the level expanse of the prairie. "Here they'll see us. Better we stay mounted. Ahrd willing they'll think us merely three trespassing Asyth, not worth the bother of chasing."

That hope was rapidly damned. One at least of the Lykard possessed eyes keen as Bracht's, for in a little while they were visible, and visibly changing direction to approach the interlopers. They drove a small herd before them, their bellicose intent made clear by their abandonment of the wild horses as they urged their mounts to a furious gallop, charging through the scattering herd. The wind carried their shouts and Calandryll saw them unship bows, nock arrows, leaving no doubt of their purpose. He saw Bracht unsling his bow, reins looped about his saddle horn as he steered the stallion with his knees alone.

"We can outrun them," Calandryll bellowed.

"They look to fight us," Bracht returned, and loosed the tether connecting packhorse and stallion. "They leave us no choice."

Did he hear relish in the Kern's voice as Bracht turned the big black, whooping, riding headlong at the charging Lykard? Certainly, there was a savage smile on the warrior's face. Katya, he saw, had drawn her saber, presumably no more confident than he of effective archery from the back of a running horse, and was turning her grey after the stallion; with one last regretful groan, he unsheathed his straightsword and slammed his heels fierce against the chestnut's flanks.

They drew closer, the Lykard battle shouts matching Bracht's whooping now, arrows humming, the metal heads flashing deadly in the sunlight. Calandryll saw a brown-haired man tumble backward from his mount, a shaft driven deep into his ribs. He ducked low along the chestnut's neck as answering shots whistled overhead. Felt one pluck hairs from his scalp, another tug at his sleeve.

Then the two lines came together and he forgot all doubts as he saw a warrior, his face snarling, aim an arrow at his chest. He turned in his saddle, desperate to avoid the killing shot, urging his horse on, looking to close the distance and use his blade. He saw the man's right hand loose the bowstring, that weapon discarded on the instant, in favor of a sword, and felt a blow, like a hard-flung fist, against his left shoulder. The Lykard's face grinned triumphantly and he felt a surge of terrible anger, that this unknown clansman should seek to slay him, to halt his quest. It expelled all other considerations save survival and he rode his mount directly at the man, the straightsword raised high as the Lykard brought up his own blade. He smashed it aside, his blow continuing down, across the chest, carving a line over the warrior's leathern tunic that parted to spray blood. He cut again as the Lykard's horse skittered, slicing back as he passed, hacking at the man's spine. The Lykard screamed and jerked upright, arching, tumbling sideways from the saddle.

Momentum carried him on through the flurry of combat, ducking under a flailing sword, stabbing, hearing a grunt of pain answer the judder of steel on bone, vaguely aware of Bracht and Katya parrying, thrusting, their blades glinting, reddened. He swung the willing gelding round in its own length to charge back, downing a man who already wore two of Bracht's arrows in his side, and saw the fight was ended. The Lykard lay bloody on the trampled grass, their horses stamping and whickering nervously. Bracht licked at a cut hand; Katya was unmarked.

"Katya—the packhorse!" Bracht snapped. "Calandryll—help me with their animals."

"Do we take them?" he asked, and Bracht shook his head: "No—we strip them and turn them loose. They'll likely join the wild ones then, and not return home to warn the ni Larrhyn. We buy ourselves time."

He nodded and sheathed the straightsword, swung down from his saddle. He felt something jar then, and a fierce pain, like lightning, flash down his left arm, his side. Abruptly, sweat formed cold on his face and he began to tremble. He shook his head, the world for

a moment swimming, as if water blurred his vision.
He held the chestnut's reins in his left hand and
tugged them to walk the gelding clear of the carnage.
The animal tossed its head and he lost his grip as the
pain burned fierce, the reins falling loose. He turned
his head and saw feathers dyed crimson and yellow, a
length of dark wood protruding from his shoulder. He
touched it with his right hand and the pain was a
thunderclap that burst inside his skull.

He did not realize he had fallen until he saw
Bracht's face above him, concern in the blue eyes.

"Ahrd!" he heard the Kern gasp. "You're hit."

"Aye," he said, or thought he said; he was not sure,
because all the world went black then.

15

PAIN dragged Calandryll from the insensate comfort of unconsciousness like a hook reeling an unwilling fish from the ocean's depths. It was undeniable, for all he fought it, and he opened his eyes to the sound of a shrill cry he dimly realized was his own. He saw Bracht's face, the blue eyes narrowed in concentration, the mouth a thin, intense line; he saw the bloody dirk in the Kern's right hand, an arrow, no less gory, in the left. He tried to rise, but strong hands pressed him down and he heard Katya say, "Lie still," and something else that he could not make out, for the pain came back in a great wave that swept over him and dashed him back down into the darkness. Then that was washed away in red light and he saw, as though from a distance, outside himself, the heated blade, glowing, that Bracht pressed to his shoulder, the agony so fierce that he writhed and bucked against Katya's restraining grip, the pain mounting until his mind escaped again and he sank back into the darkness.

Sometime after—he had no idea how long—he felt his face and hands wet, his shirt drenched, the world became black, save when great flashes of silver light illuminated the prairie. Vaguely, he realized the storm had come, the thunder like far-off drums beaten in arrhythmic time, the lightning a series of disjointed flashes that barely registered on his blurred vision. He knew, dimly, that he sat a horse, and that the animal galloped, for it seemed each hoofbeat drove a fresh wave of agony through his body. He wondered, in some part of his mind not entirely occupied with the pain, how he remained in the saddle, and thought that likely Bracht had tied him there: he did not believe he could any longer ride unaided. It did not matter. The drumming ferocity of his wound absorbed all his attention, that fiery core palpitating tidal over his consciousness, drowning other concerns, save the fear that the nausea it induced should void his belly. He closed his eyes, lids shuttered tight, gritted his teeth, and willed the pain to abate. It ignored him and he slumped, head drooping so that it bobbed with the movement of the horse, the darkness taking him again.

When next he opened his eyes the rain had ceased and the storm marched westward on stilts of pure silver light. A wind blew chill against his face, though that burned, and he shivered, his mouth dry, his throat parched. He thought to take a drink, but when he reached for his water bottle, he found his right wrist lashed to his saddlebow, his left arm strapped tight across his ribs. He tried to call out, but all that emerged was a croaking sound, lost on the wind. He blinked, not sure whether rain or tears dimmed his sight, and saw his horse was linked to Bracht's stallion, that Katya rode close by, leading the packhorse. She saw his head move and called something, but he failed to hear it and closed his eyes again, grateful that their pace seemed slowed and the pain a little less.

After that it was dark and he felt no movement, becoming slowly aware that they had halted and that he lay supine, a fire nearby. He did not think it rained now and wondered why his face was still wet, and why his body burned and chilled in alternating spasms. He moaned as an arm came around his shoulders, lifting him, and recognized Bracht's face close to his. The Kern spoke, but once more the words were indistinct, muffled by the fog that filled his mind, and all he could offer in answer was a garbled muttering. He gave up the attempt—it cost too much—and rested shivering in the circle of the Kern's arm as Katya spooned broth between his lips, her face a blur too vague he could recognize the concern there. He swallowed what he could and closed his eyes again, wanting only to sleep, to flee the pain.

It returned with movement and he cried out as he was lifted to his feet, not wanting to sit astride the chestnut, nor suffer the pounding of another day's ride.

"You must," he heard Bracht say, the words faint, like a shout carried on the wind. "This place is too open. We must find woodland."

He grunted and ducked his head in acceptance, teeth clenching as he was pushed up onto the saddle, cords wound about his legs, his arms. With his right hand he clutched the saddlebow, head spinning, the sunlit grassland shimmering, as if he looked through water, or at a mirage. He began to shiver, and knew that he was feverish, that sweat burst from his skin, and that soon the pain would start again.

Dera be with me, he asked. *Help me to bear it.*

He winced as the chestnut stamped, protesting the indignity of the lead rein, then groaned as the first steps impacted up from hooves to body, to his shoulder, kindling the fire there anew. When Bracht quickened the pace, lifting to a canter, he moaned, deep down, struggling to hold back the sound, to trap it behind his grinding teeth. He was not sure he could stand it, and when the pain came back in full measure, and the fever rose to dull his wits, he felt his senses reel: it was almost welcome, for it took him to a place inside himself where he might escape for a while.

It seemed not long, certainly not long enough, be-

fore he felt himself lifted down and heard a voice say,
"Now, gently. Careful! Aye, down here. Hold him."

His eyes felt gummed, his throat an arid channel
too parched, too constricted, to let out words. Fire
burned inside him and he thought it strange he
should feel so cold when he knew such heat. He shuddered as fingers of ice caressed his chest; screamed as
they probed his shoulder. Was he taken by the Lykard,
that they tortured him so? Surely his comrades would
not inflict this suffering? He fought the hands that
held him down and heard Katya's voice, urgent in his
ear.

"Calandryll, you're safe! We're hidden in woodland
and you can rest now. But you must let us examine
your wound. Lie still, if you can."

He nodded, or thought he did. Moaned agreement;
or thought he did. He could not tell because his body
bucked then and a scream emerged as the fingers applied themselves once more to his shoulder.

"Ahrd! Hold him down lest he tear himself worse."
That was Bracht, he knew. "The wound's inflamed.
Cursed Lykard . . ."

"Was the shaft poisoned, then?"

Katya's blunt question brought new fear, assuaged a
little by Bracht's response: "No, but it went deep. The
muscle's torn and he lost blood. I must clean it
again."

The fingers went away a moment, then returned. A
roaring filled his ears then and the darkness came
back, riding a red-washed crest of agony that took
him and carried him off so that he knew no more until he next opened his eyes.

SUNLIGHT filtered through branches, gold and green
with the leaf-spread above. Birds sang and the air
smelled of woodsmoke and humus; a horse snorted,
and from nearby came the splashing of a stream, the
murmur of voices pitched low. He felt weak: to rise
seemed too much effort, so he merely turned his

head, seeing thick trunks encircling a grassy clearing
cut by a beck, the horses hobbled on the farther side.
He eased his unsteady head around and saw Bracht
and Katya sprawled by a small fire, their tunics hung
from branches, the warrior woman's mail shirt glinting, bright contrast to the black leather that covered
the Kern's torso. Their bows and the quivers lay close
at hand, and they had both removed their swordbelts:
it seemed they felt safe in this bosky refuge.
Calandryll smiled as the realization dawned that he
saw clearly, that no fever sweat clouded his vision,
nor did he shiver and tremble, and the pain was become a dull, steady aching, such as a hard-struck
blow might leave behind. He sighed, venting his relief, and both faces turned on the instant toward him.

"Praise Ahrd, you're conscious." Bracht came to
squat at his side. "I feared for a while . . ."

The hawkish face split in a grin, leather-clad shoulders shrugging, the gesture finishing the sentence
lucid as any words.

"We were concerned," said Katya, her smile radiant, a hand reaching out to brush lank hair from his
brow. "You were sore wounded."

"And now?"

His tongue felt furred, his mouth swollen. Bracht
rose, fetching a cup from the stream, dribbling the
clean, cold water gently between Calandryll's lips. He
drank greedily as the Kern said, "Now you mend. In
a while we can go on."

"In a while?" He frowned, not knowing how long
he had wandered in the fever's grip, nor how long he
had lain here; only that each day afforded Rhythamun
a better lead. He moved to rise, and gasped as the ache
flared fire, sinking back. "How long is a while?"

Bracht shrugged again and said, "As long as it takes
you to heal. The Lykard fired close—only luck, or the
gods, saved your life—and you were cut deep. Better
had I doctored you there, but that was too risky, so we
lashed you to your horse and rode away—which did
your wound no good."

"Where are we now?" asked Calandryll.

"Safe in woodland," answered Bracht, "where the Lykard are not likely to come."

"Shall they not track us?"

"The storm hid our trail." The Kern shook his head. "And we're far from the fight now."

"How far?" Calandryll demanded. "How many days ago was I wounded?"

"Five," Bracht said. "For most of that time you raved with fever. We rode three days and for two have waited here."

"Bracht cut the arrow out," Katya explained, "and cauterized the wound, but still you lost blood and suffered the ague."

A dreadful fear gripped Calandryll then and he turned his head, looking down, laughing in heady relief as he saw his arm still whole; bandaged, but still attached to his shoulder.

"You remain entire," Bracht said, recognizing his alarm. "Weak yet, but in a little while you'll be sound enough."

"Bracht is an excellent chirurgeon," added Katya, "and well versed in herbal lore—you've him to thank for your life."

The Kern grinned at her praise and said modestly, "You played your part, and were Calandryll of lesser fiber he'd have succumbed."

"My thanks to you both," Calandryll murmured, "but should we not go on? Rhythamun . . ."

"Is where he is," said Bracht firmly, "and we here until you're full-healed. Do we go on now, then likely I should need remove that arm."

"Better you have two for that battle," Katya said. "And what he gains by our delay, we shall likely make up by crossing the Cuan na'Dru."

Calandryll saw a shadow pass over Bracht's face at that, but still the Kern nodded and said, "Aye," then smiled, rising. "And now—do you eat? We've venison."

Calandryll had not thought of his belly, but on

mention of food he realized he was hungry and smiled his agreement.

"You've taken only broth since the fight," Katya told him. "Good red meat will help restore the blood you lost."

"Venison?" he asked.

"Bracht brought down a deer," she explained, and chuckled. "This woodland is filled with game—we've eaten well since coming here."

He studied their surroundings with greater attention then, seeing the clearing ringed with beech and ash, a scattering of majestic oaks. Above, branches spread a dendroid filigree across the sky, dappling the glade with shifting patterns of green-hued light. Birds fluttered there, and busy squirrels, insects filling the warm air with a lazy buzzing. All around, the boles clustered thick, mazelike and protective, shading the hurst so that it seemed the clearing was the only place the sun penetrated. It felt very safe, the great trees imbuing the glade with a sense of calm, of tranquillity, as if Ahrd promised refuge here, safety from pursuit: he thought this was a fine place to hide and heal.

"Here." Bracht interrupted his contemplation, returning with a plate stacked high with venison, wild onions, even a few potatoes. "Eat this, and then I must examine your wound again."

Calandryll took the plate and began to eat, surprised at his appetite. It was none too easy, managing with but one arm, but still he succeeded in devouring most of the meal and set the platter aside with a contented sigh.

Bracht loosed the cloth binding his arm and eased his shirt from his shoulder, then with Katya's assistance stripped off the bandage. Calandryll frowned as he saw the puckered flesh, still an angry red, and the dark stain that covered one side of his shirt, but when the Kern touched the healing wound, he felt only a memory of the earlier pain. He watched as Bracht fetched a greenish compound to which the Kern added a little water, stirring the mixture to a paste before smearing it liberally over the wound, then winding a fresh bandage in place.

"Is this needful?" he asked as his arm was once more strapped to his side, and Bracht said, "Aye. For a day or two more you'd best not move the arm. Now, drink this."

Calandryll took the cup he offered, sipping, grimacing at the bitter taste. Bracht chuckled and said, "Drink deep, mend fast."

"I'd not known you for a healer."

Calandryll drained the cup and passed it back, feeling the draught seep warm through his insides. His eyes grew heavy and he yawned.

"Such things we learn young in Cuan na'For." Bracht's reply seemed to come from a distance. "And until now there's been no need."

"In Mherut-yi, when Mehemmed attacked me . . ." Calandryll yawned again, unable to finish the sentence.

"There was a true healer there," Bracht said, his voice faint, almost lost beneath the drowsy buzzing of the insects, the plashing of the beck. "And had we one now, you'd mend the faster. This is herb lore, no more. Such cures as warriors need, when they've no ghost-talker to remedy their wounds."

"Even so," Calandryll murmured, the thread of his thought slipping fast from his mind as sleep overtook him, "you do well enough."

If Bracht replied, he did not hear, for his eyes closed then and he lay back, head pillowed on his saddle, the woodland sounds a lullaby that sang him gently into slumber.

He woke to a different song: to the hooting of owls and the rustling of those creatures that inhabit the night. The sky was a curtain of blue velvet, silvered by a full moon that painted the undersides of drifting clouds, transforming them to ethereal castles, canyons, and mountains. He saw bats wing silently overhead, and from beside the stream came the glow of a small fire that outlined his comrades, casting red light over Katya's flaxen hair, its smoke tempting with the smell of roasting meat. He eased a little upright, resting on his good arm, the movement catching Bracht's attention, the Kern rising to bring him food, and another cup of the bitter herbal brew. He drank it without protest and ate greedily, once more surprised at his appetite, then sank back, content to sleep, to let Bracht's medicines do their work.

Two days he spent like that: sleeping, eating, the arrow wound healing, the torn muscle knitting. Frustration he set aside, aware that he was still weak, and that he would need his strength to ride, to fight. He was content for now to rest, listening to the sounds of the wood, watching the horses, or the Kern and the warrior woman practice their swordwork. He thought, idly, that perhaps the concoction Bracht gave him lulled him, or that perhaps the trees themselves—especially the oaks, that Bracht said held the spirit of Ahrd—played their part, for the rustling of their leafy branches was a gentle melody and the play of light and shade their limbs cast was a soft fascination that eased his spirit and seemed to lend him a measure of patience. But on the third day he woke invigorated, no longer drowsy, and stronger, wanting to rise and test his arm.

This Bracht allowed, agreeing that he might take his food by the fire and walk a little, removing the bindings that pinned his damaged arm with a warning against attempting exercise too vigorous.

He felt somewhat dizzy at first, in the way of a convalescent recently risen from the sickbed, but that soon passed and he gloried in the regaining of his mobility, impatience returning as he recovered. Bracht set him to working the arm, gently, and that wise, for the muscle needed time yet to heal and it would be some while before he got back its full use. His shoulder remained stiff, and he could not articulate it fully, but that would come; of that he felt no doubt.

"You can ride, at least," the Kern decided after a few days. "But with care—you'll not have the full use of that arm before summer."

Which, Calandryll thought, cannot be long in coming. And with that, felt impatience chafe again.

"And if we must fight?" he asked.

"Hope there's no need," Bracht answered bluntly. "You'll not be much use."

"Not with a bow," Calandryll admitted. "But with a blade?"

"Better you avoid swordwork," Bracht returned. "That arm's half your balance, and in a running fight, off horseback . . ."

He shrugged. Calandryll scowled, knowing he was right. "We cannot hide here until summer," he said.

"No," Bracht agreed. "So we depart tomorrow."

Calandryll's scowl became a grin at that and he nodded eagerly.

"How long before we reach the Cuan na'Dru?"

"Perhaps seven days, if no Lykard cross our path," Bracht answered. Then, softer, "And if the Gruagach grant us entry."

Calandryll ignored the Kern's doubt. Surely it must be as Katya believed—that the Gruagach, Ahrd's guardians, would not hinder their passage, but aid them. Was their quest not, after all, the salvation of all the Younger Gods? How then should those who served Ahrd oppose them? "I think they will," he said.

"Perhaps."

Bracht's reply was soft, dubious, and that evening, after they had eaten, he rose and walked away into the trees. Calandryll opened his mouth to ask what he did, but Katya clasped his wrist, shaking her head.

"He goes to pray," she murmured, watching the Kern disappear among the timber. "He's still no great liking for this idea of entering the forest."

"I'll not believe the Gruagach will prove our foes," Calandryll declared.

"Nor I," said Katya. "But we are not of Cuan na'For, and Bracht's doubts are very real."

"Then I pray Ahrd answers him," Calandryll replied.

If the god favoured the Kern with such assurance, Bracht made no mention of it when he returned, only coming back to the fire and settling on the grass to hone his sword, not speaking, his dark face thoughtful so that his companions forbore to question him. Instead they watched and waited until he was done, and then he only declared himself ready for sleep, suggesting they depart soon after dawn.

MIST shrouded the woodland as they left the glade, leaves and grass glittering with dewdrops, the sun a promise glowing faint through the dense canopy of branches. The path Bracht took was no more than a deer trail and their going was slow, hindered by low-hanging limbs and undergrowth, as if the hurst were reluctant to see them depart. By sun's set they were still within its confines, and it was not until the next morning was some time advanced that they saw the trees thin and the prairie commence beyond, the grass shifting under the caress of a warm wind, the sky a brilliant blue, cloudless. A single oak grew close to the edge, smaller than its kin within the heartwood, but nonetheless sturdy. Calandryll reached out to touch a branch, voicing a brief and silent prayer that Ahrd grant them safe passage to the Cuan na'Dru.

It seemed the god did not hear him, or exercised no power over the open country, for a little while after they emerged from the hurst they saw riders, a group of ten or so, off to the west.

Bracht mouthed a curse and Calandryll called, "Are they Lykard?"

"None else," returned the Kern. "Not here."

"What do we do?"

Calandryll looked toward the horsemen, back toward the wood. That was sufficiently deep they might escape pursuit, but to return was to give Rhythamun more time, with no sure guarantee the Lykard would not again find them when they reemerged. Ahead was only open prairie, rolling, but devoid of safe cover.

"Ride," Bracht said tersely, and drove his heels hard against the stallion's flanks.

Their mounts were rested from the sojourn in the hurst and lifted willingly to a gallop. The Lykard riders followed suit, not moving to intercept, but running parallel, matching pace rather than giving chase. Then Katya shouted and Calandryll turned in his saddle, looking to where she pointed, seeing a second group a little closer, to the east and behind them, positioned to cut them off from the woodland. Bracht saw them and cursed again, calling over the drumbeat pounding of the hooves.

"They guessed we hid there. Or the ghost-talkers found us."

"Can we outrun them?" Calandryll wondered.

"We can try," the Kern shouted back. "We've little hope of slaying so many."

Calandryll urged the chestnut to a faster pace, thankful that his shoulder was healed enough it gave him no pain; cursing it for the delay that had given the Lykard that chance to find them. He glanced around, seeing the two groups no closer, making no attempt to attack. It was as though the Lykard herded them, like wild horses, and he wondered, if that was so, to what destination. Escape seemed impossible, save they could elude pursuit until night fell and lose the horsemen under cover of darkness, and that hope slender if drachomannii employed occult powers to locate them.

They charged on, flanked by their unwelcome escorts, always just out of bowshot, over the grass toward a low ridge.

The farther side ran down into a wide swale, boggy and covered with rank vegetation. Eastward, the ground water pooled, black and noisome, starting a narrow stream; westward, the going was little better. In both directions, more horsemen waited, sealing all exits save the facing slope. Bracht snarled and sent the stallion charging down, across the marsh.

The quaggy ground slowed them, the horses plunging, snorting as hooves sank in, sucking reluctantly free, insects rising in black swarms, the air fetid with marsh stink. As they reached the firmer ground of the far ridge a line of horsemen showed, coming almost casually to the crest, a living barrier across the questers' path. They halted there, with arrows nocked and angled down; Bracht's oath was furious.

Calandryll set hand to swordhilt, halted by the Kern's sharp voice: "No! Draw that and we're dead."

"What else should we do?" Calandryll spun the chestnut, seeing all avenues of escape cut off.

"Pray," Bracht grunted. "But draw that blade and we die here."

He walked the stallion forward, a few paces higher up the slope, looking to the center of the line, where a single rider moved out as though to greet him. His face was grim as he raised a hand in mockery of formal salute.

"How fare you, Jehenne ni Larrhyn?"

"Well enough, Bracht ni Errhyn," came the answer, husky. "The better for seeing you again.,"

Calandryll knew that he should have suspected this, but still his mouth gaped open as he stared at the woman. She sat a horse of pure white, unblemished, its trappings a dark scarlet chased with silver, a match to the rider's leathers, its hooves stamping as if it were eager to charge, wickering, infected, he thought, by the malevolent undercurrent in the woman's deceptively mild tone. She was, he saw, beautiful, as a falcon or a hunting cat is beautiful, lithe and sleek, grace combining with predatory hunger. That shone in her green eyes, those blazing from the fine lines of her tanned face, white teeth showing in a wide smile as she removed the leather cap she wore and shook out a great mane of red hair that spilled over the shoulders of her tunic. She wore a falchion akin to Bracht's, but made no move to draw the blade, nor offered any other offensive sign save in the glitter of her eyes and the threat that underpinned her words.

"I had hoped we should meet again. Indeed, I prayed we should."

"And now we have," Bracht returned, his own voice deceptively casual. "What now?"

Jehenne ni Larrhyn's laughter floated on the wind. To Calandryll it sounded unpleasant as the stagnant odor rising from the swale.

"Why, now I would offer you the hospitality of my camp, Bracht. You and your companions."

"We ride for the Cuan na'Dru," Bracht said.

"Over Lykard grass. No matter—you shall commune with Ahrd soon enough. You've my word on that."

"I've werecoin." Bracht gestured at his saddlebags. "Four thousand varre."

"So much?" Jehenne's brows rose in perfect arcs; she bowed gracefully. "You flatter me."

"I'd make peace between us," Bracht said. "The werecoin in payment for what affront I offered."

Jehenne laughed again and Calandryll knew that hope was lost. "We shall discuss it," she declared, "in my camp. Do you follow? Or . . ."

Her left hand swept round, indicating the archers to either side, the horsemen watching from along the hollow. Bracht ducked his head in agreement: there was scant alternative, save to die.

"Good." Jehenne smiled. "I'd not see you cut down, not here. You deserve a better end."

"Which you've in mind?" asked Bracht.

"That, too, we shall discuss," she returned. "Now—do you accompany me?"

She turned the white horse, not awaiting a reply, and Bracht urged his stallion up the slope.

"This is Jehenne ni Larrhyn?" Katya whispered, not really asking a question. "What did she say?"

"She invites us to her camp," Bracht explained.

"Invites?" Katya glowered at the bowmen spread along the ridge. "That she may crucify you?"

"I believe," Bracht said carefully, "that such is her intention. But first she looks to amuse herself."

Katya spat, her grey eyes stormy. Calandryll asked, "Will she not take your offer of werecoin?"

"Jehenne?" Bracht laughed, a single, cynical bark. "I think not. At least, not for my life, but for yours . . . perhaps."

"I'll not leave you," Katya said.

Bracht looked at her then, and smiled fondly. "Does she agree to that exchange, I ask that you, too, accept it," he said, his voice gentle. "She'll not let me ride free, but there's a chance you two can go on. She's no quarrel with you, save that you ride in my company."

"Does she harm you," Katya said, steel in her voice, "then I've quarrel with her."

"And more," said Calandryll, "we are three. The spaewives, the Old Ones, all have spoken of three on this quest."

"It may be," Bracht murmured as they crested the ridge and the Lykard bowmen parted to let them through, forming in a solid mass about them, "that Jehenne breaks that pattern."

"She cannot!" Katya cried.

"That's a word for which Jehenne has little liking," said Bracht. "And we ride Lykard grass; we are in the territory of the ni Larrhyn, where Jehenne's word is the law."

His face was set in resolute lines and Calandryll saw that he held no doubt but that he was doomed to suffer crucifixion. Neither did there seem much doubt but that Jehenne intended to extract her full revenge for the slight offered her: that Calandryll had sensed in her voice, seen in her eyes. He forced a measure of

calm upon his racing thoughts, desperately seeking
some solution to this impasse.

"The ghost-talkers," he said at last, as their escort
lifted to a canter, Jehenne at their head, "might they
not scry our purpose? Might they not prevail on her
to set us free?"

"The one, perhaps," Bracht answered. "The other?
I think not."

"But surely if they know it," Calandryll insisted.
"If they scry what Rhythamun will do? Surely then
she must heed them."

Bracht laughed again, no more humorous than before. "Jehenne heeds her own voice and none other,"
he said. "And save she allow the ghost-talkers their
divination—which I'd doubt—they'll likely look only
to please her."

"We can, at least, try," said Calandryll.

"Aye," Bracht replied. "As I shall seek to persuade
her to take my werecoin and set you two free."

"No!" Katya cried.

"If it comes to that, you must." Bracht reached
across the space between them to touch her hand. "I
ask you do it."

"Does she harm you," Katya returned, her voice
low and hard with anger, "I shall slay her."

For a man confronted imminently with painful execution, Bracht's smile was bright, the eyes he turned
to Katya filled with admiration. His words, however,
were sober: "We've hope while we still live—hold to
that! And does Jehenne make good her promise, remember how we met, and why. This quest of ours
does not end with my death. It must not!"

Katya's eyes flashed angrily, as if the rage she felt at
this turn of events became directed at the Kern, for
his calm acceptance. She tossed her head, an angry
gesture, denial writ clear upon her face, mouth opening to voice a negative that Bracht halted with a
raised hand.

"Should you attack Jehenne, she's but to order it
and every blade in the ni Larrhyn camp will taste

your blood. I'd not see that; or know my folly results
in your death. Neither yours nor Calandryll's. Does
she nail me to the tree, then I ask you bear it and go
on. Find Rhythamun and take the Arcanum from
him; take it to Vanu, as we vowed to do. Does that
not outweigh the importance of my life?"

Calandryll saw Katya's eyes cloud with doubt, saw
her teeth catch at her lower lip, biting so hard he
thought she must draw blood.

"I'd command you," Bracht said, soft and urgent,
"but I've not that right. Rather, I ask for your
pledge—that you'll not spend your life uselessly, but
live to continue our quest."

It seemed, for an instant, that the warrior woman
would refuse. Her right hand bunched, rising, the fist
descending to strike against her thigh, so hard her
horse skittered, dancing sideways, bringing a harsh
warning from the Lykard. Then she shook her head,
not in refusal, but in resignation, her voice low as she
said, "You've my word on it. And Jehenne ni Larrhyn
my curse, must I keep it."

Bracht smiled tightly and nodded. Then grinned,
pitching his next words too low their escort might
hear him.

"Of course, should the chance arise you might slay
her without harm to yourselves . . ."

Katya nodded in turn. "My word on that, too," she
promised.

"And mine," said Calandryll, surprising himself as
he realized that he undertook to slay a woman who,
as yet, had offered him no harm. No less surprised to
know that he would, did it come to that, slay Jehenne
ni Larrhyn in cold blood should she execute Bracht.
The thought of his comrade's death chilled him, as if
he contemplated the amputation of some part of himself. They had grown close this past year, that he had
known, but not, fully, how close, not until now, when
he was forced to consider the severing of their bond.
Closer than any brother, he thought, *and closer than
ever I was to my father. Aye, does Jehenne make good*

her threat, I'll put steel in her belly without com-
punction; I'll measure my mercy to hers.

He was not aware how grim his face became until
Bracht clapped his good shoulder and said, "We live
yet, my friend."

"Aye," he grunted.

Bracht favored him with a solemn stare and said,
"That pledge I had from Katya I'd have from you,
too."

"You have it," answered Calandryll. "That, and the
other."

"Then I'm content," Bracht said.

They fell silent after that, each encompassed in the
web of their own thoughts, riding at a steady canter in
the midst of the ni Larrhyn warriors, who eyed them
with the incurious looks of men observing animals
bound for slaughter. Calandryll, in turn, studied the
Lykard, noticing for the first time that several among
them were women, though save for the obvious dis-
tinctions of gender there was little enough to tell
them apart from the men. All wore leathers, similar
to his and Bracht's, but of shades of brown, rather
than black, and sewn with plates and studs of metal
that were both decorative and defensive. Falchions
and sabers were sheathed on waists, or slung across
the shoulders, and all carried bows; a few had small,
short-hafted axes or broad-bladed knives in saddle
scabbards. Their hair, like their tunics and breeks,
was brown, from dark chocolate to the red of
Jehenne's, the men's worn in long plaits, the women's
loose. Their faces were tanned dark, stern, their eyes
no less so. In none did he see hint of sympathy.

They rode until late in the afternoon, angling a little west of north, and then, where a shallow strath, a
stream running down its length, indented the prairie,
came upon the ni Larrhyn camp.

Bracht had described the nomadic shielings of
Cuan na'For, but they were things he saw as com-
monplace and his words had done little to prepare
Calandryll for the reality of the encampment. That

came as a surprise, and despite their circumstances, he found his scholarly interest aroused as he gazed on the great mass of movable dwellings. They spread across the valley bottom, hiding the grass beneath motley leather, save where avenues and alleyways were shaped by the placement of the tents. Or were they, properly, tents, he wondered, for as they came closer he saw that the canopies were mounted on great, many-wheeled carts, and only around the periphery of the encampment were the pavilions set upon the ground, like the poorer dwellings that spring up about the great mansions of a town. But even those were spacious, and he recalled Bracht's words— that the young men and unwed warriors of each clan family pitched their tents around the periphery, sentinels over the core. There were, he estimated, perhaps two hundred souls present, and most of them come out to greet the returning party. To either end of the valley, penned in corrals, or tethered on picket lines, were horses, a multitude of horses, filling the warm air with the scent of their flesh and droppings. It was as if a village was built in the strath, but one that might up and move on the morrow, shifting on the whim of its inhabitants. Or, he corrected himself, Jehenne ni Larrhyn's word, for she was clearly in command here.

That was obvious as she rode her white horse down the slope to where the outermost tents stood, the first people there, parting as she reached them, saluting her and calling questions that went unanswered as she walked her mount along the widest avenue. Behind her, the warriors of the escort were more forthcoming, and Calandryll listened to them explaining that Bracht ni Errhyn was taken, with two strangers. To his surprise, the onlookers made no overtly hostile moves, only stared, talking among themselves until the procession was gone past, then following toward the center of the camp.

Jehenne was already halted there, where carts stood either side of the stream, approximating a village

square. She dismounted as her retinue arrived, tossing
her reins to a waiting man who led the horse away,
turning to speak with the two who stepped forward.
These, Calandryll guessed, were the drachomannii, for
they stood out among the rest. Their hair was not
plaited, but worn loose and decorated with colored
shells and feathers, their faces painted blue and white,
and instead of tunics they wore long, sleeveless
leather robes. They looked to be in their middle years,
neither old nor young, and they deferred to Jehenne,
bowing and smiling as she praised their skill in locating the three. Calandryll thought to cry out, demanding that they apply their occult talents to a scrying,
but a bow jabbed his ribs and a gruff voice ordered
him to dismount. He obeyed, and was promptly cut
off from the ghost-talkers by a ring of warriors whose
hands rested threateningly on their swordhilts; he
could only stand, nervously waiting as the horses
were led away.

Then the circle parted and he saw Jehenne again,
the ghost-talkers dismissed, splashing across the
stream, taking hope with them as the woman beckoned. A hand pushed him forward and he walked to
face her; her smile held malice.

"Come, you're likely hungry." She gestured at the
closest, largest cart. "I'd be a poor host, did I not offer
you refreshment."

The invitation was mocking in its urbanity, eliciting a humorless smile from Bracht, a scowl from
Katya. Calandryll, torn between fear and fascination,
moved to follow as Jehenne climbed the ladder reaching to the cart's deck, pausing at the foot to add, "Perhaps best if you leave your weapons."

There was little they could do but unbuckle their
swordbelts and pass them to the watchful escort before mounting the ladder.

They stood then in a kind of vestibule, facing a
leather curtain that two men drew back to reveal the
interior. It was opulent, a dramatic contrast to the
outward appearance of the pavilion. Thick carpets

covered the floor with bright patterns, scattered with
great piles of vivid cushions, the walls hung with
some silken material, pale yellow. Pomanders hung
from the roof, their scent sweet, and a circular table
of dark red wood stood low in the center, a jug and
cups there. Jehenne motioned at the cushions and the
three settled themselves as she barked orders, the
warriors turning back sections of the roof, letting in
sunlight. Jehenne passed through a second curtain,
this silken like the drapery, its parting affording a
brief glimpse of a sleeping chamber, all pastel shades
and no less luxurious. Calandryll stared about. Two
men and a woman sat facing him, two men by the
exit; all were armed and none spoke, their expressions
unfathomable. Jehenne returned moments later, her
sword and tunic removed, revealing a russet shirt that
drew taut across the full contours of her body as she
sank gracefully to the cushions, her smile speculative.

"I am remiss," she beamed with horrid pleasantry.
"Take wine with me."

She motioned, and a man filled cups, passing them
round. Whatever fate she planned, Calandryll did not
think she intended to poison them; he sipped, barely
tasting the tart vintage.

"Do your companions understand us?" This to
Bracht, who answered: "Calandryll, aye; but not
Katya."

"Then we shall converse in the Envah," Jehenne
declared in the lingua franca, "that there be no mis-
understanding between us. You spoke of werecoin . . ."

"Four thousand varre," Bracht said.

"You gave me great insult," Jehenne returned.

"For that affront I ask your forgiveness. For what I
did, I offer you the four thousand varre in compensation."

Bracht's tone was earnest and it seemed Jehenne
considered the offer. Or, more likely, Calandryll
thought, toyed with the Kern, toyed with them all.
There was about her an air of knowingness that

seemed to him a thing apart from her desire for revenge, and he felt, intuitively, that she held back some knowledge.

"I named your father my price," she said at last. "And that was not so much, but still he compounded the insult."

"He'd not see me crucified," Bracht said. "For which you surely cannot blame him."

"No," Jehenne allowed. "But you . . . I can blame you, and easily."

"Aye," said Bracht, "or think yourself well rid of a poor husband."

"Would that have been the case?" The green eyes turned a moment toward Katya. "You once thought otherwise. Do your affections now find another home?"

Bracht's expression was answer enough; Jehenne chuckled. Bracht said, "Might four thousand varre not assuage the hurt?"

"Might I not have that and satisfaction, both?"

"Were you devoid of honor, aye. But I do not believe you devoid of honor. Do you take the werecoin and your vengeance, together, then are you better than some common bandit?"

"I am ketomana of the ni Larrhyn." For an instant the casual mask dropped and Jehenne's voice grew sharp, her eyes flashing dangerously. "My word is law here."

"I've no doubt of that," Bracht agreed. "But still . . . it would not be honorable."

Calandryll guessed that his words were directed as much at the other Lykard as at Jehenne, that Bracht sought to gain some leverage, if not for himself, then for his companions. He waited for Jehenne's reply, his own mind racing as he sought some gambit he might use, some way in which he might assist Bracht.

"Perhaps," Jehenne murmured, her expression bland, "there is something in that. But what you did was hardly honorable."

"Then punish me," Bracht said. "Let my companions go. Take the werecoin for their lives."

Calandryll heard Katya's sharp intake of breath; saw, from the corner of his eye, her body tense. He held himself still, concentrating on Jehenne's face, and saw her smile again.

"Are their hands not stained with Lykard blood?" she asked.

"We were attacked," said Bracht quickly. "We sought no fight, but your folk came on us and offered us no choice."

"You trespass on our grass," came the woman's reply. "What should they do, save attack?"

"It was an honest fight," Bracht said, "and they were seven to our three. Surely that might be settled with werecoin."

Jehenne was seated apart from her fellows and Calandryll's gaze flickered from her face to theirs. He was uncertain what he saw there, but sure now that Bracht sought to sway them, that they, in turn, might influence their leader.

"It might," Jehenne admitted. "Though a question hangs thereon—why do you cross my grass?"

Bracht paused before replying, turning briefly to Calandryll, his eyes framing a silent question; Calandryll nodded.

"We hunt a man," Bracht said then. "A half-blood of the ni Brhyn who names himself Daven Tyras."

Jehenne nodded and Calandryll saw unfeigned amusement in her eyes. He felt cold shock as he sensed this announcement was not unexpected, staring at her, wondering what it was she held back.

"Why?" she asked bluntly.

Again Bracht paused, as if weighing the situation, as if he balanced revelation against the likelihood of disbelief. Calandryll felt an ugly certainty descend and said, "She knows," and saw Jehenne's eyes narrow, fixing on him.

"What do I know?" she demanded coldly, raising a

hand to silence Bracht's reply. "No! Let this young outlaw tell me."

Calandryll swallowed wine, not tasting it. There was nothing gained by prevarication, he decided; perhaps lives lost by concealment. Gart and Kythan had expressed disgust at the notion of shape-shifting; perhaps these Lykard would feel the same. He set down his cup and said carefully, "Daven Tyras is a shape-shifter, gharan-evur. His body was taken by Varent den Tarl of Aldarin, whose life, in turn, was taken by a warlock named Rhythamun. Rhythamun seeks to raise the Mad God; we seek to prevent him."

"Ah." Jehenne's response was deceptively mild; it confirmed his worst suspicions. "You quest to save us all from Tharn."

"Aye," he cried fiercely, unable to help himself in face of her indifference. "And do you halt us, then you condemn the world to chaos."

"So I had best let you go? You and Katya, and Bracht, too?"

"Aye," was all he could say as Jehenne laughed.

"A poor attempt." She chuckled. "Daven Tyras warned of your cunning tongue."

"You know him?"

Bracht's question was sharp, as if he, not the woman, commanded here: Jehenne favored him with an angry glare, no longer masking her expression. "I know him," she said. "Is he not, in part, at least, Lykard?"

"He's gharan-evur!" Bracht rasped. "That body is a skin he uses, nothing more. In Ahrd's name, Jehenne! Do you shield him, you condemn your soul."

"And you wriggle to escape your rightful fate," she returned, her voice spiteful now. "Just as Daven Tyras said you would."

"Ahrd!" Bracht grunted. "He's seduced you with his lies."

"As you once did," she retorted.

"Let your ghost-talkers scry us," Calandryll asked. "Let them examine us and you'll have the truth."

"Of that, too, he warned me," said Jehenne. "That you have magic in you to deceive the ghost-talkers. So—no; their part was done when they found you. The rest is mine."

Calandryll groaned as he felt hope dwindle, its faint flame doused by Rhythamun's subtlety. The sorcerer outthought them, left behind more defenses than the raised corpses of dire-wolves. He saw it now: that the mage used the truth itself to thwart pursuit, that he took Jehenne's lust for vengeance and molded it to his own needs.

"Blind vengeance?" he heard Bracht demand. "Ahrd, woman, if it's blood you must have, then take mine. But let these two go!"

"And take your werecoin in their place?" Jehenne resumed her guise of affability. "Your life and four thousand varre for their freedom?"

"Aye," Bracht said.

"No!" Katya cried, speaking for the first time, rising partway from the cushions in her urgency, so that across the table the watching Lykard grasped their dirks. She sank back, but still her voice was fierce, her gaze intent on Jehenne's face. "Listen! What Bracht, what Calandryll, tells you is the truth. I am of Vanu, and the holy men of my land sent me to find them, to secure the Arcanum that it might be destroyed. Spaewives and sorcerers have scried there must be three to secure that end, and if you slay Bracht, you grant Rhythamun the victory. Slay Bracht and you've the world's blood on your hands!"

Jehenne's brows arched in open mockery. "A pretty speech," she remarked. "But tell me, what is the Arcanum?"

It was Calandryll who answered: "An ancient book that tells where Tharn was banished by the First Gods. The gramaryes of unlocking, Rhythamun has already. With the book, he may find Tharn's tomb and raise the Mad God."

"I see." Contempt dripped from Jehenne's words. "A magic book, a shape-shifter, holy men from a land

beyond the Borrhun-maj; and you three questing to
save the world . . . Such a tale as the bards spin. Filled
with romance, but little substance."

"Let your ghost-talkers scry us," he asked again,
desperately. "Let them determine the truth."

"Or you deceive them." Jehenne shook her head. "I
think not; I think I shall judge this."

Calandryll looked at her face and saw no hope. Her
eyes were cold now, and if any amusement remained
there, it was the malevolent humor the contemplation of their fate afforded her, a dreadful satisfaction
that she might, at last, take her revenge for the slight
Bracht had given. All else, to this woman, was inci-
dental: there was a madness in her, born of pride, a
gift to Rhythamun. He looked to the other Lykard,
not so familiar with the folk of Cuan na'For that he
could be sure he read their expressions aright. Their
features were composed, impassive, but in a few eyes
he thought—or hoped—he saw a measure of doubt.

"Do you fear the truth so much?" he asked, aware
he clutched at a straw, not knowing what else to do,
save concede Rhythamun the victory. "Are you afraid
the ghost-talkers might deny you your vengeance?"

Jehenne's hand flashed out and he jerked back as
the contents of her cup splashed over his face. He
wiped it clean, wondering if he had achieved anything
save to stoke the fires of her anger. Had she worn a
blade, he had no doubt it would have been steel that
touched his flesh. He watched as she composed herself, the effort visible.

"Your fate I've yet to decide, but you serve yourselves ill with these feeble fantasies." Her voice was
sharp as any blade, her eyes furious as they fastened
on Bracht. "I had expected a measure of courage from
you, Bracht ni Errhyn. Not that you'd look to hide behind this tissue of lies."

"You hear only the truth," Bracht said quietly.
"What lies there are come from Rhythamun. But
you've not the ears to hear them, nor the eyes to see
the straight path."

Jehenne's lips stretched in a wide smile, prompting Calandryll to think of a cat as it contemplates a trapped mouse, enjoying the suffering of its victim. "I see the path clear enough," she said. "It leads to a tree, where you shall hang nailed. Where the birds shall peck out your eyes and the dogs gorge on your flesh. You are judged, Bracht ni Errhyn, and on the morrow I shall crucify you."

Bracht nodded once, his dark face like granite, denying her the satisfaction of his fear. He said, "And my companions? Do you take my werecoin for their lives?"

"That, I shall sleep on," answered Jehenne, and turned to her followers. "Now take them away."

16

THEY were taken from Jehenne's opulent wagon
to another, smaller and empty of such luxury,
but comfortable enough for all it smelled of leather
and oiled metal, as if customarily used for the transport of materials. Its covering was hide, tight-stitched
and windowless, the entry curtain a single flap that
was laced shut behind them. Plain cushions were
scattered over the bare planks of the floor, and when
Bracht pressed an eye to the curtain, he announced
two men stood below, likely more guards invisible beyond. Enclosed, they were in a twilight fusty from the
afternoon's heat, with little to do save stretch on the
cushions and curse their fate.

"He thought ahead of us," Calandryll said, his
voice bitter. "With the memories of Daven Tyras to
guide him, he uses Jehenne's hatred to thwart us."

"Aye," said Bracht, "but where is he? Not here, I
think, for were he, surely he'd come to gloat."

"What matter?" asked Katya. "We're doomed."

Her voice was husky, as if she fought back tears, or
held rage in narrow check. Calandryll saw Bracht
reach out to touch her cheek, gently, his reply soft.

"I am, it seems; but perhaps not you or
Calandryll."

"What?" Now scorn, frustration, entered the warrior woman's tone. "She's mad, and sees what lies between us—she'll slay me for that; Calandryll for the fact of his friendship."

"Perhaps not." Bracht's voice grew thoughtful. "Her claim on me is valid, but against you the only charge can be the slaying of those seven warriors, and I offered werecoin for that. By the ways of Cuan na'For, it must be the kin of the dead who decide the aye or nay there."

Calandryll heard Katya moan, her response muffled as her head sank, her hair falling in a flaxen curtain about her face, that held in both of her hands.

"And do they decide to let us go? Are we to ride on, while you hang nailed to a tree?"

"Aye," said Bracht. "As we agreed."

Katya's shoulders trembled, and from between her hands there came a sound Calandryll did not at first recognize: he had never thought to hear her weep. He watched helplessly as Bracht set an arm about her, drawing her close, so that she rested against his chest. He was surprised she made no move to escape the Kern's embrace, but lay against him as he stroked her hair, his voice a calm murmur in the darkness.

"Rhythamun is gone from here, else we'd have seen him. He must, therefore, continue on his way, and you must go after him. Listen"—he held her chin, turning her face toward his—"Jehenne will nail me to the tree, surely; but no man lives forever, and you've still a duty to perform. You've not let what's between us halt that yet, and you shall not now. You must not! I think I likely sowed sufficient seed among these ni Larrhyn that Jehenne shall be forced to agree to the acceptance of werecoin for your lives, or stand doubted as their leader. And in my saddlebags are the tokens of safe passage to see you safe over the lands of the other clans. If you can, learn where Rhythamun goes; if not, go on to the Cuan na'Dru, and seek Ahrd's guidance. But go on you must, or all we've done—and all there is between us—comes to naught."

His smile was resolute and in a while Katya nodded. Delicately, he brushed her cheeks, though in the shadows it was too dim that Calandryll might see if tears lay there. He thought they did, but then Katya sighed and straightened, seeming almost to regret such demonstration of frail emotion as she shifted from the compass of Bracht's arms. Though not far, composing herself, leaning back against the cart's side, her shoulder hard against the Kern's.

A thought occurred to Calandryll then, and though he felt scarcely confident of any success, still he considered it worth the voicing.

"Does Jehenne stand alone in judgment?" he asked.

"She commands the clan," said Bracht. "She was elected ketomana."

"And the ghost-talkers have no say?"

"Not in this, save she ask it of them. I see your gist, but you heard Jehenne's word on that—she'll not let the ghost-talkers scry us. There, too, Rhythamun showed his cunning."

"She said he warned against me." Calandryll frowned, unwilling to forgo the least avenue of hope. "But not, I thought, against you or Katya."

"It matters not," said Bracht. "My offense is known, and in that Jehenne's word is final. Were Katya of clan blood, then aye—she'd have the right to demand a scrying—but Vanu born, she's no such claim."

"The gods curse him!" Calandryll snarled. "He foresees each chance and seals the way."

"Likely the gods do curse him," Bracht said, his grin tight. "But the defeating of him they leave to us. Or you, come the morrow."

"You said that while we live we've hope," Calandryll returned. "And we live yet."

"Aye." Bracht snorted somber laughter, self-mocking. "But even I am not always right."

"There's no chance we might speak with a ghost-talker?" Calandryll was not yet ready to give up all hope. "None at all?"

"Save Jehenne agree it—which she'll not—no," said Bracht.

"There must," said Calandryll, "be something we can do."

"If there is, I cannot see it." Bracht shrugged, sighing. "Rhythamun set his snares too well, my friend."

Calandryll's teeth ground angrily together. With fast-waning confidence he asked, "Sword-trial? May we not challenge Jehenne's dictate?"

"Not where I am concerned," answered Bracht. "In your case, perhaps, though even then—because you are not of Cuan na'For—Jehenne might refuse you. And your shoulder's not full-healed yet."

"But I am hale," said Katya. "Could I challenge her?"

"Do the dead's kin accept my coin, you'll have no need," Bracht told her. "Do they refuse, or Jehenne seek to override them, then you might ask it. Whether Jchenne would agree, or not, rests with her. But for me, such a course is denied."

"And does she refuse," Calandryll asked, "what then?"

Bracht offered no immediate reply, then, quietly, said, "She'll order you slain. It is Lykard custom to behead offenders."

Such a death was, Calandryll thought, a better end than crucifixion, but no more welcome. "The Younger Gods," he muttered, frustration lending a note of anger to his voice. "Burash and Dera, they've aided us ere now—shall Ahrd not play his part?"

"Pray that he does," said Bracht. "But I think I'll not be there to see the outcome."

"Three," Katya murmured in a voice almost too low the others might hear her. "Three was ever the number. Save we be three, how shall we succeed?"

Bracht offered no answer, nor could Calandryll think of any response. It seemed, truly, that Rhythamun had snared them, and whether it was Bracht alone who died on the approaching morrow, or all of them, they had no chance now of defeating the mage. He groaned, tilting his head back against the leathern walls, staring into the shadows as his mind roved in search of a solution.

FOOD came before he found any answer, delivered by a silent Lykard woman, two men flanking her with drawn blades, no more talkative, even though Bracht demanded to know whether or not his offer of werecoin was conveyed to the families of the dead, cursing them soundly when they failed to reply. The woman simply set down the basket she carried, her eyes darting from one face to another, and withdrew between the swordsmen. They, in turn, stepped back and closed the curtain, lacing it tight.

Outside, night had fallen. Within the cart-borne pavilion, the gloom, of both sight and spirits, heightened, and the prisoners fumbled for the contents of the pannier.

"They might, at least, grant us light," Calandryll complained.

"And give us the chance to fire this wagon?" Bracht shook his head unseen. "Too great a danger, my friend."

"Had I but the chance, I'd set torch to their whole camp," Katya said, low and angry.

"The blame lies with Jehenne," Bracht murmured. "Not the clan."

"They follow her," the warrior woman snapped. "They obey her."

"As is the way of Cuan na'For." Bracht's voice was mild. "Save she go against clan law, they must."

Katya snorted. Calandryll, extracting a haunch of meat from the basket, said, "Still, they feed us well enough."

And that was true: the meat he found was venison, and while they must pass it from hand to hand, tearing with their teeth, it was good, with it a stew of cold vegetables, bread, cheese, even a flask of the tart wine. Such donation of creature comforts surprised

him, until he thought that likely it was the hospitality customarily offered the condemned, and that the
stronger Bracht was, the longer he should suffer his
crucifixion. After that, the food lost its taste and he
ate mechanically, from instinct rather than appetite.
He thought, as he chewed, that of them all, Bracht
seemed the calmest, for all the Kern faced the least
palatable fate. For himself and Katya there remained
the chance of escape; Bracht was denied that hope, yet
he showed no sign of fear. He was, Calandryll decided, a truly courageous man. It did not occur to him
that he gave no time to his own potential demise, but
thought entirely of the Kern.

Bracht, in turn, appeared concerned for his companions, and when they had eaten went to the curtain, asking that they be allowed to perform their
toilet. Once more Calandryll was surprised by the odd
courtesy of the Lykard, for they were promptly
brought from the wagon, albeit under guard and sepa-
rately, and escorted to leather-curtained latrines
downstream of the wagons.

It was embarrassing to perform such personal duties surrounded by watchful men, but still it gave him
the opportunity to study the camp a little further.

Fires were lit now, the largest at the center, where
the largest carts stood, and he saw that folk were
gathered there, seemingly engaged in argument. Their
voices were muffled, but he thought that he heard anger, and once saw Jehenne on her feet, gesticulating
furiously, and the two ghost-talkers. What it meant,
he had no idea, nor, when he was returned to the
prison cart, could Bracht enlighten him, save to suggest hopefully that the matter of the werecoin was debated.

There seemed little more to say after that, except,
perhaps, their farewells, and those none wished to
voice, still clinging, against all odds, to the impossible
hope of some miracle. The debate was a background
murmur, no more distinct than the ever-present

sounds of the horse herds, and in a little while they composed themselves to sleep.

Discreetly, Calandryll piled cushions at the entrance, as far from his companions as he might contrive. He thought perhaps their good-byes would be intimate, for Katya, rather than finding a place separate from Bracht as had always been her custom, stretched out beside the Kern, and Calandryll saw the silver of her mail-clad sleeve fall across the subfusc leather of Bracht's tunic. He turned his back and closed his eyes, endeavoring to block his ears, too. Those organs, however, refused to cease their work, and though he buried his head beneath a cushion, still he could not help but catch snatches of their low-voiced conversation.

"I'd not lose you," he heard Katya say, and Bracht's reply, "You've not yet."

Bodies shifted, the cart's deck creaking slightly with the movement, and Calandryll felt his cheeks grow hot, no more able to dull his hearing than halt his breath.

"We vowed," he heard from Bracht, the Kern's tone shocking him, for it was filled with pent longing, and denial; and Katya whisper, "But then we could not know."

"Even so," came Bracht's voice, "we vowed—until the Arcanum is destroyed."

"Then likely never," he heard Katya respond.

"If Ahrd wills it so," Bracht murmured. "But a vow is a vow, and I'd not see you dishonored."

"Honor!" Katya's voice rose, then softened again. "Is that so important, now?"

"Aye," Bracht said, gently earnest. "Yours and mine. I'd not go to my death robbed of that, nor have you discard yours on fate's whim."

Katya's response was lost as Calandryll found another cushion to add to his barrier. His head grew hot, the cushions stifling, smelling faintly of horses. He thought perhaps he would escape Jehenne by suffocating, but then he heard the woman laugh softly, and

Bracht chuckle, though the cart did not creak or sway as he anticipated. Instead, something struck his barricade and Bracht's voice came clear to his burning ears: "We hide nothing, Calandryll, and you've no need to hide yourself."

He pushed up then, grateful for the fresher air, and saw the Kern with a second cushion ready to throw; he smiled, gesturing surrender.

"I thought," he began. "I thought that . . ."

"Aye," Bracht said, "and your tact is appreciated."

"But this is an honorable man," said Katya. "And so you may sleep comfortable."

In her voice Calandryll heard respect, and love, like a hymn of praise, and he wondered, as he lay back, if he, in such circumstances, could exercise equal restraint. *Shall I ever know?* he thought as, like some welcome thief, sleep stole his senses.

HE was surprised to realize he had slept, for it seemed more appropriate that he should have spent the night awake, contemplating his life, holding vigil over his condemned friend, or worrying at his own fate. But light falling across his face and the gruff voices of the Lykard roused him and he opened his eyes to see a guard beckoning.

Again he was taken to the stream alone, washing, snatching what glimpses he could of the waking camp. The sun was barely over the horizon, heralding a high, bright day. Ground mist curled among the tents; cookfires burned, the central bonfire a smoldering pile now; children scurried among the carts, and all along the watercourse, folk bent to their own ablutions. When he was done, he was returned to the wagon, where another basket waited, this filled with bread and fruit, cheese, a jug of water.

The prisoners ate and waited: they could do no more.

Then, as dawn became morning, the curtain was flung back and they were summoned. A dozen warriors surrounded them, bringing them to the camp's center, where Jehenne stood, the drachomannii at her back, a knot of Lykard, men and women, to either side, their faces grave. These, as if accorded some special status, occupied the square formed by the wagons. The other folk—the entire camp, it seemed—looked on from a little distance, all silent.

"The kinfolk of the dead," Bracht murmured, indicating those closest to Jehenne with a jut of his chin. "Best I speak—does she allow."

The escort halted, shoving the prisoners forward, and for long moments, Jehenne studied them without speaking. The sun struck fire from her red hair, sparking over the platelets that decorated her leathers. Her left hand was clasped loose about the hilt of her sword, her right fisted at her side. Her eyes were alight with horrid anticipation, her smile predatory.

"Judgment is delivered," she said at last, slowly, savoring the words, a gourmet at a ghastly feast. "For the insult given me, and the slaying of Lykard warriors, his trespass on our grazing lands, Bracht ni Errhyn is condemned to death."

She paused; still all the onlookers remained silent. It seemed even the horses were still. Overhead, Calandryll heard a raven croak.

Then, her eyes intent on Bracht's face, as if hungry for sight of fear there, she said, "You shall be taken from here and crucified." Her right arm came up, her fist opening to display the nails she held. They were long, sharp-tipped, with heavy, flattened heads. "With these shall you be nailed to Ahrd's tree—the god shall judge you then! Be it his will, these nails shall find no purchase, and you go free. Be you truly guilty, then you shall hang there until death release you, your bones testament to your iniquity. So are you judged."

Calandryll heard breath come sharp from between Bracht's teeth, but the Kern's face remained impassive, and though his tanned skin paled a fraction, he showed no overt sign of fear. Instead, he ducked his head, once, meeting her gaze to demand, "And my comrades? My offer of werecoin?"

Jehenne's full lips pursed then, her eyes narrowing, angered by her victim's stoic acceptance. For his part, Calandryll felt his stomach turn, his skin grow cold, not sure whether in awful sympathy or fear for his own life. He squared his shoulders, standing straight, determined to show no more weakness than Bracht demonstrated. Though his eyes were fixed on Jehenne's face, from the corner of his right he saw Katya glaring at the woman, her proud features flushed with rage.

"That is accepted." Jehenne's voice was thick, throbbing with barely controlled fury, her knuckles white as she clutched the nails. "They shall watch you hung on the tree and then may depart. But heed me—do either of you come again across my grass, you shall die as he does!"

Her face was a beautiful harpy's mask as she signaled, and a man came forward to hand Bracht his saddlebags. The Kern fetched out the leathern pouch containing the money, passing it to the closet ghost-talker. The shaman loosed the drawstrings, spilling bright coins into his companion's hands, and announced formally, "Werecoin is paid; gold for blood. Let there be no talk of vengeance."

Bracht smiled then, and nodded, as though satisfied; Calandryll thought Jehenne would spit her ire. "A boon," Bracht said.

"No!" Jehenne's voice was strident. "Nothing!"

"It is the custom."

This from a ghost-talker, echoed by the other. Among the Lykard closest to the woman a grey-haired man said, "It is the way, Jehenne," the rest murmuring agreement.

Jehenne snarled aloud and gestured reluctant acceptance.

"I'd know of Daven Tyras," Bracht said. "Where does he go?"

The woman laughed, injecting the sound with con-

tempt. "You pursue that fiction? Do you think any
here believe your lies?"

"Where does he go?" Bracht repeated. "That I speak
the truth of the shape-shifter, I think you know. Do
you league with gharan-evur now, Jehenne? Do you
worship the Mad God, as does he?"

Calandryll was unsure whether Bracht sought genuinely to glean information, or to enrage the woman.
If the latter, he succeeded, for her face grew mottled
and fire danced in her eyes, her lips stretching tight
over grinding teeth. In that instant, she seemed truly
insane, and he thought she might draw her blade and
end the Kern's life there and then.

Instead, in a voice barely controlled, she said, "No
gharan-evur, he, but a man of vision. He rides for the
north, escorted by chosen warriors, to speak with the
Valan and the Yelle on my behalf."

Bracht's eyes narrowed at that, and Jehenne
laughed triumphantly, enjoying his puzzlement.
"Aye," she continued, gloating, "to parley with the
ketomannii of those clans, to bring them my offer of
alliance."

"Alliance?" Bracht asked. "To what end?"

Again Jehenne laughed.

"Why, that all the clans of Cuan na'For join together in one great force and ride south. Beyond the
Gann Peaks, Lysse lies soft—ripe for the taking."

Calandryll gasped, seeing in this a grand and terrible design: further evidence that Tharn's malign will
influenced men, thus furthering his own resurrection.
Civil war in Kandahar; in Lysse, Tobias speaking for
invasion; now this talk of war between Cuan na'For
and Lysse. It seemed that madness grew apace
throughout the world, men preparing for such blood-
baths as would make dreadful offering to the Mad
God. "Insanity!" he heard Bracht shout, and thought
that on the faces of more than a few of the assembled
Lykard he saw doubt.

Then Bracht said, "The Asyth will refuse such
madness; my father will never agree."

"Then your father, and all your clan, if need be," Jehenne returned, "will perish. All those who deny the dream will perish."

"You are seduced by a warlock!" Bracht shouted. "Daven Tyras is a shape-shifter, a father-slayer, whose goal is the raising of the Mad God! You deliver your clan to damnation, woman."

"Silence!" Jehenne's voice was a whiplash, accompanied by a curt gesture that brought the guards closer, their hands firm on the prisoners. "You wriggle like some grubbing worm, but none will heed your lies."

Calandryll stared, sure now that she was Rhythamun's creature. Whether consciously or unwittingly made scant difference: in her ambition, her lust for vengeance, she gave herself over to the mage, aiding him in his dreadful purpose. He felt himself hauled back, the guards pressing close, but in the moments before their bulk hid him from the onlookers, he thought he saw the doubt grow. Had that been Bracht's purpose? To reveal to all the ni Larrhyn the path their leader chose? It seemed a philosophical question as he was manhandled away and set upon his horse, Katya to his right, beyond her, Bracht.

Horsemen closed about them, driving them across the stream, through the cluster of carts, toward the farther wall of the valley. As they began to climb, Calandryll saw Jehenne in the lead, distinctive on her great white horse, the two ghost-talkers behind, then a group of folk who, unlike the guards, seemed to talk among themselves. They topped the ridge and lifted to a canter over the grass, a hurst barely visible in the distance across the flat prairie. The morning was as yet early, but already warm, the sun a bright disc above, shining indifferent from a sky of startling blue, broken by a handful of orphan clouds. When Bracht spoke none moved to silence him, as if their escort respected the condemned's last farewells.

"This is a good day to die, though I'd sooner it were in different manner." His smile, Calandryll thought, was grim, belying his cheerful tone. "No matter—you're saved, so listen. No," this softly, to Katya, "weep not, but heed me—does Rhythamun truly carry word of this mad alliance to the Valan and the Yelle, then he must linger in Cuan na'For and you've the chance to find him."

"We two?" Katya's voice was strained.

"If need be," Bracht said firmly. "And be you still set on entering the Cuan na'Dru, then I urge you ride wary. Seek first the oaks of the edgewoods and ask leave of Ahrd that you may go into his forest. Do you encounter the Gruagach, and they prove unfriendly, then turn and ride hard away. Do not go where the Gruagach forbid. I'd have your word on that."

Katya moaned an affirmative; Calandryll said, "Aye."

As he spoke, he noticed that their escort attended Bracht's words, their customarily impassive faces registering some measure of surprise, as if this talk of the Cuan na'Dru and the Gruagach impressed them. No less, he thought, it fed the seeds of doubt Bracht looked to sow. For all the good that did, he told himself as the distant hurst came nearer, for none seemed likely to argue Jehenne's judgment, and Bracht, therefore, should still be nailed to the tree.

"We've come a long way, we three," the Kern said, "and I'd have you know I could not want for better comrades."

"Nor I," said Katya, the simple words coming slow and choking from a throat constricted by grief.

"I'll never know a truer friend," said Calandryll, his own voice husky now. "And be it in my power, your death shall not go unavenged."

Bracht nodded, casting a wary glance in the direction of the guards. "Let Rhythamun's defeat be your revenge," he murmured, then grinned. "Save that opportunity we spoke of present itself."

Calandryll ducked his head in silent promise.

"So, Jehenne being in somewhat of a hurry, I think," Bracht added, "I bid you both farewell. May

Ahrd and all his kindred gods go with you, and when I'm on the tree, do not linger. Jehenne's leagued with madness now and might well renege on her promise."

Calandryll saw some of their escort frown at that, but none spoke. "Farewell," he said.

"Farewell," said Katya, and on her cheeks he saw tears glisten, silver as her mail. "And know this—that did we bring the Arcanum back safe to Vanu, then I'd have wed you; did my father say me nay, even so I'd wed you."

"Then I die content," Bracht said solemnly.

They fell silent then, the steady pounding of the hooves measuring out the distance to the hurst. Calandryll felt his own cheeks wet, and raised a hand to wipe them, his teeth pressed hard together, praying desperately that some miracle take shape, that Ahrd intervene, that a *byah* emerge from the ever-closer woodland to deny Jehenne.

None came, only the trees, no longer a blur on the heat-hazed prairie but a distinct shape now, a small copse, leafed green with fresh spring growth, dominated by the single oak that thrust gnarled limbs like widespread arms outward from the edge. Jehenne halted there, beneath the shadow of the tree, studying the great trunk awhile before dismounting, tossing her reins to a warrior who led the horse away. The drachomannii, likewise, sprang down, falling to their knees with raised arms and spread fingers, chanting a prayer. The escort slowed and reined in a little way off, beckoning the prisoners from their saddles, awaiting Jehenne's word before bringing them closer.

She stood spraddle-legged, hands on hips, her face triumphant as she watched them brought before her.

"I'd ask Ahrd's mercy," Bracht said, answered with a brief nod.

He shook off the hands that held him and paced toward the oak. The ghost-talkers rose, stepping back, and he set both hands against the rutted trunk, murmuring low, then knelt with upraised arms and bowed head. *Now!* Calandryll shouted into the throbbing silence of his mind. *Now save him! Ahrd, if you'd see us victorious over Rhythamun, send a* byah *now. Deny Jehenne and save this man who quests to save you and all your kin.*

Only bird song and the gentle rustle of wind-stirred leaves answered him, and he saw Bracht rise, turning from the oak to face the red-haired woman.

"So, my peace is made—do what you will. But remember your promise, that my comrades ride free."

Calandryll felt Katya's hand fasten tight on his forearm, her fingers digging hard into the muscle. He covered it with his own and they stared, aghast, as Jehenne reached beneath her tunic, extracting the two nails. She passed them to the ghost-talkers and called for warriors to take Bracht, to hold him against the tree.

"There's no need."

His voice was defiant and Calandryll saw Jehenne's lips thin as the Kern set his back to the trunk, his arms lifted to either side.

So vast was the ancient growth that even then wood showed, grey-green, past his hands, the branches overhead casting gentle shadows across his face. He braced himself square, and cried in a firm voice, "Go to it, then, and Ahrd curse your soul."

Jehenne snarled, disappointed by his courage, and snapped harsh orders that sent two muscular warriors to the tree to clutch Bracht's wrists and hold him fixed against the trunk. In their free hands they carried hammers, the shafts wrapped with leather, the heads dull metal, and heavy. Jehenne passed a nail to each ghost-talker and the shamans came forward to set the points against Bracht's palms. The warriors raised their hammers. Jehenne smiled, green eyes fixed intent on Bracht's face, and said in a voice filled with horrid gloating, "Now go to it."

As one, the drachomannii intoned, "Ahrd's will be done," and the hammers fell.

Calandryll stared in dreadful fascination, unable to turn his gaze or close his eyes, transfixed by the awful spectacle. He felt his own palms tingle, his hands tightening involuntarily into fists. Beside him, Katya moaned deep in her throat, and her grip tightened unnoticed on his arm.

Bracht shuddered as the metal pierced his hands. His head snapped back, hard against the tree, tendons bulging down the length of his neck as he clenched his teeth, refusing to cry out. His eyes opened wide, bright with pain, and sweat burst from his forehead.

The hammers rose, and fell again.

Blood sprang red from Bracht's palms, trickling over the skin, dripping onto the oak's trunk. His mouth stretched in ghastly facsimile of a smile. The nails extended a finger's length from his hands.

Once more, the hammers fell. Once more, Bracht's body shuddered. But still the nails remained extended, as if they found no purchase in the wood. The warrior to Bracht's left paused, casting a puzzled look at the ghost-talker by his side. Jehenne shouted, "Strike harder!"

Both hammers lifted; fell. The nails went no deeper.

Now both the warriors faltered in their work, looking to each other, to the ghost-talkers. Calandryll felt hope flicker, a tiny kindling, and called silently on Ahrd, pleading for mercy, for a miracle. "Harder!" screamed Jehenne.

The hammers thudded, metal on metal, with all the weight of the warriors' thick arms behind the blows: uselessly, for neither nail seemed able to enter the oak's wood, but went no deeper than the depth of Bracht's palms. Calandryll's gaze was locked on his comrade's face, so he did not see Jehenne's expression, but he heard her strangled cry, as though she, not her victim, were racked with pain. Then all who watched gasped in awe, staring dumbstruck as, slowly, the nails moved, outward.

The warriors holding the hammers stepped back a pace, staring, awe and something close to fear in their eyes, and Jehenne shrieked, "No! Strike again, and harder!"

The two men stood irresolute. One, tentatively, lifted his hammer, halted by a ghost-talker, who raised a commanding hand and said, "No. Leave be."

All stood in silence then as the nails moved, inexorably, pushing clear of Bracht's palms, falling loose. Red-tipped, they fell to the grass at the Kern's feet, and where they had pierced his flesh there came a green exudation, as if the unbroken bark of the tree oozed sap to expel the nails and fill the wounds. It bulged from the holes, running like some gentle balm over the skin, covering the blood, dripping to join the crimson spotting on the grass below. Calandryll gaped as he saw the agony go out of Bracht's body. The eyes, no longer filmed with pain, cleared; the wide-stretched mouth relaxed, the awful rictus grin becoming an almost beatific smile. Loud and clear, Bracht cried, "Praise Ahrd!" Then his eyes closed and he slid down the trunk, crumpling limp on the sward.

Calandryll felt his forearm burn as blood flowed again to nerves numbed by Katya's grip, that released as the warrior woman ran to Bracht's side, cradling his head, her grey eyes triumphant as she stared at the green-painted wounds. The exudate congealed now, crusting over the holes, melding with the broken skin so that it seemed no nails had driven through. In moments no trace of wound was left in either hand, only faint stigmata, pale marks of new-grown, greenish flesh.

"Ahrd has judged this warrior and found him innocent."

The ghost-talker stared, no less awed than any there, at Bracht.

His fellow drachoman echoed him: "So it is. Ahrd rejects the nails—this man is judged innocent."

"No!"

Jehenne's shout was a banshee scream of frustrated rage. Calandryll saw her blade flash from the scabbard, lifted high as she darted forward. He thrust out a foot, tripping her, and she sprawled headlong on the grass. Cat-quick, she recovered, rolling and springing to her feet, fury and madness blazing in her green eyes as she continued toward the unconscious Bracht. Katya, no less swift, set down his head, rising in a crouch, ready to defend him bare-handed. Calandryll hurled himself forward, crashing into the woman, to send her down again as all around the watching Lykard began to shout. He clutched her wrist, an arm locking about her throat as she shrieked and struggled to throw him off. He was aware of boots stamping close by, then of hands upon him, dragging him clear, thinking the ni Larrhyn would give Jehenne her way, roaring, "Ahrd judged him! Ahrd claims him guiltless!"

As he was lifted to his feet he saw that others held Jehenne, and that her sword was taken from her, and that while she fought the restraining hands, they held her firm, the dark faces of the Lykard confused and frightened.

"Slay him," she moaned, spittle flecking her contorted lips. "I command you to slay him! Slay them, all three!"

"You blaspheme."

Both ghost-talkers interposed themselves between Jehenne and Bracht. Beyond them, Calandryll saw Katya return to the Kern's side, kneeling to fold his hands across his chest, clutch his head to her bosom.

"Slay them. I am ketomana of the ni Larrhyn and I say you shall slay them."

"No!"

The ghost-talkers stepped a pace forward, their arms raised in denial as Jehenne wailed, struggling to break free. It seemed to Calandryll they spoke in unison, though perhaps their words only came too fast, pitched in tones too similar to distinguish one from the other.

"Ahrd's holy oak rejects the nails—would you deny the judgment of our god?

"This man is saved, and no Lykard may raise hand against him for fear of damnation.

"Ahrd has judged him and found him true. Let all know this. Let word be passed to all the camps—that Bracht ni Errhyn rides innocent across our grass.

"None may deny our god.

"See! Are his wounds not healed? Does Ahrd not give him back his life? This is a mighty thing we have witnessed, and who would deny it would deny Ahrd himself."

"I would deny it."

Sudden, horrified silence fell at Jehenne's words. So shocked were the warriors holding her that they let loose their grip. A voice cried, "Blasphemy!" Outrage showed stark on the faces of the ghost-talkers. The woman moved a step toward them and they fell back a pace, as if afraid she would somehow contaminate them.

"You voice blasphemy."

"Still I'd slay him. Them!"

"This cannot be."

"It can. It shall be."

Calandryll felt the hands upon his own arms fall away, saw disbelief on all the staring faces. Jehenne stooped to retrieve her sword.

"Do you deny Ahrd, then you are no longer ketomana of the ni Larrhyn.

"Put up your blade and let these three ride free."

The ghost-talkers were echoed by the rest: "Aye. No blasphemer may lead us."

"She'd deny Ahrd himself."

"Madness, as the ni Errhyn said."

"Werecoin was taken."

Jehenne flourished her blade, turning in a slow circle, her eyes challenging. Calandryll tensed, ready to spring again, wondering if he might first snatch a sword, his wound-weakened shoulder forgotten.

"Do you this, Jehenne, and you are damned."

"Then I shall be damned."

The ghost-talker paled. His fellow said, "This woman may lead us no longer."

"Then I shall lead you no longer. But I shall have my revenge!"

"To slay a helpless warrior?" The voice came from over Calandryll's shoulder. "You are bereft of honor, woman."

Another said, "I took his werecoin e'en though my son was slain. Agreement was made."

"Aye," said all the crowd, speaking now with one voice.

"You deny our god and steal our honor."

A ghost-talker thrust an accusing finger at Jehenne, who barked scornful laughter and said, "You speak of honor? What of my honor, that Bracht ni Errhyn sullied?"

"Of that, Ahrd has delivered holy judgment," the ghost-talker replied, his voice hoarse with the shock that sprang his eyes wide, cracking lines through the paint upon his face.

"But I have not."

The falchion Jehenne held darted out; the ghost-talker drew back his hand, a heartbeat before his finger was sliced off. From the gathered Lykard there came gasps of stark disbelief, close followed by an angry grumbling, and Calandryll thought they might fall upon the woman, the tables firmly turned.

"Does she thirst so for blood, then let her try for mine."

Katya spoke in the Envah, her voice cold, steely as the fury that clouded her grey eyes, as though a storm raged there, flashing dangerous lightning. It silenced the mumble of protest, drawing all eyes in her direction. Gentle as a mother lowering child to cradle, she set down Bracht's head, rising to stride forward, glaring at Jehenne.

"This . . . creature . . . would refuse the judgment of your god; she'd slay a man unable to defend himself; she'd renege the promise of werecoin. She sullies the honor of the ni Larrhyn." The words came hot and clear, answered with a nodding of heads, muttered agreement. "Aye—Bracht warned of that, and he spoke the truth. No less when he told of Rhythamun, who has seduced this foul woman. Remember that when I have defeated her—that the body of Daven Tyras is but a mask worn by a sorcerer, who'd raise the Mad God and bring all the world down in chaos. Do you pursue the crazed dream he sowed in her mind, then you league with madness—with a god damned by his own parents, who'd see Ahrd, and all the Younger Gods, destroyed. Do you as Jehenne would have it, then you folk of Cuan na'For lend yourselves to Tharn's design."

She paused, her body tense, her eyes angry and defiant. Calandryll applauded her subtlety—that she thought, even then, to turn the moment to advantage, to thwart Rhythamun. On the faces of the Lykard all about him, he saw doubt grow, becoming certainty, a rejection of Jehenne's proposed alliance.

"It shall not be," said one ghost-talker.

"Word shall be passed," said the other. "To warn of this mage."

"There shall be no alliance," promised the first.

Katya nodded. "Then give me my sword and let this be settled," she said. "Let this creature try for her mad vengeance."

There was a moment of silence, of confusion, then one of the ghost-talkers cried, "So be it," and a warrior hurried to fetch Katya's saber, passing her the blade with a respectful bow. She hefted the weapon as a circle formed, she and Jehenne at the center, eyeing each other with unfeigned loathing.

"Your life is mine," snarled the flame-haired woman.

Katya tossed her flaxen mane and smiled coldly. "Then try to take it," she challenged.

Jehenne needed no further prompting: swift as a stooping hawk she sprang forward, the falchion weaving a glittering pattern before her.

Katya stood her ground, the saber rising bright, deflecting the Lykard woman's attack, returning it so that Jehenne's advance halted and they moved a little way apart, circling, testing each other with feints and thrusts, parry and riposte. Steel clashed on steel, each woman seeking the other's measure, Jehenne driven by rage, by the madness that blazed in her eyes, Katya by bold determination, in defense of the man she loved and the high purpose of their quest.

Calandryll could only watch, one among the fluid ring of onlookers, moving back, to the side, granting the combatants room as they shifted, this way and that, seeming for the moment evenly matched, the outcome unguessable. He saw Jehenne feint a cut at Katya's head, turning the blow to launch a darting thrust at the chest, and the Vanu woman parry, riposting a sideways slash at the Lykard's belly. Jehenne danced back, undaunted, her smile savage as she sprang away, seeking to use Katya's momentum to turn the flaxen-haired warrior woman and hack the falchion across her momentarily exposed spine. Katya, in turn, leapt clear of the blow, answering it with her own, so that Jehenne's blade was flung out, only her speed saving her from the return stroke.

They each stood their ground awhile then, trading blow for blow, the day loud with the sharp clatter of blade on blade. Then, as Katya brought up her saber to oppose a descending cut, Jehenne stepped closer, her left hand reaching down, to the dirk sheathed on her right hip. Calandryll shouted a warning, though he had no need, for Katya saw—or sensed—the movement and locked her left hand about Jehenne's wrist before the dirk could slash across her lower belly. For long moments they stood face-to-face, the Vanu saber raised, holding off the Lykard falchion, Jehenne straining to bring the dirk into play, Katya pinning the weapon between them. Then she hooked a boot about Jehenne's ankles and pivoted, leaning away as the falchion came down, letting Jehenne's own strength unbalance the redheaded woman.

Jehenne yelled as she fell, Katya still holding her

left wrist trapped, the Vanu woman's boot slamming down against the right. The tip of Katya's saber rested against Jehenne's throat, lightly, but sharp enough a pinprick of scarlet showed there. Jehenne's face contorted, no longer lovely, and in a hoarse voice she snarled, "Do you end it, then? I'll not plead for mercy, be that your thought."

Katya shook her head, the sun striking points of brilliance from the silvery gold mane, and her full lips twitched in a small smile. "I'd not expect it," she said, in the Envah still, so that, Calandryll realized, all there should understand her and not, afterward, have chance to claim the duel unfair, or won with trickery. "No—I'd not slay a helpless enemy. Such is your province."

She loosed her grip and sprang back as Jehenne spat insane fury and leapt to her feet, falchion and dirk, both, extended. From the crowd, Calandryll heard a murmur of approval; for his own part, he thought, he would have driven the blade in and sundered Jehenne's head from her neck, without such honorable display of clemency.

Katya, though, seemed confident, and, indeed, her action appeared to have rendered Jehenne less, rather than more, cautious. It was as if that sparing of her life served to stoke the furnace of her rage, provoking her to careless desperation, for she now attacked with a wild disregard for defense, seeking to drive Katya back and batter down the Vanu woman under the sheer fury of her onslaught. Falchion and dirk swung and probed, Jehenne seeking an opening denied her by Katya's self-control, by the flaxen-haired woman's sword skill. Each thrust, each stab, was parried, and as they circled, Calandryll saw that Katya led her opponent on, persuading Jehenne to expend her strength, while husbanding her own. It seemed she fought entirely defensive now, looking only to hold off Jehenne's enraged assault, but Calandryll saw that she moved only a little, reserving herself, while Jehenne paced and darted and hacked in a fury of energy that painted her face with sweat and brought the breath in heaving gasps from between her stretched lips.

Once, it seemed the dirk had found a home in Katya's ribs, but she shoved Jehenne away, smiling still, even though a fine line of red coursed over the silver of her mail. Once, the falchion scored a cut upon her thigh, but not deep. And the saber scored its own wounds—over Jehenne's ribs, the tunic parted, stained with a red brighter than the leather; blood ran from a forearm, over the fingers that held the dirk; platelets hung loose, jangling, below the thrust of Jehenne's breasts—but none serious, small hurts that went unnoticed in the fury of combat, ignored as the Lykard woman pressed in, seeking to drive through Katya's defense.

They shifted toward the tree and Calandryll moved to place himself between them and Bracht, who still lay unconscious, thinking that perhaps Jehenne might sacrifice herself to slay him, or that a random blow might strike the Kern. He was surprised to find that the ghost-talkers, too, and the warriors who had wielded the hammers set themselves as living barrier against such accident. He chanced a look at Bracht and saw his comrade as though asleep, his features tranquil, his hurried glance drawn back to the duel by a sudden gasp from those still intent on the fight.

The two women were closed again, Jehenne's dirk held back from Katya's throat by the saber, the falchion trapped between ribs and the Vanu woman's left arm. Then Jehenne twisted, drawing back the dagger, so that Katya's blade sliced down through empty air even as the dirk was rammed forward, not seeking to stab, but slamming the fist that held it against Katya's jaw. Calandryll saw her eyes start wide, unfocused for an instant, and Jehenne leer in feral triumph as she snatched her sword arm clear and swung the falchion back, then forward again, at Katya's neck.

It seemed that Katya, stunned by the blow, must stagger helpless, as the falchion hacked down her life.

It seemed to Calandryll that time slowed in that instant, each minute detail enacted with agonizing languor. He saw the bright steel of the falchion swing toward Katya's throat; saw the warrior woman take one horribly protracted step backward: not enough to save her life. He saw her take a second, her knees bending, and thought the blow to her jaw had unwitted her. Then, still slow as dream's inertia, he saw the falchion pass close over her head, so close the flaxen hair was ruffled and long strands drifted, severed, on the blade's passage. He saw Jehenne turned by the force of it, the dirk moving forward and across, instinctive defense, even as she shifted her weight to reverse the stroke. He saw Katya gather herself, no longer falling, but lunging forward, the saber outthrust, propelled by her straightening legs and all the carefully harbored strength in her slim body.

It took Jehenne in the side; before the dirk could move to fend it off, before the falchion could riposte.

Time resumed its normal pace then, as the saber slid half its length between Jehenne's ribs and the flame-haired woman's scream split the silence. It seemed to Calandryll the sound held less of pain than outraged anger. Katya twisted the blade as she withdrew the steel, no longer gleaming silvery, but dulled now. Jehenne swayed, coughing crimson bubbles that burst and spattered over her lips and chin. Her face was haggard as she raised her blade, taking one unsteady step toward Katya. Almost casually it seemed, Katya swung the saber across the Lykard woman's belly, and Jehenne grunted, spitting blood, and doubled over, sword and dagger both falling from her grasp as she crumpled. She fell on hands and knees, and for a while rested there, her face hidden behind the curtain of her sweat-lank hair, her breathing a horrible, bubbling exhalation. Then she shook her head and moaned something none could hear, and sank down with a final, heaving sigh, and lay still.

There came a silence then that stretched out, as if none present could quite believe Jehenne ni Larrhyn was defeated, was dead. It seemed as though even the insects buzzing over the grass, the birds in the woodland, the waiting horses, were stilled; the wind itself seemed muted. Katya stood, head lowered, the bloodied saber at her side, her face solemn, even grim, no triumph, nor satisfaction, in her expression. It was as if she honored her slain foe.

Then the drachomannii spoke, again in singsong unison: "The combat was just.

"Jehenne ni Larrhyn was tested and found wanting.

"From her own mouth she damned herself.

"By blade was she tried, by blade was she defeated.

"Let all who saw know this, and tell it—that Katya of Vanu fought with honor, and in honor was victorious."

Calandryll saw that Katya frowned as the shamans intoned their ritual chant, and moved to her side, translating the words. She nodded, tearing a handful of grass with which to cleanse her blade, sheathing the weapon. "And now?" she demanded. "Shall they send us on our way, or grant us shelter until Bracht recovers?"

Calandryll could offer no answer, but one of the ghost-talkers approached then, his expression tentative as he ducked his head and said, "I speak your language. No Lykard will offer you harm, for we shall send word to all the camps of what has happened here, and all shall know of Jehenne ni Larrhyn's blasphemy, and that Ahrd looks with favor on Bracht ni Errhyn. Be it your wish, we shall carry him back to our camp, and he shall rest there until he wishes to leave. The sap of Ahrd's holy tree is in his veins now, but be our healing skills needed, then they are his. And yours."

He paused as Katya glanced down, seemingly aware for the first time of her own wounds. She dismissed them with a careless gesture, fixing the shaman with her stare.

"And shall you pass word of Rhythamun? Daven Tyras?"

"That shall be done," the drachoman promised. "From camp to camp the word shall go—that Daven Tyras is outcast, to be slain on sight. Ahrd has judged Jehenne, and all shall know her dream of alliance was a madness, born of this Rhythamun's seduction."

"Still we'd pursue him," Katya said. "For he carries with him a book that we are vowed to bring to Vanu."

"None shall prevent you," answered the shaman, "and be he slain, then all he has with him shall be delivered to you, wherever you may be on the grass of Cuan na'For."

"So be it, and our thanks for that." Katya inclined her head. "But for now, do we bring Bracht back to your camp?"

"As you wish it." The ghost-talker bowed, turning to call in his own language, sending men hurrying to fashion a litter from the pollarded growths that flanked the edges of the hurst.

THEIR return was met by all the camp, and a great cry went up as Jehenne's body, slung across her white horse, was seen, another at sight of Bracht, still unconscious, on the litter. The ghost-talkers rode ahead, shouting news of the crucifixion and its outcome, of the combat, and of Daven Tyras. Word spread fast and awed faces looked up at Katya as she rode between the wagons, her eyes intent on Bracht, troubled.

They were brought to Jehenne's wagon, which, by custom, was now theirs to command, and Bracht was laid upon a bed of silk. Impatiently, Katya allowed the ghost-talkers to dress her wounds, going, once they were done with their ministrations, to Bracht's side. The Kern appeared unharmed. The wounds in his hands were mended, the flesh there sound, no longer even shaded with the greenish hue of the sap that had flowed out to expel the nails and heal him. Save he had seen it happen, Calandryll would not have known his friend had suffered any hurt. But still, as dusk fell, Bracht slept, and none could say when—or if—he would awake, for none had ever seen a man survive that ordeal.

"He lives," Calandryll said, as Katya gently bathed the peaceful face, her own creased with worry, "and we—you!—won an advantage this day."

"Save he wakes, that shall be lost." Katya set aside the cloth, not looking at Calandryll, her voice defiant. "For I'll not leave him, and Rhythamun is powerful. I know not what magicks these ghost-talkers command, but I wonder if they own such gramaryes as may halt that mage."

"Aye," granted Calandryll. "And so we can only wait."

"Until he wakes," said Katya, smoothing Bracht's hair.

17

B RACHT slept on, peaceful as a babe, as dusk darkened into full night. Lykard came, their silence respectful now, to show where lamps were stowed in compartments ingeniously built into the wagon's walls, containing food and wine, to offer invitation to the communal feast that would decide the clan's new leader. Katya refused to leave the Kern's side, but Calandryll elected to attend, aware an honor was done them and thinking the ni Larrhyn might be insulted did they both refuse, and also that he might well learn something of value.

It seemed to him impossible that Bracht should not awake: Ahrd had saved his life and surely would not now condemn him to a living death. The strange slumber was, he told himself, some part of the healing process, some necessary thing, that Bracht should fully mend, in spirit no less than in body. He shuddered at the memory of the nails entering the Kern's palms, and told himself no man could swiftly recover from such ordeal, that this unduly long sleep was equally part of Ahrd's blessing. Too, he felt a strange embarrassment at remaining in the wagon, the soft conversation of the previous night, Katya's unhidden concern now, prompting a feeling that he intruded on their privacy, like some voyeur, spying. It was irrational, and Katya gave him no reason for such emotion, but still he felt it, and left her alone with Bracht, promising to return once the feast was done.

Outside, the moon hung full over the strath, attended by a sweeping panoply of courtier stars. Fires burned, painting the night with red-gold light and coruscating sparks, the air warm and filled with the odors of roasting meat, so strong they overcame the scents of horse flesh and leather. The largest fire was close by the stream and he found the drachomannii there, and other faces he recognized now, belonging to those who had attended the crucifixion and the subsequent duel. They turned toward him as he approached, unreadable until a ghost-talker smiled a welcome and motioned for him to take a place to one side of the shamans. He bowed his thanks, as yet a trifle apprehensive, knowing some among them for kin to the warriors he had helped kill, but it seemed no grudges were held, those canceled by the payment of werecoin, and he settled on the grass, his hand soon filled with a brimming mug, a platter set before him, listening intently to the conversation, the arguments, ranging back and forth around the circle.

These, he soon realized, were the most prominent of the clan, the decision makers, men and women speaking as equals to determine the path the ni Larrhyn should take. None seemed to much mourn Jehenne's demise, and he guessed she had not been overly popular. Neither did any speak for pursuing her dream of clan alliance, for her intended invasion of Lysse. In that at least, he thought, some setback was given Rhythamun's design, that shedding of sacrificial blood denied the mage and the insane god he worshipped. Jehenne's body, he learned, would be taken far from the camp on the morrow and left for the wild dogs to devour, in dishonor: her blasphemous rejection of Ahrd's judgment denied her the customary practice of tree burial, the body laid in ceremony on the branches of an oak. Of greater interest was the

ghost-talkers' repeated promise that word would go
out to all the shamans of the Lykard, and from them
to the ghost-talkers of the other clans, that Daven
Tyras spoke for none save himself, and was a shape-
shifter and a patricide, against whom all should join.
In this debate, Calandryll took part, for the ghost-
talkers urged him to tell all he knew of the warlock,
elaborating on what Katya and Bracht had already
said.

He spoke then of the quest, seeing no reason to prevaricate, and told them of Varent den Tarl's coming to
Secca, and the long journey across Kandahar and into
Gessyth; of finding the Arcanum in Tezin-dar, and
how Rhythamun had snatched it from them; of their
return to Lysse and their pursuit into Cuan na'For.

When he was done, he saw all their eyes studying
him gravely, with admiration, as though he were
some mythic hero, woven from the fabric of a bard's
imagination, and experienced a further flush of embarrassment that he sought to hide behind his mug.
That was never allowed to go empty, wineskins circu-
lating constantly, carried by women and young men
who eyed him with awe, and as the night grew older
and the clan folk fell to discussing who should now
lead them, he feared drunkenness.

He sipped then, not wishing to lose his wits, fleet-
ingly amused by the memory that it had been that
state that had first introduced him to Bracht, then
concerned again for the Kern, seeking opportunity to
question the ghost-talkers. Fruitlessly, it transpired,
for all they could tell him was what they had said
before—that ere now, a man crucified had hung on
the tree until he died, and none been saved—and offer
reassurance that they were confident Bracht would
awake when Ahrd willed it; though when that might
be, they could not say.

Dawn was close before the feast ended, and
Calandryll longed for sleep himself. He had succeeded
in remaining—unlike most there—sober, but his head
swum from the babble, and his belly felt overly full;

he was thankful when finally a leader, Dachan, was elected and the gathering began to disperse. A trifle unsteady, he rose to his feet, climbing the ladder into the wagon to find the lamps pinched out, Bracht and Katya dim shapes in the farther chamber, the Kern's head pillowed on the warrior woman's outthrust arm. He shrugged off his tunic, pulled off his boots, and sank gratefully onto the cushions. It seemed he slept on the instant.

And woke as soon, gaping at Bracht's puzzled face.

He opened his mouth to speak, but a callused hand clamped down to silence him and Bracht pointed warningly to the sleeping chamber, where Katya lay, touching a finger to his own lips as he beckoned Calandryll to follow him.

Amazed for all he had felt—or convinced himself he felt—confident of Bracht's recovery, Calandryll snatched up his tunic and his boots, going after the Kern into the pearly-grey stillness of the false dawn. After the excitement of the night, the camp slept yet, the fires burned down to embers, the air chill. Calandryll's own exhaustion was evaporated by the delight of finding his comrade awake, and he beamed hugely as they crouched by the ashes of the central bonfire, studying Bracht's face, shaking his head and chuckling, unable to resist clutching the Kern's hands to peer wonderingly at the unblemished palms.

"What happened?" Bracht's voice was hushed, his blue eyes narrowed, perplexed. "I remember the nails . . . the pain . . ." His mouth tightened at that memory. "But no more than that."

"Ahrd saved you," Calandryll said, and told him everything.

As he spoke, Bracht examined his hands, turning them this way and that, rubbing curiously at the palms and the backs, as if not quite able to believe the evidence of his own eyes, the evidence of his survival. When Calandryll was done with the telling, he sat silent for a while, digesting all he had heard. Then, as though relegating the wondrous to some hinder part of his mind, said, "So Katya slew Jehenne, eh? And now the ghost-talkers send out word to slay Daven Tyras?"

"Aye," Calandryll confirmed. "But Katya—and I think her likely right in this—remains uncertain they'll succeed."

Bracht nodded and said, "I, too. The drachomannii of Cuan na'For have many skills, but they are not sorcerers of Rhythamun's standing. Save they act in concert, I doubt they have the strength to hold him."

"Will they not," asked Calandryll, "act in concert?"

"How?" Bracht shrugged, gesturing at the slumbering camp. "This is as large a gathering as any, and there are but two of them here. In ones and twos, I think Rhythamun must find them weakling foes."

Calandryll saw the slender hope their quest might find its ending in Cuan na'For dissolve, and sighed.

"You thought to find our work done for us?" Bracht laughed, slapping a hearty hand to Calandryll's shoulder. "Not so easily, my friend. But simpler—we've free passage now, no further need to hide from the Lykard; and likely news of Daven Tyras along the way. Even are the ghost-talkers unable to slay him, they'll at least pass word from camp to camp and thus make the finding of him easier."

"Save he shifts his shape again." His optimism dampened somewhat, Calandryll grew once more practical. "Save he takes another's body."

"Even then," declared Bracht. "For does he assume a new identity, he must leave behind the old. With word passed, should the body of Daven Tyras be found, then the new vessel will be known—some warrior will be missing, and we may learn his description."

"Still he's ahead of us," Calandryll said.

"Aye, but the ghost-talkers—all the clans now—are valuable allies." Bracht's cheerfulness remained undimmed, as though his survival, perhaps the oak sap that mingled with his blood, imbued him with a dauntless vitality. "And so we must hold to our design—go north from here to the Cuan na'Dru and seek passage through the forest; perhaps emerge before him."

There was, in his confident statement, none of the doubt he had previously evinced at the prospect of entering the great central woodland, and when Calandryll looked, in some surprise, at his face, there was none visible there, only a smile.

"That tune is changed," Calandryll murmured.

Bracht frowned then, as if himself surprised at his confidence, and ducked his head in thoughtful agreement. "It is," he said, and paused. "I know not why, save perhaps . . ."

He held up his hands, staring at the palms. Calandryll waited. Then, slowly: "Ahrd gave me my life; the ghost-talkers say the holy sap runs in my veins. Surely, then, Ahrd will grant us passage."

"And the Gruagach?" asked Calandryll.

"They are the guardians." Bracht shrugged, some slight shadow of his old trepidation crossing his face. "But still they serve Ahrd, so perhaps they'll not deny us. And we've but the one way to find out, eh?"

His good humor returned in full measure and he rose to his feet, stretching, staring about as if surveying a world newfound, or one he had thought to have quit, its regaining rendering it the sweeter. Certainly, his smile was wide, and he drank the air, savoring its mingled scents of woodsmoke and horses and leather.

"I think," he said at last, "that we had best depart as soon we may. Katya's wounds are not severe, you say?"

"Cuts," Calandryll assured. "None serious, and all tended by the ghost-talkers."

"They've great skill at healing." Bracht nodded. "And your shoulder? That mends?"

"Apace." Calandryll flexed the hurt joint, forgotten until now. "Your own skills are considerable."

"Let's hope they're not needed again." Bracht

grinned, sketching a bow, and rubbed his belly. "Now—I'd eat. There's food in the wagon?"

Calandryll nodded and rose to join the Kern as Bracht set foot on the ladder.

The false dawn had given way now to the first true brightening of the sky, and birds were singing, while from the corrals came the snorting and shuffling of waking horses. A band of fiery red stretched across the eastern horizon, lanced with brilliant gold as the sun edged upward, the radiance striking in through the parted curtain, brightening the wagon's interior even when the leather was dropped closed behind them. Katya stirred, turning beneath the bed furs, a hand blindly searching to her side. She mumbled something in her sleep and then, abruptly, her eyes snapped open and she sat up, the searching hand reaching instinctively for her sheathed sword.

"All's well," Bracht said. "Save I'm mightily hungry."

His voice burned sleep's fog from her eyes and she flung back the furs, springing from the bed in a tumult of flaxen hair, legs and arms bare and tan under the shirt that was all she wore. Her saber was flung aside, and in a rush she fell upon the Kern, enfolding him in her arms, her momentum such that they tumbled together onto the cushions. Calandryll could only stare as her lips pressed firm to Bracht's, his reaction threatening to rescind those earlier, honorable promises. Then Katya pulled away, pushing tousled hair from her face, her eyes alive with delight and wonder. She knelt beside him, taking both his hands, staring at the palms.

"Why did you not wake me?" she demanded, the accusation in her voice belied by her smile, radiant as the rising sun.

"You slept so sound." Bracht reached out, brushing a flaxen strand from her cheek. "And earned your rest, I hear."

Her smile waned a little at that reminder, but then

she nodded and said solemnly, "Like you, I keep my vows."

"To Jehenne's cost." Bracht grinned, far less concerned than she with the moral niceties of life-taking. "And these?"

He touched the cuts—already healing, Calandryll saw—on her arm and thigh. Katya shrugged. "Nothing," she said. "They were no more than scratches, and the ghost-talkers applied salves and chanted words. But you . . . I feared you'd sleep forever."

"I feel greatly rested." Bracht chuckled. "And very hungry."

Katya glanced round, at the compartments and cupboards lining the walls, reaching to open the closest, the movement shifting the hem of her shirt to expose a length of smooth, brown thigh. Embarrassed afresh, Calandryll looked away; Bracht stared appreciatively, and as she caught his eye, Katya seemed to become aware for the first time of how little she wore. She blushed prettily, still smiling, and tugged the shirt down.

"You likely know where food might be better than I," she murmured, suddenly demure. "Do you look, while I dress."

"Happily," Bracht announced, deliberately misinterpreting; answered with a flung cushion as Katya returned to the sleeping chamber, firmly drawing the curtain behind her.

Grinning, Bracht rummaged through the cupboards, finding wine, hard biscuits, a little cheese and some smoked meat. All this he set on the table, and though none was particularly fresh, he consumed it all with gusto as Calandryll, preferring to await the rising of the camp and the more appetizing breakfast that promised, watched. Katya emerged dressed, settling on the cushions as Bracht ate. She smiled still, her eyes soft as she studied the hungry Kern, but had regained her usual composure.

"When do we leave?"

Bracht washed down a mouthful of biscuit with a

long swallow of wine and said, "Likely they'll insist on feasting us when they find me risen, and to refuse that would be an insult . . . Tomorrow, then?"

"Each day sets leagues between us and Rhythamun," Katya returned, "and I doubt the ghost-talkers can stop him."

"Calandryll spoke of this, and I agree." Bracht nodded. "But still, to go now would be a slur on Lykard honor. And a day may be enough that the ghost-talkers locate him."

"How?" asked Calandryll, intrigued.

"They speak, one with another, over many leagues." Bracht shrugged, as if this were a thing so commonplace it begged no questioning. "How, I know not; only that they do."

"So they may advise us where he is," murmured Katya. "But not halt him or slay him, you think."

"They may try," said Bracht, "but I do not think they'll have much success."

"And think you we shall?" Calandryll wondered.

Bracht chuckled, shrugging. "It seems we are chosen for that task," he said, "and we've come too far to let doubt assail us now. We go on—and what comes, comes."

"Aye." Calandryll smiled back: the Kern's enthusiasm was infectious.

BRACHT'S surmise that his awakening would be greeted with a celebratory feast proved correct. The sun was not much higher above the horizon before the camp began to rise and the ghost-talkers came to inquire as to his condition. Finding him awake, healed, and in excellent spirits, they sang Ahrd's praises and declared a banquet must be held later that day. So awestruck were they, it was an afterthought to examine Katya's wounds, and only Bracht's earnest intervention—weighted by his newfound status— reminded them of the need to send on word concerning Daven Tyras. That, they promised to do, but more immediately they insisted Bracht present himself to all the gathered ni Larrhyn.

A shaman to either side, Katya and Calandryll in attendance behind, he was brought to the warrior elected in Jehenne's place. Dachan ni Larrhyn hailed him as an illustrious guest, embracing him and promising whatever aid he might require before summoning an honor guard that paraded him ceremoniously through the camp. Warriors—male and female—who short days before would have slain him on sight came out to greet him; mothers brought children for him to touch, as though that contact would somehow confer, in surrogate, Ahrd's blessing; folk with wounds long past all hope of healing asked that he touch their disfigurements. Bracht played his part well, beaming hugely at the crowd, as if they had never been enemies, clasping hands, holding giggling children aloft, and Calandryll found himself reminded of those victory parades about which he had read, long ago, in Secca, when some conquering general paraded the streets, a servant in the chariot at his back, whispering the reminder that the victor was mortal, lest pride overtake him.

Such reminder was not necessary in Bracht's case, for when his parading was finally done and he was allowed to return to the wagon, he flung himself down, declaring gruffly that such pomp left him weary and he needed wine and quiet, adding the promise that they should depart on the morrow, before their quest was mired in clan hospitality.

First, though, there was the feast, and before that, news from the ghost-talkers.

They came almost humbly, as the afternoon lengthened toward evening and the cookfires filled the air with the odors of roasting meat. Bracht sat with Katya and Calandryll on the steps of the wagon, trying hard to ignore the awe-filled stares of the children who watched them from a distance, not quite daring to draw close to so prestigious a figure, but intent on observing him—and, he pointed out, with

great amusement, to Katya, the soon-legendary warrior woman from the north who had defeated Jehenne
ni Larrhyn in single combat.

The ghost-talkers—Morrach and Nevyn were their
names, the three had learned—bowed, waiting at the
ladder's foot. Bracht welcomed them courteously and
beckoned them inside, offering them wine, which
they took with murmured thanks, gradually relaxing
as the Kern evinced no signs of abnormality or pride,
but only those of a human warrior eager for the news
they brought.

"The warlock who calls himself Daven Tyras skirts
the Cuan na'Dru," Morrach said.

"Likely afraid to chance Ahrd's wrath," added
Nevyn, prompting Calandryll to wonder if they always spoke in unison, the one completing the other's
sentence as though mind and voice were shared between them.

"He rides westward," Morrach continued; "Around
the edgewoods," said Nevyn.

"With the six elected by Jehenne," said Morrach,
Nevyn echoing: "Still in the shape of Daven Tyras."

"How far ahead?" asked Bracht.

The ghost-talkers exchanged a glance and Morrach
said, "Forty days or more."

"He was last seen by a camp of the ni Brhyn," said
Nevyn. "Nine days ago."

"By now he's likely on Valan grass," said Morrach.

"And the speaking grows harder," said Nevyn.

"Though the drachomannii of the ni Brhyn endeavor to contact the Valan," Morrach promised.
"And will send word back."

"We depart on the morrow," Bracht said.

Morrach frowned then, and Nevyn's lips pursed.
Morrach said, "Do the ghost-talkers of the Valan learn
what he is, they'll seek to take him."

"Shall they be able?" asked Bracht.

Once more the shamans looked one to the other
and Nevyn said, "This we do not know."

"But they will attempt it," said Morrach. "And riders go out from the ni Brhyn camp, hunting."

"Rhythamun is powerful." Bracht spoke slowly, choosing his words with care, tactfully. "Down the ages of his ill-won life he's accrued such occult strength as few sorcerers may claim. I'd not belittle the skills of Cuan na'For's ghost-talkers, but I think that none have faced such as Rhythamun before. And plain warriors will stand no chance against him."

Morrach nodded, understanding, though it was Nevyn who replied, "Even so, they shall—Ahrd willing!—attempt it. Whether they be successful, or not . . . that rests with our god."

"And you'd face him," said Morrach. "No?"

"We would," said Bracht solemnly. "But that is a duty given us by fate, or the Younger Gods, and we've no choice in it."

"Nor we," Nevyn said.

"Nor," added Morrach, "our fellows. Ahrd grant the Valan agree, the attempt shall be made."

"Then I pray Ahrd grant them success," Bracht murmured. "But still we three must leave tomorrow."

"What hope have you of overtaking him?" demanded Nevyn.

"He's forty days, perhaps fifty now, ahead," said Morrach.

"He skirts the Cuan na'Dru, you say?" Bracht waited as they ducked their heads in agreement, then: "We ride for the holy forest."

Stark surprise showed on the faces of both ghost-talkers. Morrach's hand shaped the sunburst sign; Nevyn stared, as if struck dumb by Bracht's calm announcement. His fellow said, very softly, "You look to pass through the forest? The Gruagach . . ."

"Serve Ahrd," said Bracht. "His guardians. Do we three, too, not serve the god? You say Ahrd's sap runs in my veins now, no? Then shall the Gruagach deny us passage through, when we ride in defense of Ahrd and all his kin?"

"Even so," Nevyn whispered. "To dare confrontation with the Gruagach is not a thing to take lightly."

"I do not," said Bracht earnestly, glancing at his hands. "Before . . . Jehenne did what she did to me . . . I'd no great desire to run that risk. I'd hoped to find Rhythamun before he reached the Cuan na'Dru. But now—save we venture through the forest, we must likely remain ever behind him. And do your fellows fail to take him, then he goes free."

"It may be you shall succeed." Morrach sounded doubtful. "The sap is in you, aye; and that may prove token of safe passage."

"For you," said Nevyn. "But for your companions?"

He turned, encompassing Calandryll and Katya with a troubled glance. "We take that chance," Calandryll offered.

"We ride, as Bracht has said, in defense of Ahrd," said Katya. "Shall his guardians not see that?"

"Perhaps."

Still Morrach sounded unconvinced; Nevyn sat silent, his face clouded with doubt.

"We shall attempt it," Bracht said firmly. "We must—else Rhythamun elude us and continue northward across the Kess Imbrun."

There was authority in his voice and both ghosttalkers bowed their heads in tacit acceptance. "We shall pray for your success," said Morrach. "As shall all our fellows," said Nevyn.

"Our thanks for that," Bracht returned. "And word will be given to us, of what your fellows learn? Of what transpires, do they confront Rhythamun?"

Again, the shamans nodded their agreement, and Morrach said, "You need but ask, in any camp."

"What is known to one is know to all," said Nevyn.

"You serve Ahrd well," Bracht said.

"We do no more than our duty," Morrach replied.

"Would that we might do more," said Nevyn.

Bracht smiled and said, "This is service enough."

The ghost-talkers left them then, voicing further assurances that whatever news they gleaned should be instantly communicated, and the three set to readying their gear for departure. Dachan had promised them supplies sufficient to see them through to the next Lykard camp, and they had little enough to occupy them, save the stitching of leathers, the honing of blades, the small tasks attendant on the journey. Calandryll had thought Bracht might go about the camp again, but the Kern expressed himself loath to suffer such attention more than he must, and so they lounged within the wagon, the entry curtain drawn back and panels in the sides rolled up to ventilate and light the interior, aware of the curious children still huddling outside, the more adventurous daring to approach the steps and peer in.

"I feel like some freak," Bracht muttered as a small, dark face showed briefly at the entrance, disappearing with a squeal as he looked up. "An exhibit in some mountebank's show."

"You're a hero," Katya declared, mocking him with her exaggerated solemnity. "They've never seen such as you."

Bracht grunted, frowning, then grinned. "But is it only me they seek?" he demanded. "I suspect you are no less an attraction. You are, after all, the slayer of Jehenne. There are doubtless stories in the making even now—of how the woman from the north defeated the finest swordswoman of the Lykard."

He spoke in jest, teasing, but still Katya's face clouded and she shook her head. "I've no great pleasure in that," she said quietly. "What I did then, I did in anger—because Jehenne would have slain you—I take no pride in it."

Her conscience was, Calandryll thought, fine-tuned. His own was likely roughened, coming more to Bracht's pragmatic way of thinking—that Jehenne would have slain them all, and so had earned her death. Had his been the sword opposed in that duel, he did not believe he would, in the least, mourn the

taking of Jehenne's life. But on Katya's face he saw
genuine regret, and wondered at the tenets that governed the ethics of Vanu.

Bracht, too, recognized the warrior woman's unhap-
piness, and said softly, "Calandryll told me of that
duel, and I say you had no choice but to fight her. Had
you not, we'd all likely be dead now, and Rhythamun
free to go on. If you must blame someone, lay that
charge at Jehenne's feet, or Rhythamun's, for it's not
your burden."

Just as his conscience grew harder, Calandryll
thought, so was Bracht's softened: a year ago he could
not imagine the freesword Kern offering such comfort. It seemed they each reacted, the one upon the
other, for the better, their company changing them.
He toughened, no longer the scholarly prince, the
pampered aristocrat, while Bracht softened, his mercenary ruthlessness tempered now with consideration. Like pebbles in the stream of fate, he thought,
rubbing one against the other as the current shifted
them, accommodating to one another, rough edges
smoothing, weaknesses eroded, the core the stronger
for that.

He saw Katya smile, setting her doubt aside, returning to the mending of a frayed sleeve, and Bracht
watch her awhile, his eyes gentle, before he, in turn,
went back to his work.

THE day grew older, the sun moving toward its setting, and in a while Bracht rolled down the leather
flaps and drew the curtain closed across the entrance.
Calandryll lit lamps and they stowed their gear in
readiness for a swift departure. Soon evening shed
blue light over the valley, the glow of the cookfires
brightening, the smell of roasting meat pervading the
wagon. Then drums began to beat, a sonorous cadence
that drew steadily closer. Bracht sighed and set to
combing his long hair, muttering something about
ceremonies. Intrigued, Calandryll went to the curtain,

looking out to see a crowd gathered, Dachan to the fore, Morrach and Nevyn at his side, each with a hide drum slung from their shoulders, beating the slow rhythm with long sticks of polished wood, and a great throng of folk beyond, all their faces expectant.

The drumbeats softened and Dachan took a pace forward, crying out in a great voice that carried through the camp, "We would honor Bracht ni Errhyn and his companions. Do you come feast with us?"

Calandryll felt a hand upon his shoulder and turned to find Bracht there, stepping out from the wagon to stand upon the ladder and answer formally, "You do us great honor, Dachan ni Larrhyn, and we accept in gratitude."

Over his shoulder he murmured, "Come. Bring only dirks."

Calandryll thought him regal as he went down the ladder to meet Dachan's embrace, a shout of approval rising at that, the drums lifting to a crescendo and dying away. Formality, too, as men and women pressed in to take Bracht's hand, surrounding him and bearing him off toward the central fire. Katya, no less, was swept up in the acclamation, and Calandryll felt somewhat ignored, the least of the three, as he followed behind.

It suited him well enough, for it gave him better chance to observe and listen than he had had the previous night, when he had been the focus of attention. Now that distinction belonged to Bracht, and to Katya, and he was able more to play the scholar, and take note of Lykard customs as the feast proceeded.

It was unlike any banquet he had attended in Secca, and what little formality appertained was cursory. They were seated to Dachan's right, Morrach and Nevyn to his left, the elders and most prominent warriors of the clan completing the circle closest to the fire, the lesser members in ranks behind. Bracht was offered first choice of meat, served wine before the rest, Katya after, and then Calandryll himself, and that did serve to conjure memories of his father's pal

ace, himself the least of the den Karynth there. The
very least now, he thought with wry amusement, proscribed outlaw, a price on his head. Should he one day
return, as Bracht had come back to Cuan na'For, to
win such acclaim? To overturn his brother's ruling?
Even overturn Tobias? He chuckled at the random
thought. Did it matter? Now, more than ever, he felt
no wish to be Domm; that was a duty he left cheerfully to Tobias. Save, it occurred to him as the wineskins passed round and a great platter of succulent
venison was given him, it seemed Tobias, albeit unwittingly, played Rhythamun's game. He looked
around the fire-lit circle of smiling faces, thinking
that had Jehenne had her way, these folk would even
now be readying themselves for war with Lysse, seduced to that bloody cause by Rhythamun's subtle
blandishments. And that all he had heard in the crossing of his homeland suggested that Tobias took the
same road. Were his brother successful, then the
Domms of Lysse would agree to war with Kandahar,
and that, as with the warlock's meddling in the affairs
of Cuan na'For, must surely serve to pave the way to
the Mad God's resurrection.

He grew somber then, thinking that surely forces
beyond his understanding moved in the world, and
that whatever promises the Younger Gods had made
him, he, and no less Bracht and Katya, were but three
pawns in some incomprehensible game. Could they
truly hope to win? Rhythamun was so far ahead, and
he had no confidence the ghost-talkers might halt the
mage, less that they might defeat him. Yet surely
those shamans commanded powers greater than anything he might hope to bring against the warlock, and
if they could not prevail, then how should three itinerant freeswords? Faith, his comrades had urged; but
was that enough? Burash and Dera had both spoken of
powers that would aid the quest, but in terms so
enigmatic as to leave him no wiser as to their effi-
cacy, nor any more enlightened as to how Rhythamun
might be defeated—should they succeed in gaining on

the warlock. Faith, he thought, was ofttimes a very hard thing to hold.

"Ahrd, but you've a miserable look! Is the wine soured? Or have you enough of feasting?"

He turned, abruptly shamefaced at his doubts, to see Bracht grinning cheerfully, a smear of grease across his lips, a brimming mug in his hand. He smiled ruefully and shook his head, murmuring, "I thought of Rhythamun, and all he does."

"Put it aside," Bracht advised. "For now enjoy the night. Come the morrow we commence our journey, but this night is for enjoyment. We've new friendships to cement, and an easier path before us—drink to that."

Calandryll's smile warmed and he voiced a silent prayer of thanks for such a comrade. "Ayé," he said. "You're right."

He drained his mug, shouting for more wine, deciding that it could not hurt. They were safe here, surrounded by warriors who would now, he suspected, defend them with their own lives if need be; and ghost-talkers with their strange magicks to pass word and bring news of the warlock. It came to him that this was the first time in long weeks they had been, truly, safe, and he elected to take Bracht's advice, relaxing.

Even so, he avoided excess, and saw that his comrades followed suit, eating their fill and drinking heartily, but neither consuming so much the morrow's ride would prove uncomfortable. For himself, he ate until he felt his belt draw tight about his waist, and after that ignored the meat that still passed round; likewise the wine, taken in slow sips as he felt a pleasant languor seep through him.

Not so their hosts, for long after the carcasses of the deer were reduced to bare bones the wineskins continued to make the rounds and the Lykard brought out drums and pipes, the bards of the clan composing songs that rose like the sparks coruscating from the fire into the night. They sang in the tongue of Cuan na'For, and Calandryll wondered if he saw Bracht blush as they wove their tale of the Kern's ordeal and the great quest he pursued. Certainly, Katya appeared embarrassed as Bracht translated those verses describing her part, casting her in the role of savior, a mysterious warrior woman come to defeat Jehenne and thus save the ni Larrhyn from dishonor. Calandryll himself, he noticed, was allocated by far the lesser part, little more than a companion, attendant on the Ahrd-favored hero and the flaxen-haired woman. He minded not at all, for it gave Bracht little opportunity to jest at his expense, but still was glad when the singing took on a more bawdy tone, with choruses that all the camp took up.

It seemed the Lykard were set to drink and sing the night away, and already there were folk succumbed to the wine, their eyes glazed and their voices slurred, some slumped and snoring about the circle. In time the bards grew hoarse and ceased their rhymes, and gradually the rest quieted, the singing giving way to individual conversations. Women began shooing reluctant children to their beds and warriors set to reminiscing, often enough, Calandryll heard, about battles with the Asyth, though such tales were told in a spirit of comradeship, with the valor of old enemies praised highly as that of kinsmen, and Bracht joined in without sign of affront. There was in these people a simplicity and a generosity of spirit that seemed to Calandryll lacking in the more sophisticated societies of Lysse or Kandahar, and he warmed to them, thankful that they were no longer foes.

In a while Bracht murmured to him that they might find their beds without giving insult, and for that he was grateful. He took Bracht's cue, rising and bowing, expressing his gratitude to Dachan and the others, who promised again that they should be seen off with filled packs and an escort for at least part of the way. Morrach and Nevyn, themselves looking not entirely sober, declared their intention of seeking further contact with their fellow ghost-talkers before morning, and the three returned to the wagon.

They were ready enough to sleep, somnolent from so much food and more wine than they had drunk in longer than any could remember. Calandryll stripped off his tunic and collapsed onto soft cushions, drowsily tugging at his boots. He wondered idly where Bracht would make his bed this night, his speculation ended by the Kern's soft words, bidding Katya sleep well as he ushered her courteously into the sleeping chamber. The warrior woman smiled and nodded, closing the curtain behind her as Bracht loosed his belt with a heartfelt sigh.

"Ahrd, but I doubt I could survive overmuch of such hospitality," he grunted as he hauled off his boots.

Calandryll yawned in answer, stretching luxuriously on the cushions. They were very soft, and he felt no desire for further conversation, only to sleep. A pleasant torpor gripped him, reducing Bracht's low voice to a distant drone. He heard the sound of a body settling, then Bracht's snore. He sighed contentedly and gave himself over to sleep.

IT was long past the middle of the night when he woke, but not yet dawn, the darkest hours, the camp silent, Bracht's snoring a dull murmur, little louder than the splashing of the stream. He grunted, burrowing deeper into the cushions, not wanting to be awake, nor sure why he was until he felt his bladder protest. He cursed then and fumbled his way across the deck to the entrance, pausing as Bracht muttered something, whispering his explanation. Bracht mumbled an inarticulate reply and turned on his side; Calandryll went out into the night.

The moon was low in the west, its face scarred with streamers of cloud, more rack blown on the wind that had got up, soft and warm from the east. From beyond the wagons came the nighttime snuf-

fling of the horse herds, and somewhere a child cried
once and then was quiet. The central fire was a glowing mass of red beside the stream, its dulled light revealing the sprawled bodies of those too drunk to find
their own beds. Calandryll blinked, his eyes yet
gummed with sleep, squinting as he climbed down
the ladder, his caution exaggerated. He yawned, feeling damp grass beneath his bare feet, and made his
way to where the Lykard had dug their latrines,
scarcely awake as he vented the pressure that had
roused him. It seemed that even the hardiest of the ni
Larrhyn had given up their celebrating, for all the
wagons stood dark and still.

Save one, he saw as he returned, recognizing it for
that occupied by the ghost-talkers. A lamp burned
there, painting a thin thread of yellow between the
edges of the outer curtain, and he supposed that the
shamans went about their occult business. He marveled at their fortitude, for they had seemed to drink
as much as any at the feast, and had seemed no less
inured to the wine's affect than any others. Perhaps
they had some magical trick, he thought, that overcame weariness and wine, grinning sleepily as it occurred to him that such a gramarye could be most
useful, and that had he possessed such a knack he
might not now be here, creeping barefoot through a
Lykard camp.

He slowed as he saw the narrow ribbon of light
grow wider, than become blocked by the dark shape
of a body, the curtain falling back into place behind as
the man climbed silently down the steps. He grinned
again as he thought that ghost-talkers, like any mortal men, were after all prone to the ordinary weaknesses of excess, assuming the shaman attended those
offices he had just satisfied. He was too far distant,
and the encampment too night-shrouded, that he
could make out which it was, but then he paused,
confused, as he saw the figure went not toward the latrines, as he anticipated, but in the opposite direction;
and furtively it seemed. He wondered then what

brought the man out, creeping like a thief in the night
through his own camp, and found himself moving
stealthily, watching, wary; then dismissed his own
presentiment as groundless.

This quest, as he had thought earlier, changed him:
he saw shadows where there were none, found suspicion where only friendship existed. No doubt the shaman had some business that required the darkness for
its doing, or went to Dachan on some pressing errand.
He shook his head, telling himself the prickling he
felt along his spine was nothing, the night wind, or
the aftermath of wine. But still he held to the shadows as he went back, not yet quite awake enough it
immediately registered that his course took him naturally after the furtive figure.

He was a fool, he told himself. He saw some innocent errand and read into it alarums: sleep and wine
fogged his mind, rousing phantoms. He stopped, wiping a hand through the damp grass, transferring its
moisture to his face, the cool wetness dissolving
sleep.

Sleep, but not suspicion, for as his eyes and mind
cleared he realized that Dachan's wagon lay across the
stream, not this way, and surely, did the ghost-talker
go seeking some herb, some night-blooming flower, it
must lie beyond the camp, and he would take a horse.
Thieflike himself now, he trod with instinctive caution, taking care to make no sound as he went after
the shaman, curiosity and embarrassment mingling,
for surely there was some innocent explanation.

Then he saw the man's direction—toward the
wagon where Bracht and Katya slept—and shook his
head, laughing softly at his misplaced suspicions: the
ghost-talkers had kept their promise and spent the
midnight hours communicating with their fellows.
They had gleaned some piece of information and one
of them brought it to the wagon. No more than that:
he translated help as threat. Feeling guilty now, he
paced swifter forward, opening his mouth to call out,
to save waking his sleeping comrades.

Then his mouth snapped shut and his eyes narrowed, doubt flaring anew. Always before the ghost-talkers had acted in unison. He had not seen them apart; they spoke together, as though a single mind commanded the two mouths. Yet this man was alone, and if he carried news of such import it could not wait for morning, would he come alone? Surely, were that the case, they would come—as always—together.

Calandryll saw the figure reach the ladder's foot and pause, peering round, as does a man wary of discovery, not as one come with helpful news. His suspicion seemed no longer groundless, for there was something mightily wrong in this stealthy approach: cat-footed, he drew closer, hugging the shadows the surrounding wagons cast. The shaman started up the ladder and alarm replaced all thoughts of tact as Calandryll saw him reach beneath his long robe and moonlight glitter on steel. He burst from the shadows, caution discarded, running toward the man as his shout split the silence of the night.

The figure sprang down as the moon emerged from its mask of cloud and he saw Morrach's face; saw, too, the dirk the ghost-talker clutched. He halted his headlong charge, slithering to a crouch, arms spread wide and defensive as the long knife angled toward his belly. Beneath its mask of paint, Morrach's face was twisted in an ugly leer, and in his eyes there burned an unholy light, radiating pure hatred. Calandryll felt it, as if the shaman's glare fell hot upon skin gone suddenly cold. The man was no longer the friend, the ally, who utilized his strange powers to aid the quest, but clearly an enemy; no less clearly intent on slaying Calandryll.

He sprang back as the blade slashed for his belly, and heard a feral growl burst from Morrach's mouth. He shifted again as the man closed the distance between them, the dirk probing, hungry to kill, his mind racing even as he danced clear of the thrust. Morrach seemed possessed, driven by some inner fury, mumbling and growling as he slashed and cut, not expertly, but with such ferocity that Calandryll had no chance to close and grasp his wrist, but could only avoid the vicious attack.

He shouted again, and heard voices raised in answer, dulled with sleep and not particularly alarmed. Likely, he thought as he sprang aside, sucking in his belly to avoid a sweeping blow, the Lykard assumed two warriors woke and quarreled drunkenly. He cursed them for their lack of concern and yelled once more, louder.

"Bracht! Ware magic!"

"Aye, and greater than any this vessel commands."

Spittle flew on Morrach's words, and the knife darted out, swift as a striking serpent. Calandryll gasped, shocked bad enough only those reflexes honed and hardened on the quest's long road saved him from mortal wound. He spun clear, feinted to his left, and chanced a kick at Morrach's knife hand. The ghost-talker made no attempt to avoid the blow, but neither did it affect him. Indeed, it felt as though Calandryll's foot landed against dead flesh that absorbed the kick, feeling nothing, the reaction spilling his balance so that he slipped on the damp grass, falling.

He heard a triumphant shriek and rolled desperately aside, fetching up against the wagon's ladder as Morrach crashed down, the dirk driving hard and deep into the soil. The shaman sprang instantly to his feet, his long tunic swirling as he rounded once more on his intended prey. Calandryll felt the wooden steps at his back and feinted to the right, blocked by Morrach; feinted leftward, and was again blocked.

"Mine!" The voice was animal, as though whatever power utilized the ghost-talker's body animated unwilling cords. "At last it ends!"

The dirk drove forward, low and angled up, seeking the soft entry of the belly, below the cage of ribs. Calandryll twisted, his shirt torn by the blade, and locked both hands around the wrist.

He felt himself hurled back, propelled by a terrible strength, far greater than the ghost-talker's wiry body could naturally possess. Fingers closed on his throat, and as he felt his windpipe shut and stared in horror at eyes that blazed madness, he knew with a dreadful certainty that he faced not Morrach, but Rhythamun.

He gasped the warlock's name and heard it answered, triumphant: "Aye, fool! Thought you I'd not know when these feeble things looked to oppose me? You thought they'd the power to halt or hold such as I?"

He strained against the arm that drove the dirk steadily closer to his belly, wine-scented breath fetid in his nostrils. In the glaring eyes he saw Rhythamun's hate, as though the sorcerer looked out from the shelter of Morrach's skull, glorying in his impending victory.

"Three only may succeed, fool. But soon there shall be but two, for you die now."

He felt the dirk's point touch flesh. He felt his lungs strain, empty, his head pound. The painted face blurred behind a curtain of red; the muscles in his shoulders and arms burned, weakening under the remorseless pressure. He felt hope take flight, leaving him.

Then, suddenly, the pricking in his belly was gone and his heaving chest filled with welcome air. He fell against the ladder, pushing himself aside, anticipating a killing thrust. Instead, he heard the clash of steel on steel, and as his watered vision cleared, saw Bracht, dressed in no more than a breechclout, facing Morrach with extended falchion. He felt hands on him and heard Katya's voice, urgent in his ear.

"Calandryll, your sword!"

He snatched the blade and darted forward.

"Rhythamun!" he croaked as light flared from the surrounding wagons. "Bracht, Rhythamun possesses him!"

"Then Rhythamun dies in this body," came Bracht's grating answer.

And insane laughter from Morrach.

"Think you it be that easy? Then strike—and see."

The ghost-talker's arms rose, wide to either side, inviting Bracht to attack. The shaman capered, leering horribly, making no attempt at defense as the Kern raised the falchion. Calandryll stared, aghast, aware that Lykard tumbled from their wagons now, torches raised, and voices, in alarm, demanding explanation.

"No!" he cried, loud as his bruised throat allowed, seeing the warlock's intention, guessing that the fell gramarye employed would likely continue to animate the body even after death; and that did Bracht succeed, the slaying of a ghost-talker might likely turn the ni Larrhyn against them all. "No, don't slay him!"

Bracht halted his stroke, confused. The horrid laughter tittered into silence, and Morrach's face turned toward Calandryll.

"You learn wisdom, but it shall avail you naught. One or the other, it matters not."

He sprang at Bracht, the dirk probing for the Kern's chest. Bracht turned the blow, stepping aside, moving beyond the range of the far shorter blade, confused as he risked a glance Calandryll's way. "Not slay him? Then what?"

Calandryll came closer, calling hoarsely for the puzzled Lykard to stand back. Katya moved past him, long-legged in only her shirt, the saber held ready, so that all three formed a loose circle around the figure of the shaman. From the crowd, Calandryll heard Dachan shout, "What is this? In Ahrd's name, Morrach, what is this?"

"Rhythamun possesses him," answered Calandryll. "By some sorcery, he owns Morrach."

"He lies! They all lie! Slay them, in Ahrd's name!"

"Morrach? Where's Nevyn?" Dachan yelled. "Is this magic? Who speaks the truth here?"

"I do," said Morrach's mouth; "I do," said Calandryll.

"Put down your weapons," Dachan ordered. "No man may raise his hand against the drachomannii."

"Aye," echoed Morrach. "On pain of death. But they did—slay them, then."

"I do not understand this," Dachan said.

"What's to understand?" asked Morrach. "Slay them."

Dachan faltered, looking from one to the other. Calandryll said urgently, "Ask why he comes at this hour, with knife in hand. Ask why he comes alone."

Dachan frowned at that, eyes narrowing. "Find me Nevyn," he ordered. And: "I say again—put down your weapons."

"Aye, put them down," said Morrach.

The encircling Lykard pressed a little closer, their torches glinting on the swords they held, lifted now. Warily, Bracht lowered the falchion. And with a shriek of dreadful triumph, Morrach launched himself forward, slashing at the Kern's throat.

On the instant, the falchion rose, clashing loud against the dirk, forcing it up. Katya sprang then, like a great blond feline, the saber cutting at the shaman's back. Dachan and all his folk roared in outrage. Calandryll screamed, "No!" and brought the straightsword round in a sweeping arc that sent Katya's sword rattling clear of the man.

"My thanks," mocked Rhythamun, from Morrach's lips, and the ghost-talker's body turned, swift as Katya, to send the dirk thrusting once more at Calandryll.

Unthinking, his action simple reflex, Calandryll deflected the blow. Dirk and straightsword met. Sparks flashed, and on Morrach's face, the leering smile was transformed. Surprise glittered in the burning eyes even as the knife darted again. Again Calandryll turned the attack, and this time Morrach groaned, as if pained.

Realization dawned and Calandryll cried, "Praise Dera! Hold him!"

He smashed another blow aside as Bracht and Katya leapt forward, clutching the shaman's arms.

Morrach was still possessed, still commanded an

unnatural strength, enough that man and woman both were lifted off their feet, but their weight, combined, slowed him and prevented him, for the moment at least, from using the dirk.

A moment was all Calandryll needed. Even as Dachan shouted, and the Lykard moved forward to prevent him, he raised the straightsword and brought the flat of the blade down against the shaman's wrist.

Morrach screamed then, his hand snapping open, the dirk tumbling to the trampled grass. Calandryll stepped closer, pressing the sword to the man's chest. Morrach struggled, flinging his captors about, his mouth stretched wide, a thin, high keening wailing out, his eyes no longer burning hateful, but agonized now, as if the blade glowed red-hot, its touch seared him. Calandryll lifted the straightsword from the chest to the man's face, the flat across his parted lips.

Abruptly, Morrach's shrieking became an awful bubbling moan. His body stood suddenly rigid, eyes and mouth both opened wide. A red mist, like fog lit with internal fires, spewed from between his lips, swirling about the blade. The Lykard halted their advance, staring. Calandryll breathed the heady scent of almonds and shouted Dera's name like a battle cry as he swung the straightsword through the mist. It writhed, fleeing the steel, streaming from the ghost-talker's mouth to coalesce, glowing, in the air above him as the fire dimmed and quit Morrach's eyes. The last of it gone from the shaman, Calandryll held the sword defensive, ready to strike again, and for an instant a face, contorted in dreadful rage, took shape within the vapor. Then it faded, the almond scent with it, stirred by the night wind, and was gone. Morrach shuddered, moaned once, and went limp, his eyes closing, his head falling to his chest.

Calandryll stared at where the apparition had been, its afterimage burning still on his vision, thinking that he had, for the first time, seen Rhythamun's true face. He lowered his blade as Dachan said, close and ominous, "Ahrd, if you've slain him . . ."

"I've not." Calandryll lifted the shaman's chin so that the ketoman might see Morrach still breathed. "I've saved him. Dera willing, he's himself again."

Dachan frowned, perplexed, and gestured for men to take the unconscious ghost-talker. "This requires explanation," he said, no longer so hostile, but still not yet assured. "You say Rhythamun possessed him?"

"Aye," answered Calandryll. "And Dera saved him. And us."

He prayed, silently, that he spoke the truth.

18

THE ghost-talkers' wagon grew crowded when
they carried Morrach back, finding Nevyn
stretched out among the scattered paraphernalia of
their art, an ugly bruise darkening the blue paint upon
his forehead. Morrach was settled on cushions, sleeping babelike, Nevyn groaning as Dachan's lieutenants
sought to wake him with water-soaked cloths and
burning feathers. Calandryll, Bracht, and Katya were
summoned inside by the puzzled ketoman, and more
lamps were lit as the ni Larrhyn clustered all about,
anxious to learn what strange thing had happened this
night, and if their shamans lived.

"When he and Nevyn communed with their fellow
ghost-talkers, then Rhythamun must have learned
what they did and somehow seized control of
Morrach." Calandryll gestured at the unconscious
shamans, speaking in the Envah, that Katya might
understand what was said. "I warned you he's a sorcerer of terrible power. I'd wager he used a gramarye
to send his spirit back, and took hold of Morrach—
had him overcome his fellow and sent him to kill us.
Or one of us, at least, for he said that one would suffice; that save we be three we must fail."

"To possess a ghost-talker?" Dachan studied him a

while, troubled, seeming not yet entirely convinced. "To make Morrach his creature, his murderer?"

"I know not the way of it," Calandryll answered, "but that he did ... You saw his animus quit the body."

"Aye." Dachan shuddered at the memory.

"And Morrach urged Bracht to slay him," pressed Calandryll. "What should you have done then?"

Dachan was silent a moment, his eyes hooded, his dark face suddenly haggard. "Likely slain you on the spot," he said at last. "Or ordered you executed."

"Again," murmured Bracht, prompting a shame-faced smile from the Lykard. "Rhythamun is mightily cunning, my friend."

"And will stop at nothing to halt us," said Calandryll. "'Though we may learn from this night's events."

He was about to elaborate, but a woman called out then that Nevyn woke, and all their attention turned to the shaman.

"Ahrd!" Nevyn opened bleary eyes, sitting up. "What happened?"

"Morrach sought to murder these three, or one of them." Dachan indicated the questers. "They say he was possessed by Rhythamun."

"Ahrd's holy tree!" Nevyn shook his head, and groaned; a man lifted a cup to his lips and he drank, turning when he was done to observe his supine fellow. "Morrach? He lives?"

"Calandryll drove out the warlock's spirit, or so it looked." Dachan shrugged again, helplessly. "There is much I cannot understand."

Nevyn raised inquiring eyes to Calandryll, who said, "My sword was blessed by Dera. She told me it should then hold power over magic, and so it does." He shook his head as Nevyn looked again at Morrach. "No, he lives yet—I put the flat against him when I saw he was possessed."

"He used no edge," Dachan confirmed. "He claims this Rhythamun seized Morrach while you tranced."

Nevyn sighed and took a compress to hold against his face. "We looked to fulfill our promise," he murmured. "To commune with our fellows and obtain word of Rhythamun. Aye, that must be the way of it. Ahrd, but he's powerful then!"

"Do you explain?" asked Calandryll.

Nevyn nodded, regretting the movement, wincing, and said, "We opened the way, from ghost-talker to ghost-talker, northward. Between the last of the Lykard camps and the first of the Valan there was a . . . disruption . . . a darkness that intruded. Ahrd, but that must have been Rhythamun! It grew; I remember that. And that it was . . . evil. I looked to end the contact, and when I emerged, Morrach was on his feet. I spoke to him—he struck me. After that I knew nothing, until now. Rhythamun must have possessed him, as Calandryll says." He groaned, not now in pain, but in something close to fear. "If he can do that . . . can possess one of us . . . what can he not do?"

"He's a powerful enemy," Calandryll agreed. "But still we may turn this to our profit."

"How so?"

It was Nevyn who spoke, but the question was writ clear on every face there as all turned toward him.

"We know now that he may use the ghost-talkers against us," he said slowly. "In what he did to Morrach, he showed his hand."

"Poor comfort, that," Bracht murmured. "Must we then avoid all camps along our way?"

"Perhaps; perhaps not," Calandryll replied. "Messages can be sent to warn of what Rhythamun can do, so that all the ghost-talkers of Cuan na'For are alert to his stratagems. Perhaps he has some gramarye he can employ to intercept that message, or—knowing he failed here—he'll guess it; but I think he'll likely avoid the camps now."

"And ride the harder for that," said Bracht.

"But likely without further aid," returned Calandryll. "Knowing Daven Tyras can expect no

ready welcome, he'll surely be forced to hide, for fear
the drachomannii unite against him."

"Which we shall," promised Nevyn. "And now we
know he's able to insinuate his foul magicks into our
minds, we can ward against him."

Calandryll nodded, a thin smile on his lips. "You
see? By revealing his power, he weakens himself. I
think he must travel alone now."

"He's likely still the warriors Jehenne sent with
him," Dachan reminded them. "And if he can possess
a ghost-talker . . ."

"He's the use of their horses," Bracht said. "At the
least."

"But not the hospitality of the camps," Calandryll
argued. "Even does he shift his shape again, he must
ride in the form of a ni Larrhyn, no? Nevyn, once
we're gone—not earlier!—can you send word of all
this?"

The shaman grunted confirmation.

"Then let word be sent," urged Calandryll, "that
all the camps beware the ni Larrhyn riders."

"To slay them?" asked Dachan, tugging on a plait,
his expression dour. "There's little honor in that."

"No." Calandryll shook his head. "I'd see no more
innocent folk slain for Rhythamun's sake. Say only
that they be turned back—given no aid; neither
horses nor more food than they need to reach the last
camp they left behind them. Do any seek to go on,
then they must be Rhythamun, or his creatures.
Thus, we may deny him further assistance."

Dachan nodded; Nevyn said, "It shall be done."

"A day, at least, after we depart," Calandryll
warned.

"And you shall have all the aid we can give,"
promised Dachan. "Spare mounts, supplies, an
escort—ask and it shall be yours."

"My thanks." Calandryll ducked his head in gratitude. "But I think there's no need. Speed is our ally
now, and packhorses will only slow us."

"No more than hunting," said Bracht doubtfully.

"We'll not stop to hunt"—Calandryll's grin stretched wider, and he chuckled, beginning to enjoy this turning of the tables—"for we'll find our food in the camps along the way to the Cuan na'Dru."

"With ghost-talkers likely to turn against us?"

Bract's voice was harsh. Calandryll motioned him silent, grinning at his startled visage. "Listen," he urged. "Rhythamun knows—for now, at least—that we are here. He knows we live still, and therefore that we shall continue after him. The ghost-talkers along the way shall be warned against him, against all of Jehenne's warriors, but"—he raised his hand again as Bracht opened his mouth to argue further—"if the ghost-talkers we encounter seek no communication while we are in their camps, nor send any word of where we are, or where we go, Rhythamun can learn no more. At best he may discover where we've been, but only that."

Bracht frowned, digesting the notion. Beside him, Katya pursed her lips and spoke for the first time.

"There's sense in that, I agree. But what if he possesses a ghost-talker before we come on a camp? Then we might well ride into the arms of a murderer who wears the face of a friend."

"I suspect he can only exercise his magic while the ghost-talkers employ theirs." Calandryll looked to Nevyn for confirmation: received it in a nod, soon followed by a groaned curse. "And it looked to me that Morrach fought the gramarye. Even though Rhythamun's magic overcame his will, still the signs were on his face. You saw his eyes?"

"They burned with madness," Katya said softly. "As though some demon looked outward from inside his skull."

"As did the eyes of the dire-wolf we slew," Calandryll murmured. "I think that save he possess a man utterly, taking the body for his own, his evil shines like some fell beacon, and so must be noticed."

"There's more," Nevyn said eagerly, then winced. "Ahrd, but my head hurts!"

"Can you not mend it?" asked Dachan.

"Not yet." The shaman grinned ruefully. "Until these three are gone, I'll not employ my powers in the least, for fear . . ." He glanced significantly at Morrach, still unconscious, and Dachan grunted his understanding. "Until then I'll suffer. Now listen—it seems to me that Calandryll speaks sense, and you've no need to fear further assault from my brethren. Had Rhythamun been able to possess us both, do you not think he'd have sent me with Morrach?"

"I wondered at that," Calandryll said. "When I saw only the one man come from the wagon."

"Aye." Nevyn remembered not to duck his head. "Do we not always act in concert? Is there any camp with but one of us?"

Dachan and Bract, both, shook their heads.

"Always two, at the least," said Nevyn. "In the larger camps, three, even four sometimes; but never the one. Do you not see it? Were Rhythamun able to seize Morrach and me together, then he'd surely have sent us both about his filthy business, but he did not. Therefore, I believe he could not: he is able to possess only one."

"Aye." Calandryll grinned. "I see it."

"You've a quick mind," complimented Nevyn, and turned smiling to the others. "Two, at least, in each camp, and Rhythamun able to use but one of them. The closest camp to this is five days ride distant, so before our friends arrive there, word can be sent. And even does Rhythamun learn of their coming, and take possession of one ghost-talker, then surely the other must know it. Such magic cannot hide itself, but must be seen."

"And the one possessed be taken," said Calandryll. "Even such strength as Morrach commanded cannot stand against a whole camp."

"Aye, he'd be held until you came," said Nevyn, smiling. "And do you use your blessed sword again, the gramarye shall be expelled."

"So we may ride free," said Calandryll.

"Save he dream up some other kind of obstacle," Bracht muttered.

"As doubtless he will," Calandryll retorted, chuckling, pleased with himself now. "But shall that sway us?"

"No," said Bracht firmly, and began himself to chuckle. "In Ahrd's name, it shall not!"

"Morrach wakes."

The woman's voice recalled their attention to the second ghost-talker and all fixed a wary gaze on the shaman. Nevyn, with a grunt of discomfort, knelt at his side; Calandryll drew his sword, a precaution. Morrach's lips parted to emit a sound part sigh, part moan, and his eyes fluttered open, blinked, and then flung wide as he cried out, his shout filled with loathing. Nevyn took him by the shoulders, speaking softly, urgently, in their own language, and Morrach whimpered, clinging to his fellow as does a child awakening from a nightmare cling to its father. For a while Morrach trembled, his teeth rattling, his long face drawn, his eyes glazed, seeming to search inside himself. Then, slowly, his shuddering eased and ceased, he clenched his teeth, took a long, deep breath that whistled out like a hymn of thanks, and raised his head.

"Ahrd be with me." He stared around, drinking in the sight of the familiar wagon, the familiar faces. "Is there wine?"

A man filled a cup and the shaman drank it down greedily, wiped his mouth, and passed it back, rising to prop himself against the wagon's side.

"Ahrd be with me," he repeated, in the Envah now, "and grant I never more know such horror. Better you cut me down."

"Better you live," Nevyn said. "As do you, thanks to Calandryll and the goddess Dera."

Morrach stared at Calandryll's blade, a hand extending, almost reluctantly, to touch the steel. When all his wary fingers found was cold metal, he sighed, essaying a tentative smile.

"You've my thanks for that. Ahrd! I looked to murder you."

"Rhythamun looked to murder me," returned Calandryll. "Or any one of us."

Morrach nodded and said, "I know. I felt him in me." He shuddered at the memory, his eyes hollow, and turned his face to Nevyn. "Are you bad hurt, my brother?"

"A sore head,"—Nevyn smiled—"no more."

"Praise Ahrd for that," murmured Morrach. "And none others came to harm?"

"None," confirmed Nevyn. "Now do you tell us what you know?"

Morrach's eyes said that he had sooner forget, but he ducked his head in agreement and said, "We tranced. We spoke with Tennad of the ni Brhyn, and as we spoke there came a darkness—a fell clouding of the aethyr, as if some malign thing invaded—that came into me."

He broke off, shuddering anew at the recollection. Nevyn murmured for more wine and passed him the cup, waiting as his fellow drank. Morrach drained the cup and held it in both hands, tight, his knuckles tensing white as he continued.

"I knew it for Rhythamun's animus—I fought against it, but it was too powerful. Ahrd, but it was strong! It overcame me. I became its puppet! I saw you knew and struck you down. Forgive me. I left you, not caring whether you lived or died, and went seeking these three." He released his grip on the cup just long enough to gesture at the questers. "I—or Rhythamun, in me—thought to find them sleeping. To slit all their throats, or as many as I might. But then Calandryll came at me and we fought; and then all three were there, and I heard myself call for Bracht to slay me, the animus thinking that did he put his sword in me, Dachan would command him slain and thus their quest be ended. That there are three is important—Rhythamun knows that, that there must be three. Then Calandryll touched me with his sword and I .. Ahrd, but I knew pain then! It was like fire in my veins." He stared in wonder at the blade, shaking his head and smiling. "Cleansing fire, for even as I burned, I felt the animus quit me. The next I knew, I was here."

"Praise Ahrd you wake entire," said Nevyn.

"Praise Ahrd—praise Dera!—Calandryll bears such a sword," said Morrach. "And that he had the wit to use it as he did. A slower-minded man would have cut me down."

Calandryll sheathed the blade then, confident now that Rhythamun's fell gramarye was utterly dispelled. "He sought to use you," he said. "But he overreached himself."

Swiftly, Nevyn explained all they had discussed, and when he was done, Morrach nodded, smiling firmer. "Aye," he declared, "it must surely spin fate's wheel against him. What shall he do now, think you?"

"He travels ever northward, toward the Jesseryn Plain," Calandryll replied. "The god, Horul, rules there, and so it's an unlikely site for Tharn's tomb. More probably, he looks to cross the plain and the Borrhun-maj, too. It's our belief the Mad God lies beyond."

"How shall you find him on the Jesseryn Plain?" asked Morrach, his face twisting in disgust as he added, "What if he takes another's body there?"

"Ahrd willing, we shall emerge from the Cuan na'Dru ahead of him, and it seems the shape-shifting takes time and effort. I think he'll hold the form of Daven Tyras for a while, and so we'll recognize him." Calandryll paused, frowning as an unwelcome thought crossed his mind, and said hesitantly, "Though without the aid of the ghost-talkers to the north to warn us where he goes, we must guess at his path."

"Does he look to reach the Jesseryn Plain, there are few enough descents into the Kess Imbrun," offered

Dachan. "And only one convenient to the path he seems to take."

"The Daggan Vhe," murmured Bracht, amplifying as Calandryll's eyes flashed a question, "the Blood Road—where the warriors of Cuan na'For met the last invasion of the Jesserytes."

"Then we'd best ride hard for the Daggan Vhe," Calandryll said.

Bracht nodded and turned to Dachan: "In this your offer of help would be useful."

"Name it," said the ketoman.

"Food to see us through to the next camp, and one good horse apiece," Bracht asked, adding for Calandryll's benefit, "our supplies we can distribute, so no one animal is overburdened. We ride one, leading the fresher mount. That way we shall travel faster."

Calandryll voiced agreement, and a request of his own: "An escort, too. Of warriors who know those Jehenne sent with Daven Tyras—against the possibility that Rhythamun ensorcels them and sends them back to oppose us. To the edgewoods of the Cuan na'Dru, at least."

"Pray Ahrd no ni Larrhyn need raise sword against kin," Dachan murmured, "but aye, you shall have all that. When shall you depart?"

Calandryll glanced toward the wagon's entrance, suddenly aware the last of the night had passed as they talked, that between the curtains there stood a band of light, herald of the burgeoning day. He looked to Bracht and Katya, who nodded as he said, "Now."

Dachan, in turn, nodded, barking orders that sent warriors hurrying from the wagon. Katya said, "I'd bathe, if we've time. I've the feeling it shall be long ere we enjoy that comfort again."

"Swift, though," Bracht warned. "We bathe and eat, then we're on our way."

"I'd accompany you," Morrach announced, "save I fear my talents should prove more danger than aid."

"Better you remain for that reason," Calandryll

agreed, smiling, that there be no sting in his words. "And you've messages to send, besides. Nor, I suspect, is Nevyn's head yet sound enough for hard riding."

"Aye," Nevyn answered, grinning. "There's truth in that."

"We shall pray to Ahrd," promised Morrach. "That he ward you, and grant you success."

"Our thanks, then." Calandryll rose, bowing. "And farewell."

He quit the wagon, Bracht and Katya at his back, the Lykard crowding round separating to grant them passage, with awe-filled eyes and shouts of good wishes. They went to the stream, bathing hastily, and emerged from the shelters to find breakfast awaiting them, and Dachan with their own horses, saddled and ready, with three spare mounts, those, too, saddled, and all the bags filled.

"I've chosen twenty to side you," the headman advised them as they ate. "All know the warriors Jehenne sent, and they've my orders to obey you. Be it needful, then they'll slay the others."

"Ahrd willing, it shall not come to that," said Bracht.

"I've the feeling Rhythamun runs now," said Calandryll, "and likely won't spend time holding warriors to his geas."

Dachan nodded, his lean face expressing the hope Calandryll spoke true. "I'd ride with you myself," he said, "but with Jehenne only recently dead, I had best remain here."

Calandryll swallowed a last mouthful of bread and smiled. "You do enough already," he told the Lykard. "And you've our thanks for that."

"One thing more," Bracht asked, standing. "I'd send word to my parents that I live, and that the feud is dead."

"It shall be done," promised Dachan, clasping them each in turn by the hand. "The ni Errhyn shall know.

Ahrd, once the bards are done composing, all Cuan na'For shall know! The god go with you, my friends."

"And with you," Bracht said, and grinned at his companions, fiercely. "So, do we ride? We've a mage to meet."

Now Calandryll learned, truly, what it meant to ride fast. Without need to husband their horses' strength, or avoid contact with the Lykard, they sped across the grasslands. Where before they had alternated their pace, cantering at times, but as often moving at no more than a trot, now they held to a steady canter, each with a riderless mount in tow. As one animal tired, so they transferred to the other, back and forth, as would, Bracht explained, a warband striking into hostile territory. They ate and drank in the saddle, thundering remorselessly northward, sending herds of wild horses scattering from their path, the dog packs running yelping from so large a group. They slowed only when the sun set, rendering the footing treacherous, and then proceeded at a fast walk until full night fell and they made camp, dining on the ample provisions Dachan had provided. At first light they went on, and in two days reached the next camp, sighting the wagons clustered in the lee of a small hurst just as the sun sank beneath the western horizon.

They were welcomed there, with respect and curiosity, and brought before the ketoman, Vachyr, and the drachomannii, of whom there were two, Dewin and Pryth. These confirmed that word had come from Morrach and Nevyn, warning of Rhythamun's gramaryes, and that it had been passed on. Of the sorcerer who wore the form of Daven Tyras, they could say no more than that he had gone through the camp long days earlier, and that none of his escort had returned.

They slept the night in Vachyr's camp and rode out as it woke, continuing for five days before coming on a group of the ni Brhyn led by a warrior named Ranach. Here, too, they were made welcome, fed and offered the use of the headman's wagon, Rachan embarrassed by his familial connection with Daven Tyras. This camp numbered three ghost-talkers—Ovad, Telyr, and a woman named Rochanne—who reported much as had Dewin and Pryth: that none of their kind had sensed further interference in the aethyr, nor knew where Rhythamun was now. It seemed that the sorcerer had disappeared, for since that last sighting in the ni Brhyn camp none had encountered him, neither in Lykard territory nor Valan. Indeed, after possessing Morrach, he looked to have disappeared from the face of the world.

"Surely he's not yet reached the Kess Imbrun," Bracht said as they sat by Rachan's fire.

"Save he employ sortilege, no," said Rochanne. "Through use of magic, he might; but it would seem he prefers to travel in human form."

"Stolen form," grunted Ovad, his lined face sour with distaste.

"He told me once that he was able to transport himself through use of magic," Calandryll offered. "But only did he know his destination."

"The gharan-evur are limited by their choice," said Telyr. "A mage with the power to work that spell could readily assume a form that might travel faster than can a man—become a bird, a horse—but does he shed the body of Daven Tyras, then he becomes trapped in his new shape until he finds another."

"And to take that requires time," Katya murmured.

"Aye." Telyr favored the Vanu woman with a curious glance. "You know something of this."

"The holy men of my country told me something of it," she replied. "But I know only that the shapeshifter must become familiar with his victim before he may affect the possession."

"He spent time with Daven Tyras," Calandryll said.

"And so will likely hold that form," Telyr declared.

"To take the form of a beast would be easy—to shed it, far harder."

"Magic's worked easier by men," agreed Ovad. "I believe he'll hold the body he has until he finds one more useful to him."

"What of his own?" asked Calandryll, remembering the image that had formed as Rhythamun's animus quit Morrach's body. "In Dachan's camp I saw his face."

"You saw his pneuma," answered Telyr. "The face of his spirit."

"The gharan-evur forsake their natural form," Rochanne expanded. "Their physical being is left behind when they work their filthy magicks. What you saw was Rhythamun's true face, revealed in the aethyr."

Ovad spat into the fire, clearly finding such discussion unpleasant. "Rhythamun exists only as pneuma," he said. "As an elemental force—a spirit. The body he was born with is long gone into dust, so what physical shape he has is that of his latest victim."

"So most likely he'll remain Daven Tyras," said Calandryll thoughtfully. "Until he finds another— likely some luckless Jesseryte."

"Aye." Ovad nodded. "I'd guess it so."

His two fellow ghost-talkers voiced their agreement; Calandryll said, "Then it must be as I thought—he avoids the camps."

"Guessing we're alert to his gramaryes," said Telyr. "Aye, I'd reckon it so."

"Then we've still an advantage." Calandryll looked to Bracht, smiling tightly. "He'll not have reached the Kess Imbrun yet, not traveling in human form."

Bracht ducked his head, returning the smile; like a wolf, Calandryll thought, scenting its quarry on the wind.

"And he must eat," the Kern said, glancing at the three ghost-talkers. "No?"

"Daven Tyras must eat," Telyr confirmed.

"And none to feed him," Bracht said, musing. "All the camps warned against him, closed against him."

"By now every ghost-talker in Cuan na'For will know what he is," said Rochanne. "He'll find no welcome betwixt the Gann Peaks and the Kess Imbrun, nor from the Eastern Sea to the Valt."

Bracht's smile grew wider. "I wonder then," he said softly, "what the men with him make of their sudden outlawry."

"Dera, aye!" Calandryll gasped. "I'd not thought of that. Might they turn against him?"

"Do they attempt to enter a camp, they'll learn what he is," said Telyr, "and save he binds them with magicks, they'll go against him. No warrior of Cuan na'For would side with the gharan-evur."

"Nor are likely to overcome him," grunted the skeptical Ovad. "A warlock such as you've described could slay six with ease."

"And take the shape of one," said Rochanne.

"But still with need to eat," Bracht said. "And consequently slowed by his need to hunt."

"And does Ahrd grant us passage through the Cuan na'Dru," Calandryll said, "then we may well emerge ahead of him. We can reach the Daggan Vhe before he does, and so—even does he wear a new face—we need but halt the single man attempting to reach the Jesseryn Plain."

"He'd not attempt the same passage?" Katya wondered. "You're sure of that?"

"The Gruagach would never grant him entry," Rochanne said in a tone of utter conviction. "And I'd doubt me even such a mage as Rhythamun could defeat them. No, it's my belief he'll look to skirt the forest."

"All rests with Ahrd, it seems," said Telyr, "and the Gruagach."

Bracht glanced at his hands then, and Calandryll thought that upon his comrade's face he saw a flicker of doubt, but the Kern's voice was firm as he said, "If the god's green sap truly runs in my veins, then surely they must aid us."

"You can but attempt it," Telyr murmured.

"Aye." Bracht ducked his head, his smile resolute. "That we shall."

"And we pray for you," Rochanne promised.

THEY left that camp as early mist skirled among the alders of the hurst, soon burned off by a sun that heralded the beginnings of summer. They held pace as before, league after league consumed beneath the pounding hooves, racing steadily northward, toward the Cuan na'Dru. For days they traveled through an empty, sun-washed landscape, and then, as they broke camp one morning, they saw stormheads build great grey cloud castles in the sky to the north. By midmorning their pace was slowed by driving rain, thunder booming, the grass beaten down under the onslaught. The streams they forded were angry, swollen by the downpour and foaming, but still, driven by the urgency of the quest, they rode as swift they might, reluctant to concede the slightest advantage to their quarry.

It seemed now they had, for the first time, a genuine chance to gain on Rhythamun, to beat him to the Kess Imbrun and take the Arcanum from him. How they should do that, Calandryll was not sure, and did not much welcome the time the storm afforded him for such contemplation. The cloudburst transformed the sunny grasslands to a dark and miserable vista, locked in a gloomy twilight punctuated only by the stark scintillation of lightning, driving thoughts inward as frustration at this slowing of their progress grew. He endeavored to push doubt from his mind, but it was as though the suddenly dismal landscape, the seemingly endless curtain of water that flooded down, forced unwilling introspection on him. That Ahrd's strange guardians should allow them passage through the Cuan na'Dru he did not doubt; every ghost-talker he had spoken with was of the same opinion: that Bracht's failed crucifixion marked him as one favored by the god. And had Burash not come to save them from the Chaipaku and bring them swifter than any dared hope across the Narrow Sea? And Dera appeared on the road to Gannshold, to set that power in his blade that could overcome magic? Perhaps that, he thought, was the answer: that he should face Rhythamun in combat, his goddess-blessed sword against the sorcerer's fell thaumaturgy.

The thought frightened him. That he realized as a great peel of thunder echoed across the sky and his horse danced in alarm. Rhythamun's power he had seen, and for all the mage's gramaryes had not yet succeeded in defeating him, or in halting the quest, still he felt the stirrings of raw terror at the prospect of confronting the warlock in open fight.

Faith, he told himself, as he urged the nervous horse on. *The Younger Gods are on our side, and surely we must win.*

Surely . . . But in his heart, deep, there lingered a doubt he could not entirely snuff out.

No matter; he wiped rain from his eyes, knowing that he had no choice. Even should he die in that battle, he was committed. To turn from it was unthinkable, would unman him. Bracht had not turned from the crossing of Cuan na'For, for all it held the threat of dreadful death; and Katya had exiled herself from all she knew to pursue their goal. His determination, then, could be no weaker. Onward in faith, he told himself. To the Cuan na'Dru and beyond, to the Kess Imbrun. To the aptly named Blood Road, where, perhaps, all this long quest should end.

As if in approval of his resolve, he saw the sun then, at that exact moment, striking from between looming banks of black cloud, shedding light over the grassland, a great, radiant shaft, such as had illuminated Dera as the goddess stood beside the Gannshold road.

"Aye, faith," he said, unaware he spoke aloud.

And then the heavens vented one final blast of sound and the rain blew away to the south, the sky above cleared to a high, fierce blue, and the wind was warm again. Birds began to sing, and from the prairie came the sweet perfume of rain-washed grass, rising with the vapor that drifted up as the sun shone hot.

It was late in the afternoon, the sun westering, and before them stood a ridge, misted as the soaking grass dried. They crested the summit and by common, unspoken consent halted there, Calandryll staring in awe at what lay before them.

The grass ran down gently to flat land, and then ended where a wall of green darkness spread beyond the limits of sight across the prairie. From east to west and farther north than the keenest eye could range, it seemed as though shadow was painted over the grass, as though the northern limits of Cuan na'For were marked by that vast darkness, as though a great and silent black sea lay there. Calandryll heard Bracht say, "The Cuan na'Dru," softly, his voice reverent. He stared, daunted by the immensity of it. He had thought the woodlands of Kandahar were large, but they were no more than copses set beside this enormous forest, its extent unimaginable, limitless, it seemed. Silent, he followed Bracht down the slope as the setting sun washed the treetops in red light, the great forest seeming to blaze.

They camped that night on the grass, by a little beck that meandered careless, babbling softly, and at dawn set off again, riding hard. The escorting Lykard, Calandryll saw, were solemn-faced, as though wary of approaching this holy place, and, indeed, he felt the presence of it, as if the dark swath that filled all the horizon now cast its spiritual shadow over the land.

Three long bowshots away, close on noon, the escort slowed pace and the leader, Nychor, brought his mount alongside the three questers.

"By your leave, we'll ride no closer," he declared. "Without the drachomannii to intercede . . ."

Bracht nodded, understanding. "Wait here," he said, reining in. "At least until we enter."

Nychor smiled his gratitude. "We'll watch you approach," he promised, "and do the Gruagach grant you entry, wait until tomorrow's dawn."

His tone, and the way he eyed the forest, suggested he doubted that permission would be given. Bracht smiled, himself by no means easy, and passed the rein of his spare mount to Nychor.

"Take these back to Dachan, with our thanks." He turned to Calandryll and Katya. "So, come."

Not waiting for a reply, as though anxious to confront a test without delay, he drove his heels against the black stallion's flanks and galloped forward. Swiftly, his companions tossed reins to the nervous Lykard and thundered after him.

It seemed to Calandryll the air grew quiet as they came closer to the Cuan na'Dru. Insects darted over the grass and birds flew above, but their noise seemed subsumed, swallowed by the stillness of the forest. A wind blew, soft, the constant rustling of the prairie barely discernible, even the drumming of hooves dulled, overwhelmed by the silence of the trees that now filled all his vision. Rowan and blackthorn grew about the perimeter, and ash, elder, like outguards or acolytes to the greater trees that rose over the lesser species. The oaks dominated, mere saplings among their cousins of the edgewood, but rising vast-trunked a little farther in, with massive limbs imperiously outthrust, all hung with leaves like shining green jewels. They were majestic, and he felt their power.

Bracht slowed to a walk some distance off, and then reined in. Calandryll and Katya followed suit, none speaking as they dismounted, leading the horses slowly forward until the Kern raised a hand, wordlessly bidding them halt.

"Wait here."

He gave Katya his reins, and for a moment she clutched his hand. Calandryll saw his face was grave, set in somber lines. Then he nodded once and released her grip, walking forward, much as he had, Calandryll thought, gone to his execution. The sun stood overhead now, and all the forest shone green, patterns of shifting shadow dappling the ground between the outermost trees as Bracht approached. Calandryll watched him skirt a clump of blackthorn, moving cautiously toward the closest oak.

He reached the tree, a youngster by its size, but still massy, and fell to his knees, his arms flung out, the fingers of both hands spread wide. What he said was spoken too soft to hear, and too far distant, but after a while he rose and pressed both hands against the furrowed bark, his head bowed. For long minutes he stood thus, then turned away, walking back to his companions. His face, Calandryll saw, was still set in solemn lines, impassive, unreadable. When he spoke, his voice was equally muted.

"I know not if Ahrd deigned to hear me. We must wait."

"Not enter?" Katya asked, her question met with an expression almost of outrage.

"Without permission?" Bracht shook his head. "That would be sure death."

He turned, silently pointing. Calandryll looked to where he gestured and saw, almost hidden among the tangling of undergrowth, the long grass, the white of bones, the dulled glint of metal. His eyes alerted, he saw the edgewoods were a boneyard, that the mortal remains of men lay there, all twined with roots, become part of the wood. There, a rib cage thrust up; there brambles wove a thorny mask over a skull; an elder hoisted a carapace of bone, the branch extending from the socket where once an eye had sat; the parts of a man hung from a blackthorn.

Glum doubt assailed him, and must have expressed itself on his face, for Bracht said, "Some were slain by the Gruagach; others were sacrificed," and shook his head as Calandryll gasped in horror, explaining, "not lately. Long and long ago. Now only those foolish enough to enter without permission fall prey."

"To the Gruagach," Calandryll said very softly.

"Aye." Bracht smiled, briefly and without much humor. "Do you see now why I was reluctant to enter here?"

"I do," Calandryll murmured. "But now?"

"Now we can only wait," Bracht answered. "If we are to cross the Cuan na'Dru, it must be with the Gruagach's consent."

"How shall we know that?" Katya demanded. "That they grant us the crossing?"

"We shall know," Bracht said. "They'll come to us, or not."

"When?" asked the warrior woman. "How long must we wait?"

'Until they come."

Bracht shrugged; Katya said, "And if they do not come?"

"Then we've a long ride. Nychor and his men wait until the dawn: I think they'll come ere then, but if not . . ."

"We must ride around?" Katya flung out an arm, gesturing at the vastness of the woodland stretched before them. "Around this? Be we forced to such a detour, Rhythamun must surely escape us."

Bracht ducked his head, and as the warrior woman's face grew dark with frustration said, "Be that the way of it, then that way we must go."

Katya's grey eyes narrowed, her lips pursing as if she would argue, but Bracht preempted her. "Heed me," he said in a tone that closed her mouth tight on any argument, "I'll not allow you to go in there, save with the consent of the Gruagach. I'd not see your bones join those others so foolish as to make that attempt."

"You'd prevent me?" she asked, her gaze speculative as she studied his determined face. "With force?"

"I would," Bracht said. "You mean too much to me that I'd see you die so senselessly."

"Then," said Katya, a smile of resignation curving her lips, "I suppose we must wait."

✣   ✣   ✣

THEY took the opportunity to eat. Cold food, for none
wished to offend the god by taking kindling from his
forest, and afterward busied themselves with grooming the horses and checking gear. It was makework: a
means of passing hours that dragged slowly by without indication Bracht's prayers had been heard, each
of them wondering if consent would be given, if the
Gruagach would come; and what those strangeling
creatures would prove to be. They spoke little, for
when they did, it seemed inevitable their conversation should veer to discussion of Rhythamun's progress, and then frustration mounted, which Bracht
sought to quell, for fear Ahrd take offense and deny
them help. Off to the south they could see the Lykard
setting up shelters for the night, their horses cropping
contentedly, though all the time the warriors turned
nervous faces to the forest, wondering no less than
the three what should be the outcome of their unprecedented request.

The afternoon aged toward evening, the lengthening of the day as summer neared serving to fuel
their impatience. Katya strode restlessly along the forest's edge, constantly peering inward as irritable fingers drummed a tattoo against her scabbard.
Calandryll joined her for a while, but her nervousness
served only to renew his own doubts and he chose to
settle on the grass, endeavoring with scant success to
sleep. Bracht seemed the only one calm, squatting
cross-legged, his face fixed phlegmatic on the timber,
as though he momentarily anticipated some sign, or
was resigned to the waiting.

The sun closed on the horizon, that dark with its
covering of trees, and a new moon climbed the eastern sky. The air assumed the blue shades of dusk;
birds flocked homeward to their bosky roosts. And
Bracht's stallion whickered a challenge, stamping, its
ears flattening back on its plunging head. The chestnut and the grey, too, began to fret.

Instantly, Bracht was on his feet.

Calandryll rose to join him, and Katya came running from her inspection of the woodland, all of them staring toward the timber.

The Cuan na'Dru was draped with shadow now, ghostly, forbidding in its sheer immensity. Ghostly, too, were the shapes that moved within the darkness, flitting from trunk to trunk, silent despite the detritus littering the forest floor. They were impossible to define: they moved too furtive, leaving only an impression of huge eyes, limbs longer than a man's, a preternatural agility.

Calandryll had half expected a *byah* to appear—that manifestation more comforting for having once been seen—to speak, bidding them enter, but these things were infinitely more menacing, and he felt his skin grow cold as his eyes struggled to discern them.

He could not, even as they drew closer, moving past the oaks to the outer growths of elder and rowan, to where the bones lay. It was as though they remained constantly on the periphery of his vision, never quite in focus, but always shifting too swift, too sudden, for his sight to hold them. He heard them, though, as they flitted ever closer; not speaking, it seemed, but communicating with soft whistles, sighs, murmurs, such as the trees themselves make, when the wind stirs rustling through the branches.

He thought of the syfalheen of Gessyth, of Yssym and his kin, who had, at first, seemed very strange, but proven true friends, and told himself that these creatures—the Gruagach, of that he had no doubt—were no more odd, nor any more dangerous. But then he remembered the bones, and wondered if he only sought to reassure himself.

A hand fell unwittingly to his sword, reflex action as a shape stepped closer still, picking a delicate way among the thickets of blackthorn, halting in the bushes' shadow. It raised an arm, long, oddly jointed fingers curling in an unmistakable gesture.

"Come," Bracht said in a soft, almost hesitant voice.

Calandryll felt saliva fill his mouth, and spat as he took the chestnut's reins. To his side, he heard Katya let out her breath in a long, wary sigh as she followed Bracht toward the waiting figure.

The Kern led his stallion forward, halting on the edge of the wood and calling, "Do you grant us entry into Ahrd's holy forest?"

The Gruagach beckoned, and in the fast-waning light Calandryll saw that its elongated fingers were tipped with sharp claws. It was difficult, in the twilight, to be sure, but he thought its skin was a mottled fusion of green and grey, like the bark of some ancient tree, and when it opened its mouth, he saw serrated teeth set in double rows, like a shark's. Its eyes were huge and pale, the pupils vertical slits, overhung with ridges of bone that sloped dramatically back to form a broad forehead, the nose vestigial, a flat hump that flared wide over the nostrils. It spoke, or seemed to, the sound a fluttering whistle, and gestured again.

Calandryll saw Bracht's shoulders square as he led the stallion toward the strangeling creature. The Gruagach stood immobile as the Kern approached, and then extended one long arm, pointing at Bracht's right hand. The man, in turn, thrust out his arm, the hand suddenly grasped, turned this way and that as the Gruagach brought it close, examining it, sniffing it, touching the healed skin with a delicate claw. It whistled then, answered by a chorus from the darkness, and let go its hold, moving away. Bracht stepped a pace forward and the Gruagach fell back, as though, satisfied, it was now unwilling to stand too close, or to allow itself to be clearly seen, moving with such fluid grace it seemed not to walk, but to glide, drifting from the shelter of the thicket to halt again, beckoning, beneath an elder.

Bracht followed, and it seemed to Calandryll that the hedge of blackthorn parted, shaping a narrow avenue into the edgewood. The Kern led his horse in, Katya behind, and then Calandryll, glancing back to see the thicket spring up impenetrable, the glow of the Lykard fire a distant spark off on the open grass. Ahead stood ash and rowan, all filled with the subtly shifting shapes of the Gruagach, their guide leading them steadily deeper, past the outer palisade of trees to the great oaks that formed the true forest. The creature halted there, beneath the wide boughs of a mature oak, so still it became invisible, seeming no more than some offshoot of the great tree until it waved its long limbs and emitted a series of fluting notes, like the call of a night bird.

Its language was incomprehensible and it clashed its sharp teeth in frustration as it saw the three questers did not understand, pointing at them, then at their horses. Bracht studied it a moment, and then, tentatively, set foot to stirrup. The Gruagach nodded enthusiastically and the Kern swung into the saddle, ducking low as the branches of the oak threatened to strike his head.

"How can we ride through this?" Katya indicated the now-moonlit forest with a jutting chin. "By day's light, perhaps, but by night?"

The Gruagach whistled, the sound somehow indicative of irritation, and Bracht said, "Do as it bids."

Katya shrugged and mounted; Calandryll followed suit, seeing the Gruagach nod approvingly and turn, motioning them to follow as it loped away.

It ran swift as a horse, using all four of its limbs, leaving them no choice but to heel their mounts in pursuit, praying no low-hanging branch would sweep them from their saddles.

None did. Indeed, just as the blackthorn of the edgewood had parted before them, so it seemed did the oaks, affording them clear passage into the forest, so that in a little while they grew more confident and sat upright, chasing the racing Gruagach ever deeper into the heart of the Cuan na'Dru.

The creature remained a constant distance ahead,

only just visible, though its brethren were soon lost,
seen but occasionally as shadows that flitted through
patches of moonlight. Calandryll saw that they swung
with prehensile agility from tree to tree, seldom
touching the ground, apparently preferring to travel
through the canopy of overhanging boughs rather
than along the forest's floor. They were, he surmised,
arboreal, reminded of the monkeys he had seen in the
jungles of Gash, and the one he followed, therefore,
elected to lead the way . . . To Ahrd? He supposed so,
for it seemed impossible that they should be able to
travel so fast without divine intervention, the horses
no longer nervous, but galloping now, freely as if they
traversed the open spaces of the grasslands, sensing
what their riders' eyes denied. The oaks grew thick,
and while their wide-flung limbs and heavy roots denied undergrowth much purchase, still it was not possible so swift a pace could be maintained without
accident. They rode in single file, and he at the rear,
but still, beyond Bracht, he saw trees stand directly
athwart their passage, with boughs hung so low as to
deny even the horses a clear way. Yet the Gruagach
ran and they followed after, and even though it
seemed they charged directly into a barrier of solid
trunks and interwoven limbs there were no obstacles,
no hindrances, as if the oaks dissolved before them,
moving aside on agile, dendrous feet. More than once
he chanced a backward look, and saw only trees, impenetrable, behind.

And all the while, at first unnoticed in the urgency
of their ride, there grew a sense of peace, of tremendous calm, that rose to a point undeniable, at which
it became a palpable thing. Only then did Calandryll
realize that since entering the wood he had heard the
natural night sounds of a forest: the rustle of breeze-
stirred leaves, the trilling of night birds, and the small
cries of nocturnal beasts, the pounding of hooves on
ancient soil. Now there was another silence, not the
forbidding stillness that had marked the edgewoods,
but one of venerable tranquillity, akin to the quietude

of a temple. It seemed then that time fell out of gear, that the motion of the horse beneath him slowed—though he knew somehow that he still rode at breakneck pace, impossibly swift—becoming a rhythmic sensation, gentle as the rocking of a boat on a calm sea. All around the timber blurred, like shapes seen through water, unclear, shafts of moonlight lancing in random patterns through boughs that swayed and danced to some unheard music. Like a dream, he thought.

Not a dream, said a voice inside his head, strangely familiar. *Did you not seek to cross my forest?*

"Aye," he answered, the word torn from his lips and carried off on the unnatural wind of his passage.

And did you think I should refuse you, when Bracht asked it of me? Have I not twice shown him my favor? The once in Lysse, and again, when I healed his wounds?

"You have," Calandryll replied, recognizing the silent voice now, remembering the *byah* that had warned of Rhythamun's treachery. "And I thank you for it."

How else should I treat with those who defend me, save by granting what aid is mine to give? To the farther edge of the forest the Gruagach shall bring you safe.

"And shall we find Rhythamun then? Shall we be ahead of him?"

That is not mine to know. Calandryll sensed a hesitation in the god's words. *He has not entered the Cuan na'Dru. Nor shall, for not even he can withstand my guardians, nor come within my aegis unharmed.*

"Then surely we must outpace him."

Perhaps. For my sake and yours, hope it be so.

"Denied the camps, forced to hunt his food—surely he must be slowed. The men with him must surely learn his nature and turn from him."

Aye, for they are only misguided. But even do they, still he has such power as may overcome them.

"He has slain them? Taken their horses?"

And likely more.

Now Calandryll felt a great regret in the voiceless communication, such as made his skin prickle with horrid anticipation. "What do you say?" he said.

That such as Rhythamun live beyond the pale, beyond mankind's compassion, or human feelings. That six lives are as nothing to him, save steps along his fell path. That six men may provide such as he with more than only mounts to bring him onward, but be his meat, too.

"He becomes a cannibal?"

Calandryll spoke low, struck with the horror of that likelihood, no more for the advantage of speed it must surely afford the warlock than loathing for the act itself.

I say it may be. I cannot know for sure—only that Rhythamun inhabits a place of darkness where few men venture.

"Then we must catch him before he reaches the Kess Imbrun; before he enters the Jesseryn Plain."

What aid is mine, I give you, and my blessing with it. More than that, I cannot. But know that all we Younger Gods are with you.

Ahrd's voice rustled into silence, like a wind departing trees. Calandryll sat stunned, leaving the chestnut to pick its own way after Katya's racing grey. Would even Rhythamun sink so low? he wondered, knowing the answer even as the thought formulated, spitting disgust from a mouth that seemed suddenly tainted by the contemplation of so filthy a deed. By all the gods, he deserves to die.

That his comrades, too, had heard the god, and held similar conversations, he saw when Katya turned a paled face back, horror widening her eyes. Beyond her, he saw Bracht gesture angrily, and heard a curse float by. Unspoken, all urged their mounts to greater effort, thundering through the heart of the Cuan na'Dru without concern for pitfalls or obstacles, utterly confident that Ahrd himself loaned divine aid to their quest and would not, while they remained within his domain, allow them to come to harm.

How long that passage lasted was impossible to tell, for they rode beyond the laws of time, sped by the god himself, so that as night brightened into dawn they saw before them the ending of the forest, the rising sun striking brilliant through the timber of the northern edgewoods.

Their guide halted there, waving them on before fading back into the timber, and they went on, northward, the horses fresh, running eagerly as if they had not already galloped through the night, over more leagues than might be encompassed in so short a time. For that, they all gave thanks to Ahrd, but underlying their gratitude was a terrible doubt that despite all their efforts Rhythamun would still reach the Kess Imbrun before them, would take the Daggan Vhe down into the great rift canyon and lose himself in the unknown land that was the Jesseryn Plain.

19

CENNAIRE studied the two men with an enigmatic smile, aware that she held their lives in balance in her slender hands. For all they carried the long dirks favored by the Kerns sheathed on their belts, and their swords set carefully within easy reach, for all they were hard-muscled, still she was confident she might slay them, did it come to that. Indeed, it might be the quicker way to obtain the information she sought—to disable the one and slay the other before his brother's eyes: a token of her power.

And yet, not knowing why, she hesitated.

Perhaps she grew a conscience. Perhaps it had something to do with the loyalty she sensed in them, palpable as the desire, the curiosity she smelled oozing from them. She had found them readily enough for Gannshold still buzzed with rumors of the skirmish they had fought, the trick worked on those Kerns hostile to Bracht ni Errhyn, to whom these brothers were, in some obscure manner she did not entirely understand, related. Gart and Kythan ni Morrhyn, they were named, and she had found them, her way paved with seductive smiles and tentative promises, in this hostelry called The Horseman's Rest.

At first they had been suspicious, but her courtesan's wiles had charmed them enough that before long they boasted of their part in her quarry's escape. There were few enough men could resist her when she fixed them with her huge brown eyes, attentive on their every word, leaning forward so they might catch a glimpse of cleavage, her musky scent heady in their nostrils, and these had proven no exception. Save, her preternatural senses told her, that they held something back. That the three she sought had come to Gannshold and quit the fortress city, she learned soon enough, but their destination, that was withheld—and it was that knowledge her master would have her discover.

She had debated the swiftest means of unlocking their secret, realizing as she sat with them, utilizing all her powers, that likely overt violence was not the key. Behind their boasting, behind their desire for her, she had sensed some greater concern, and behind that, hot and steady as the blood in their veins, the certainty that they would die before revealing that secret knowledge. Their loyalty transcended the physical and she had known past doubting that each would fight her to the death, would sooner see his kin sacrificed than besmirch the honour that lay at the core of their existence. In that they were very different to such as Darth, and that—to her surprise—had touched her, prompting her to doubt. It was a kind of pride, but different to that Menelian had evinced, a loyalty, a bonding, that she did not understand in any articulate fashion, but rather felt deep in her being, as if it struck some mysterious responding cord that she could not readily define.

It was a dilemma, for the knowledge they held she must have—on pain of failure, of Anomius's displeasure—and she had left them with the promise that she would return later that day, allowing herself a little time in which to order her disturbed thoughts.

She had found an answer of sorts and gone back to the inn, to the private chamber they had arranged for

the tryst, with at least the possibility of an alternative
to their deaths. Now she wondered if she should use
it, or the more direct method.

They had bathed and dressed themselves in clothes
that smelled a little less of horses, and that she found
appealing. Equally that they treated her not as some
harlot to be bought and used, but as a woman of gentle birth. One they desired, certainly: that particular
odor emerged powerfully from beneath the scents of
soap and recently applied oils. Also a tremendous curiosity, a wariness akin to that of an animal not entirely satisfied with the overtures of a stranger. They
hoped—this overwhelmingly obvious—to bed her; but
they did not yet trust her. Did they know her for a
revenant, did they learn that she hunted the questers,
they would, she was sure, oppose her to the limits of
their fragile human bodies.

That thought amused her: that were she to reveal
herself they would fight her and die. To own such
power was intoxicating, but there was also that other,
unfamiliar, awareness. Respect? She was not sure, only
that she felt an odd reluctance to take their lives, a hesitation she had not known with Menelian or Darth, a
thing that troubled her.

Her decision was made unwitting, born of instinct
and emotions she did not comprehend.

She joined them in the emptying of one bottle, bidding them remain seated as she rose, playing the part
of serving maid as she went to the table by the window, where more wine waited. Furtively, she unstop-
pered the little vial she had purchased, the spilling of
its contents hidden, the colorless liquid blending instantly with the dark red wine. She brought the bottle
to them, filling both their cups and her own, drinking
deep—it would have no effect on her—while they
drank deeper.

The bottle was soon drained. The two Kerns
beamed slackmouthed, observing her with glazed and
lustful eyes.

"Ahrd, but this vintage is powerful." Gart's words came slurred. "My head spins."

Kythan chuckled, lolling in his chair, threatening to turn it over as he nudged his brother. "Surely you'd not so offend this lady?" he mumbled, raising an empty cup in toast to Cennaire.

She favoured him with a radiant smile and said, "Tell me of Bracht and his companions. Where do they go? Why do they quest so?"

THE night was passed as Cennaire drew the shutters closed over the windows of her room and lit two candles for all the early morning sun shone outside, and even in the mountains the days grew warm. Checking her door was bolted shut, she fetched the ensorcelled mirror from its wrappings and set to polishing the gleaming surface, absentmindedly studying her reflected image as she sought to compose her thoughts, not yet ready to utter the words that would replace her face with that of Anomius, wondering at the enormity of all she had learned and what it meant for her.

As a child she had heard the ancient tales of the Godwars, of how Tharn had waxed prideful, vying with his brother Balatur until all the world lay in ruins; of how the god had gone down into madness, and his parents, his creators—Yl and Kyta—had set him and his sibling both aside, banishing them to a dreaming limbo, their places taken by the Younger Gods. And she had forgotten, as children do, that in such tales there lies often truth; as an adult, she had thought nothing of such things, being, as is the way of the full-grown, far more concerned with her own affairs than with such vague matters of theology and myth.

Now it seemed the seed of truth in those old tales sprouted, preparing to spring up full-blown again—if what she had learned from Gart and Kythan was true. She frowned a moment, then smoothed her unlined brow, her lips pursing. Of how Anomius would take this startling news she entertained little doubt: he

would want the book, the Arcanum. Of how it might
affect her, however, she could only guess, and that
with little enough certainty.

The ugly little sorcerer held her heart, and thus
held her in sway, his to command on threat of destruction. That he would order her to follow, she did
not doubt; that he lusted still for revenge, she did not
doubt. But should she secure him the Arcanum . . .
what then? Would he, like this other, seek to raise the
Mad God? Did she want that?

It felt strange to ponder such matters, as if the fate
of the world lay in her hands. This world she knew;
such a world as Tharn would make, were he resurrected, would surely be a stranger place. And could
the Mad God feel gratitude for those who brought
him back? She smiled, wryly, thinking that a priest
might better answer those musings than a heartless
courtesan, a revenant created by fell magic. Indeed—
her smile became a cynical chuckle—a priest,
whether of Burash or Dera or the tree god, Ahrd,
would likely condemn her out of hand, for all her existence was Anomius's doing, and she no say in it,
save to obey.

She thought then, her smile dying, what concern of
hers was the world? It had treated her unkind enough,
and why should she hesitate to advise her master that
the Arcanum was the goal of her quarry's quest? But
still she did, for reasons she could neither articulate
nor define.

She had the knowledge now, but what was she to
do with it? Anomius yet held her heart, and even
though he rode with the Tyrant's army, and could not,
without consent of the Tyrant's Sorcerers, return to
Nhur-jabal, still there must come a time. And then,
did she hold back this truth, surely he would snuff
out her existence, spitefully. But if she told him,
would the world she knew end? Did she bring him
the Arcanum, would he still have use for her, or cast
her off, redundant?

It was an imponderable problem, a thing of doubts

and ethics, which she was ill-equipped to consider. To Cennaire, life was a simple matter of pleasure's attainment and the avoidance of pain; and were the Mad God raised, she did not know which might take precedence. She felt certain of only three things: *that Anomius would want the Arcanum for his own; that Anomius was mad; and that it was likely impossible to deceive him*. And a fourth, she thought, slowly setting down the scrap of silk as she stared into the glassy surface of the mirror—*that Anomius holds my heart, and therefore I must be very careful*.

Slowly, she began to speak the words he had taught her.

The mirror darkened, then filled with shifting colors even as the air was filled with the sweet scent of almonds. The swirling hues eddied, like colored oils in water, resolving slowly into the sallow features of the mage, all bulbous, wart-pocked nose and pale, demanding eyes. Cennaire leaned closer as he spoke, his voice a whisper.

"What have you learned?"

"Much," she said. "Things change."

"Tell me."

His voice, for all it came rustling and faint, was imperious. Cennaire paused a moment, pink tongue flicking over full lips, then said: "They have left Gannshold for Cuan na'For. They still pursue Daven Tyras, but he is not Daven Tyras."

"I know this. He is Varent den Tarl, or was."

"No. Before that he was Rhythamun. He is ancient . . ." She almost said, "older than you, even," but caught herself. ". . . centuries old, and the grimoire is not a grimoire."

"What riddle is this? Speak plain, woman, lest you know my anger."

"This Rhythamun took the shape of Varent den Tarl, that he might secure a chart from the archives in Lysse. He tricked Calandryll and Bracht into traveling to Tezin-dar to secure the Arcanum . . ."

"The Arcanum?" Stark surprise edged the wizard's

voice blade-sharp. He brought his face closer to the glass, his watery eyes wide an instant, then narrowed. "Do you tell me they pursue the Arcanum?"

"You know of it?"

"Of course. What sorcerer has not heard of that book? By all the gods, that tome is power incarnate! Go on."

"He—Rhythamun—seized it, carried it back to Lysse. They followed him . . ."

"The Vanu woman, she's with them?"

"Katya, aye. She went with them into Cuan na'For."

"So, that mystery resolves." In the glass, Anomius nodded, rubbing at his nose. "Doubtless the hierophants of Vanu scried what was afoot and sent her out. But still the three, only? And into Cuan na'For?"

"Aye, with Rhythamun far ahead, in the shape of Daven Tyras."

"The easier to cross the grass. Riding northward?"

"So I was told."

"Ah, quite. By whom?"

"Two Kerns, Gart and Kythan, of Bracht's clan."

"How did they know?"

"Bracht sought their aid."

Cennaire told of Jehenne ni Larrhyn's pledged vengeance and the help the brothers had given, all they had told her. When she was done Anomius grunted and asked, "You're sure of this?"

She nodded and said, "I employed a decoction to loosen their tongues; such as ensures the truth, without memory after."

. "You let them live?"

He sounded surprised. Cennaire nodded again: "I saw no worth in slaying them. And I was seen with them—had they been found dead there might well be questions asked about me."

Anomius grunted, tugging for a moment on the hairs that clustered within his nostrils. Cennaire waited.

"So. Gone into Cuan na'For after this Rhythamun, you say?"

"So I learned."

"Northward," Anomius murmured thoughtfully. "The Arcanum in Rhythamun's hands; the three in pursuit. No doubt Rhythamun looks to raise the Mad God, to curry favor with Tharn. Well, he shall not! No, that prize shall be mine!"

"How shall you take it?" Cennaire asked. "Cuan na'For is vast."

"Cuan na'For is no more than a step along the way." The wizard's eyes grew distant as he thought. "Aye, and the Jesseryn Plain, too. Does this Rhythamun look to raise Tharn, then he looks beyond the places known to men. I'd hazard a guess he travels for the Borrhun-maj and beyond."

"Surely the Borrhun-maj marks the world's limit."

"And what should a creature of the bedchamber know of such matters?" Anomius snarled laughter, scornfully dismissing her comment. "The limit of one world is but the beginning of another. Aye, I'll wager that's where he goes, and they after him."

"Do they survive this Lykard woman."

"They've the gods' own luck. How else did they trick me? It's my belief they will, but now I know what game's afoot and can better play my hand."

Quickly Cennaire asked, "How shall you do that? Do you come to Lysse, or Cuan na'For, to take up the chase?"

The wizard's ugly face darkened at that and he raised his hands, displaying the bracelets that gleamed dully about his wrists, shaking them as he shook his head.

"I cannot while these cursed ornaments fetter me."

Before he had opportunity to continue, Cennaire asked, "Where are you now?"

"Marching eastward from Kesham-vaj," came the sullen answer. "The Tyrant's chosen to secure his coastline ere we assault Fayne Keep. That shall be our final conquest, he says, and before we go against that

fortress, we must take Mherut-yi and the other sea-
ward cities."

And so cannot return to Nhur-jabal, thought
Cennaire, *where my heart beats in your magical box.*
Aloud, she said, "What would you have me do then?"

"Go after them," said Anomius.

"Not after Rhythamun?"

"No. I begin to perceive a design in this affair.
Burash! Had I the freedom of Nhur-jabal's
libraries . . ." He hesitated, delving in his nose. "But
no matter—it's my guess those three are foreordained
to hunt him, and so have the better chance of finding
him."

He fell silent, lost for a moment in contemplation.
Cennaire thought she had never seen him so uncertain, sensing his plans changed to accommodate this
new information. Patiently, she waited for him to
speak again, and after a while he ducked his head,
muttering to himself, then speaking, louder, to her.

"That must be the way of it: it explains the presence of the Vanu woman. Aye, their quest is likely
now to take the book from Rhythamun, and if that be
their destiny, then they're the more likely to succeed.
In the finding, at least."

"But not the taking?" Cennaire asked.

Anomius chuckled—a horrid, bubbling sound—and
said, "Perhaps; perhaps not. Rhythamun must command powerful magicks to have got so far, and do
they confront him, the outcome may go the one way
or the other. Whichever, it changes our game."

"How so?"

Anomius spat contemptuously. "Because the three
are now important to me, fool! If foreordained they
be, then slaying them loses me a greater prize. I'd
have the Arcanum for my own, and now it seems
they lead me to it. Aye, they become my allies in this
game—like hounds that point me to my prize."

"Surely they'll not lend themselves to aid you?"

In the mirror, Anomius ground his yellow teeth.
"By all the gods," he snapped, "am I ever served by

fools? Of course they'll not aid me, do they know what they do. But unwitting, then they shall."

Cennaire bristled at his insults, concealing her irritation with the long-practiced skill of her old trade, her face calm.

"Listen," Anomius told her, "Calandryll, Bracht, the Vanu woman, would seem to have some clue to Rhythamun's direction. If I guess aright, they're on his trail, and with far better chance than you of finding him. Does he reach the Jesseryn Plain, then likely he'll take another's form and prove the harder to find. So . . . your task now is to join them."

"Join them?" Cennaire could not conceal her surprise. "I thought you sought their deaths?"

"I did," came the answer, "before this news. In time, I'll still have my revenge, but for now they become useful to me. No, you'll aid them, rather than slay them. You'll find them and go with them. Stay with them until they find Rhythamun, then take the Arcanum. That above all! If you must slay them to take the book, do it. But the book is the thing! Bring me that and I've power beyond imagining. Even leave them live if you must, only bring me that book."

His excitement was a palpable thing, intense enough it seemed that even separated by so many leagues, by all the width of the Narrow Sea, still Cennaire could smell it flooding out of the mirror. She watched him wipe spittle from his fleshy lips, smiling now, like a miser contemplating his hoard, or a ghoul a grave. Warily, she said, "They're long gone into Cuan na'For. How shall I find them? How shall I overtake them?"

"They go north," he answered, "across the grass. If this Lykard woman seeks to revenge herself on Bracht, then they must travel cautiously, and that must surely slow them. I'll provide you with such a steed as shall outrun the wind itself. As for finding them . . ." He paused, gnawing at his lower lip, then nodded, chuckling. "Aye, they go northward to the Jesseryn Plain, so they must cross the Kess Imbrun.

That chasm has few enough crossing places, so they—
and Rhythamun, too—will look for the closest, the
easiest; and that is the way the Kerns call the Blood
Road, the Daggan Vhe. You'll go there and, the gods
willing, arrive before them."

Cennaire doubted the gods would be willing to further a design likely to result in their destruction, but
that thought she held to herself. To Anomius, she
said: "I've scant knowledge of Cuan na'For, nor are
there roads or towns. How shall I find this Daggan
Vhe without delaying to inquire of folk unlikely to
bid me ready welcome? And how persuade the three
to take me with them?"

"The finding you can leave to me; the persuasion I
leave to you. Burash, woman, were you not a courtesan?" Anomius gestured impatiently. "You've a
horse? If not, go out and purchase one. Time is our
enemy now, and I'd not see it wasted. Heed me! Take
only what you must—no more than will fill your
saddlebags—and on the instant. Ride north along the
Gann Pass, and immediately you're clear of prying
eyes use the mirror again. You understand?"

Cennaire said, "I do," and began to speak again, but
the sorcerer waved her silent, ending their communication with an abrupt gesture, so that she could only
watch, frowning, as his image wavered, the almond
scent wafting once more as the glass cleared, becoming a silver-surfaced vanity, innocent.

She sat a moment, lost in thought, then shrugged,
stowing the mirror back in its protective sack. It
seemed impossible that she could now catch up with
her quarry, and yet Anomius had evinced no doubt
that his glamours would bring her to them, or to
where they went. She wondered how he might affect
that meeting as she began to gather up those things
she deemed necessary to her journey.

THE sun stood some little distance past its zenith as
she rode her newly purchased horse out through the

gates of Gannshold. The soldiery there eyed her appreciatively, their lewd comments ignored, as were the warnings against a lone woman—and especially one so lovely—venturing without escort into Cuan na'For. She was thankful she had bought riding gear in Lysse—breeks of soft brown leather and a tunic to match—for it meant she could sit astride the roan gelding. What equestrian skills she possessed had been learned in childhood, on plodding farm horses, and she doubted her ability to travel far riding side-saddle, as was more usual for ladies. Indeed, she felt little enthusiasm for this ride at all, for while she was now immune to most of the physical discomforts suffered by those whose lives were governed by a beating heart, still she felt the steady pounding of the saddle against her buttocks as she steered the gelding along the pass.

Walls of sheer grey stone rose to either side, footed with scrubby bushes, the band of sky above streamered with mares' tails of high cirrus, dotted with the dark shapes of wheeling birds. Cennaire lifted the roan horse to a canter, leaving the city's north gate behind, proceeding along the flat roadway until the canyon began to rise and Gannshold was lost in the distance. At this time of day there were few enough travelers venturing the pass, and those she encountered she ignored, soon finding herself alone as she climbed a defile that curved around the base of a lesser peak. She slowed there, her mount straining as the altitude began to take effect, though she herself felt no discomfort, and let the animal walk the final league to the egress of the cut. The road widened again here, devolving on a mountain meadow part encircled by a rushing stream; she recognized it from Gart's and Kythan's description, seeing here and there mute evidence of the fight in the churned ground and the broken arrows that still littered the grass. This was, she decided, as good a place as any to halt and obey her master.

She reined in, walking the gelding over to the

stream, tethering the animal to a larch, and fetching
the mirror from the saddlebag.

For a moment, she waited, listening, her preternatural senses telling her she was alone, but still took
the precaution of walking in among the trees before
she unwrapped the glass and spoke the gramarye.

The scent of almonds joined the resinous perfume
of the larches as the mirror's surface shifted, shimmering colorful, revealing Anomius's unlovely features, puckered with irritable impatience.

"You take your time, woman."

In the mountain-girt silence his voice came loud. "I
had to buy a horse," she said defensively, "and ride
clear of the city."

"Where are you now?"

"In the pass. High up, in a meadow."

"Alone?"

"Aye, nor any near as best I can tell."

"Good. Hold up the mirror and move it round that
I may see."

She did as he bade her, standing and turning the device in a slow circle, thinking all the while that she
had not known he could see more than her face
through the glass, storing that information as she
stored all the little tidbits she gleaned, against their
future usage.

"It will do," came his voice. "Now look at me."

She brought the mirror back before her face.
Anomius asked, "You've a blade of some kind?"

Cennaire nodded, touching the dagger sheathed on
her waist. "A knife," she said.

"Show me."

She drew the dagger, holding up the blade.

Anomius nodded and said, "I must teach you another gramarye. Listen now, and carefully."

He spoke slow syllables, guttural words that
seemed torn from deep inside his scrawny chest, the
almond scent strengthening with their utterance.
Cennaire listened attentively, and then, on his order,
repeated each word. They were hard of saying, as

though the product of a language designed for tongues other than human, and it took some time before she had them right and Anomius pronounced himself satisfied. Even then, he had her repeat the sentences until they came fluid, the one after the other, in what, to her, was a meaningless babble.

"Good enough," he declared, and chuckled maliciously. "If not, you've a lengthy walk. Now bring your horse where I can see it."

Cennaire wedged the mirror between a low-slung bough and the trunk of a larch and fetched the gelding from its placid grazing. She brought the horse to stand before the glass, awaiting her master's further instruction.

"Take out that knife," he ordered, and she obeyed.

The gelding snickered, stamping fretfully, as if sensing something amiss.

"Hold it firm," Anomius said, "and speak the gramarye."

Cennaire began to voice the words, the almond scent thickening, heady, stronger now than the piny smell of the timber or the horse's drying sweat. In the mirror, Anomius spoke with her, an echo that seemed to lend power to the spell. The gelding ceased its fretting, its head drooping as though the arcane syllables were a soporific.

"Kill it," said the sorcerer. "Cut its throat and repeat the gramarye as you do it."

She took hold of the gelding's halter and drew the knife, once more mouthing the words as she drove the blade deep into the animal's neck, severing the great artery there. The horse shuddered, air whistling from its flared nostrils. Blood spurted in a long, thick jet when Cennaire withdrew the dagger, but the gelding remained on its feet, only trembling, as if the outflowing of its life was no more irritation than a bothersome fly as she completed the glamour.

"That was well done," Anomius remarked. "Now wait."

Cennaire stooped, wiping the dagger clean on grass,

seeing, as she rose again, that the pulsing blood slowed, coming in a trickle now. The horse sighed, sinking down, rolling heavily onto its side. For a while it lay there, busy flies gathering about the great dark pool of crimson, crawling industriously over its neck. Then it shuddered again, and heaved, its eyes opening as it lurched to its feet. Where the knife had cut its flesh, the skin seemed to writhe, binding over the wound until only a drying clot remained. The flies transferred their attentions to the richer pickings that puddled the grass.

"Now you've a mount," said Anomius. "And one that will bring you to the Daggan Vhe. Ride!"

Cennaire hesitated a moment. "Do I need call on you," she asked, "what then?"

In the mirror, the wizard's ugly face wrinkled. "Call only if you must," he said. "There are shamans in Cuan na'For with powers to sense such a summoning, and they're best avoided. Indeed, avoid what folk you see, and call me only at direst need. When you reach the Kess Imbrun, call then, if it be safe. Above all, do not let the three know I'm your master."

"And do they find Rhythamun, and I be with them?"

"You'd best be with them." Tacit threat hung on his words. "But then, use your wits. Rhythamun may well know you for a revenant, but if I guess this game aright, the three have the means to conquer him. Let them, and after, take the Arcanum."

"Think you they'll allow me?"

Anomius's image twisted with sour laughter. "I doubt me that"—he chuckled—"but you'll find a way. How, I leave to your wits and wiles; only secure me the book. When you have it, call on me. Now go!"

The scent of almonds faded as he ended the spell. The mirror reflected only the larches and the blue sky, Cennaire's face. She studied herself a moment, arranging strands of raven hair, then put away the glass and turned to the horse.

It stood docile, its tail flicking idly, more, it seemed to the woman, from habit than because the flies were irksome. When she looked at its eyes, she saw them dulled, emptied of life. That commodity, she thought, seemed Anomius's to command. Her's, the horse's, both belonged to the wizard: she wondered if he valued the one any more than the other. *But still he has my heart*, she reminded herself, *and while he holds that I can only obey*. She climbed astride the gelding and turned its head toward the egress of the pass.

When she drove her heels against the animal's flanks she was taken by surprise. The roan snorted and broke into an immediate gallop, almost spilling her from the saddle. She clutched the pommel, letting the reins hang loose, more concerned with holding her seat than directing the beast, which, anyway, seemed not to need such ordinary management. It charged headlong over the meadow, ignoring a lesser trail in favor of the wide road that cut deep through the backbone of the mountains. Its hooves rang loud on the stone as it ran, thundering as if it charged into battle, the pace impossible for any normal animal to maintain. This, though, was no longer a normal horse, and it showed no sign of faltering as it hurtled along the pass, so that in a while Cennaire hung the reins from the saddlehorn and locked both hands firm about the leather.

She felt the wind of their passage whip her face, spilling her hair loose to stream behind her, the rocky walls flashing by in a blur of motion, hoofbeats echoing behind. Soon she was more confident, content to let the ensorcelled horse run, its stride, for all its unnatural speed, comfortable enough that she no longer feared a tumble. It appeared that Anomius's thaumaturgy endowed the roan with an agility, a surefootedness, to match its speed and stamina, for even when the ground became broken, littered with rockfalls from the slopes, or fallen trees, still it held its pace, charging around obstacles or leaping over them. Cennaire needed only to clutch the saddle and

stay astride, for which her own sorcerous strength
proved ample, and before long confidence became enjoyment.

By late afternoon, she was through the heights of
the Gann Pass, the retreating sun throwing long shadows over the descent into Cuan na'For, and as dusk
settled across the prairie, into the foothills. By midnight, she was on the grass, the revenant gelding still
running at breakneck speed, slowed no more by darkness than it had been by ascents or obstacles.

On and on it ran, unwavering, guided by whatever
weirdling instinct Anomius's glamour had imparted,
moving of its own accord from its northward line to
a northwesterly direction. Wild dogs barked in anger
as it thundered through their dens, and horses whickered as it disturbed their sleep. Several times
Cennaire saw fires burning, and twice came close
enough to see the outlines of great leather-tented
wagons against the flames, but if she was seen, she
was gone before the observers had time to mount a
pursuit.

Night darkened toward morning and still the gelding ran, onward through the brightening of the false
dawn and the ascent of the sun. Little, brightly colored birds rose in chattering flocks from the grass, and
overhead black-winged predators rode the sky. The
wind blew warm, though to Cennaire it felt cool,
chilled by the sheer speed of her passage. Once that
day she saw riders nearby, and tensed, thinking they
might seek to halt her. The gelding ignored them,
charging inexorably toward its destination, and
though they brought their own mounts to a gallop,
shouting challenges, they could not match its pace,
and after a while gave up.

Cennaire felt a heady sense of power then, such as
she had only experienced before in her dealings with
men. It seemed she flew, unstoppable, her ensorcelled
mount an automaton, untiring, unwavering, she like
some goddess, borne ever onward by such a steed as
the world could only dream of, beyond man's touch.

She shouted laughter that was lost on the wind, and when next she saw riders felt no fear, even though they stood across her path. What they thought as she charged them, she could only guess from their startled expressions and half-heard shouts. One man, she saw, nocked arrow to bow, but before the shaft was loosed the gelding was on them, and the bowman's mount squealing and tumbling as the roan crashed headlong past, no more deterred by living barriers than any other. Arrows flew then, and behind her Cennaire heard cries of outrage, briefly, for she was soon outdistancing the warriors, their pursuit falling off as their worldly horses foundered.

The leagues and the days were swallowed, the sun rising to chart its path across the sky and give sway to the moon, that orb falling down past the western horizon to accord the sun fresh passage, the cycle repeating, timeless: Cennaire rode on, no less inexorable. How many days had passed since she quit Gannshold, she forgot, for time grew meaningless, the ride a thing entire to itself. She knew only that she crossed all the vastness of Cuan na'For at a speed no mortal creature could hope to match, and that surely she must come to the Kess Imbrun before her quarry, for they were fleshly beings and subject to fleshly demands, delays, and hindrances beneath such as she.

And then, on a day when the sky was banked with great castles of massy white cumulus, she saw before her a barrier that stretched wide and dark across the grass, farther than her eyes could see, running out to east and west, so far northward it seemed to fill all the world. Like a sea, it was, an ocean that swayed and stirred under the wind. She felt the gelding change direction then, turning further west, as if reluctant to come too close to that great shadow that filled the heart of the grasslands. She made no attempt to correct this new course, for as they drew closer she saw that it was an ocean of trees, and knew it for the Cuan na'Dru, the holy forest, home of the god Ahrd, and somehow knew that to enter there was

to die, no matter what sorceries Anomius employed
to grant her existence. She felt a kind of fear then,
turning in her saddle to study the enormous woodland, aware of its presence as though it were some
sensate thing, a gestalt entity comprised of all the
myriad trees that grew there; and all, she knew deep
inside, in what, did she yet own such, she would
name her soul, opposed to her and the task imposed
upon her.

It came to her then that her mount had avoided every stand of timber along the way, hursts and copses
alike. For sake of speed, she had assumed, the grass
offering a clearer path, the woods, no matter how
small, obstacles that should, inevitably, slow it, or
sweep her from the saddle. Now she thought that
likely the god had a presence in the trees, in every
one, and that the glamour Anomius had placed upon
the roan horse sensed that and directed the animal
around, clear of Ahrd's influence. She eyed the Cuan
na'Dru warily then, leaving the horse to find the way,
thinking that Ahrd could have little truck with one
entrusted with the Arcanum's seizure; and then, ap-
pended to that thought, that Ahrd and all the Younger
Gods must surely look with favor on those who
sought to destroy that threat to their existence.

Aye, she mused as the forest flashed by and the day
aged toward evening, surely the Younger Gods must
grant a boon to their savior. And surely the Younger
Gods must have such power as could restore a revenant's heart, and find it in their own to forgive past
transgressions, were such a service done them.

But still Anomius owned her heart. Still it lay ensorcelled in that pyxis in Nhur-jabal, and even though
the bonds placed upon the wizard by the Tyrant's sorcerers denied him ready access to the palace until the
war in Kandahar was ended, at some time he must return there. And what then? Then he would hold her
being in his hand, and he was mad, and he was her
master, and he could destroy her with a word.

Still, there was, perhaps, some thread here that she

might weave to a tighter pattern should opportunity come: she locked the thought in her mind as the sun went down and the Cuan na'Dru fell dark.

She rode through another night and into another day, and still the great forest lay to her right, vast and impassable, a dendriform wall, transformed by the sun into a barrier of shifting green shadows from which, she noticed, her undead mount kept a respectful distance. It seemed she could almost sense Ahrd's presence, for along all the length of the edgewoods there was a kind of stillness, a ponderous solemnity, and she grew uneasy, wondering if the god looked out, watching her.

Toward noon, however, she was distracted by a curious sight. In the grass ahead she discerned the signs of a camp. Not one of the great clan gatherings, but such as a small group of travelers might make, the grass flattened, the remains of a long-cold campfire visible at the center of the trampled circle. Of itself that meant little enough, but as the gelding brought her closer she saw the signs of combat, corpses sprawled, picked over by wild dogs and carrion birds, a patch of dried blood, rusty red, as if something—or someone—had been butchered. She saw two heads separated from their accompanying bodies, and a torso devoid of limbs, the amputations strange to her, for it seemed unlikely the wild dogs would gnaw so precisely. She thought perhaps a fight had taken place and the losers been ritually mutilated, and thought no more about it, though she felt oddly glad when the littered battleground was left behind.

The gelding thundered on through the remainder of the day and then, when night was fallen, shifted direction once more. By the moon's silvery light, Cennaire saw that they had reached the western edge of the Cuan na'Dru, and that the forest now stretched out northward. How far, she could not guess, for when the sun rose, it seemed still endless, and for all her mount's supernatural speed, it seemed they must run forever with the trees ominous at her elbow.

Another day and most of another night they continued, and then, a little before dawn, she saw that the great stands of timber thinned, the massive oaks fewer, giving way to elder and rowan, thickets of blackthorn that straggled out as if reluctant to concede dominance to the prairie. As the sun came up she saw that the Cuan na'Dru lay at her back, and that ahead there again stretched the great grass sea, swaying and rustling in the wind. She felt a lightening of her mood then, the dendroid weight lifting as the forest receded shadowy behind, though in the deepest and most secret part of her mind she stored those musings she had entertained as she rode within Ahrd's aegis.

THE sun stood at its zenith as she saw another shadow impose itself upon the landscape, this a curving black line that meandered vast across her path, as though an enormous river of darkness flowed over the prairie. At first she felt confused, wondering what fresh obstacle this was, and why the gelding made no attempt to alter its course, but instead raced headlong onward. Then, as the afternoon aged, she realized that she had reached the Kess Imbrun and that what had appeared a river of night was the shadowy immensity of the rift canyon.

The gelding halted scant feet from the rim, as abruptly as it had commenced its englamoured gallop, so that Cennaire was flung forward, almost unsaddled, clutching at the beast's neck, wide-eyed as she stared down into the depths of the chasm. Her nostrils wrinkled then, offended by an odor of decay as she felt the horse shudder and hauled herself upright. The smell came from the animal, and she frowned as she dismounted, springing a step backward as the equine lips parted to reveal a clutch of sickly yellow-white maggots that fell squirming onto the grass. The rotten stench grew stronger and she hurried to unlatch her saddlebags, carrying them a little distance off, remaining there as she stared at the horse.

It seemed that, the animal's task dispensed, it no longer enjoyed the protection of Anomius's spell. It decayed before her eyes, its hide shrinking, stretching tight over the bones beneath, the dull eyes liquefying, oozing amorphous tears that ran slowly over the suddenly shrunken cheeks. The wound in its neck opened, exposing blackened flesh from which more maggots spilled, and then the legs folded, depositing the moldering body in an ungainly heap. Bones thrust out as the skin split and the wind became pungent with the odor of rotting organs. Briefly, Cennaire caught the waft of almonds amid the putrid stench, and then both were gone, the gelding's corpse desiccated, as if many days dead.

Cennaire turned away, her stomach offended, taking deep breaths until the last memory of rot was banished. Then she looked about. South and east and west lay the grasslands, the northernmost limit of Cuan na'For; ahead was the Kess Imbrun, a barrier as dramatic, as imponderable as the Cuan na'Dru. She walked toward it, going down on hands and knees as she came to the edge, for it seemed the depths called out, a siren song that threatened to suck her in, seductive, urging her to succumb and cast herself off, to fly down and down to the rocks below. She stretched flat on the grass, the sheer immensity of the cleft sending her senses reeling, dizzy, as she peered down a vertical face of dark red stone, seeing, far, far below, a thin thread of glittering blue that she guessed was a river. The farther rimrock was hazy in the distance, several bowshots away, crenellated with folds and buttresses infinitely more majestic than any man-built constructions. Nhur-jabal itself, she thought, awed, might be lost in that chasm, like a child's toy house dropped into a well. Some way off, eastward of her position, she saw the rimrock split, a steep-walled gully descending at an angle, widening where it bled out onto a broad ledge that traversed a buttress, a trail

of kinds evident there, winding precipitously downward: the Daggan Vhe, she assumed.

Cautiously, she wriggled back, and only when she
was some several paces from the rim did she stand
upright again and assess her situation.

She was alone and now unhorsed. Food and drink
were meaningless to such as she, casual pleasures she
could easily do without, but to be on foot was a matter of concern. Had her quarry already reached this
lonely place? And if they had, what should she do?
She ran to her saddlebags, hurriedly locating the mirror and speaking the gramarye that would summon
Anomius. The scent of almonds reminded her of the
decaying horse and she brought a perfumed handkerchief from her tunic, holding the cloth to her nostrils,
startled by the wizard's voice.

"You've reached the Kess Imbrun?"

"And the horse died!"

"It was already dead." The sorcerer chuckled. "It
served its purpose, though its remains shall still
help."

"I'm alone!"

"Ah well, not for very long." Anomius seemed not
at all disturbed by her discomfort; rather, he appeared
greatly satisfied. "Be my calculations aright, then the
three you seek are not yet come. When they do, they
shall find you there."

"How can you be sure of that?"

Cennaire looked around, the emptiness of the landscape pressing in, a psychic weight. Anomius grunted,
his bulbous nose flaring in momentary irritation.

"Do you doubt me?"

"No." Cennaire shook her head nervously. "But are
you sure?"

"As much as my thaumaturgy permits, aye. Did
that steed I gave you not cross the grass faster than
mortal mount might manage? Has it not brought you
to the Daggan Vhe?"

"If the Daggan Vhe is a track that goes down and

down into the canyon, then aye. But it's a trail for goats or flies, not men."

"Men use it." He waved a peremptory gesture. "Listen, you've but to wait and they'll come."

Cennaire studied his unsightly features, her doubt visible, for he said, "I've scried all this with magicks beyond your comprehension, and I tell you that no matter what start they had, you've overtaken them. Rhythamun will have taken that trail and likely reached the Jesseryn Plain ere now, but your quarry's yet to come there."

"And so I'm to wait?"

"You'll do as I bid."

His tone was commanding, brooking no dissent. Cennaire was surprised to realize that her eyes were moist: she dabbed at them with her handkerchief and murmured, "This is a very lonely place."

In the mirror, Anomius snorted. "Do you grow feelings now?" he asked scornfully. "Remember that your heart is mine, and you'll do as I command."

Cennaire nodded, crumpling the handkerchief in her fist as she muttered, "Aye."

"Good. Then you've but to wait, and when they come they'll find a poor, luckless woman, whose horse has died, leaving her stranded, alone."

"And what shall I tell them I did out here? They'll hardly take me for some Kern woman."

"Aye, there's that, but I've given the matter some thought," Anomius agreed carelessly. "It's not unknown for caravans to venture trading out of Lysse, and that shall be your story—that you rode with one such expedition. It fell foul of the northern clans and there was a fight. You alone escaped, fleeing helplessly until your horse died."

"And shall they believe that?" asked Cennaire.

"Why not?" came the sorcerer's reply. "You're there, the remains of your horse are there. How else should you come to that place? Faith, woman! These are honorable folk we deal with, and they'll take pity on you, and look to aid you in your plight."

He invested the word "honorable" with massive contempt. Cennaire nodded again and said, "What if they send me back, southward?"

"Then I've another stratagem to devise," he answered, "but I think they'll travel alone and their sense of honor will require they aid you. Aye, I think they'll take you with them to the Jesseryn Plain. Along the way, you'd best make yourself indispensable." He leered, chuckling obscenely, "After all, there are two men and but the one woman. Save they share her, one of them must surely find your company attractive."

He looked away then, as though distracted by some occurrence beyond the mirror's range, and said, "Aye, a moment only." Then, to Cennaire, "I am summoned. Our glorious Tyrant calls me. Do as I instruct you, and when you can safely speak again, summon me."

He mouthed a gramarye and his image faded on a wafting of the almond scent. Cennaire sighed, staring at her reflection. The journey to this place had taken some toll, her clothes dusty, stained by travel, her hair fallen loose. She resisted the instinctive impulse to tidy herself, instead using her handkerchief to remove what little cosmetic remained upon her face: if she was cast as some fugitive traveler, then she had best look the part.

After that she waited, her role easier by the moment, for it seemed that she was the only human in all that emptiness, and she felt the weight of it afresh. She watched the sun go down, birds winging southward across the red-washed sky, and the filling moon rise pale to the east, attended by the filigree of bright-twinkling stars. The day's heat waned, the breeze cool and gentle, smelling of dust and stone from the vast darkness of the Kess Imbrun. Far off, wild dogs howled, their cries faint and distant, and it occurred to Cennaire that few living things came close to the great chasm, as though its very vastness, its emptiness, erected a barrier. From choice, to alleviate the

discomfort she felt, she elected to sleep and dozed
lightly, curled in the deep grass.

She woke as the sky paled toward dawn, pearly
grey at first, then shining silver, brightening as a band
of gold spread along the eastern horizon and, like a
fast-drawn curtain, blue spread across the firmament,
shot through with brilliance as the sun climbed majestic into the heavens. She made perfunctory toilet,
drawing her hands through the dew-damp grass and
cleansing her face, standing up to survey her surroundings, wondering how long it should be before
here quarry came in sight, pushing aside the thought
of what she might do if they failed to appear. And
then she heard hoofbeats, a faint drumming, distant,
but, so her preternatural senses told her, coming
steadily onward, toward her. She listened a moment,
frowning, for she heard but a single horse where she
had expected three. Wary, she ran a little way from
the ingress of the Daggan Vhe and crouched down,
the high grass hiding her.

The hoofbeats came closer still and she discerned a
lone rider, whose animal flagged, as if driven to the
limits of its endurance. It and the burden it bore came
into clear sight and she gasped, swiftly stifling the
sound as she studied the features of the rider: a man,
his hair a sandy color, his nose crook-bridged where it
had once been broken, his eyes brown.

Daven Tyras, she thought, confusion and alarm
mingling. *Rhythamun! What do I do?*

Her instinct was to fetch out the mirror and call on
Anomius for advice, but then she thought that likely
the approaching warlock would sense that summoning and turn his power against her—and
Anomius had hinted at the power he commanded.
Sufficient, she thought, to destroy her: she opted for
caution and sank deeper into the grass, watching.

The sandy-haired man rode close to the chasm and
halted, climbing down stiff-limbed, as if he had ridden
long and hard. His horse blew gusty breaths, head
drooping, its hide creamed with sweat, the shoulder

trembling, exhausted. The man dropped the reins and walked to the very edge of the Kess Imbrun, and Cennaire congratulated herself on remaining hidden as she watched him raise his arms and shout strange words into the stillness of the morning. They seemed to resonate against the walls of the chasm, echoing back, filling the air with crackling, invisible power, the strong, sweet scent of almonds. The rimrock of the canyon seemed to shimmer with the strength of his magic, the very air distorted. Cennaire felt her long hair prickle and sank deeper into the grass, losing sight of the man for a while, willing the fear she felt be gone.

This one, she thought—knew!—she would not confront. The occult power he wielded was too great: she could feel it in her bones, in the membrane of her flesh, and she felt a terrible certainty that Anomius was right in his assumption that only the three she sought held the key to his defeat. She watched in tremulous silence as he lowered his arms, thankful when the oppressive weight of his magic eased and the air grew once more still.

She watched as he went to the weary horse and rummaged in the saddlebags, bringing out the makings of a fire, a tinderbox, and chunks of dried dung. Watched still as he arranged those things and sparked a flame. Then, despite all she had seen in both her lives, thrust a knuckle between her teeth and bit down hard to prevent herself gagging as she watched him prepare his meal.

Now she understood the nature of the dismembered bodies she had seen, the reason limbs were missing, as if the corpses had been butchered: butchery was what it was.

She watched as Rhythamun set part of a man to roasting, casual as if he spitted a haunch of venison or a rib of beef over the fire. The sweet, porky smell of sizzling human flesh overcame the scent of the grass, and Cennaire fought the urge to vomit, thinking wildly that for all she had done, for all Anomius had made of her, there yet remained depths to which she would not—could not!—sink. She felt a dreadful revulsion, and that became a kind of clarification—that this creature she observed was sunk lower into evil's mire than any living thing should go; that whatever ends were sought, limits existed still, past which a step like this carried a being beyond the pale of understanding, beyond the pale of reason.

She swallowed the bile threatening to spill out as Rhythamun gnawed on his horrible feast and tossed the bone aside. Watched as he rose and strolled to the rimrock of the chasm, peering down as if in anticipation of some arrival.

Whatever he had summoned did not come that day, or the ensuing night, which Cennaire spent huddled in the grass, afraid for the first time since Anomius had made her what she now was; not until noon of the next, awful day.

Then, climbing up through the heated haze that shimmered the light along the edges of the Kess Imbrun, she saw riders ascend the rim of the Daggan Vhe. Five men on small, shaggy horses, all clad in outfits of cotton and leather and link mail, short, heavily curved swords sheathed on their waists, bows slung in leather buckets behind each saddle, and lances booted before. They clattered and clinked as they surmounted the precipice and halted, heads hanging, their eyes vacant, looking nowhere.

They were short, she observed, and—when Rhythamun barked a command that wafted the almond scent of magic heavy on the morning wind and they dismounted—bowlegged, with long, oiled hair hanging in ringlets from beneath their conical helmets, nets of mail cut with eyeholes dangling from the forward edges. Each, like sleepwalkers, raised the concealing metal veils, and she saw their faces were broad and squat, the cheekbones high and steeply slanted beneath angled eyes that seemed almost feline in their yellow hue. Their skin was the color of old, oiled leather, darker than any Kern's, and cut deep with lines that radiated from the eyes and the mouths, curving down from nostrils to lips, so that their ages were unguessable. Three wore mustaches, thin and waxed, sweeping in parentheses to the lower edges of their angled jaws; two sported beards, thin, stiff triangles of blue-black that jutted proudly despite their shambling, entranced posture.

She watched as Rhythamun inspected each one, carefully; as would, she thought, a man inspect a horse he thought of purchasing, checking posture and muscles, assessing stamina and strength and speed. Then she heard the wizard speak again, and again smelled the scent of almonds on the warm wind, and again stifled a cry of surprise as the Jesseryte warriors snatched out their swords and set to fighting.

It was a brief and bloody combat that, at the end, left one standing alone, the rest stretched bloody on the grass, he cut, though not badly, his sword and the wide-bladed knife he had used smeared from hilts to tips with gore. Rhythamun laughed obscene approval at that victory, and waved his hands, mouthing guttural words that sealed the man's cuts and sent him to pitching the slain, one by one, into the depths of the Kess Imbrun. Another command, another waft of almond scent, and the horses followed the men, tumbling over and over into the chasm to crash, lost, onto the rocks below.

Then Rhythamun beckoned the surviving Jesseryte toward him.

Cennaire watched as the warlock clasped his hands tight upon the man's shoulders, the almond scent stronger now, surpassing all other smells as Rhythamun spoke, each word seeming to burn on the air, a fierce, red glow growing between his mouth and the Jesseryte's, the sense of power palpable, like the enormity of a building storm. It seemed then that the grass bent, blown by an occult wind, and Cennaire crouched lower, afraid, knowing that this wizard was one mightier than Anomius, and that if he sensed her presence she must surely be dead, or worse.

Even so, she could not tear her eyes away, and consequently saw the sudden rush of indescrible power that flooded between Rhythamun and his victim as the arcane chant ended and the mage possessed his new body.

What had been Daven Tyras fell, like a string-cut puppet, down into the grass. For a while the Jesseryte stood, head hung, long streamers of spittle dangling from his lips, his yellow eyes blank. Then, as if the connecting strings of his mind were tugged by a new master, his head snapped up and his eyes focused. He laughed, and Cennaire flinched at the naked obscenity of the sound. He wiped the drool from his mouth, glanced, chuckling, at the body of Daven Tyras, and stooped to bring a small black book from under the shirt. It was a slender volume, insignificant save in the sense of power that radiated from it, an aura that set Cennaire's teeth to clenching, her skin to tingling. It was, she knew beyond doubting, the Arcanum, and for a sole, wild instant, she thought of rushing forward to snatch it from the warlock's hand. But what then? He would destroy her—of that she felt no doubt—and neither Anomius or her own revenant strength could protect her from his magicks. She forced herself to calm, to stillness, watching as Rhythamun dragged the vacated body to the precipice, tossing it after the others.

Then he mounted the one remaining horse and rode it down into the Daggan Vhe.

Cennaire remained where she was until the last echoes of the descending hooves faded into the vast silence of the chasm, and then a while longer, reluctant to risk discovery, convinced that even from the depths of the canyon Rhythamum could strike against her. Finally she crept, slowly and cautiously, to the rim, flattening there to peer down. Far below a toylike shape moved, dark against the sun-baked rock, its progress inexorable as a spider's down a wall. Cennaire watched until man and animal were no more than a blur, and then indistinguishable from the shadows cast by the overhanging bluffs.

Slowly, no longer so frightened but still confused, she retreated from the edge of the Kess Imbrun to settle in the grass, thinking over what she had seen and learned.

In all the world, she thought, she was the only one to know Rhythamun's new face. She glanced at the satchel containing the ensorcelled mirror—should she summon Anomius and tell the wizened sorcerer what she knew? How should he then command her?

To go after Rhythamun?

That was a notion for which she felt scant appetite.

And, a further consideration, had Anomius not told her the three questers alone held the unlocking of the shape-shifter's magic?

More—the thoughts tumbling one over the other in wild array—might this not be a gambit she could use to her advantage? She alone knew Rhythamun's Jesseryte face—which must surely provide a bargaining point with the three. And Anomius had ordered her to join them, to inveigle herself into their company. How better, then, than to offer guidance to the wizard's new shape?

And more again: if they commanded the magicks that might defeat Rhythamun, might they not also command such power as could free her heart, release her from Anomius's dominance? Surely, in return for what she might now offer, they would aid her in that.

She nodded, staring unblinking into the face of the high, hot sun, a decision reached: she would not bring out the mirror to commune with her master, but seek to use this knowledge to her own advantage. What she now knew, she would communicate to the questers alone—carefully, maintaining her role—and look to bend events to her own gain.

Satisfied, she settled down to wait.

✠   ✠   ✠

When she saw the riders approaching, she felt genuinely thankful, for her own sake, as if she were, truly, lost. She watched them, crouched in the grass, until she was certain they were not clansmen, then rose, waving and calling.

They came toward her at a canter: a beautiful woman, whose flaxen hair streamed out, glinting in the morning sun, mounted on a grey horse; a dark-skinned Kern astride a big black stallion, his hair black and bound in a long tail, his eyes hard and blue as he sighted her; a younger man, tanned dark, but Lyssian to judge by his features and the sun-bleached mane that he wore in the Kernish style, his expression puzzled.

Cennaire ran toward them and they slowed, eyeing her curiously, hands lightly touching their swords' hilts, glancing round as if anticipating some trick, wary of ambush.

"Praise all the gods you've come," she cried. "My name is Cennaire."

THE END, OF THE SECOND BOOK.